A primary school teache
England, my first book was an
ears watching Newcastle United. I have a love for the
sport of Ice Hockey and this was partly the inspiration
for some of the technology used by the character of
Archie. The other inspiration came from my love for
the science fiction stories of the 1970s onwards: films
and TV series such as Star Wars, Battlestar Galactica
and Buck Rogers excited me. I used to sit balancing a
tray on my knee, eating my tea as I watched them with
my mum, dad and sister. I also used to love the old
Flash Gordon and Buck Rogers black and white series
from the 1930s. The city of Tenebria is based on my
love for Mega City One in Judge Dredd: my favourite
character in the comic 2000AD for which I used to run
to the paper shop every Saturday morning.

A regular programme contributor to Newcastle's
various ice hockey teams until their eventual demise, I
switched back to following and writing about my local
football team: Whitley Bay. Since then, when I haven't
been teaching, planning and marking, I have been
writing the Albie trilogy which has been many years in
the making: the science fiction series that has taken my
life to emerge.

I would like to thank, my wife Odessa, who has
humoured me in all my bizarre hobbies and
obsessions. My two incredibly clever and funny
daughters Hol and Jas, who have both shared my love
for a good, and not-so-good science fiction story. My

mum and dad for funding my weekly comic dose and allowed the likes of Judge Dredd, Rogue Trooper, Dan Dare… to fill my head in between my TV doses from the likes of Dr Who, Blakes Seven et al.

Thanks also must go out to my super proof readers: 'Parky', Mairi, Chris and me Mum: thanks for your willingness to help out and all the time you spent spotting my mistakes.

My unbridled respect goes out to Mr Trevor Storey who put my ideas into the most amazing cover I could have imagined. Who knew there was so much talent on Tyneside?

Thank you to the friends and family who have encouraged me along the way. My Friday writing days have been a godsend to my mental health!

Finally, also thank you to all those people who are reading this. I hope you enjoy it and are looking forward to the next Albie books.

Albie Book I: Fugitive of Tenebria

1

The dark tunnel reeked of neglect. Its crumbling, rounded walls, thick with algae, hadn't been touched for years; decades even. No matter how hot it was above ground, this micro-climate was always cold, a cold that chilled to the bone with the constant winds that dashed through the close, rotting walls. A steady stream of water trickled down the sides and into a constant stream that ran throughout the tunnels: a city's debris constantly on the move. The momentary feeling of calm that had descended on the labyrinth was about to tragically change.

The figures that stumbled through the shadows took no notice of the rubbish swirling around their feet.

"Quiet," hissed a savage voice from the gloom, "You'll have every uniform in the district down on us." The glare from the whites of his eyes was all they could make out as he turned around but it was enough to make them stop. Pushing himself to the head of the column he urged them all to squat down, the filthy water swimming around them. He was the obvious leader of the group and the others quickly stepped aside, shuddering as they pressed their backs against the slimy, damp walls. He made his way forward. They listened to the trickling sound as it ran away from them but they could make out a different sound from up above: they could hear a steady stream of beats...music.

"There…" he whispered and at first his group couldn't make out what he had spotted but they could feel a warm but fresh breeze blowing. A chink of light shone upon the tunnel wall ahead and their eyes were drawn upwards to a small grille. They hardly noticed the water running down their backs and around their feet. They were in touching distance of the city of Tenebria.

Some had doubted they'd make it this far or that it even existed. But through the grille, big enough for a single person to squeeze through, stood the city of their dreams. The shining city where the beautiful ones lived: people who glowed in the sunlight and whose lives seemed blessed. The air was never stale or polluted: always pleasant, warm and fresh. They knew that above ground you never felt the clammy drag of damp clothes or the chilling grip that the Underworld held for all its unfortunate inhabitants.

Huge towers, dwarfing tree-lined plazas, climbed into the glorious sky. Transparent walkways reached out from one to the other. Great glass fronts watched over these plazas on every side, broken only by huge screens that flashed with constant messages. These called and bewitched the lucky residents with vibrant images of happy, perfect-looking, gorgeous people. Their life wasn't a daily struggle to survive: it was glamorous and flawless. The perfectly-controlled weather was never too hot and never too cold: simply perfect for its inhabitants. Who couldn't be happy there? Paradise: and it was just through that grille.

Hearts were beating faster and they continued to ignore the damp. They waited for the signal. All had lived below ground for as long they could remember, in the tunnels that ran under the city, carrying away the city's waste. Most had lived far below in the ruins of cities abandoned long ago: cities that had been swept by the immense tidal waves and devastating floods.

Now the beat of the city was calling them.

"Once you are out there you are on your own: remember that..." he warned them. "Spread out and head for the outskirts of the city, it'll be safer there." He couldn't make out their faces and was glad; he preferred not to know how frightened they were. He didn't want to know anything about any of them: that was except one. She was smaller than the rest and had the widest, brightest eyes he had seen. He had no idea what colour her hair was in this gloomy underworld: all their hair had the same dirty, matted style. He did think, however that she might probably be quite fair. She was pretty: he had certainly noticed that. All through their climb from the underworld he had lingered near the back of the group, chatting to her when he could…he'd miss her: it would be too risky for them to stay together – too much of a target for the troopers: the city's police who ruthlessly rounded up anybody from the underworld. Their life would then be one of forced labour in one of the many factories that served Tenebria.

After stealing a glance at her darkened form, he climbed to the grille, pulling out from his ragged coat what looked like just a simple grey stick. A gasp from the group made him freeze. "How come you've got a domitor?" A stocky man asked him suspiciously. "Only a uniform would be able to get one of them." The leader snapped angrily back at him:

"If I was one of them I could have saved myself a lot of bother long ago, so unless you want me to take you back down…" The stocky man shook his head looking up at the city lights and stepped back into the shadows.

The leader stepped up and, silhouetted by Tenebria's lights, placed one end of the domitor onto a plate to one side. A faint humming accompanied the grille's opening. Anticipation grew.

Artificial light filled the tunnel, but though harsh to their eyes, it was beckoning them, welcoming them, luring them.

Without a word, one by one, they stepped up to their guide, muttered thanks and using his cupped hand as a foothold they pulled themselves above ground. The last one reached down a hand to pull him up and he closed the grille in the same way he had opened it.

They had reached their promised land. All their efforts had been worth it. The air tasted sweet to their polluted lungs. They felt giddy just inhaling it. Unable to move, they marvelled at the skyscrapers that dwarfed them. Like the world they had just emerged from, they didn't belong here. It was hard to imagine that they were even of the same species that had created this sprawling metropolis. Some just kept turning like windmills, round and round, unable to take it all in: the beauty, colours and cleanliness. A kaleidoscope of colours danced above them. Even though it was night-time the city still shone and the beats still drifted from the towers around them, holding them entranced like a spell. This had to be heaven. They were bewitched.

The beats were joined by a throbbing sound that grew in strength until it filled the air.

The gentle breeze that had lulled them now became a whirlwind and the softer glare of the city was filled by the stark brightness of a searchlight.

"Rippa, rippa, rippa."

The sound filled their ears.

"Rippa, rippa, rippa."

The sound they had dreaded. Panic gripped hold and suddenly the group was heaved from its revelry. The leader frantically fought to open the grille again. Thankfully it began to slide open. Without thinking, he leapt back into the familiar, icy waters. He heard the screams of his group as gunfire from above reverberated around him. All he could do was stare up at the sky as both gunfire and screaming suddenly stopped. They had come so close, how had the uniforms known they were coming? A small, dark shape appeared at the hole before landing nearly on top of him showering him in sludge and slime. It was his small friend; she was shaking violently and her arm was hanging limply by her side.

"They were waiting for us," she gasped, "One ripper … loads of uniforms…we never stood a chance." She sobbed, holding her injured arm.

"Come on, we've got to get out of here before they come down." The thud of marching boots echoed above as he dragged her up, she winced as he grabbed her arm but said nothing as bolts of light flew past them and the boots grew louder. Half dragging her, he led her back along the tunnel and they were out of sight by the time the first set of boots landed in the water.

The black and silver troopers they had feared soon poured through the grille. The grim sound of metallic orders crackled from a radio located on a dark visored helmet. A domitor, just like the one that had opened the grille, was waved up and down the tunnel. A light appeared at the top of the domitor as the uniformed figure switched off his radio. With a wave of his hand, he ordered silence. Listening to the trickling at his feet he could just make out the sound of frantic footsteps leading away to his left.

"This way!" he ordered, "Tell His Lordship we are in pursuit. Make sure the Predavator craft search above ground for any survivors."

Another officer watched as more uniformed troopers dropped down into the hole in the ground and didn't flinch as a wrenching sound ripped into the air and the Predavator craft lifted off to carry out his instructions. A sleek silvery craft with short stubby wings either side of its curved body, it rose effortlessly, two searchlights on its front scanning every corner of the square. They scoured the four huge towers that looked down on them on all four sides. Not one of the city's intruders moved.

Dropping down into the tunnel he studied the open grille and snarled as he spoke once more into the communicator in his helmet.

"Tell him also that the group have used a domitor…but make sure you aren't in the same room as him when you do…he's not going to like that!"

The sun rose on another beautiful day in

Paradise. Soon, millions of Tenebrians would be emerging from their apartments and buildings to begin their day with a pleasant stroll to work through their sterilised city. For them the sun always rose and shone brightly upon them. They were always warm thanks to the city's weather stations that made sure their days were never bothered by cold or rain. Their night would have been a relaxing sleep, oblivious to all but their own little domain. A single, overlooked, drop of blood lay on the warm pavement; all that remained of the night's attempted breakout. The bodies were swiftly removed to be reprocessed by orange overall-wearing workers and the scene quickly 'sanitised'. That drop of blood would condemn one of the workers to a place in one of the underworld's factories if it was spotted. The world above ground was, once more, spotless and uniform: trees, buildings in their regimented rows and exact in size and detail.

The tunnel was silent as the boy stared up at the grille. Just old enough to be considered an adult, despite his sleight figure, he certainly knew how to take care of himself. His thin arms hid their great strength and he had never been outrun by anyone. Able to blend in perfectly with the filthy walls of the tunnels he called home, he was constantly aware of every sound around him, his manky coat and trousers were badly fitting and like a second skin. His hair was thick with dirt, amongst other things. It was impossible to judge what colour it had originally been: sprouting from his head like a multitude of snakes seemingly with a life of their own. Slung across his chest was the strap of a bag crammed with what most would have called junk but to him were the treasured possessions of a lonely underground life.

The bright lights above had attracted him for as long as he could remember. They winked and flashed, trying to lure him out from his hideaway. His hands gripped the bars tightly, hoping to move them just a fraction so that he could get that little bit closer to a world that seemed strangely familiar – a world from his past.

Every day at the same time he would journey to one of these grilles to watch the early morning activity and every morning no matter where he was watching he was treated to the same sights. The sight of men and women dressed in immaculate, brightly coloured clothing: each of them wearing the same coloured, shiny material that dazzled Albie. Albie: that was his name, not that anybody had called him that in years. To him it looked like the people were floating like gods. The one thing he didn't like about them was their faces. Despite their dazzling clothes and hair and the enormous, brightly lit buildings they swanned in and out of, their expressions were fixed with blank expressions and eyes that never shone. They hardly ever seemed to notice each other, staring straight past each other or down, preferring to remain in their own little worlds. They were so intent on getting to where they had to be that their heads were rarely lifted from their feet. Albie had always thought himself to be quite clever because he didn't need to look at his feet when he ran. In fact, he could do a lot of things: leap, roll, climb and run without even noticing his feet. So how come he was trapped down in the tunnels and the world below while they were enjoying the warmth above?

There was one group who didn't wear the same bright clothes. They wore black with silver metal patches on their knees and arms and some kind of hard hat: he seemed to remember it was called a helmet. A dark reflective material covered their eyes: he didn't trust them because of this and the bright people were frightened of them too. Every time they appeared, people would push each other to move out of their way. In this way they were able to move quickly through the crowds. They would sometimes appear in flying crafts that made that "ripping" noise: once again making everyone bustle away. He wasn't surprised when people ran away from those crafts: their noise was deafening and they made his body shudder and his insides churn. He made sure he was never close enough to one to feel the full effect of its engines.

Turning his attention back to the busy street he noticed a pair of brightly coloured shoes stamping toward him. Smiling, he recognised them: he knew that wobble anywhere.

In complete contrast to the rest of them, every part of the owner of the shoes always gleamed: right up to a gleaming smile and glint in her eyes. She had the brightest, most perfect teeth he had ever seen. Often, she smiled at the others but they hardly ever returned the compliment. They were all so serious and they would stare down at her, as if they didn't like her smiling so much: as if they thought it distasteful. Why did they do that? She was smaller than the rest, her legs especially. They seemed to have to work harder to keep up with the rest of the crowd and avoid being swallowed up by the charging mass of bodies. The shoes didn't help but then they were a strange lot up there.

She wandered past his hiding place and he caught the slightest glimpse of a sparkle in her eyes as her tall mass of curly green hair, matching her outfit, bounced by. She never looked down and he soon lost sight of her.

Dropping silently into the gloom, he blinked as his eyes adjusted before padding on his way. The brightness was gone now; this was his world. It was a crumbling and uncared-for world where cracked and dirty bricks replaced polished metals. He waded carefully through the tunnels that hung below the city. They removed all the city's water and sewage, making it an unwelcoming place to any troopers that ventured below ground but the perfect terrain for Albie to move about undetected.

Reaching a hole in one of the tunnels he looked down into a gaping blackness that was broken up by a number of dotted lights. This was the other part of his world. A hundred metres or so below him stretched the underworld: the ruined remains of the original city and home to some of the most vicious people Albie knew. Staying out of everybody's way had been the safest policy. The tallest ruined buildings touched the network of tunnels and it was through these buildings that Albie and the bravest and most desperate dwellers were able to move from Tenebria's tunnels to the Underworld. It was inside of these buildings that Albie had made one of his homes. He paused at the hole: his eyes still recovering from the brightness of the world above ground. He sat on the edge of it, ignoring the water that was pulling at him, listening to the sound of water raining down on the building below. He wondered what the building had been and what had destroyed it and the rest of the Underworld. He knew the bright city above had replaced the dark world below his feet but he didn't know why. His eyes having recovered from the unfamiliar light, he jumped down and was pleased to feel solid ground beneath his feet.

After jogging towards an empty doorway, he made his way down a set of steps before pausing. His smile had gone now as he scanned before him, on the lookout for anything that moved. He froze, listening to the sound of water dripping and now the sound of footsteps. They came from in front of him, moving effortlessly down the stairs.

Slowly he pulled a wooden rod from his belt. Clenching it with one hand above his head, ready to swing, he edged forwards. With his free hand he felt his way along a damp wall, towards a dark opening. He could hear the steps as they grew louder; they were heavy and there were many.

Glancing above him he could just make out some long pipes below the dark metallic roof: cold from years of inactivity. In one movement he leapt, hauling himself on top of the pipes as lights appeared in the doorway he had been approaching.

He lay silent and still, not daring to breathe, as two slight figures with laboured steps dashed below him one supporting the other, followed by three, maybe more, dark uniformed figures with slower, heavier ones. Each uniform carried a long grey object with a light that made him squint. They scanned the darkness with these, exploring every corner of the squalid corridor.

"I'm sure they came this way," one said as he kicked over a pile of old boxes directly below his hiding place. Another figure ran a light carefully along the wall, picking out strange symbols stencilled into the wall long ago next to the opening. There was an air about this one – he stood straighter than the others and kept apart from them. The others looked at him uneasily. Above them, Albie sensed fear behind their visors as the uniforms rushed about searching every single nook and cranny.

The tall figure's dissatisfaction was obvious as he impatiently tapped his boot with the red stick in his gloved hand. A red, unblinking and inhuman eye blazed under his visor, scouring every corner. Standing right below the boy he slowly looked up but despite a familiar feeling in the human part of him, could not make anything out. He shone the light on his weapon around the pipes but could see nothing. He stood motionless, tapping his stick-like weapon into his gloved hand. The same type of weapon that had been used by the fugitives he was seeking. They had dared to pollute his city with their disgusting bodies. They would pay...that was clear but his mind was distracted. Only troopers carried them so where had they got it from?

He could sense something about this derelict room but he just couldn't work out what it was. Kicking a nearby crate out of the way he turned towards the others who flinched as he spoke; his voice devoid of emotion.

"There's nothing here now, they must be trying to crawl back to the slime-hole they climbed out of. Keep searching for them and the domitor they stole. Keep searching until you have it. Nobody stops until we have it back!" With that the others ran off, relieved to be on the move and away.

They soon disappeared, leaving the tall figure behind. The beam of light that shone from one end of his stick crawled across the ceiling, inching towards the youngster's hiding place. Albie, lying full length and clinging to the pipe above was struggling to hold his breath and was desperate to breathe: but he daren't. The glow danced past his hiding spot. The figure below gave such an air of menace that it terrified Albie: his orders were always carried out instantly and without question.

The light scanned the walls one final time then the figure muttered angrily and stormed off in the direction the others had taken.

Finally, Albie could breathe again. A mouth full of dust and dirt made him want to cough but somehow, he managed to control this urge.

Dropping down from his hiding place, the young figure let out a sigh of relief, sucking in air for the first time since he had been so rudely disturbed. He shook the dust from his long-matted hair, daring to finally break the stillness with a quiet cough.

He was used to them coming around. They were always trying to stop his type from getting above ground. He'd seen them use those objects to blow their targets away or leave them convulsing on the ground. He'd also seen his kind carried off by them, never to be seen again, just for trying to get something to eat. Yet, he had rarely seen that one before. To him they all looked the same but that tall one was different, he seemed detached, vaguely familiar even…but he couldn't think from where.

He patted the trusty bag slung over his shoulder; he wouldn't go hungry for a while. Listening out once more, he set off through the doorway and down endless metal steps. They clanged every so often when he stepped on a loose one; sending his heart racing but nobody came to bother him so he began to relax. Eventually he reached the barricaded opening that was the entrance to one of his many hideaways. He liked to keep moving, it wasn't good to stay in the same place for too long – made it easier for them to find him.

Silently pulling aside a rusting sheet of metal, he crawled inside, replacing it as he wriggled through. He laid the contents of his bag in the wheeled metal trolley that lay next to the clammy, ripped mattress that served as his bed. He loved this trolley. It had a handle at one end so he could push it around and a big basket that he had filled with all his clutter. He wondered what it had been designed for and why the small wheels wobbled so much. Pulling his long brown coat around himself, he lay down, closed his eyes and drifted off to sleep. He dreamed of the world he could only wonder at through the cold grille bars.

2

She sat high up in the Edu-suite, staring at the blank screen ahead of her waiting for today's lesson to load, twirling thin wisps of red hair that had dropped down from her high-rise hairdo with one hand, while the other was idly nudging the touchpad on her chair. It hovered ever so slightly lower then higher then to the right.

"Tissa!" noted the Roboteach model 3000 far below her as it patiently waited for the lesson to load. "Stay in your allotted space until the end of the session. Failure to do so could result in injury for yourself or your colleagues and removal of social points." Warning issued, a hushed murmuring returned to the domed room. Her colleagues shook their heads in disappointment, not only did she have hairs out of place but she fiddled. Why didn't she make the effort to stay in touch? They'd lost count of the number of times their chairs had been buffeted by hers. Either side of her were always the last two seats to be taken, even though she was usually one of the first to arrive. She was always the last to adopt the latest styles: her hair, her clothes could be out of date for hours, days sometimes. She was emotional: sometimes so bubbly and other times crying openly in public. She just didn't act like...like a Tenebrian. Surely, she'd be better off in the factories or with the workers: outside of the wall? Away from them!

Their cool exteriors annoyed her and upset her in equal doses. She loved being happy...friendly...she loved expressing her emotions! So many things made her feel that way: the warmth of the sun, the look and feel of the plants in the Bio-farms and Plazas and most of all being with her mother: talking to her ...hugging her. All of these things were a part of her that she had to avoid showing in public. The others' aloofness was upsetting to her. The way they could walk into the same room, every school day and look past her or through her every time: as if she wasn't even there. She'd tried being like the vast majority but it hadn't been her. She couldn't help the way she was so she went out of her way to put up her happy visage: if only for her own sanity.

Be cheerful!
Be positive!
Smile!

She would repeat those phrases daily like a mantra to keep the negative feelings at bay. Once she left the safety of her mother's apartment it was a fight to keep positive and she never knew why. Her clothes were the same style as theirs: right down to the same shimmer and glow of the material, same colour (usually) and swish her dresses made as she walked. Even her hair was usually the same, although she found it hard not to keep touching it: just to check it was still all in the right place. This meant sometimes it was slightly out of place: but she couldn't help it! She tried, oh how she'd tried, but the more she worried about it the more she wanted to touch it: make it right!

Her gradings were always good, the Roboteachs thought so, although she knew never to put down what she really thought: she'd learnt that lesson early on. A week of exclusive, intensive extra adjustment in Civic Duty Classes had seen to that. The headaches had lasted for days after that one and when she had returned back to her class the others had isolated her even more. After that she certainly knew that 'happiness' was not as important part of Tenebrian life as 'fulfilment and service'.

The rest of her class, circling the domed roof of the building in two rows of hovering, padded armchairs, turned their pristine heads towards the screens directly opposite them as they began to glow.

"Advanced Civic Duty Lesson 45. Please put on your VR headsets." announced the screen. Each of the sixty students did as they were requested and the murmuring stopped. Their attention was totally focused on the images that flashed before them. Each student wore the same blank expression as they soaked up the information: except Tissa. She shuffled and fiddled, making her seat wobble as it hovered in mid-air. The students next to her and below her tutted their annoyance as they were momentarily distracted but their attention was quickly returned to their screens. The whole room glowed as their clothes reflected the bright colours glowing on the screens. The VR headsets that covered their ears and eyes echoed with the same monotone and emotionless Tenebrian voice. Tissa found its voice soulless but managed to concentrate on listening.

"…duty of Tenebrians is to pair with the correct partners that are chosen for them. Their genes are matched according to Directive 51. Touch *here* to learn more." Around the room, each student's arm reached out to touch a spot in front of them and the voice continued.

"Directive 51 was introduced early on in the City's development to avoid the errors made by the Human Race in the past. By controlling the way genes were combined, the city was able to remove undesirable emotions such as anger and depression from the population: for more - press *here*." Some students reached in front of them but Tissa had heard it all before and didn't. She kept her thoughts to herself. She continued listening to the voice but felt her concentration waning the longer it went on. The introduction of images of war and aggression which flashed across their screens made the room glow red and orange as flames and explosions ripped across their screens. Tissa reeled at the scenes she witnessed. The tears welled up in her but she was the only one. Around the room, stoic faces shone in the reflected colours.

Finally, the screens all faded and returned to their blank states. The students one by one carefully removed their headsets, still looking perfect, and using the small touchpad, lowered their chair down to their allotted spaces on the floor. They waited for their classmates to descend. Tissa was the last. Her hair was unravelling and her make-up was streaked down her face from the tears that she had shed. As she landed, the Roboteach informed them.

"Make sure you complete your assignments this afternoon. They have been sent to your accounts: due in tomorrow. That will be all. Good day." It swivelled its robotic face back to its screen in the corner and paid no more attention as the students filed silently past it.

Tissa remained in her seat, trying to compose herself as she sobbed, ignoring the smirks and disparaging glances as the others passed her. Eventually, she too slipped out of her chair and as she headed towards the door, Roboteach's red eyes swivelled around to her and its synthetic mouth began moving.

"Extra assignment for you, Tissa: Emotion Control Module 13 due in tomorrow. Good day." Its head swivelled back around and she left, her head bowed but still sniffing. She couldn't wait to get back to the safety of her room. Maybe she'd visit the Bio-Farm that afternoon. It usually enabled her to get back to normal after upsetting sessions.

One figure was waiting for her in the corridor. She smiled sympathetically. Her hair and clothing were still as pristine as the moment she had left her room. She gave an attempt at a smile which Tissa returned half-heartedly.

"I can help you with the Emotion Control

Module…" she offered but Tissa shook her head.

"Thanks, but I'll be okay." She headed up the corridor leaving the figure behind. Giving a momentary look at Tissa's figure, she looked up at the cameras watching her from either end of the corridor. Hoping to avoid attracting any more attention to herself, she headed in the opposite direction.

He always had the same dream. He was living in the bright city with a woman he calls mum. There is a man that he sees occasionally but always briefly, furtively. He's called something like Moran in public but dad in private. He is important and seems stern. He always smells the same: clean…almost sterilised. Not like his mother who smells…nice in a relaxing kind of way. It is a smell he would watch her put on every morning and he would almost drink it in.

His mother and father both look fabulous: bright clothes and perfect hairstyles of the latest colours. That changes when his mother hurries him out of the warm and comfortable apartment she and Albie lived in. They hide from the men in the black and silver uniforms, round corners and behind the bright moving screens that are everywhere. Finally, they descend into the squalor of the Underworld, with its crumbling, ancient brickwork, freezing waters and pungent smells. It always ends with his mum crying and cradling him, surrounded by debris in a dark, dirty but familiar place.

Wiping away some water from his eyes, he sat

up. For some reason he always felt tight, tense and often angry after these dreams. His hands were usually clenched tightly into a fist and his head often hurt.

He missed her but he knew he needed to look after himself. He had no idea where she was, only that it had happened years ago and that he had had to move on. He had no pictures of her, except in his head and he only had one of those. In it she was slim, always with the same curly, black hair. She would make him laugh all the time, even when everything had turned wrong, her smile was always there whenever he needed it. She had taught him how to survive down here and the years they had spent in the tunnels had been the toughest but most satisfying of his life. He tried to remember his dad but couldn't. He only remembered being taken to a grand building in the middle of a giant green with trees leading up to it. Once there, people would do tests on him and other times he would just sleep but those were the times he had the strangest dreams: dreams he had chosen to forget.

In the dim light from outside, he chose a silver packet that crinkled as he pulled it from his trolley. Feeling the smooth surface, he ripped it open with his teeth before spitting the wrapper out – he liked the taste of the inside bit, even though the outside looked more interesting. Shoving it all in one go; his cheeks bulged as he chewed. The taste exploded in his mouth but he still felt hungry for something else. He'd have to search the big food dumps for some more supplies before they disappeared.

He sipped some water from a plastic bottle. Enjoying the taste, he screwed the top on. He knew where to get the best water from. The tunnel water tasted disgusting and made him ill but there was one spot where there was a big water tank. He knew just the spot to dip his bottle in without being noticed by the Tenebrian workers that occasionally visited the hundreds of pipes that led from there into the city. It was delicious: probably the same water the Tenebrians drank! He slipped the bottle back inside his shoulder bag before walking over to the edge of his home. Leaning against the exposed metal and concrete wall he looked out on the dark landscape below him. Fires dotted about served as the only light: their reflections dancing on the waters that covered all but highest land and the tallest of the ruined buildings. They also told him that he wasn't alone down here; there were other people here, both good and bad. Enormous columns stretched from the waters up to the roof of his world. Above lay the bright city, the neon and the glamorous people and below lay starving, desperate groups of people with barely enough food to stay alive. Down here there was only night, up above the glare seemed never-ending.

He looked out from his 'fortress', watching boats crossing between the relics from another time, another world – once mighty buildings – crumbling away. His eyes followed a single light, probably a boat, as it crossed the rippled darkness; a larger light appeared above it, moving quickly. He felt the familiar ripping noise as it circled the boat. The noise began to tear through his body even at this distance. He could hear cries from the boat then the next thing he knew there was a flash and the boat was gone and the cries were no more.

The ripping noise continued as its light picked out the nearest fire. More cries and parts of a nearby building crumbled into dust following another flash. He was mesmerised as the scene was repeated again and again until all sign of light and life had disappeared. Satisfied with its work the craft peeled away, approaching the static figure as it did so. The hairs on the back of his neck stood on end: there was another feeling of familiarity. The beam fell on him; he suddenly remembered what he had just seen and what he needed to do. Grabbing his bag, he threw back the metal sheet before pushing away the barricade that threatened to collapse upon him. A flash signalled the destruction of his den as hot flames burned his neck and burning fragments flew at him. Taking two steps at a time, he finally paused once he had rounded the corner.

Daring to peek, he saw his home fall away from him, into the water below.

Without waiting, he knew he had to keep running. So, he ran up the stairs in full view of the waiting craft through a giant hole in the brick wall that had appeared. He was an instant target. More flashes hit the building but he always managed to keep a step ahead. The stairs shook with each explosion and he staggered to the top before tumbling into a pile of crates that blocked his way.

He couldn't summon up the effort to move any further. The craft hovered, trying to spot him, its light piercing the stairwell below him. Gradually it rose up, scanning as it did. He hauled himself away from the entrance and under the crates.

Holding his breath, he waited as a red beam crisscrossed the corridor – systematically searching every corner. It would find him sooner or later; he'd have to get out. Looking up he remembered the gap in the roof that only hours earlier he'd dropped through, stocked up with food and looking forward to a well-earned rest. Now, his 'home' was no more.

From his bag he pulled out a three-pronged hook with a rope attached to one end. He waited until the beam was at the far end of the room before summoning up his last ounces of strength to throw the hook through the gap. He tugged and it stayed firm as the beam approached him. His muscles burned as he hauled himself slowly away from the danger zone. He had just squirmed to safety through the hole when this latest hiding-place was momentarily lit up and masonry and wood sent flying. Crumbling bricks fell away from the metal roof he had just climbed through. Where once the centuries-old blackened brick building had stood; now there was only an inky darkness.

He sat silently listening to the sound of destruction below. Only moments earlier he had been a good leap away from building to ceiling, now one slip and he'd plummet to his death. The water that had trickled down the walls of the once-proud building now rained down on the piles of bricks far beneath his feet. He was stuck between two worlds. The darkness beneath and the glare of the city whose sewers he now stood in.

Shaking, he edged further into the sewer-pipe before daring to stand. He didn't care where he went – anywhere would be better than here, he was tired, wet, cold and always alone.

He was unhappy, it was dangerous enough out in the sewers when he was constantly on the move, never mind having to sleep there. He had no idea why the 'rippers' had blown up his hide-away but he knew that he'd have to find a spot to hide himself. There was trouble brewing; he could feel it. He'd seen a lot more uniforms in the sewers and the rippers hadn't stopped patrolling the surrounding waters and buildings. Explosions had become a regular part of the soundtrack to his life of late and he was getting a bit fed up with them.

Wandering through the murky streams, he stopped for breath by his favourite grille, hoping to see his smiling and tottering friend. There she was, slightly smaller than the people around her but nevertheless his face broke into a smile for the first time in twenty-four hours. She was dressed identically to his previous sighting; however, her clothes were orange (previously blue) and her hair was like a red tower (it had also been blue). He noticed that everybody else about her was dressed in an identical manner. They were all tottering about (with more success than her) on the same kind of raised shoes.

He was so fascinated by them all, he failed to spot her looking straight in his direction. Rooted to the spot, his eyes followed her as she stumbled closer. His mind told him to move, but his body refused, aching from the cold, the wet and the lack of sleep.

She drew closer and closer.

"What's this?" she mused as she approached. Kneeling down with some difficulty in her tight skirt next to the sparkling silver bars of the grille she touched a single dried spot of blood.

"Blood?" she gasped. She then gave a start as she saw a pair of delighted and wide eyes staring up at her.

She stared back.

He could see sadness in those eyes but also colours on her face – not the dirty blotches that decorated him but red eyes and cheeks and orange lips. Her clothes were immaculate to him, they crinkled and shone: unlike his tattered, scratchy outfit.

A swift jolt to his leg broke his stare. Breaking free with a lash of his free leg, he spun round. A dark, uniformed figure stumbled back as he turned around – visor hiding its face.

The uniformed figure was unclipping its weapon when Albie instinctively kicked out again, knocking the weapon from its hand and out of sight. The speed of the young boy's reaction saved him. In one movement he leapt forward, knocking his opponent into the filthy stream where there was a dull thud. Pausing only to snatch his grey weapon, Albie ran off into the shadows.

Above ground the girl was still concentrating on the grille in the pavement.

"Hello…hello down there!" She waited for a response but none came. All about her gasped as the girl knelt next to the grille, apparently talking to herself. She tried to pull it open, putting her hands around the bars as she did so.

Behind her, a crowd of perfectly dressed bodies had gathered. They gasped at the unusual sight of someone on their knees – it just wasn't the way to act. The girl was completely oblivious: her efforts with the grille held her full concentration.

The crowd quickly moved back as a troop of uniforms arrived.

"Citizen, stand away!" they ordered as they ran towards her. Their voices sounded mechanical from behind their visors and facemasks. They drew their domitors that hung by their side when she took no notice.

Those members of the brightly decorated (but identically dressed) crowd that had remained to watch from a safe distance held their breath as they did so, not daring to warn the youngster and get themselves involved.

"Move away now, citizen!" they repeated, maintaining their distance. They looked unsure as to what to do when faced with such disobedience from one so young. They stood motionless as if willing her to take the initiative. Were they waiting for orders? Throughout all of this the girl had carried on calling down into the dark, blissfully unaware that anybody but her existed above ground.

The tense standoff was broken by a panicked scream:

"Tissa!" A woman raced across the empty paved square. She ignored the onlookers cowering behind the trees that lined the perimeter. The startled girl and the troopers around her spun round surprised to see the crazed woman rushing towards them.

At the sight of the weapons that were now aimed in her direction she froze, just managing to stop in time. Only her stack of orange hair still moved.

"Please don't shoot. She's my daughter," she pleaded, raising her hands as far above her head as her tight dress would allow.

As Albie ran through the slimy water, his mind was racing from his encounter. He had not heard such a sweet voice since he had lost his own mother. As he rested, leaning against the walls of the dank tunnel, he remembered the brief moment he had felt warmth sweep across his chilled and aching body. A kind of calmness had descended upon him too and it had felt so good. The hustle and bustle of everyday survival in the Underworld faded into the background. The harshness reality had been momentarily suspended but glancing down at the grey weapon he had picked up, brought his mind back to the present day. His soaked trousers and bruised, cut feet made him wish he could follow her sweet voice into her world.

Cold, unpleasant-feeling objects slipped past his feet as he made up his mind: he had to get out.

Pointing one end of his new possession at the opposite wall, he pressed one of the lightest coloured buttons. A bright flash accompanied a screech. He jerked and was flipped back, sending him crashing from wall to water. His whole body shook as he sank into the filth. Spluttering and thrashing, he finally steadied himself.

Picking himself up, he stared first at the dark smoking burn on the spot he'd been leaning against, then the untouched wall opposite. Making a mental note of the end that had sent him tumbling; he made a vain attempt to squeeze the sludge out of his dripping clothes. He examined the weapon again, this time pointing the hot end away from himself before pressing the darkest buttons. The resulting flash and screech was accompanied by flying rubble and dust that once more knocked him down. As he flicked back his knotted locks, liquid and congealed objects flew behind him. He began to do something he hardly knew he could do – he laughed. It was more like a strangled choke but it felt so good!

His target was now reduced to rubble and bare snakes of metal. The extra stench of the river far below him crept through the hole and plunged into the dark. Studying his handiwork, he glanced out and could see the familiar dotting of fires reflected on the ripples of the vast waters below.

Footsteps, splashing as they approached, brought him once more back to reality. He blinked as light started to fill the tunnel. Turning to run, he could hear shouts followed by quicker splashes. Before the approaching beams picked him out, he scuttled off.

He'd become so used to dodging patrols down here that he hardly thought about it as he squeezed effortlessly into a small drainage pipe. Submerged, the water that trickled over him barely registered. Only his nose could be seen; he was just another piece of debris amongst the jetsam of his underworld.

"…you better find it or else it's the factories for you…" The shape he had earlier upended stumbled through the tunnel towards him. Panicked, short breaths accompanied the feet that waded along the tunnel. Albie waited as they faded away and was just about to emerge when he froze.

More figures had arrived, flashlights probing. He waited as they examined his handiwork: the hole and the drop beyond it, the scarred wall. Radios crackled – he had no idea what they were saying but he was ready to strike if they spotted him: weapon in hand, feet poised to launch him forward. The cold was beginning to bite. Still the beams inched along the walls: he had to remain where he was. He desperately tried not to shiver as he lay: soaked and covered in sewage. The longer they poked about the rubble the harder it became for him to control his actions. His body was telling him it wasn't happy and wanted to be somewhere else while his brain told him that to move would mean discovery.

Stealing a peek, he could make out four bodies bent over: still studying the wall. The cleanliness of the top half of their uniforms contrasted starkly with the curved, grimy walls around them and the sludge that constantly dragged at their once-shining boots. Even down here, their armour gleamed – knee and elbow-pads and chest armour. The radios attached to their helmets constantly buzzed and chattered. Despite their sweeping glances, Albie remained hidden.

A long-tailed creature climbed over his head and dived back into the water. Unable to stop himself, he gave a slight start, sending out a series of ripples. Had he given himself away? Gripping his toy tightly he inched his finger towards one of the coloured buttons and waited to pounce. A cry further up the tunnel attracted his visitors' attention.

"Positive ID: it's them, the man and the woman with the domitor." a metallic voice echoed and as quickly as they had arrived, the Uniforms were gone. The quiet trickle and dripping of the water was the only sound. His faced emerged and, coughing, he spat out the contents of his mouth. His long-tailed friend looked back at him from the entrance to the pipe before carrying on its journey. Sitting up, he watched the glow of their lights that quickly disappeared around the corner. He listened until all the faint splashes in the sludge had gone before he emerged fully – dripping and smelling worse than usual. Trying his best to rid himself of many undesirable objects, he took one prouder look at the hole before he set off back to the grille where the girl had spotted him.

3

"Promise me!" screamed her mother but Tissa

wasn't listening…couldn't listen. Her mind was alive, buzzing with the day's events. It *had* been a boy, trapped below ground, and there *had* been blood next to the grille. He had needed her help, she was sure of it. She could hear her mother's voice, hammering away, at the back of her mind but just couldn't come back to the here and now. She looked up at her. Still fighting with her flood of thoughts, she momentarily watched her; as if in a watery bubble. The sound vibrated around her: muffled and incomprehensible. Her mother's mouth moved rapidly but incomprehensibly. She was shaking and her make-up was smeared in all directions as she wiped ever more furiously to stem the flow from her red, puffy eyes. Her arms reached out to Tissa and suddenly, like a child's bubble mixture popping, the wall around her vanished and she felt herself being dragged into the tightest embrace. She was being squeezed as her mother shook.

"…do not go near that grille…or any grille…again. Do you hear me Tissa?" Her voice had softened in between the quieter sobs. "You almost had us both in the factories." Her mother's grip softened until Tissa was able to rest her head on her mother's shoulder. They were both crying: one from fear, the other from frustration.

"I'm sorry, mum. But there was a boy down there. I saw him! He was trapped and needed my help."

"Forget him. His kind and ours must never mix."

"But why…?" she began but was instantly

interrupted.

"…just because that is the way it is. If we start asking questions and acting away from the norm then our good lives will be gone."

"But, I just want to…"

"You mustn't even think about it or you will become one of them and I, for one, don't want to even think about what it might be like…" They both froze as the crackle of radios and heavy boots filled the corridor outside. Were they coming for them? Gripping each other tighter, they waited as the steps drew closer. The radios grew louder and clearer. The bang on the door would be next. However, the boots walked past and it was not their door that shook with the force of the fists. It was two apartments down. Tissa's mother relaxed her grip on her daughter and in that moment, she was away. Tissa raced to the door, ignoring her mother's strangled cry. The door to the corridor opened and Tissa stepped out in plain sight of the black-clad troopers. A guardian swooped over her head, narrowly missing her but she still stood, transfixed by the scene unfolding two doors down. She was the only other person in the corridor. Her mother didn't dare move.

They listened to the cries from the apartment and the robotic instructions of the guardians to remain calm and come peacefully. Tissa could hear a brief struggle and a trooper was flung back through the door, colliding with the wall opposite. As he stood up, Tissa could see the dent the metallic armour had made. The guardian fired a swift pair of darts and it was over.

Please, Tissa. Come back in before you are spotted…" she urged, barely able to whisper. "Tissa…" Her pleas fell on deaf ears again. After five tense moments, Tissa whispered to her mother.

"It's Armand and his mum. They are being…" but before she could utter another word, two bodies were carried out by the troopers, their bare feet dragging along the carpet.

Armand: he had always been such a nervous type. She had liked him for that because he had kept himself to himself. He hadn't been extravagant, obsessed with his looks. She had often smiled at him and he had never looked away. He had always given her the same, reserved little wave and grin in the twenty years she had known him. She had always known him. Rarely talking to anyone he had been studious, kept his head down so why was he being taken away?

His head lolled from side to side as he was hauled by his arms. She wanted to cry out, pull him away from them but her feet were firmly planted. One of the troopers bringing up the rear turned to look at Tissa. They stood studying each other momentarily. Tissa's distraught eyes couldn't see any kind of emotion or body language to indicate whether he felt any kind of sadness or remorse. He hardly looked human behind the dark visor. He began to raise his domitor.

Tissa's mother summoned up the courage to step towards the door. She grabbed her terrified daughter and shut the door. It slid silently and swiftly shut. She instantly locked it and pulled her daughter into her bedroom before her knees gave way and she sank onto the edge of her bed.

Her eyes were wide and wild. She once again anticipated the heavy fist on their door but once again it did not arrive. She sat in shock, unable to look at her daughter.

"But why take them?" Tissa finally broke the shocked silence. Still gaping at the blank wall, her mother said nothing. Finally, Tissa sat down next to her and took her quivering hand. Her mother turned to her.

"Who knows? I heard a rumour they were in contact with her former partner…"

"Armand's birth father?" Tissa gasped and her mother nodded. "But what is so wrong with that?"

"It just is," her mother sighed. "It interferes with our job to keep the city working efficiently." Her mother trotted out the phrase they had had drummed into them from an early age. "Everyone has…"

"…their role!" Tissa finished for her. "But why is seeing your birthing partner not allowed? Why is it so wrong?" The questions began to gush but her mother turned her head away to gaze once more at the blank space. Tissa waited but no answer came. She decided, now was the time to ask the question that had been burning within her for so long.

"Who was my birth father? What was he like?" Her mother's face turned red and once again she began to shout.

"No! I will not talk about him. I love you and

that is all you should need to know! Now go to your room, finish your HomeStudy and go to sleep. I have to try to work this evening. Goodness only knows how I am going to do that after all of this. Stay in the flat and out of trouble! You hear me?" Tissa looked bewildered by the venom and fury that her mother had mustered up and meekly nodded.

Without another word she trotted off to her room and locked herself in. Her mother fought to control the sobs that engulfed her once more. That had been a part of her life that she had been forced to forget. She often thought of him, of their Pairing day. It had been the happiest time of her life. But now she had to move on. Tissa was all she had left to remember that period by. Sentimentality was not permitted in Tenebria.

It was dark above ground when he returned to the grille, which seemed strangely subdued after all the excitement of the day: almost too quiet. Sniffing the air for any unusual smells, he could smell the troopers' uniforms from far off, there was nothing different. It wasn't what he expected to smell but he half-hoped her sweet smell would still be lingering. He was sadly disappointed.

He reached for the bars that had always imprisoned him in his labyrinth of subterranean passageways. They still stood firm. There was no sign of any troopers or onlookers from above. Where had she gone – was she alright? He tugged at the bars half-heartedly, lacking the strength to maintain any real effort. He felt decidedly unhappy in his cold and clammy state and needed warmth. The only place he could think there might be some was above ground.

Remembering the weapon he now carried, he poked the bars with it. He had seen the uniforms use their weapons to open them so why couldn't he do it now? His frustration grew: taps on the bars quickly grew to angry beatings. He growled at it but that made no difference either. Defeated, he slumped back, staring dejectedly up at the bars to his prison. The lights above continued to wink at him. He wanted to be drawn in…be part of it. The stream he sat dejectedly in sapped his strength, along with any warmth he had had, as it flowed over and around him. He leaned his head against the dank walls and stared up at the bars. He didn't care if the Uniforms caught him. He had had enough of fighting to survive and being alone.

Finally, a small plate, on the left of the bars, no bigger than a hand, caught his eye. The flashing lights danced across its shiny surface and ideas started forming. He casually tried to prod it with the new weapon in his hand. He was too far away. He folded his arms and tried to bury his face into his coat. It was cold and so was he. In fact, he was frozen and he'd have to do something about it. From somewhere a voice from his past echoed.

"Believe!"

He returned his gaze to the grille.

"Believe!"

Like a shot, he leapt up. Nervously he held one end of his 'stick' to the panel and held his breath.

To his amazement, a click was accompanied by a

whirring noise. He could not believe his eyes as his prison door slid open. Punching the air, he splashed the water everywhere and the smile that covered his face was joined by tears that smeared the dirt down his cheeks. He cried out for the first time in many years.

"Yes!"

The moment he did so, he realised how stupid he'd been. Instinctively he ducked into the smallest space he could find: a crack at the foot of the tunnel wall, the wind from below sucking at him as he held on. Blinking, he waited. The moment he popped his head out would he meet the same fate as his home and the people in the boat?

But nothing happened. The lights still winked and glowed and the grille remained open.

He crept back towards the hole. Plucking up the courage he waved his new toy slowly through the hole. Nothing happened.

His hand edged upwards. It emerged above ground.

Still nothing happened.

All he had to do was climb out. However, he was suddenly frightened to leave his prison. The cold kept clawing at him, urging him to stay down there: where it was safe. But his hand felt warm and the warmth was spreading to his arm. His body and mind were in conflict but he knew, deep down which would win. The more of him that emerged above ground the better he felt. In one last push he took the plunge, rolling out onto warm concrete where the evening sun had lingered. He closed his eyes and he was at last warm.

Paradise was his!

He lay unmoving for an age: not daring to open his eyes in case it was all a dream or there was a Uniform standing over him. At last he managed to open his eyes. He couldn't help but let out a gasp at the sight that greeted him.

Four enormous identical buildings towered over him with endless rows of windows: some still lit. Rows of enormous, thin plants on long stalks surrounded the square he lay in. They gently swayed in the breeze their upper sections rustled gently, adding to his unexpected moment of calm. Signs on the buildings flashed dimly – not the loud colours that he had seen during the day but softer pastel shades, despite the pictures and symbols still looking the same.

He lay on his back, the stars above him unobscured by bars. A light breeze blew over him: not like the foul-smelling winds that blew through the sewers: this felt fresh, welcoming and sweet. He gulped it in, closing his eyes with each breath and sighing loudly, enjoying the heat on his back. Even if it turned out to be a dream, he thought, he would still be happy just to have imagined it.

At the back of his mind he could hear a distant, steady beat. It grew and grew. His insides began to shudder and shake. His eyes opened instantly. He knew that sound. It was a ripping noise and it was growing louder. Scanning the sky, he immediately realised how exposed he was. How had he let his guard down so much? The memories of the morning's massacre filled his head yet his body ached so much that he couldn't move. The concrete's warmth lulled him as he wafted to drift back; he felt so tired. His eyes wanted to close: let consciousness slip away. But the ripping sound grew louder. His body began to react to the jarring and suddenly he was awake. He had to move.

Jumping to his feet he could see that he was in an enormous square. Steps led up to the buildings lining the outside but he had forgotten the golden rule of survival – stay alert and in the shadows. Between two towering blocks that disappeared into the night sky, a light was approaching, accompanied by the juddering throb he had become so familiar with.

Instinctively he ran: towards the nearest building. Hurling himself behind a pillar as the ripping grew nearer. He waited, the sound sending shivers through him. The light crept closer. The Predavator circled the perimeter of the square: scanning the ground. The long line of pillars that ringed the square wouldn't hide him for long as it scanned the forecourt he was sheltering in. He found himself counting down the pillars as they were lit up by the approaching searchlight. Glancing behind he made out the shape of two dark tinted glass doors with a steel opening panel just like the one on the sewer bars. He would have to try to get into the building.

As the craft edged closer to his hiding place, he could feel the air being whipped up by its engines. The cold gripped him once more. Steeling himself he sprinted the ten metres to the doors before placing his weapon onto the panel. Expecting the doors to open, he waited anxiously but nothing happened. The only object that was moving was the Predavator as the glass-panelled fronts to his left lit up, one by one. The searchlight's glare was getting nearer. It jumped from panel to panel as he tugged frantically at the bars on each door. He kicked them, hoping for a miracle but they wouldn't give. He squealed like an animal, all the time tugging at the door and turning to see how much time he had left.

He gave a final pull before he made a run for it and to his complete surprise they swung open. He dived in, rolling until he careered against a wall opposite. By the time he was able to take stock of his surroundings the doors had closed and the Predavator was continuing its search of the buildings in the square.

The glare of a single light that shone at him was painful. He buried his head into the soft floor. Slowly he lifted it but his eyelids remained firmly clamped together. He forced himself to open them a crack. Then his ears were attacked by a horrible squealing noise: like a dying creature. The first thing he could see was a figure jumping up and down, slapping her hands together.

As he got used to the glare the figure came into focus. He smiled as he looked up at his saviour. Stupidly high shoes combined with shiny green dress. The smile that now spread across her face revealed a perfect, white set of teeth. Freckles on her face stood out as if she'd painted them on.

"It is you, it is you," she repeated in a suppressed

high-pitched screech, "I knew you'd come…I've been watching the entrance since I got back…boy I was in such trouble… but I managed to bypass the release key for the door and here you are…and…oh no! You've got a domitor…how did you get that…we've got to get rid of it?"

He hardly understood a word she was saying, it had been a long time since anybody had ever said anything to him and the only sounds he had remembered were the crackles of the communicators on the uniforms' radios.

Despite all of this: he felt safe. He managed to ignore her twittering as he marvelled at the floor that felt so furry and warm: it had to all be a dream! He rolled majestically about in it – this was far better than his old mattress – if only she'd stop screeching at him.

Finally, her twittering and his rolling were interrupted by footsteps descending the metal stairs. He sprang to his feet; years of constant danger in the sewers had trained him well. Tissa stopped giggling and ran to a side-door as the steps grew nearer.

"Quick: in here!" Her furious pointing along with the impending arrival spurred him into action. He grabbed his prized possessions, the stick and his bag, before slipping through a door into a long corridor.

As they stepped through the door that had slid open before them, strips of light burst into life above them. He backed up against the wall, unsure of what to make of this. He was used to running for cover whenever a light flickered. The sounds of gunfire and exploding masonry usually followed it. The lack of any reaction from his new friend helped him to relax slightly. However, he still wasn't happy with the situation and felt far from calm.

When he turned around, she'd gone. He made a sound – a cross between a cry and a grunt – as he spun on the spot: looking up and down the corridor, he warily studied the flashing light strips above.

The door he had come through moments earlier began to slide shut. He took aim with his weapon at the door and readied himself for an explosion.

A hand gripped his arm, dragging him through another door that itself swiftly slid shut. Pulling himself away from the hand he ran into something low and soft that sent him tumbling.

"It's only me," a voice giggled. Hearing the familiar, quieter voice, he gratefully sank into the welcoming, soft floor.

Opening his eyes, he noticed he was being watched. His companion was pointing at herself and repeating the word "Tissa". Eventually, he repeated the word and was rewarded by a gleam of brilliantly white sparkling teeth: perfectly formed. He repeated the word and this time she smiled, clapped then led him into another room with glass on all the walls.

He jumped back as an unkempt, filthy but somehow familiar boy appeared before him. For the first time he was able to look at himself. He carefully studied the reflection, and then compared it to Tissa's. She did likewise.

She was spotless – perfect skin, hair and teeth

but there wasn't a clean part of him, his hair was long and matted while his teeth were black and rotten. They stood staring at the others' reflection, neither daring a peek at the other. Albie reached out to touch her reflection, half expecting everything to disappear and find himself back in the tunnels again. Tissa wrinkled her nose and her expression changed.

"Phew, you stink!" she informed him. "I'm sorry to be so blunt but it's true." His smell had become overpowering: an unpleasant combination of sewage, dampness and body odour.

"Tissa!" She repeated it and pointed at herself again. This time he smiled, pointing at himself but remaining silent. It was a start she thought.

"We're going have to do something about you – you won't get very far looking or smelling like that." Although he didn't know what she was saying, he grinned at her with all his black teeth then cautiously shuffled forward as she invited him to step into a tiled room that had opened out in front of them.

The walls were smooth and shiny. A row of coloured buttons in the wall each had their own nozzles below it. A dial on the left-hand wall had two arrows on it facing in opposite directions: one red and the other blue.

He tapped each of the walls in turn with his weapon. Every time he did it he put his ear to the wall and waited. Tissa tapped him on the shoulder making him spin round. She gently tried to take hold of the domitor clutched tightly in his hand but he snatched it away from her.

"You don't need that...no-one's going to hurt you," she reassured him but he still wasn't letting go. He backed away and, in the process, managed to press one of the buttons. A bright pink liquid shot towards him. Instinctively, he dived out of the room sending Tissa flying. Rolling over he aimed the domitor at the buttons on the far wall.

"No!" cried Tissa just as he was about to obliterate the tiled room, "It's only a shower!" Bemused, he reluctantly lowered his weapon.

"It cleans you..." she told him "...and you don't need that!" Holding out her hands she motioned towards the domitor. He handed it over. Pleased with this major step forward she decided not to interfere further as he stepped back into the shower fully clothed.

Turning the dial, she watched his expression change from suspicion to enjoyment as water shooting out of a grille in the ceiling grew warmer and warmer. He stamped his shoes sending dirt flying. The water trickling down his grimy clothes changed colour to a thick brown as he experimented with the buttons. Pink liquid shot out once more and he began to enjoy dodging the liquids that spat out of the wall. Blue liquid then purple shot out. He tried to spray his friend as she laughed at his antics.

For the next hour he giggled at this new toy and gradually the water colour changed from near black to just a grey tinge. He couldn't remember ever making the kind of sounds he was making now but he felt totally at ease...and happy.

Finally, Tissa cried "Enough!" and the water slowed to a trickle. He decided he had tired of this game and clambered out still fully clothed. A trail of dirt continued to run down him onto the carpeted floor as his footsteps trailed from the shower into a corridor.

Traces of colour could be seen through the muck that had virtually covered him from head to foot. Tissa could make out a faded red jacket.

"How long have you been down there?" she wondered but didn't get a reply. His trousers were in a similar state while his boots had lasted well and looked newer.

She led him into an enormous cupboard filled with rows upon rows of clothes. Rails of trousers stretched to his left with tops to his right. Thick coats sat above the trousers with thinner versions opposite. He gulped and stared, stared and gulped. He sighed then whistled, whistled and sighed. His head shook as he struggled to believe the sight of so many clothes.

Tissa on the other hand was charging up and down the aisle, muttering to herself.

"Blue…too last week…turquoise…that's more like it…flares…nobody wears them…shiny…yep…ooh; that will look good…and they could pass for a man's clothes."

He had no idea what she was doing and didn't take any notice, the array of colours fascinated him. Stretching his arm out he ambled along, pausing to stroke a type of fur or make plastic clothes shimmer. His daydreaming was rudely brought to a close as Tissa finished her search with a cry:

"That'll do nicely!" she cried, "Come on…" she grabbed him and skipped into another room. "There!" What do you reckon?"

His eyes followed her arm to an outfit that she had laid out in front of him; it sparkled blue, captivating him. Everything he'd ever worn had been pre-soaked in sewage or caked in mud, certainly he'd never seen anything like this before.

"Go on then, put them on." Tissa commented as he stroked the trousers and shirt. He finally realised that she meant for him to put them on. She stood at the door and looked at her uncomfortably.

He waited. She still stared. He kept glancing at the door and she finally got the hint and left the room. It wasn't until the door swished shut behind her that he started to change.

Outside, Tissa was considering the next stage of his transformation. She started typing instructions into a keyboard that had slid out from the wall. A leather chair slid out next to it and a long and thin, frosted glass cylinder slowly dropped from the ceiling. At the same moment a screen appeared in the wall.

He proudly emerged through the door, smoothing himself down. Tissa looked him up and down – there was something not quite right about him. Okay, his hair was still in series of matted knots (she'd fix that later) and there were still traces of dirt on his face (nothing another good shower wouldn't get rid), but something wasn't right. She just couldn't put her finger on it. Glancing down, it came to her – he had no shoes and scruffy (and hairy) bare feet were never really likely to make a comeback – not smelly ones anyway.

She led him to another cupboard where rows of shoes sat neatly on seemingly endless shelves. His eyes lit up when he spotted a black pair of leather boots that had numerous pockets – both seen and unseen. He immediately set about his old clothes, pulling out knives, nails, rolls of wire…all the tat he had convinced himself was so important to his continued existence. Tissa had never seen so much rubbish – if he was going to pass himself off in her world – it would all have to go. There was plenty of time for that…now, it was time for a facelift. Giving him a moment to put on his new shoes and tuck his trousers into his boots, an action that made her shudder, she led him out into the corridor once more.

He, almost looked the part now, from the neck down. The big giveaway was the mass of snakes that were trying to escape from his scalp. Even his lengthy shower and the variety of coloured liquids had had little effect.

Tissa led him back into the main room, to the screen on the wall on which was a picture of him as he was now – complete with muddy patches.

"What do you fancy?" she asked, remembering he hadn't a clue what she was talking about. "How about the bald look?" The image on the screen was suddenly robbed of hair, "A bit severe I think…what about a Mohican?" He laughed at himself.

"…floppy fringe?" He pulled a face, having

realised what she was trying to do to him. Various styles appeared before them, he pulled a face or she dismissed them with phrases such as "too yesterday", "too last week" or "nobody would ever be seen dead like that". In the end they settled on "short but not scalped".

Tissa moved him in place below the glazed cylinder. As it grew closer to his 'snakes', he began to panic. He still trusted his friend but the moving object was severely testing his faith in her. At first, he tried not to appear alarmed, but as it drew nearer his fears grew. He focussed on the whirring sound that grew louder – adding to his unease.

At the last moment he dropped to the floor, rolling to the corner of the room whilst grabbing a knife from his new boots. The noise immediately stopped as Tissa impatiently punched a key on the keyboard.

This tense figure, waving his knife at the motionless cylinder, was beginning to annoy her. "Look there's nothing to be frightened of..." she spat out, "it's only going to cut your hair…like this." She pointed at the screen on which even his image was starting to look annoyed at him, as if to tell him not to be such a coward.

He stopped cowering, summoning up the courage to put his head into the base of the cylinder and the whirring began again. He shuddered as unknown objects whizzed about his scalp like a whirlwind.

However, the whirlwind started to slow down

and the sound of cutting blades became the sounds of a struggle. The snakes were fighting back: his hair didn't want to be cut and certainly not the way Tissa and her machine had decided. Still trying to impress, he hardly flinched but inside his stomach was churning. He couldn't move. While the machine had a tight hold, his hair was determined not to give in. He cried out as he felt his hair being tugged from his scalp. Pushing against the cylinder's base he was still unable to free himself, the groans of struggling motors grew above him and smoke started to spiral out of the top of the cylinder.

Tissa had stopped smiling reassuringly at him and was furiously typing on the keyboard next to the screen. The image of him on the screen had been replaced by a sandstorm. He fought to free himself from the machine's tight grip but despite their attempts it wouldn't budge or stop. A screeching noise grew inside the cylinder as the smoke grew from struggling motors.

Just when they thought they couldn't bear the piercing noise any more there was a blue flash directly above his head, thick smoke billowed from the ceiling and silence fell upon the room.

Tissa stared at the smoke pouring from the machine. She couldn't move. Every bit of her wanted to pull the stupid machine off Albie but her feet wouldn't do as they were told. She clenched her fists tighter and tighter to urge herself forward but she couldn't do it.

A sudden cry snapped her from her trance. It was

Albie, and he was crying. Tissa pulled the cylinder up and with Albie's help managed to slide it off his head. She breathed a sigh of relief: his head was intact although she couldn't say the same for her machine.

He whistled then let out a chuckle. Despite the thick smoke above his head he was unharmed. A peculiar, watery foam rained down on him and the smoke was gone.

Pulling himself out of the tangle of metal and wires that snaked around, he looked at Tissa, who was still in a state of shock.

Once this had passed she studied his hair. He still had a mass of snakes but at least they weren't down his back any more and didn't look quite so dirty and untidy. One day somebody might even think they looked good – but that time was a long time off she thought.

"Well you won't be able to blend in with the Tenebrians anytime soon…" she muttered.

Tissa's face dropped as there was a buzz from the door. Albie leapt out of sight, into the clothes cupboard as Tissa tried to hide any trace of him. The delay had obviously annoyed the person at the door as another short buzz was accompanied by a long, drawn out one. Tissa ran to answer it. Tapping the screen by the wall she could see the face of her block manager in an extremely annoyed state. He was the man who looked after all the apartments in the block – all 20 000 of them and their little 'problem' would certainly not have been missed by him.

"What are you doing in there?" he growled. He looked as if he had just woken up and was rubbing his head furiously.

"It's okay, just a blow-out on my hairstyler, we'll get it fixed in the morning…"

"Where's your mother?" he grumbled back, still holding his forehead.

"She's at work, but I'll get her to sort it out, I…" Tissa tailed off, it wasn't going well.

"You'd better…" With that he stumbled off up the corridor, muttering. Forgetting him, Tissa eased herself onto a bed that had appeared from a hole in the wall without even thinking of changing into night clothes. It had all been too much excitement for her, she had no idea what she was going to do with her new friend but she had a feeling life was about to take a new twist – for the better or worse she had no idea. Whichever way it went she'd sort it out: something her mum always said to her:

"Don't regret the choices and mistakes you make, just make sure you learn from them." Her mother's voice tailed off and for now so too did thoughts of her visitor as exhaustion took hold of her, dragging her gratefully to sleep.

4

After a fitful night's sleep, Tissa wished she couldn't hear the crackle of radios and the sound of marching boots in the corridor. She tossed and turned, fighting to ignore them. Suddenly her eyes shot open:

she remembered the events of the previous night. Fists pounded on a door two apartments along. Throwing back the plastic bedcover her thoughts immediately turned to Albie. Rushing through the door, she scoured the filthy room, her mind raced with all the possibilities: had he sneaked out while she slept? Had he been captured? Where was he now?

A grunt from the clothes room made her jump. A pile of clothes in the corner was stirring – her worries were eased when a mass of snake-like hair emerged from the middle of the pile. Albie emerged extremely disorientated.

Her brief moment of ease ended with a hammering of gloved fists on the door.

"Open up, citizen!" They shuddered at the familiar metallic voices but were stung into action. Leaping up, he mimed holding a domitor. She understood and raced to the shower – just as the door to Tissa's apartment exploded inwards, sending metal shards raining into the room.

Uniforms poured through the door, covering every corner with beams of light. They wasted no time in picking out the intruder to their city. The lights converged on him as he leapt to avoid the inevitable shots. Tissa grabbed Albie's weapon and flung it across the room where he caught it in mid-air. Bolts of energy followed his flight as he landed with a spin so that he faced the intruders. A bright beam screeched from his weapon. The wall behind the invaders melted as he grabbed Tissa's arm. They ran past the troopers as they lay on the ground, their heads still ringing from the blast and covered in debris.

Radios, alarms and the buzzing of bare wires filled the air. He grabbed his faithful bag before pulling the coughing Tissa through the smoke, dodging sparks of electricity, and into the corridor. He stood, uncertain which way to go but now it was Tissa's turn to pull him up the corridor.

As they dashed up the passage, bolts screeched past them blowing neat circular burn holes in the doors ahead of them. He swung round, pushing his friend to the floor as another bolt fizzed past them. Black smoke snaked up from the charred wall that she had been in front of.

"How did you…" she began but the far end of the corridor exploded as Albie sent a bolt screeching back at their pursuers.

They slipped through the door that slid open before them, leaving the burning fumes and acrid smoke temporarily behind.

"Thanks," she whispered, trying to catch her breath in between coughs. He just grinned – despite being disorientated he was quite enjoying himself. Tissa was not impressed with the state of his teeth – not the perfect sets of dazzling white everybody she knew had but an uneven, broken set with a few missing just for good measure.

"Uuurgh!" she commented – "you need a good dentist." He seemed to like the sound she had first made and repeated it, laughing.

"Uuuurgh!" he repeated, listening to the sounds behind the door.

"Good thinking – maybe now's not the best time: this way!" She once more took hold of his hand and they scurried down the corridor and around the corner.

He was glad she knew where she was going because to him, every passage was the same; from the painted metallic walls to the pale, soft carpets. Even the pictures with constantly changing patterns featured the same colours – rotating and twisting. He didn't like this. Below ground everything had its own uniqueness: from the burnt-out wrecks to the rotting wood and ancient buildings collapsing through old age. He could spend ages exploring them, studying what remained of their ornate pillars, ceilings and sculptures: his favourite sculptures were of strange four-legged creatures with wild manes and the most vicious looking teeth he'd ever seen.

These newer buildings were filled with painted arrows and bare walls: they weren't welcoming at all. His old spots had been extremely cold but safe, and even though they had been wet and the wind blew straight over him, they were his homes and they were safe. Nobody had bothered him before last night or had even known he was there. Now it seemed that the whole city was after him and he did not like it.

"In here," Tissa called, "no-one will be coming for ages – it's the holiday…and I know the code!" She pulled out of her pocket a small, plastic tablet with coloured grey buttons that rested neatly in her hand. Pressing them, she touched the pad on a metal-plated door. There was a single beep, the pad lit up then the plate door slid open. She ushered him inside. Finally, she breathed a sigh of relief as it closed slowly behind her.

He stared at the huge, domed room which she had led him into. Screens flashed high above them on the walls while rows of chairs stood empty in a circle on the ground. They each had a headset hooked on one arm and a touchpad on the other.

It was into one of these that Tissa flopped. Albie followed suit, his head was spinning with all that had happened to him in this new world. There had been little time for either of them to think clearly about anything since she had opened the door for him a few hours earlier. She didn't even know his name yet they had saved each other's lives with barely a word said. Looking at him she knew he would stick out like a sore thumb. He had the clothes but he was dishevelled, he still reeked, his teeth were nearly rotten and he couldn't understand her. She shuddered as she realised the danger she…they were now in: she was hiding a fugitive. She'd seen enough on the tele-wall to know what happened to those people who defied the troopers. Putting her anxieties to the back of her mind she turned her attention back to Albie who was busy studying his chair.

"This is the Edu-suite," she informed him "it's where we learn about all sorts of things – how to behave, what to wear, when to wear it, where to get it, how much it costs…" He just looked blankly at her.

Touching the pad on her chair's arm she pointed at one of the screens as it automatically lowered to meet them.

"Do you like these? It's my work so far…" she chattered as pictures of people in different clothes flashed before them; some featured Tissa but most had blank faces. There were pieces of writing – some small and black, that held no interest for him, but there was other writing that was bold and colourful which fascinated him.

"That was an advert I designed for a sale at…" Tissa hesitated as she looked at him – his face showed no inkling of understanding her so she stopped.

"We'll have to start at the beginning…" she muttered as from her chair she switched on the pad set into his chair. Her fingers quickly swept over her pad then she stood up and placed headphones on him.

Reluctantly, he let her slip them on, this was her world after all, and she hadn't let him down so far. He tried not to think of the episode with the hair machine. The chair started moving. He squirmed then relaxed when she laid her hand on his arm. The chair rose effortlessly towards a screen high upon the wall. He threw her worried glances as he rose but decided to put his trust in her.

The chair rose higher and eventually stopped level with a screen that flickered in front of him. A voice bombarded him with what he thought was nonsense. He could not understand anything that was being said to him: it was just like his new friend's voice but a thousand times faster. Images on the screen flashed past him at the same rate but he found himself unable to tear himself away from them. He drifted into a trance: his eyes glued to the screen.

As he sat transfixed, Tissa studied the action outside. The plaza had become a hive of activity. Predavators flew in and out every few minutes and that penetrating sound was everywhere. Luminous orange barriers were being set up at each entrance, all manned by at least four black uniformed bodies. The enormous screens around the plaza flashed brightly coloured messages:

"Do not panic!" and

"This is a controlled situation for your safety."

"Return to your residences."

Eventually these were replaced by calming patterns and soothing voices.

A familiar figure was standing by one of the barriers; "Mum," Tissa muttered and immediately reached for her mobile communicator. She watched the figure as it rummaged inside a pink bag, pulling out a small, similarly-coloured object and held it to her ear.

"Mum, it's me…I'm inside the building…no, don't tell the troopers…please don't: it's important! I'm okay…call you later – I'm okay: honest! I love you."

She forced herself to switch the communicator off. There was no way her mum was going to be able to get to her without discovery.

Twenty metres above her, Albie was staring at the now-blank screen. His face looked as if it had been punched. His eyes were open but there was no recognition there. His cheeks were red and sweat dripped down him. The headphones were to one side of his head and his arms were hanging limp over the side of the chair.

A groan indicated he was coming around as his fingers began to twitch.   She dashed across to a pad on the wall and began lowering his chair. He had even less idea where he was and she could do without any broken bones from a fall. She slipped a brightly coloured tablet into his mouth.

"Suck this: it'll help with some of the after-effects of your intensive learning course." He obeyed and soon his face returned to a more-normal colour.

There were more groans as the chair slowly settled back on the floor. Tissa removed the headphones then returned them to the arm of the chair.

"It's okay, you'll feel better after a drink – everyone feels dehydrated the first time." He took a sip of a clear liquid she held out to him and the fazed expression was replaced by a squinted stare. To his amazement he realised he could clearly understand what she was saying.

"What…?" he asked unsurely.

"You've just taken an intensive language course," she replied "it'll be enough to get you through."

He nodded, leaning back on the chair and closing his eyes; images and words were still flashing through his mind. He certainly didn't feel like using his newfound language yet.

Tissa looked out the window again but although there were no new developments, now she couldn't see her mum. Sounds of movement in the corridor pulled her away from the scene. Dashing across the room she looked at a screen to the side of the door. It showed the view outside the door – nothing happening there. Pressing the screen another view appeared, this time showing the whole corridor. She was shocked to see the corridor filling up with black and silver-clad bodies. Turning to warn him, she could see he was still dazed.

The moment they stepped out they would be recognised but what else could they do? Her eyes desperately scanned the room; every screen, chair, desk and wall then she saw their way out. It was only a small ventilation grille just above all the screens but it was a way out. How were they going to reach it? She looked at the body next to her, still coming around. He wasn't going to be any help.

The chair! It was just what they needed. Squeezing in next to him, she steered the chair using the pad on the arm to propel them higher, above the screens and towards the grille.

The chattering radios and robotic voices in the passage grew closer and clearer. They needed to hurry.

The speed of the rising chair added to her anxiety and every second was like an hour. Her heart pounded even quicker. She furiously wiped the sweat from her brow without a care for her make-up. She was struggling to keep control of the gently rising chair as her fingers slipped across the pad. Each unexpected movement made her grip both herself and Albie. It was not a good time for his increased animation. They tipped backwards and forwards and her grip on the chair grew less and less.

The search outside drew closer while the chair seemed to be ascending slower and noisier with the two of them perched on it.

"How did you get so heavy?" she asked Albie but he was still not ready to reply. They drew nearer the grille, eventually stopping within touching distance of it. Using Albie's head as a lever, Tissa climbed onto the two arms and balanced there. She reached out for the grille, expecting it to open easily, but it wouldn't budge. She pulled again but it remained tightly shut. Wrapping the fingers of one hand around the bars of the grille, she began searching her pockets. Unfortunately, all she could come up with was her communicator and a make-up set.

"Got any bright ideas?" she asked Albie.

As if flicked on by a switch, Albie suddenly came to with a start. Looking around, he first noticed the precariously balanced Tissa above his head then gasped at the drop to the floor.

The chair tipped with his movement, catching Tissa off guard. She screamed as she stumbled, her free hand flapped and the make-up set sailed down, smashing into pieces. Tissa grabbed hold of the grille with both hands.

Below them the door slid open. Two uniforms appeared, their domitors raised before them, their feet crunching as they stepped on the remains of Tissa set.

The searchers carried on, completely unaware of the efforts above them. Carefully pulling his arms back into the chair to avoid dislodging Tissa, Albie remembered his domitor. Easing it out of the chair he held it out for Tissa to grab. Hanging with one hand, she swiped out at it but it was just too far away.

Albie looked at the chair, trying to work out how to move. A cry outside made the troopers below turn and race back into the passage. Once the room was clear, he glanced at the pad on the chair arm and pressed. The chair surged down then forward, crashing into the wall below Tissa. She couldn't hang on any more and she fell.

With a stifled scream, Tissa landed on top of Albie. He grabbed hold of her with one hand and the arm of the chair with the other as they began to slide over the edge.

The pair held their breath as they waited to be discovered – but nobody appeared; the room and the corridor were silent and empty. Easing the chair back down, Tissa ran to the window to look outside again; where she had earlier heard screams. Straining to see below her, she saw a troop wagon positioned in the middle of the plaza and a woman lying on the ground surrounded by troopers. Tissa immediately recognised her mother.

"Mum," Tissa gasped as she recognised the body below. Fighting back the tears, she couldn't breathe. She desperately hoped to see her mum move.

Albie stared blankly down and remembered that memory he had willed himself to forget years earlier. That day his own mother had disappeared, leaving him alone, had been blanked out of his mind. It was the only way he had been able to cope with her desertion –

she had to be alive somewhere – forgetting her had made it easier to forget how much he had missed her. Now his new friend was experiencing the same emotion.

A sigh of relief brought him back to the present day.

"She's alive…!" Tissa relaxed momentarily "…but why have they got her?" She strained to hear but couldn't.

Far below, two troopers pulled Tissa's mother up by the arms but her legs refused to support her and she slumped downwards.

"Get up, citizen!" the mechanical voice ordered her. She managed to haul herself up but stood unsteadily and her voice betrayed her nervousness.

"What have I done wrong?" she pleaded, her voice faltering as she spoke.

"You are the owner of block 1969?" droned the voice behind the visor.

"Yes…" she couldn't believe this was happening to her. All her life she had made sure she towed the line. Nothing out of the ordinary about her, the right clothes, hair colour…everything that was expected, she had done to avoid attracting unwanted attention. She had left it up to her partner, Tissa's father, to attract the limelight. Now, here she was with thousands of pairs of eyes watching her from every level of the four enormous towers that surrounded the square.

"You have been harbouring a fugitive and will be disposed of accordingly."

"No…my daughter…she's…" It was then that she remembered Tissa's actions the previous day. There *had* been someone below the ground but she had refused to believe Tissa and now her daughter was in serious trouble, never mind the dangerous fugitive she was hiding…

"Put her in the wagon. We'll find the daughter and the sewer rat she's hiding." The troopers grabbed her and dragged Tissa's mother into the back of the waiting Predavator. The sound of charging engines and closing ramp sealed her fate. While the ripping grew her mind clouded over as she fought the fear charging around her body. The moment they lifted off, she felt sick. Only one place beckoned for her…the factories.

"Noooo!" Tissa cried as she helplessly watched the craft grow nearer then rise above their position, on up the building until it rose above the smooth, curved surface of the tower's top-floor bio-dome. The ripping gradually faded from the square; every beat making Tissa's heart ache that much more. This was worse than seeing her mum lying on the ground. "It's all my fault. Why did I open the door to you? Mum would still be here!"

She beat the wall with her tightly clenched fist, each time it grew redder and redder and she pounded harder and harder until Albie pulled her away from the wall. He wrapped his arms around her, squeezing her arms together so that she could not hurt herself any more. The adrenaline pumping through was too strong for her to feel the pain in her fists.

It was the first time he had touched another human being for a long time. He just wished it had been in happier circumstances. Suddenly he felt a sharp pain in his foot from a well-aimed high heeled shoe.

"Get off me…" Tissa screamed at him as she pushed him away. He staggered and she crumpled to the floor, sobbing.

Remembering the danger they were in, he pulled her arm.

"We must go…troopers will come." He spoke so slowly and in such a deep, commanding manner that Tissa stopped and gaped at him, completely amazed. He paused, taken aback by the impact his ability to communicate with her in her own language had had. Words were spinning around his head, desperate to come out but only one word emerged:

"Come." He insisted. She was amazed at how assertive he had become. She let herself be dragged up and he set her down in one of the floating chairs. Stepping on the side of it, he motioned to her to steer and wiping her eyes, she gingerly moved the touchpad bar and they glided towards the grille above them.

Stopping at an arm's length from the grille, he rummaged through his pockets and pulled out a knife. Poking the grille's base with it, his efforts at prizing the grille open were cut short when a blast rocked the chair.

Small flicks of concrete rained down on them: revealing the metal behind. Picking up Albie's weapon, Tissa returned the compliment, scattering chairs but completely missing her target. It did however earn them more time as the troopers took cover.

Albie carried on trying to force his knife further under the grille as another shot whizzed past them – this time blowing another hole where one of the grille's hinges had been. Tissa's next shot blew a hole in the floor. Her companion put his knife away and grabbed hold of the grille. Hearing the metal groan, he forced it some more as another section of the domed roof crumbled. Tissa ducked as more shots whizzed towards them but was unable to do much more than blast the chairs on the floor. Albie concentrated on their escape route.

"Request back-up in the Edu-suite." crackled a voice below.

"Three units on their way!"

Tissa and Albie knew that time was short before they had more 'visitors'. He pulled with renewed effort at the grille. He felt a small give but still it wouldn't open. The air around them continued to be filled with laser blasts and falling concrete.

"Good job they can't shoot straight." Albie muttered. Trying once again, his fingers slipped sending him crashing on top of Tissa.

"I've had enough of this!" her muffled voice announced and her hand moved onto the chair's pad. Skillfully, she manoeuvred the chair away from the grille.

"Watch out!" She called as she took aim at the grille. He covered his head and held on as the chair rocked with the shockwaves. A hole appeared in the wall where the grille had been. The chair hovered up to the hole in the wall and instinctively Albie leapt from the chair into the beginning of a metal tunnel beyond. Tessa stayed put as shots rocketed about her.

"Jump!" he shouted, holding out his arms for her to catch.

Steadying herself, Tissa eased herself to the edge of the seat and launched herself off from the chair. Just as she did so, it erupted in flames from the force of a direct hit.

Before she had the chance to fall, Albie grabbed her with both hands and pulled her to safety. Once inside the tunnel she flung her arms around him and rested her head on his shoulder. With her mother who-knows-where Albie was all she had left.

"I'm sorry about your foot," she whispered and Albie grinned back.

"That's ok." He replied in his slow, purposeful drawl. "But we must go now." As if to emphasise the point a blast melted part of the wall. Tissa nodded and she released him. Leading the way, Albie set off. They didn't stop for breath but crawled along the cramped tunnel. The further they were from the room, the better.

<u>5</u>

Albie was able to relax now. The closeness of the walls and roof felt more like his subterranean home. With all their armour, radios and weaponry, there was no way the uniforms could follow them. Once he felt they had crept along enough passages and round enough corners he stopped for a rest.

"I'm sorry about your mother…but thank you for saving me." Normally, Tissa would have been distraught. Instead she burst into a fit of giggles as his voice resembled exactly the voice of the man who had taught her and every other child in the city to speak and read. His intensive language course had affected him more than she expected – even down to the man's higher social accent. She'd have to avoid him meeting any of her friends: not that that seemed likely now. "Thanks," was about all she could muster, it was good to laugh again she thought, in spite of everything.

Surprisingly their night was relatively peaceful. With Albie staying mostly alert and awake, Tissa had drifted off to sleep lying on his lap. The nightmare visions of her mother being led into the troop wagon woke her up in fits, but her exhaustion took hold of her and she was finally able to get more rest than the previous night.

Albie had found a spot well away from the Edu-suite to avoid being disturbed. He had kept tight hold of his weapon, falling asleep occasionally but most of the time he had maintained his watch. His thoughts were never far away from the events of the day – his clothes, hair and…all those words that were buzzing around his head. Memories of his mum were more vivid. He could picture a place, not unlike Tissa's home, where they had used the same words – but that had all stopped suddenly. The man called dad had told them to go. The two of them had left, carrying whatever food they could. His mum had led them down to the lowest level of the building and down into the world he had come to call home. From bright colours and light, they had become used to dirt and darkness. Then she was gone.

Tissa woke up with a start, banging her head as she jolted. The sound of head hitting metal reverberated along the tunnel putting her companion into a state of readiness.

"We will go down," he announced still amusing Tessa with his accent.

"Wait!" she called out softly to him before he could move on. In the available light, he watched as she pulled pin after pin from her hair that no longer resembled any known Tenebrian hair style. Clump by clump it fell about her shoulders and face as she shook her head to help her hair fall. Finally, she pulled a simple band from her wrist and dragged her hair tightly into a single ponytail. He looked amazed at the change it had made to her. She scowled at him.

"C'mon then: let's go!" she told him and, bemused by her change in mood, began crawling along the tunnel shaking his head.

They tried to crawl as quietly as possible but with every movement, the metal buckled; banging as it did so. This was accompanied by another bang when their position changed again – not exactly the mouse-like movement they would have hoped for.

The shafts linking different floors were vertical

and they had to wedge back and feet against the walls and slowly lower themselves down; this, along with the need to avoid discovery, increased their anxiety. Every tunnel was identical – flimsy metal giving their position away to all and sundry. The further they went the more cramped and clumsy they became and they found themselves making even more noise.

Suddenly, he put his hand on Tissa's shoulder, making her stop. She gave him a puzzled look that he returned by putting his finger to his lips. She listened as the tunnel settled beneath their weight. At first it was nothing but as she concentrated she could hear the faintest scuttling and beeping above the noise of the air being pumped past them. Whatever it was, it was getting closer. He motioned her past and as she moved the noise stopped momentarily. After a brief pause the scuttling started once more, this time at a faster pace.

"Let's go!" urged Tissa and they started again: faster and less concerned about the noise. The quicker they crawled, the nearer the pursuer seemed to get. Reaching a vertical shaft, they flew down, hands slowing themselves but still they landed with a thud at the foot of it.

"We've got to get out of this duct!" Tissa cried, "They obviously know where we are." He nodded grimly. Steeling himself he aimed at the end of the duct and pressed one of the lighter buttons on his stick. A bolt shot out and the end of the duct glowed red but stayed solid. He tried again with a different button – the duct glowed white this time.

As he was preparing for his third shot, Tissa

grabbed his arm and pointed above them. Looking up he made out what looked like a metal spider; blue, flashing eyes turning red as it spotted them. Two antennas whirred and the creature started clicking, obviously telling its owners where they were.

"SPDR!" she cried.

"Go!" he shouted as he let off two bolts. Tissa edged nearer the still glowing tunnel edge and, using her feet, began to pound at it. His shots were hardly having any success against the creature that still chattered away as it climbed towards there. Arriving next to Tissa, Albie added his weight to her attempts. They were frantically hammering as the SPDR reached the foot of the shaft. Red angry eyes drew closer and closer, as the beeps grew more excited.

Furiously kicking it at, the panel moved slightly as the feet continued to pound. With renewed energy they kicked again, a gap emerged and grew until it was big enough for Tissa to squeeze through. She jumped into the dark. He was just about to follow when he felt a pull on his leg. Lashing out with his other foot was like hitting a brick wall. His attacker took a tighter hold and he found himself being dragged back along the duct. His hands reached out for any kind of hold to slow the creature down but in his desperation, he made matters worse as his domitor dropped agonisingly out of his reach.

Defenceless, he was the fly in the SPDR's clutches: no matter how hard he struggled he couldn't break free. A cold metal clamp had attached itself to his ankle as the SPDR's remaining legs scuttled back up the shaft. He lashed out with his free leg but his kicks had no effect and there was nothing for his fingers to cling onto as he continued to be dragged along.

"Tissa…help me!" He called more in desperation than hope.

Tissa's legs refused to move. She'd only just escaped from that cage and couldn't go back in: she just couldn't! She shut her eyes hoping everything would go away: Albie, the SPDRS, the duct, her mother's arrest. She wanted everything back to normal. Yet no matter how hard she tried they just wouldn't and soon, if she didn't help, the only thing that would stop would be the struggles of currently her only friend.   His cries made her focus. She looked around for inspiration and spotted his domitor lying on the duct floor.

Ignoring the voices screaming at her not to, she ducked back through the hole, wriggling after him; just as his head was disappearing into the darkness.

Reaching the vertical shaft, she managed to shove the domitor into his hand. He thrust the domitor onto the SPDR's clamp and pressed the top setting. He gritted his teeth and closed his eyes, preparing for the fireball that could, quite possibly, destroy both him and the tunnel. Instead of this, blue crackles of electricity shot up the SPDR and sparks leapt out from its head before it froze with its prey dangling beneath.

The clamp released its grip and sent Albie crashing to the shaft bottom. He landed in a heap. Tissa was relieved when the crumpled heap groaned and she pulled him up, hugging him tightly.

"Promise me," she began "that if we're ever separated you'll come find me!" He wasn't sure why she was so adamant, they hardly knew each other after all, but he knew how hard it had been getting used to being alone and staying alive. She had just lost her mum: she was relying on him. It was a feeling he wasn't sure he liked.

"Of course," He replied, already confused by this new friendship: things were easier on your own he told himself…but lonelier. She hugged him once again, this time knocking the wind out of him as she squeezed tightly. Then, she crawled back along the duct.

Abruptly she stopped.

"I don't know your name. What do they call you?" she asked, sitting next to a grille, through which artificial light poured.

Who?" he asked. The last person who had talked to him had probably tried to kill him.

"Anybody…people…your mum!" There was that word he had suppressed for so long. It was now a word he was hearing quite often. Images flooded his mind…he could remember watching his mum's lips moving but couldn't recall what she was saying…He tried to move his mouth in the same way but his memories were patchy…distant….

"Al…..b….ie" he mouthed then a sound followed it "…Albie." He smiled, saying his name again with more confidence and now he could hear her…his mother saying it with such love. Then he remembered his father saying it.

"Albie…" he felt the rough but caressing strokes of his father's hand as it ruffled his hair or patted his back. Wetness filled his eyes and this time a hand touched his arm and Tissa's soft voice whispered:

"Well, hello Albie – I'm Tissa." She grabbed his hand and then they awkwardly shook hands before she pulled him once more into a hug and as she felt a wave of relief flood through her body. She wasn't alone. This close contact was going take some getting used to, he decided before turning his attention to the light beyond the grille.

The moment Albie caught sight of the compelling, hypnotic neon signs and bizarre window displays he was desperate to get closer.

Using the domitor to unlock the grille, he jumped ten metres to the floor below, tumbling as he hit the ground. Distracted by an array of flashing lights, he left Tissa, legs dangling, waiting for him to help. He held his arms to show that he'd catch her but she refused to budge.

Albie looked back at his friend who waved her hand to say she could get down herself. Reassured and impatient to explore, he set off towards the winking lights.

They were in a long, wide strip bordered by great windows filled with bright, flashing lights. Dashing from one to the other, pressing his face up against them, Albie became more and more agitated. In each window were people, not real people but plastic people. Each one's clothes appeared to be made of the same material – even the same colour. He was amazed however, at the way the figures lit up and came to life every time he stepped near. Some would simply walk on the spot swinging their arms while others would be holding hands or…putting their mouths together. Every time he stepped up to look into a window they would start moving, the light reflecting off their clothes, making them shimmer. The moment he stepped away, they would freeze and the lights would disappear again. Somehow, he knew they weren't a threat and enjoyed the power he had to turn them on and off by simply stepping backwards and forwards.

Tissa stood, amazed and fascinated by this boy: the way that the simplest and most everyday aspects of her world held such fascination for him. He zipped about lighting displays, watching models walking up and down, smiling coyly at each other and listening to the naffest accompanying music, before jumping back and laughing loudly as they stopped in awkward positions the moment he moved away.

Tissa was buzzing with questions. Where had he seen such displays before? Had he always lived below the city?

Looking down, her intention to be independent failed her so she called out for help as her backside began to feel a growing numbness.

"Albie!" she cried, he carried on leaping from window to window "Albie, can you help me to get down…" still no reaction, "Albie!" she screamed.

He stopped, turned slowly around, momentarily annoyed, then looked apologetically at his friend who was hanging above him.

"Okay, I admit it. It's too far for me to jump."

"Go on, I will catch you!" he instructed her. It wasn't that she didn't trust him to try – it was just that she didn't have the confidence in his ability to catch her.

Albie started to get cross the longer she sat there. He encouraged her, teased her but she just stared down at the floor unable to commit herself to the drop.

"I *will* catch you…" he assured her but she just shook her head.

Just at that moment, his face changed to that of abject horror.

"SPDR, behind…!" she didn't have to hear the end of the sentence, preferring to throw herself, screaming, onto him, sending both of them to the floor.

"I knew that would work," he commented, casually laughing in his superior tele-voice. Her screams instantly stopped as she prepared to launch a fist towards his stomach but froze in mid-punch:

"Troopers…run!" she cried.

"Ha! Good one." he chuckled but his good mood ended abruptly as a shot zipped past his head and a shop window shattered. Tiny fragments of glass showered the passage. Glittering armoured figures were converging on them from either end of the wide precinct. They were trapped.

Setting his domitor to its highest level he took aim at a spot on the floor a few metres away from them. The blast shattered the nearby shop windows stopping the now-annoying music and sending models crashing across the walkway and momentarily blocking the troopers' line of sight. A blast of cold, putrid-smelling air shot up through the hole in the ground.

"Trust me!" Albie whispered quietly taking Tissa's hand and they jumped into the blackness, just ahead of the blasts of the troopers that chewed into the floor where they had been lying moments earlier.

The troopers and the lights above grew smaller and less significant as they fell further and further.

6

Tissa fell. Further. Further. Albie's hand slipped from hers. She screamed his name. It wasn't the moment when her feet hit the water or when her body sank under the pungent river. Neither was it the moment she found she couldn't breathe and water filled her nose, rather the moment the biting cold took hold that made her panic. Tissa's arms and legs refused to move, frozen as she steadily tumbled downwards. Albie could have been next to her and she wouldn't have known a thing about it – darkness surrounded her as her mind started to slip away. Finally, her head emerged above the surface.

She felt a cold that she didn't think could exist anywhere. It gripped her body which refused to move. Her once beautifully-arranged hair now clung tightly to her face and down her back and there were…things in it! Her dress clung to her in a similarly slimy manner. Her bare legs and arms were being buffeted by…objects that she didn't want to consider. Waves buffeted her. Her life had taken a terrible turn.

She could feel the numbing iciness of the water and the rotting, stale smell all around her but suddenly she couldn't help seeing her mother waving, her classmates at school and rows of clothes…all moving further away, growing dimmer in her mind. The last thing she could sense was of something grabbing her roughly. She felt herself rising and being held tightly against a metal, armoured body as a ferocious wind whipped at her. She wanted her lonely life back but instead everything went black.

Albie had felt calm as they fell but the moment her hand had slipped out of his, he started screaming for her. Her body had hit the water first and immediately disappeared from sight. Albie then slammed into the surface, he too sank. The dirt of the river obscured his vision and all sight of Tissa.

Despite the stiffening of his arms and legs in the biting waters, his only thought was Tissa and the guilt he was feeling: the guilt at making her a fugitive and his part in her mother's arrest. He couldn't let anything else happen to her. He fought furiously to reach the surface, aching limbs dragging him back. As he rose, unseen objects collided with him – the results of hundreds of years of human and inhuman waste. This only made him work harder – determination driving him on and up.

Gasping, his lungs finally filled with the cold, stale air so familiar to him. For the first time he was glad to taste it. Wiping the dirt from his face he scoured the dark for any sign of his friend. Even the fires from the dark ruins around him served to trick him: casting lengthy shadows of unknown creatures. Albie fought to avoid being washed onto nearby rocks. Dejected, he slowly half-swam half-drifted towards the ruins of a building that rose out of the water. Clambering out of the watery grip his questions were answered by the sounds of two revving engines. He watched as water bikes zipped across the waves, one of them carrying a familiar passenger – unconscious, judging by the lolling of her head. The craft veered from side to side, avoiding the river debris and he cursed: Tissa was strapped to the front of one of the riders.

Albie's first impulse was to dive back into the water in a vain attempt to follow but by now, all he could see were two plumes of spray shooting into the air.

He stood, dripping, in the ruins of a once-majestic building. The intricate carvings of unhappy ancient figures above mirrored Albie's solitary figure. The feeling of losing his mother once again pushed itself into his mind. One day she had been there, the next gone. After weeks of endless and fruitless searching, he had become accustomed to his own company. A need for food had taken over in the end. Here he was now and it all felt very familiar; even though he had hardly shared two days with Tissa. Apart from the grabbing, he had felt comfortable with her but he had let her down. The promise he had given her looked extremely hollow now.

Waves lapped gently at his feet, accompanying the rhythmic dripping of soaked clothes. His head sank into his hands. Finally, anger pushed every other emotion from his mind. His hand touched something wet but reassuring. He still had both bag and domitor. He allowed himself a relieved smile as the torch at one end lit up his surroundings. He immediately switched it off, not wanting to attract any unwelcome attention to himself. Nevertheless, his spirits were lifted as he scrambled over the rubble in the general direction the bikes had taken.

He had a good idea roughly where they were heading but what he didn't know was how he was going to get to her. It was a place everybody stayed clear of. The smell of constantly burning oil hung onto everything and the closer you got to its source the thicker it became – breathing was a chore and hardly worth the effort. Immense pipes, smoking chimneys and grinding pumps of a multitude of factories dominated the landscape. The factories, some on the surface and some underground, made everything that was needed by the inhabitants of Tenebria: everything from clothes to food, Predavators to domitors. The poor wretches that toiled in these factories came from captured underground dwellers and those rejected inhabitants of the bright city. Tissa was on her way there. He had to rescue her.

Taking another breath of disgustingly stale air, Albie put all these thoughts to the back of his mind. He kept his mind on the ruins ahead of him. They were little more than piles of stones: none of the carvings and the buildings he had grown accustomed to in his part of this underground world. He was creeping through what could only be described as a wasteland: no shelter to protect or food to scavenge and in the middle of it all stood a wide metallic column, faintly glowing, stretching up until it disappeared in the gloom.

Albie found himself drawn towards it and the closer he got, the lower his spirits fell. It dominated the land around it and Albie could only guess that it was one of the many such columns that held the world above in place. Directly around it the land was flattened…without the rubble that covered every other part. There were tell-tail signs of life: tracks made by some sort of wheeled vehicles leading up to and away from the column.

He ran his hand over the smooth surface and it hummed, vibrating to his touch. Its size made him draw back, not in fear but in wonder. He'd seen the world above: the size of the buildings, the numbers of people living there…. how could this, and all the others like it, support all that?

Walking around it, studying it, he noticed a pair of doors on one side. They were tightly sealed but he knew he only had to touch the pad to the side to open them. He knew he couldn't afford to delay any more. It would still take him a day at least to reach the factories Tissa would have been taken to. It would be slow going on foot.

He was glad to leave the column behind and follow the dirt track that led to the factories. The further he drew away from it the better he felt and his pace quickened. Once the rubble either side had been replaced by mud and sand, Albie rested. Exploring the bottom of the bag slung over his shoulder he realised how little food he had left. He had no idea how long he had been travelling: when he walked it was dark, he slept when he could walk no further and it was still dark. Yet all the time Tissa's face drove him on.

Eventually there was only sand and thickets of spiky evil-looking plants that somehow managed to survive. Sniffing the air, he knew he was close. Climbing steadily up a slope, he stood at the top of a ridge.

In the valley below, clouds hung in the air as smoke rose from chimneys and vents that were massed in a complex over a murky stretch of water. In the centre of the buildings stood another column, glowing in the same manner as the others, watching everything as if it was the ruler. There was no kindness about this lord however, only an arrogantly superior dominance over everything around it: controlling and ordering all it looked down upon. Every so often a deep, threatening red light would appear at its base, penetrating the smoky gloom, slowly rising up its shaft, glowering at onlookers before vanishing into the base of the city above. The columns were visible from every part of the underworld and Albie had often sat and wondered what the rising light on each column meant but knew well enough that too close an inspection was asking for trouble. Its presence in the middle of the complex was another reason to get Tissa out as soon as possible.

Predavators circled above, probing with their searchlights, on the lookout for anybody foolish enough to trespass. On the waters that protected this spaghetti complex, waterbikers played endlessly, racing around and shooting at anything that looked challenging. Some poor individuals found themselves as moving targets, their lives nothing more than a source of amusement. The bikers were just as wretched as those they guarded: just another link in the city's chain of command.

It was this scene that Albie stared down upon. He was street-wise enough to avoid any unpleasant encounters on the way but the expanse of water that lay before him was daunting.

The best he could hope for was to avoid being used as a break from somebody's boredom. He had a feeling that this fate had not befallen Tissa, but there were plenty of other gruesome ends that she could have met: so many that he had to fight to stop himself becoming downhearted.

The longer he waited for a break in the near-constant activity, the more anxious he became. The shadows on the water never slowed, nor did his mind. He couldn't see or hear anything else. Even the odd occasion a searchlight flashed across him hardly made him flinch. He remained still and was never spotted, blending in with the rest of the ruins, dirt and mess.

His fine clothes were now coated in the same filthy layer that he had become so used to. His new clothes however, obviously hadn't been designed for a life in the underworld and he shivered as the cold clawed at him through the thin, and now mostly ripped, fibres.

So, intent on his search to get across the water, Albie failed to spot a silent figure behind him. The sudden stab of pain on the back of his neck only registered as he slumped forward into an oil-coated puddle. He felt himself being dragged by his arms then his mind slipped into…nothingness.

The air was cooler when he came to and the sand had been replaced by cold, hard rock. He was underground.

"You must be the stupidest individual ever!" A throbbing ache was the first sensation he felt. Opening his eyes, he couldn't make it much. Everything was dark, gloomy and painful. "Have you really got no sense?" The voice pierced his skull with its shrillness. Disbelief hung onto every word. "We watched you for well over an hour and it's a miracle you weren't used as target practice…you weren't even spotted, man!" The last word hung on the speaker's lips and Albie detected a sense of unfairness in its delivery, "Boy, are you lucky!"

All this came from a large, silhouetted figure that had positioned its face millimetres from Albie's face. It waited for an answer but Albie could only let out a long-drawn-out groan. He'd never known this kind of pain before, never been caught by surprise: he didn't like it. The silhouette started to become a blur and Albie could make out long straggling snakes of hair, just like the ones he had owned before his 'image change'.

"And how do you explain this?" A long-blurred shape was thrust towards him – he could make out a long and vaguely familiar object. "I suppose you were just given it!" Disbelief had been replaced by suspicion. "Come on then…where's it from?" the interrogation started once again.

Albie was trying desperately to focus on the face of his interrogator whose hair flew about in front of the one tiny source of light as if it had a life of its own. He tried to reply but all that came out was a drawn-out groan.

"Uuuurgh." He managed to focus on the object waved before him…his weapon. Lunging for it, his grab was too slow. Instead he found his hand pushed beneath a particularly heavy boot. A big black boot was now causing him a considerable amount of pain as its owner pressed harder and harder.

Gritting his teeth, Albie found the pain improved his sight – the blur became a face. The face that stared at him was still waiting for an answer. Angry eyes glared impatiently back at him along with an unevenly toothed snarl.

"Found it," he managed, his voice mimicking his interrogator's: the well – educated voice of the screen just didn't seem an appropriate voice to use. Nevertheless, the words came out so quickly that he hardly knew his mouth had opened. Being able to talk to other people was still a hard thing for him to come to terms with. The answer didn't seem to please his interrogator either as a gloved fist grabbed hold of him.

"You don't just find these lying about…" the fist lifted him up then threw him back. This didn't have the desired effect as Albie's tumble turned into a roll then a spin and ended with Albie knocking his attacker flat with an outstretched foot.

The weapon rolled across the floor and they both lunged for it. Albie reached it first but just as his hand closed around it, a yank at his leg sent the domitor spinning once more into a filthy, darkened corner.

Another lash with his leg and Albie was free. Throwing himself into the corner he was at last able to grab the domitor and spinning round, he slowly levelled the weapon at his aggressor. Realisation dawned and as it did so the attacker's face paled. His hands were slowly and instinctively raised. Albie was able to feel a moment of superiority for the first time.

Studying his interrogator's broad shoulders and muscular figure he was glad to be holding the domitor. He was considerably bigger and judging by the wrinkles on his face a lot older than Albie. He was wearing a vest top that revealed numerous scars and bruises across his arms and shoulders to go with a fine set on his face. Judging by the way his fists were tightly clenched, Albie felt certain he knew how to look after himself in a fight and considered himself to have been extremely lucky. He whistled then took a deep breath.

"How about you tell me who you are, now…"

Albie still found it hard to believe that he was able to make others understand him and as he talked, his voice became rougher and gruffer. Making a motion with his domitor indicated a sense of. It certainly had the right effect as his victim had lost his cool confidence and was now hesitantly backing off.

7

A scowl spread across Albie's face. His body was grumbling after the fight. The more worried his opponent looked, the more relaxed he felt – it was about time he dished out some of what he had just received.

"Well, I guess you're not one of them – we'd have already been toast – and there's no way any of them would have been stupid enough to stand that long next to that sludge..." mumbled his opponent. Albie stared at him with a look of growing impatience.

"...okay, we're just drifters like you, man..." Albie didn't like being called 'man' so he pulled a face to show he wasn't happy. "...okay, no 'man': We just found this old war bunker a while ago, hadn't been used for years, and it's away from their eyes and ..." His voice tailed off as he glanced quickly and nervously across the room towards a door opposite them both.

It hardly stood out as a door, only the disturbed dust around the edge showed that there was anything other than a part of the wall. No handle, just a mass of finger prints around the middle of one side where parts of the wall had been 'attacked' so that the door could have been opened.

Maybe it was the initial blow on the head but Albie suddenly realised his opponent was hiding something.

"Who's we?" he quietly asked. There was only one person in here – where were the others? Sweeping the room with the domitor he was drawn to the new door that shuddered slightly.

"Come out!" he ordered. He was trying to work out whether he liked being in control or not – was it good being the boss, all threats and shouting? He was not sure but for the time being it was necessary. He knew that the moment he showed weakness the man would strike. As the door slowly opened he could make out two sets of eyes fixed on him. The pair of hands that had appeared through the widening slit of the door were now struggling to slide it open.

Losing his aggressive stance, Albie lowered his weapon and rushed across to help.

The hands looked worn and, judging by their failing efforts, lacking in strength. Tearing across the dirt, he pulled open the door and in the dark he could make out a cowering, frightened duo.

Albie immediately softened and he offered the nearest body a helping hand. He flinched as he tried to grip a fragile set of bony fingers. The hand disappeared quickly into the gloom.

"It's okay, Sted," came a voice that made Albie jump "Faon – you too, he's okay…" Albie turned around and was met by an outstretched fist. Bewildered, he raised his own fist, sensing that the fist was not about to knock him to the floor. Again, he flinched as his knuckles were struck.

"...name's Reznor, been looking after these two for as long as I can remember: ever since I found them here..." his voice tailed off as he waited for Albie to introduce himself.

"Albie," he replied as the two emaciated shapes emerged.

Both were painfully thin and the scars that covered them indicated that they had done well to last as long as they had. Their clothes were thin, white and ripped except for a variety of scarves wrapped around their necks. Identically matted hair once again reminded Albie of his former look.

Movement brought him back to the present as the two bodies introduced as Sted and Faon shuffled forward. Sted was the slightly taller, stronger-looking and more awkward of the pair, thanks mainly to the twisted shape of his ankle. Albie couldn't help staring at it.

"...happened out there...was clearing rocks by the mine entrance when a slide hit. They left me for dead – at least it got me away. They gave up the mine at the same time."

"What did they mine here?" asked Albie, shifting uncomfortably from foot to foot trying not to look at the two wretched figures before him.

"Was one of the first iron mines when they were making the city. Mined here for decades then blew it up, with everybody in it, when they didn't need it any more. Some escaped out of other entrances but they were soon tracked down and dealt with. There was a surplus of workers – easiest thing to do with them. We hadn't been here long when they blew it…we weren't as weak as the others. Probably how we survived so long."

Faon, who had been resting on a stick, followed him gingerly out. With all her weight resting onto the whittled branch, Albie could see that every breath for her was a struggle.

"You two escaped?" Albie asked quietly. His face betrayed the shock he felt. It was all he could do to turn his face away, ashamed for enjoying his moment of power over these wretched creatures. He had been no better than the ones that had taken his only friend away from him. He knew exactly what it felt like to be frightened and he'd been able to look after himself – he had no idea how these two had survived but it was obvious that they couldn't have survived without Reznor's help.

As Faon tried to summon up the energy to speak, Reznor put an arm around her to guide her carefully to a pile of rags that looked as it if could have been some attempt at a bed. He took up the story as she gave up her efforts; exhausted.

"…Sted dragged himself from under the rocks but found himself trapped in the tunnel that led here."

"I found Faon, she'd obviously been down here for a while, they must have forgotten about it. There was very little light and no food. She must have been there since the first slide hit – she'd been treated pretty bad but doesn't talk about it."

Albie relaxed enough to study his surroundings and it was at this point that he realised he was still pointing the domitor at them, even though his fingers had relaxed.

"Sorry, guess I won't need this." He apologised. His eyes were once more drawn to the passage that Faon and Sted had been hiding in. The door had been pulled back along a giant metal track cast into the floor. The door rested on a series of small wheels but everything was rusted and disused.

The room he left had nothing in it except three piles of rags on the floor – rough bedding to say the least.

"What would Tissa have made of all this?" he wondered.

Stepping into the passage – he was fascinated by the rows upon rows of faces that stared out from one wall. Uniform in size and in the empty expressions each possessed – he couldn't take his eyes off. There were old, young, male and female, the early ones wearing ragged clothes but gradually they changed – wearing more of a uniform.

They looked more and more like the people in Tissa's city – clusters of the same coloured clothes appeared as he followed the images up the steadily rising passage.

His three new acquaintances silently watched as Albie worked his way up the seemingly endless rows and columns of staring faces. Reaching out to touch the odd one, it would fizz, disappear and then reappear when he took his hand away. On the wall behind each portrait were a tiny projector and below was a series of buttons. He randomly tapped at some: names appeared along with numbers that he couldn't make sense of.

His eyes fell on the last photo in the last column and he studied the picture – it looked familiar. There was the same expression, the same look of fear, as the surrounding pictures along with the clothes of a Tenebrian citizen, but slowly Albie realised who he was looking at.

Horrified, he slowly turned to look at Faon – she was drastically thinner but the same features and a filthy, ripped version of the same clothes stood before him.

"It's you!" He could barely utter the words, shocked as he was by the transformation from this person to the battered and bruised ghost-like creature in the room with him. Albie turned from picture to person, each time unable to believe the difference.

What would Tissa be like? Was she destined to look the same if she wasn't rescued? That radiant smile, sparkling eyes and happy demeanour that had kept him going in his darker moments: how long would she… He didn't want to even consider the state she would be in.

His thoughts were brought back to the present by Faon's coughing, her body shaking each time. He felt a guilty twinge and turned his gaze to look at Faon's convulsing and fitting figure that fought to regain control of itself.

"…like I said, she's had it rough," Reznor repeated. Sted gave her a gentle hug and she gave him a grateful but worn and tired smile.

Albie couldn't bear to look at the sorry pair sitting upon their rag mountain anymore and turned his attention to the pictures. Ambling up the passage he studied the faces and he began to recognise faces from his life in the sewers, what an easy life that'd been he mumbled to himself; only looking after number one. Faces he'd seen only fleetingly – amongst the ruins by the shore – some had dashed past whilst being chased. He'd never given a single thought to them: obviously they had been caught. He now knew what had happened whenever they had disappeared from the spot they'd always seemed to live near.

A Realisation dawned in his mind. He started to anxiously scan every photo. He quickened his pace. He looked at more pictures; back and forth, quicker and quicker, frantically searching. He started to narrow down his search, ignoring the more recent photos and the oldest ones, from down on his knees he rose as high as he could, finding himself a largish rock to stand upon, he peered closer to the highest pictures, jumping down again as he rejected them. Short breaths accompanied his actions as he began to pant with his efforts. His face had taken on aspects of all the harrowed expressions before him, each one twisted in its own way. Reznor inched his way towards him. His two companions started to panic at the increasingly frantic search before them and was on the verge of grabbing Albie to try to calm him when suddenly the searcher abruptly stopped.

He stood, panting, trying to catch his breath and stared at one picture. A tear rolled down his cheek. He was gripped by an emotion he found disturbing and was from his past: loss. Reznor eased further forward, reaching out to touch Albie's shoulder. Albie flinched then remained still. A slight breeze started to blow down the tunnel past them.

Again, Albie touched the image and again it buzzed with disapproval then disappeared. Hopeful, he pressed a button below it – a name appeared in place of the picture, but that wasn't important to him. Reznor pulled Albie's hand back and studied the picture then studied Albie before returning to the picture once more. Albie stood staring; the one tear had now become a steady stream accompanied by gasped breaths as he fought for oxygen. Tears rolled down from cheek to chin with Albie making no effort to wipe them away. Reznor understood and left Albie to be alone with his past.

Reznor watched as Albie continued to stare, occasionally and gingerly reaching out, pressing the buttons beyond the image.

"What does this mean?" he eventually asked, turning his bloodshot eyes towards the three onlookers. Sted made an effort to move so Reznor helped him up from the dirt and supported him as he stumbled over. His eyes were fixed on the picture.

"Is it your mother?"

Albie simply nodded and then repeated his question. The growing wind that whipped his hair across his face was now making him more irritable.

"What does this mean?" there was a slight edge to his voice now as his finger followed the words that had replaced the picture. The blank look on his face was met with more annoyance from Albie.

A shuffling from behind made them both start. Faon was battling against an increasing wind that was pushing its way down the passage.

"There are two locations…where they were taken from…and to…There's also the date when they were put there." It was a huge effort for her to talk but yet Faon was determined. Sted, still leaning on Reznor, offered her a shoulder to lean on.

"This was once Faon's job. She had to take the pictures of anybody who came in – they did it here. She's the electronics whizz so they had her taking the pictures of the new internees…even did mine – look!" with that he pulled out a similarly-sized picture on a thin piece of plastic. He waved it at Albie, but his mind was finding it harder and harder to concentrate on the wall and his mother's picture. Instead the growing wind was becoming more and more of a distraction. There was now a distinct ripping sound from outside: from the end of the tunnel.

Reznor, unaware, was still beaming with pride at his friend's achievements; "…and she ordered all the cards here – like one of those library things the ancients used to have…" He was glowing now and didn't seem such a sorry wretch any more, enthusing about the body he was now using all his strength to support.

Albie could no longer ignore how agitated the noise was making him – it was extremely familiar to him and gradually Reznor's expression changed. Sted was still completely oblivious to the imminent danger.

"…course she stopped doing it when the entrance collapsed. They called it an accident but…" the wind and noise began to pull harder and harder on them. Albie pulled out the weapon from his belt while Reznor lifted Faon into both his arms and they edged towards the entrance of the tunnel. Sted continued talking about the image of Albie's mother before he noticed the others were much further up the passage. Pressing one of the buttons below the picture of Albie's mother, a printed piece of plastic with her face on it emerged. He snatched it as it came out and put it in the same pocket as his own. He then tried to catch up, stumbling from side to side, with slow progress. The entrance was now bathed in light and a ripping filled the air. He had to hold the rocky wall to stop himself from being knocked down as the wind became unbearable. Reznor lay Faon down, shielding her with his body as she gasped for breath.

Albie continued to fight against the whirlwind that the Predavator was creating while the pictures flew from their mountings, slicing through the air as they bombarded the figures now flattened on the floor. He drew closer to the entrance, the back draft from the engines forcing him to work harder just to stay upright: hundreds of digital image cards continued to swim around his head.

He dare not risk firing this close to the craft: that could easily seal them beneath wreckage and rock; he'd have to draw it away from here.

Dropping to the floor he dragged himself along the stony ground, head bowed to protect his eyes he crawled forwards. Constantly spitting out dirt and dust that swirled around his mouth, he ignored the sharp pointed rocks and stones that littered the sand that now tore at him. His once-fine clothes hung in shreds.

The entrance grew larger, as did his determination, until he burst outside into the open. He ran through the tall grabbing grasses and clutching sands. Try as they might, Albie proved the stronger as he heard the steady ripping pursuing him. Tumbling, he avoided a shower of sand as a thicket of grass exploded to his left. He rolled as another tuft blew apart. Shots rang about around him – everything that could offer him protection soon disappeared upwards and he was engulfed by a sandstorm of natural debris.

He knew his pursuers would struggle to see him in all this so he allowed himself the luxury of a moment to catch his breath. Covering his mouth with one hand, he positioned himself amongst the nearest vegetation and waited for the dust to settle: domitor in hand and set to maximum.

8

Sand started to swirl upwards in the draught of the craft that hovered above. The grass whipped at

Albie as if it was pointing him out, lashing out to scratch his skin under the flimsy clothes he had inherited – why had he let Tissa get rid of his old ones? Okay, so she thought they stank – it hadn't bothered him.

Ignoring the whipping and the sand lashing at his eyes, the swirls in front of Albie began to join together like the pieces of a jigsaw. Spinning patterns merged and drifted into a face. Finally, Tissa's face smiled at him. He smiled to himself, chuckled then laughed. Tissa laughed back at him – those teeth, those perfect teeth: nothing else mattered to him. He thought about neither the blood that started to seep out of his numerous scratches and scrapes, the poor individuals sheltering down the tunnel nor the guns that would soon obliterate him if he didn't end his gaze.

He couldn't tear himself away; It was Tissa! If he could just stare at her a bit longer…

The patterns started to change and Tissa's smile changed, worry was replaced by pain…she was crying. He could almost feel the heat of her tears as they touched his bloodstained hands. She faded as the patterns changed once more.

"No! No! Give her back!" Albie screamed as she disappeared completely and he gazed up at a visored helmet that stared down upon him from inside the Predavator's cockpit like a bird of prey ready to strike. He wouldn't give it the chance. His weapon was still firmly wedged in his hand despite the sand-lashing it had taken. He screamed, so did his weapon. Bolt after bolt belted skywards, impacting inside the ship. Albie, still screaming hysterically with rage, gazed as explosion after explosion rocked the Predavator. Its metal outer panels shot in every direction. The figures inside disappeared in the fire that engulfed the sky above him. Still gaping at the destruction he had unleashed, he felt something hard hit him from behind. He just had time to see Reznor's arms wrap around his waist as they both flew before rolling out of the way of the plunging Predavator.

Pieces of Predavator were scattered, scaring and scorching as they hit the ground. Covered by the sand thrown up by the initial crash, Albie and Reznor still felt the extreme heat of the craft's destruction. Albie realised he was now indebted to this man. He was starting to question himself – he was getting sloppy. For years he'd managed without anybody else's help – that was before a brightly coloured, petite individual had come to his aid.

Albie tried to pull himself out of the dirt his face was buried in. He wasn't too keen on the crawling creatures investigating his moist mouth and face. Spitting, he pushed upwards but Reznor still lay motionless and he sure was heavy. Rolling, Albie wriggled slowly out from underneath him. Taking a rare moment to look up, he checked there was nothing else on the horizon: all clear. He knew that that would not stay the same for long.

Grabbing Reznor's arms he pulled him between the smouldering chunks of metal that would soon attract every piece of bad news in this part of the underworld. Images raced in his head while he dragged him. Even now he could picture Tissa's still-perfect looks smiling: a wicked but innocent smile nodding her approval. Was she daring him to do more damage; as if it was just a prank?

Heading back to the tunnel, he saw Sted trying unsuccessfully to half-drag Faon towards them. Sted almost slumped to the ground when he saw the state of their companion but somehow the two wretched figures managed to keep going. Albie laid Reznor gently down at the edge of the debris and was about to look for signs of life when he realised he had no idea what to look for. He couldn't see any blood: surely that was a good sign! That was all he could think of – apart from telling him to get up. Panic set in.

"Don't do this! Don't leave me here with these two!" his mind screamed. Hiding in a tunnel when everyone assumed you to be dead was one thing; but what was he going to do if they had to move quickly? It would be hundred times worse as Tissa in those high heels trying to get these two to safety.

He felt a gentle touch on his shoulder and was surprised to see Faon hunched above him.

"Let me have a look," she whispered and started pressing his chest with her stick-like fingers. The other two watched, impressed by her expertise (or appearance of it) as she bent close to his mouth. She may have been a waif but in her hands, they felt a great power was at work. "He's breathing…just stunned…he took the heat of that blast, judging by his back." Looking where she pointed, they could see scorch marks straddling his back. A groan from his body brightened their spirits but these dropped immediately as the throb of approaching aircraft reached their ears.

"Get close to the fires and cover yourselves in anything you can, they'll think the heat of our bodies is just debris, hopefully," urged Sted as he once more supported Faon. Albie, doing the same for the waking body of Reznor found the nearest piece of debris and covered the pair of them with sand barely allowing himself space for his eyes and mouth. He relaxed as the others covered themselves close by and they crouched…waiting.

A Predavator hovered above the spot. It sat there: searching and watching. Lights wandered lazily across every spot of wreckage but still the craft didn't land.

Albie sat holding onto Reznor, sweating from their closeness to the remaining fires and the fact that they were both huddled together under the sand. Fear and heat made the sweat build up on his forehead. He wasn't helped by Reznor's coming-to which was completed by occasional unwelcoming groans and twitches.

"Can't you stop?" Albie urged his semi-conscious buddy "It's a bit of a giveaway." He kept on piling up the sand that trickled away every time Reznor moved his body but he wasn't convinced that they were the least bit invisible to the prying eyes from above. The Predavator watched, motionless.

It waited. Perhaps it knew they were there and

was just waiting for them to end this stupid game. Albie glanced across at the others; luckily, they weren't in danger of giving themselves away. He found himself gripping Reznor tightly, trying to stop him making any further movements. "Stay still, will you!" he hissed quietly.

He started to nervously finger the weapon fastened to his belt: he'd been lucky once – but there was no sandstorm to protect him and the moment he burst out and took aim he knew exactly who'd come out worse. This waiting was becoming unbearable – even without Reznor's big waking form.

Luck was on his side as the Predavator changed its tune – the engines started to slow down and it gradually descended towards the crash site. Albie relaxed slightly but this newfound ease vanished as he glanced up at the spot where the Predavator had hovered – two others had replaced it – the engines combining in a rhythmic duet that made Albie's heart sink.

The first craft had touched down now and a ramp had dropped effortlessly from its back. With its lights still crisscrossing the site and the presence of the two extra craft above, the whole area was lit up as if they were in the city above. The two uniforms that emerged had little chance of being surprised in this brightness.

Thankfully Reznor had regained consciousness and seemed to understand the situation. The uniforms headed straight for Faon and Sted who had neither the will nor ability to fight and were pulled, dejected, from their hiding place to be led away to the waiting craft.

A fully awake Reznor gave Albie a shove. "Get down – they'll be coming back for somebody – they know there's a body here – but you've been cuddling me so tight, they might not think there're two of us. Bury yourself deeper – I'll distract them and make sure you get to that craft somehow – you're the only hope any of us have got." Albie understood so Reznor started to pull himself out of the sand, in the process covered his companion further.

The two dark figures duly returned and were met half way by Reznor's disconsolate figure.

"This one's clever – decided not to play hide and seek." A metallic-sounding voice joked as they led him up the ramp, "wasn't very good anyway – can't lie still can you? You'll soon relearn how where you are going."

The other crackled into life, "Tell control – no crew survivors, found three escapees though. Put the crash down to the sand again – sooner we get away from this site, the better." With that the two craft above called off their search, plunging the site into near darkness, only the landing lights of the stationary ship cast a dull glow over the scorched ground about it.

Heading up the ramp, they didn't notice Albie's slight figure sneak up behind them and onto the ship, trailing sand as it did so. They'll find out soon enough Albie thought as he nestled undetected between the pipes that ran above their heads – there was something very familiar and comforting about them, he thought.

9

Albie scanned the dim compartment below as the Predavator shook from its sudden ascent. Through a sliding door he could make out a small cockpit at the front with just enough space for two seats: one pilot and one navigator, side by side. Dials, screens and instruments spread in front of the two seats dominated the view.

A small space for two visitors to watch the screens completed the cockpit and behind them a small five-foot high door led into the main area of the ship. Albie winced as he thought about being able to get through these doors without a head injury: a difficulty that had possibly been overlooked when the ship was designed.

Stepping through the door into the rear of the craft would hardly be a relief for those with concussion as it was nearly as low on the other side of the door, he noted. The pipes that he lay on, were growing uncomfortably hot as they climbed. Backless plastic bucket seats either side of the length of the hold included an intricate set of straps that looked like they could hold even the most determined of 'guests'. The higher it flew, the cooler the breeze that blasted through the open ports either side of the fuselage. Welcoming as it was for Albie, the heat was still making it a challenge to stay where he was.

He tried to spot possible escape routes but there was only one way in or out and that was through the ramp at the back. It was wide enough for two people to

squeeze through at a time: a trooper and his heavily
shackled prisoner, perhaps.

Thanks to the whining din, Albie was able to slip
unnoticed along the pipes and finally settled on a
cooler spot to take further stock of the situation. There
was so much sand whipped up by the take-off that the
steady trickle that rained down from above went
completely unnoticed. Reznor stared straight ahead,
lost in thought, while Sted and Faon hung their heads,
defeated and expecting the worst. The uniforms
fastened them in as they lifted off, before disappearing
into the cockpit, leaving them unattended.

The sandy figure that made its way along the
pipe-work, carefully avoided those pipes that now
belted out the most heat and seemed to be connected to
the engines. As it did so, a trail of sand followed it
along the steel grating, some blowing onto the still
figures below. Reznor simply nodded as he casually
raised his head. Faon's head was hung too low to
notice but across Sted's thin face an attempt at a smile
flickered. Hope momentarily shone in his glazed eyes
as he fought to stay upright as they were buffeted by
the craft's rocking. Reznor's attempt to help was held
in check by one of his restraining straps.

The stooped figure of a uniform immediately
emerged from the cockpit, alerted by the sounds of
movement. Adjusting himself to as near his full height
as he could manage, his attention was drawn to the
steady trickle of sand that dropped onto his
regimentally polished boots. Following the trickles

upwards, he found himself face to face with a grinning sand-covered monster.

A completely sandy face joined the monster's toothy grin in front of the Uniform. Suddenly a pair of feet appeared behind him knocked him forward, his feet clanging on the grate as he stumbled. Albie slid gratefully down from the pipe, landing easily on his two feet. Swinging his stick, he hit the figure at the back of the neck. The Uniform slumped to his knees before crashing forward; his head made a resounding thud as it crashed into the fuselage wall.

The tied-up passengers held their breath as they stared expectantly at their rescuer. Pulling the body into the shadows he just grinned as he sprung back above and waited. It didn't take long before another uniform emerged. Taking a quick look around him, he stared suspiciously at the three tied securely to the side. The door had just slid shut behind him when a pair of legs wrapped themselves around his neck, knocking off his helmet and swiftly lifting him upwards. There was the brief sound of head meeting pipes before his body dropped back to the floor.

The uniform momentarily stood swaying, trying to stay in an upright position so unable to warn his comrades. Just for good measure, Albie, his hands still clinging to the pipework, swung his feet back before launching a two-footed kick that connected with the Uniform's head, which was promptly pitched into the grilling. The body lay motionless.

Albie jumped down, waving his scalded hands to

cool them down. He was still regaining his balance as the cockpit door slid open behind him. Falling onto his red-raw hands he kicked out with his feet once again, returning the entrant back through the door. Expertly back-flipping he followed the flying mass into the cramped flight deck. The pilot stared at the object now slumped onto the co-pilot's seat. Staring, his bewilderment disappeared the moment he focussed on the barrel pointed at his head and Albie's delighted smile directly behind it.

"Land, please." Albie instructed him. He did as he was asked. Once they had set down upon a desolate strip of land, Albie thanked him then motioned towards the expectant cargo of bodies strapped on the other side of the door. Releasing Albie's companions was the last thing the pilot remembered before he felt a sharp pain at the back of his neck.

In the middle of nowhere, stuck inside a craft he had no idea how to work; his quest to find Tissa was not working out the way he had envisaged. Having said that, even though its pilot and crew were 'peacefully sleeping' at his feet, Albie was growing in confidence. He had found himself coping quite calmly. Despite only knowing Tissa for a short while, he cared for her in a similar way he had cared for his mother. Strangely, there was something different and exciting about this feeling. At one time she had just been a distant figure but now he felt responsible – he'd dragged her through the vents, subjected her to robot SPDRS, pulled her down into his world and subsequently lost her. Thinking about it: some friend he'd been.

Studying his three new comrades, he realised he was now responsible for them too; if only because he was the only one who still had his strength. Faon was still struggling to move after being buried in sand and then bound. Her breath was short, more of an effort than when Albie had first seen her. Reznor was fit enough but there was something Albie felt uncomfortable about in the way he studied their former captors; he was definitely waiting for the slightest stirring to exact his revenge on them. The sooner they were away from here the better. Sted: he was much the same as Faon, weak to say the least and barely able to sit or stand without the support of the hull: a truly pitiful pair.

Turning his attention back to the figures stretched before them, he jumped as Reznor gave a cry of delight then sprung forward. Grabbing hold of the nearest helmet, he prised it off its wearer and letting the head plunge with a sickening thud of skull on metal. He repeated the trick with the other three that lay at their feet. The others watched silently, and slightly bemused, as their armour and steel-tipped boots were removed along with their uniforms; leaving four sleeping, semi-clad bodies.

"Time they got off our ship!" Reznor proudly announced as the rear door whined open. Without any ceremony he rolled the troopers out, swiftly followed by Reznor's torn clothing. Reznor turned the boots over in his hands and marvelled at them. They were so much sturdier efforts than his own shoes that had really just become another layer of his skin. His skin had been systematically ripped, scraped and scratched: well-worn would have been an insult to their endurance.

Faon and Sted sat, supporting each other as they watched their comrade peeling his footwear off, wincing as occasional pieces of skin were pulled away with his old shoes. Reznor hardly noticed them peering through their fingers, making sympathetic noises as he changed nor did he see them briefly turn their heads away to wince only to return their gaze once their morbid curiosity had got the better of them.

Albie had managed to roll himself into a uniform and taken an immediate dislike to its tightness so it was swiftly unrolled and tossed out. He did however take a shine to the silver and black chunky boots and the armoured, silver chest pad and elbow pads. Since putting on Tissa's choice of clothes he had escaped scrape after scrape but now all he had left was the equivalent of a ripped t-shirt and shorts that had definitely lost any sparkle and stylish pizazz. He mused whether she would have told him that rips were once fashionable or something stupid like that? But with chest pad, elbow pads, helmet and boots – he certainly looked the part…but part of what? That was the question the others were trying to work out. His visor concealed his expression and he certainly appeared menacing. Casually lifting his visor, he reassured them with a rotten, uneven and unkempt set of teeth that finished off an awkward and extremely lopsided smile. Life wasn't so bad if you could still manage to smile with teeth like that thought Reznor, chuckling whilst making sure his own teeth remained hidden.

Glancing outside, to check their unwanted guests were still sleeping, they closed the rear door before exploring the tightest corners of the craft. Their search proved extremely successful as food, looking like metal bars (without the tooth-crunching effect) and drink (almost the thickness of oil) were commandeered and gratefully consumed. Soon after various weapons, that offered many levels of destruction, were found in lockers dotted about the inside of the hull. It was the first time any of them could remember feeling rested and full, after only a few bites. Faon and Sted were finally able to raise serious attempts at a smile although Reznor still looked serious. Albie had taken a liking to his new visor so didn't feel like showing anybody his face for at least another hour. For the time being they were content to eat, rest and relax. Before long each was lost in their version of the day's activities before sleep took hold of them all.

Barely an hour later, Sted awoke from an exhausted slumber. He was amazed to find out that his body felt energized for the first time in years. Although he felt stiff and his muscles still ached, it was a different kind of ache. It was the kind of ache that he had known from being inactive. He rolled his neck and despite the cracking bones he felt good…no, not just good, he felt great. Stretching his arms out, he felt blood returning to his little-used muscles. Testing his legs, he stood up and after an initial stumble he felt the same rush of blood. A single wrapper from the food bar he had had just an hour earlier floated off his knee. He dreamily watched it float to the floor then steadying himself, he bent over to pick it up. He had barely had the presence to study it earlier but now he could make out the luminous letters: "Emergency Regeneration Bar".

Delighted with his new-found strength, he turned to tell Faon his discovery, only to find she had vanished. Momentary panic set in.

"Albie, Rez, Faon's gone!" he cried, shaking his comrade awake. They searched the hold, checked the ramp was still up and made sure their former guards were still out for the count outside the ship. They were but their search for Faon still met without success.

The sound of warming engines sent them storming into the cockpit. Mouths gaping, they couldn't believe the transformation in the figure that had barely been able to stand an hour before. The once-frightened abductee spun gingerly but steadily around in her black plastic pilot's seat. With a rejuvenated and exultant expression, she asked them:

"Where shall we take our ship?"

There was a relaxed air about Faon as she casually guided the ship into the air as if she had done it a thousand times before. She even had a smile – quite a novelty, thought Albie: and teeth! There were no gaps – straight, mostly perfect, apart from the odd cracked tooth and the colour: a dirty yellow. Albie had only met Tissa with better teeth.

He continued to study her with a look of amazement. She was completely oblivious to all of this and the others converged on her. She was revelling in having energy…and no pain. She was no longer the wretched pale imitation of the person she had been.

"Aren't you a surprise package?" Reznor announced to break the stunned silence. Her hands were gliding across the controls with more and more confidence and control.

"I think the regeneration bars must have an advanced cell repair ingredient. There were similar, but less advanced versions of these when I was at the Academy but nothing like this. I feel as good as new, although will probably collapse in a few hours when the effect wears off. Need to take a few with us I reckon." She mused.

"Academy?" Albie's concerns were shared: Sted took a nervous step away from his friend, looking at the other two for some reassurance. The person in the middle of it all had discovered a new lease of life; too busy playing with her new toy to explain anything to them. The Predavator banked sharply to the left, flinging them all towards the empty co-pilot's seat. Albie thought he heard their pilot cry "wheeee" to herself as they all collapsed into a heap. The next second, they were being thrown back: again, into a heap but this time against the hard and cold door which slid open sending them into a heap in the cargo bay.

This seemed to annoy Albie more than the others since he ended up on the bottom with his head gradually moulding itself to the grille. Cold air from the numerous holes in the underside of the craft added to his discomfort.

Kicking, he began struggling to speak: "Guff" became "Gruff", this in turn transformed into "Gerruff" and as the others untangled themselves he shouted:

"Get off!" He emphasised both words as if to check his jaw was still working. Finishing off with a cry of "Stop: now!" he was caught off balance once more and this time they were all sent flying via the controls onto the back of the pilot's chair. This time Albie was on top. Faon winced as he buffeted her, her fragile body still not ready for this sort of contact. But she was happy, genuinely happy. She was reborn into a role that had once given her so much pleasure. She was like a child again.

"OOOhhhh, sorry," she apologised meekly and managed to throw them a grin, "got a bit carried away." The Predavator was now hovering in a manner Albie had extremely uncomfortable memories of: without exception he had been on the outside, trying to avoid being spotted. This however was quite a unique experience – he would have preferred a spot outside, perhaps behind a concrete wall: at least then he would have had a chance to run, not be reliant upon a pilot who had developed a sudden unstable, insane and slightly suicidal streak. Straightening up, he stared at Faon and realised he couldn't picture the frightened figure he had first stumbled upon. Pausing, she finally read their concerned faces and, with a shrug, began to explain:

"I used to be a pilot, had a fabulous apartment and job – I loved it. But, instead of just doing my job, I started to notice things I didn't like – old people being carried away, families, some with young children...all being taken below the city. I wondered where these people were going...what they'd done."

"I asked too many questions to the wrong people – even my own co-pilot seemed pleased when he saw them waiting for me after an unbearably long shift.

"Asked too much, didn't you?" he had snarled angrily as they took hold of me. Don't know what happened to my home; don't even think my friends were told what had happened to me – I was just another disappearance that nobody ever questioned. We always assumed that the 'disappeared' had to have done something wrong: I certainly did. That is until it was my turn to 'disappear'."

The smile had gone along with the glow of the circuitry as she stared into the unbroken blackness of the viewing screens ahead of her.

"Never thought I'd fly again. Someone must have felt sorry for me, so they put me in charge of 'the library' as they called it..." Tears welled up in her eyes but she continued staring out, fighting the urge to cry, the muscles in her face tensed up. She quietly trembled but the others didn't know what to do. Albie had never met this emotion or situation before and had no idea how he should react while Reznor was frozen, unsure of who this person was. Was she still one of them? It was Sted who shuffled over to her and wrapped his arms around her.

"It's okay, I think we've all got a few stories to tell…It's going to be alright." She was only half listening to him as he tried to comfort her. Her eyes had become transfixed to the screens and a dot of light that grew rapidly larger as she watched.

10

Her sudden motions flung them back once more, the Predavator lurching forward and Sted's embrace was immediately ended. Her attention was now focussed entirely on a circular dial with a flashing dot cruising steadily towards its centre. It took a moment to work out what it was but the others soon realised they were at the centre of the dial and the object flashing was something they didn't want to be getting any closer.

Albie was the first to ask; "Is that what I think it is?" a simple nod told him all he needed to know, "How do we get rid of it?" Faon's hand patted a joystick and trigger in front of the other seat before quickly returning to the controls. He was just about to jump into the seat when Sted slipped quickly in before him.

"Could be fun," he casually remarked as he pulled the joystick from left to right. "How…?" Her same hand shot out, knocking a switch on top of the joystick to reveal a red firing button. She then returned to piloting the craft without any more instruction. Dials in front of him sprang into life – one of them looked like it could be a target so Sted repeated his movements from left to right. A red dot appeared on the target before disappearing when he moved it too far to either side.

Albie and Reznor felt like spare parts – and were having difficulty staying upright. Despite Faon's claims about her piloting abilities, their flight had neither been calm or relaxing. They retreated into the hold and held onto the straps dangling from the ceiling that had bound them just an hour earlier. It seemed as if the craft was bouncing as it flew and they exchanged worried glances, expecting the worse.

"Hang on!" warned Faon as both craft and passengers were tossed through the air followed by a 'crump' sound outside. Albie and Reznor ended up with bruised and battered pride, lying crumpled together on the floor. The latter rubbed his chin where the former's metal–tipped boot had been planted firmly. Albie didn't get off lightly as he removed Reznor's bony elbow from his midriff.

They were rocked again and every time they tried to untangle themselves from each other, another explosion undid their efforts.

A different sound accompanied the 'crumps'. This time a whine split the air, followed by a good deal of cursing from the cockpit. There was nothing to do but wait and hang on as best they could. The pitching continued but gradually the cursing died down – they took this as a good sign and after losing count of the number of bruises sustained they finally heard an explosion outside followed by a cheer from the cockpit. For the first time, they thought they were flying straight. Untangled at last they dared to peek into the cockpit.

As they stepped through, a jubilant Sted sat spinning himself round and round in the co-pilot's seat. Lolling his head back, he greeted them. Every time he span past their eyes, he whispered:

"I got it!" His chair finally returning to rest, he panted for breath as he struggled to recover from his sudden burst of adrenaline and energy.

Faon on the other hand cautiously scoured the panels in front, muttering irritably to herself. Reznor punched him affectionately, but gently, on his shoulder, nodding.

"That told them, eh? No messing!" Sted laughed and with the return of a second wind, carried on spinning and 'Wheeeeeing'. Faon wasn't in such a good mood.

"There'll be more. They know when one's down, they'll also know that a Predavator's not doing what it's supposed to and be after us." Reznor caught Sted's feet in mid-spin and they turned their attention to the screens ahead of them. Faon's expression remained constant: concerned, her hands once more skimming across the circuit board, while her eyes seemed oblivious to the actions of the rest of her body, transfixed.

The craft continued to cruise through the dark: the crests of the waves skimming off its hull. They were just another shade of black to add to a virtually non-existent view. Occasional dots of light appeared in the distance but soon disappeared without trace. There was a sense of nobody daring to breathe and it was Albie who eventually broke the silence:

"Where *are* we going?"

Sted and Reznor turned to look at him, his face only half-visible in the pale lights of the control panels. They exchanged a look as if they were about to tell him not to be so stupid when they too realised they wanted to know the same thing.

"Good point," was all Reznor could muster, nodding. It was an action he hoped would convince the others that he had some inkling as to what was going on and therefore had some control over it. After all, they had been stunned by Faon's sudden display of dominance. None of them had thought what would happen after they had managed to overpower the troopers, pilot the ship and escape detection.

"Can we land somewhere and think what we're going to do next?" Albie piped up, once again becoming the group's voice – a voice for forward planning, even. This surprised him since in his previous life he had rarely thought beyond his next meal. His stomach and the need to keep both it and the rest of his body in one piece had decided his actions. For the first time he had supplies and nobody was trying to blow him up (not at that precise moment anyway).

He couldn't help his thoughts turning to Tissa. She was definitely not in such an advantageous situation and he was determined to do everything he could to get, even if it meant doing it alone. His mind was filling up with the images that had decorated the tunnel– faces as haunted as Faon and Sted had been and it made him even more desperate to find a landing spot so he could formulate a rescue plan. The constant buffeting by the tips of the waves was bad for his concentration.

"Okay," replied their pilot. "Let me find a spot…"

Their hopes weren't high. They stared into the blackness and even the occasional dots of light had vanished. For all they knew they could have been intended to lure flyers to their deaths so their craft could be salvaged and traded as scrap. Albie had heard many things and he knew the lengths some would go to scrape a gloomy existence down here.

Faon had slowed her hand movements drastically and seemed to be tiring considerably after her radical transformation. Her hand started to slip on the joystick and after a sudden altitude dip accompanied one fumble, Reznor took hold of first her hands then the controls. She gratefully accepted his help. Their pilot needed rest. The adrenaline of the escape was rapidly fading.

"Open the rear door and try to find the forward searchlight controls!" Albie ordered, rushing out of the cockpit. With Faon prompting, Reznor did as he was instructed and by the time Albie reached the back the combined efforts of the other three meant he could make out patterns of light on the water as they skimmed above it. The engines whipped up spray as they flew lower and Albie had to fight the winds from outside whipping at him. Sted and Reznor watched him, unsure what he had in mind.

Clinging onto the ramp, he spread himself out onto the floor and crawled towards the edge. By now his head was hanging below the craft, desperately searching for somewhere for them to stop and rest. His head disappeared from their sight then quickly reappeared.

"Keep on this path; I think there may be something ahead." Reznor's booming voice immediately relayed Albie's instructions. Albie's head disappeared from view again.

If he'd had any more hair it would have dragged him into the water, one thing to thank Tissa for, at least. The chillingly cold spray covered his face and hands as he blinked his way through the waves. Gripping on the rim of the ramp was becoming more difficult as what warmth he had left in his hands was being stolen by the cold steel of the ramp. To make matters worse, the craft was being tossed about just above the murky, watery blackness and the ramp was becoming increasingly treacherous in the wet.

"Start slowing, there is something…"

He felt himself slipping. Wedging whatever parts of his body he could into the metal hull he held his grip at the top of the ramp, fighting the constant rocking. Craning his head further out of the craft and looking along the Predavator's belly for what seemed an age, he finally thought he could see something. He strained and blinked as he made out an object ahead of them. A large floating slab grew closer as he lowered himself even further. Jerking his head up to call out, one of his boots was wrenched from the crack it had become entrenched in. Frantically he grabbed at anything he could as he slid head first down the greasy ramp. His head slipped into the spray. Each wave was now like a hand trying to haul him into the filthy water below.

Just as his body slid to the edge of the ramp, he shot out both hands to grab the winch shaft at the foot of the ramp. The rest of him carried on its downward slide and wrenched at his aching arms but with grim determination he held on.

The spray whipped his legs as they dangled yet he managed to pull himself back onto the relative safety of the ramp. He called out for Faon to slow down but she showed no sign of having heard him. His vain attempts to shout to them were lost in the lashing waves. The floating slab drew closer and closer. Why weren't they slowing down?

Surely, they couldn't miss that great slab?

When nobody arrived, he released one hand to call out louder. Just as he did this their craft dipped just slightly too low, clipping the waters. Albie was flung backwards as the craft lurched upwards. His fingers slipped and he tumbled off the ramp into the icy depths.

He remembered his earlier plunge from the city above and even though this was a far shorter distance, his tumble was every bit as unpleasant and painful. He skimmed the surface like a stone. Each bounce smashing into a different part of him – his back first, followed by his feet before he was flung upwards to land face first. Albie began to feel his body being dragged into the depths. He knew he would be completely unable to resist their clutches and realised he had failed Tissa. Her dirty, tear-stained face, begging him to keep fighting and to find her, shimmered in front of him.

"Don't leave me!" he could hear her. "You promised you wouldn't!" He wanted to reach out to her, call out, but she faded into the inky waters.

She suddenly disappeared as he crashed onto his side: like hitting a solid wall. This final blow jarred him more than the others as did the pain that shot through him.

His body was numb.

Albie lay, waiting to sink below the water and for his lungs to fill with water, but he continued to draw in air – it wasn't very pleasant and it was wet…but he was still breathing…still breathing. It was only after he had been laid out for a few minutes, the pain wracking his body that he remembered his eyes were still shut. Although opening them made him none the wiser, he could feel his back was cold: not the numbing cold of water but the sapping cold of metal.

He tried to use his arm to push himself up but failed miserably, slumping back with an echoing bang. Rolling, he found himself illuminated. Turning his head, he took in the object he had landed upon and laughed – quietly at first but gradually gathering both fervour and volume.

Barely metres away stood the Predavator – gases spewing from its engines as they cooled down, ramp still open. A grateful, but bemused, Reznor stood gawping at him.

Albie felt physically wrecked. Every part of him ached; he was soaked through and frozen. Reznor on the other hand looked positively heroic with the spray of the waves hitting the edge of the slab that he lay on, making him sparkle in the glow of the Predavator's lights. The air from its engines blew his hair across his face and from this distance it didn't look like it was matted into a few thickened strands. Reznor seemed to be enjoying the feeling and stood surveying the sight with his hands on his hips; posing for dramatic effect.

It took Reznor some moments to stop his posturing and realise that his friend was seriously hurt. It also took a cry from Sted who had eased himself down the ramp to attract Reznor's attention. Foolish pride deserted him and he rushed over, tried to pick up Albie, who complained about every movement as Reznor struggled to carry him. In the end it took Sted and Reznor's combined efforts simply to drag him onto the craft. Faon had recovered some of her strength with another pack of nutritional biscuits that she had salvaged from the hold.

"Lay him down here," she ordered; indicating a pile of material she had stretched out across the metal floor. She opened a backpack she had discovered that looked like it might contain some medical supplies.

Albie was laid on the floor where he continued to make agonising yelps the moment anyone tried to touch him. Falling from Tenebria's basement had been nothing compared to this. Faon surprised them again by reaching into the medical kit and pulling out a long, white object with flashing lights on the underside. They blinked red at first as she ran it over Albie's knees and as Albie tentatively stretched his legs out they turned green. Faon repeated this over his body as the effects of his tumble eased. Once she had finished, Faon pulled out what resembled an old-fashioned pen. Without warning, she stuck it into his upper arm. Before he could react, Albie felt himself floating, drifting away from the cold, the aches and feelings of loss and into a place of safety and warmth.

He forced his tired eyes open to gaze into a warm yellow circle in a clear blue sky. There were long green stalks swaying in a gentle, soothing breeze. The whole scene glowed with bright colours. There was water – but it glistened in the warmth: it was blue, just like the sky. He was stretched out amongst the stalks and he thought he had slept for what seemed like hours. Stretching he was pleased to be able to stand. He touched the green shoots that stroked his legs and feet and began to walk. He felt no pain. The achiness had gone. Around him, green fields stretched out in all directions. Apart from the wind that whistled gently around him, there was no other sound. In the distance the land rose into peaks. He felt calm.

There were no dirty ruins – no bricks, no sounds

of craft above and in the distance, he could make out a figure: a familiar, silhouetted figure – young, carefree and sure-footed. He ran towards it but as fast as he ran, he still couldn't quite reach him…or was it a her? There was always another stretch to run across or hill to climb. As he ran, the greenery felt like fingers trying to hold onto him: slow him down. He called out but it made no difference he couldn't get any closer. Finally, the figure, with a brief wave, disappeared.

He sank to his knees and began to cry. He didn't know why and he didn't know who it had been but he knew that he had so wanted to reach them, hold them.

Albie turned around and the worry about the disappearance of the figure subsided. He once more felt at ease as a warming, fresh-tasting breeze blew across him. He sensed an aroma he hadn't smelt for many years and turned to the direction from which it came from. In the distance he again could see another figure: this time older but just as relaxed and full of life. He once more raced towards it, green and yellow vegetation stroking him as he ran. The further, and faster, he ran the more the stroking once more turned into a grabbing, tugging at his legs again and slowing him down. His legs finally gave way and tumbled. He wanted to climb back up but couldn't. He gasped for air but no matter how hard he tried his lungs still gasped for more. The figure's carefree nature disappeared. Its shoulders sagged and with a melancholy shake of the head, it turned away from him. With a final look at him, it wandered into the forest background before vanishing in the undergrowth.

Albie screamed and as he did so, the vegetation coiled around him like a myriad of snakes. He was unable to escape! Crashing to the floor, all he could do was call out:

"Mum! Don't...leave...me!"

11

Albie sat bolt upright. As he did so he was aware of three concerned faces observing him. Their expressions slowly changed to relief and Albie heard their collective sigh as they drew closer.

A relieved Faon gently hugged him. He felt peculiar. Before Tissa he hadn't been touched by anybody in his memory (that is without them ending up on the floor in pain) but it was now happening with increased regularity.

"Thanks..." his voice tailed off as he returned her gaze. She was becoming more and more confident: was this the real Faon? What must she have been through and what was Tissa going through now? His only image of Tissa was carefree, excitable. What would they do to her? If they had reduced this confident pilot to a shell of a personal wreck: what would they do to a dizzy dreamer of a girl?

Organising his thoughts, he pushed the others away:

"I'm okay, but we've got to find someone... she's alone...we've got to go back. I've got to get into that camp." The determination in his voice put any reservations they may have had to the back of their minds. They all started to move but hesitated as Sted pulled out a picture and handed it to Albie.

"Is this your mother…?" he asked, "…cause if it is, she's probably not there. Faon can explain better." He prompted his partner, nudging her elbow. She shot him an annoyed look and waited for Albie to process this latest development.

Albie stared at the image that had been presented before him; it had been hard being confronted with a picture of his mother after so long. What made it worse was that it had been taken after he had lost her. Seeing her face that first time had been a shock, but he had managed to blot out the memories; they would have done him no good. He had convinced himself she was gone and there was nothing he could do to bring her back but there was something in the way the others were talking to him. They desperately wanted to avoid giving him hope; a false hope that might never be realised. They patiently waited for the youngster.

Albie was in a quandary. He didn't want to be torn between the only people in his life he had cared for – one of whom he had grown so close to in such a short space of time and the other who had been out of his life for so long that she was little more than a vague vision in his head. He now held the only picture he had ever owned of his mother and he could feel himself welling up, feeling it his duty to search for her. He wanted the tears to flow as they had during his dream but his eyes remained dry. His lungs gasped quietly. If he asked more about his mother, he knew he wouldn't be able to stop himself: details, places, journeys would soon turn into more plans. Tissa would spend more time in the…in the…he realised he only had a vague idea where she might be.

Closing his hand around the picture, he shut his eyes and tried to blank his mother from his thoughts: it hurt but he had to focus on the here and now. Tissa needed him. Tears finally trickled from each eye. He yearned for the mother he had had to do without for so long but was now turning his back on. However, the frightened girl who had opened her door to his dark and undesirable world needed him more. She had become his responsibility and he had let her slip away. One thing at a time, he decided.

"Look, whatever it is…about my mum…" he was going to end up sounding callous whatever he said: "I've got to rescue my friend first: who knows what state she's in. She's only known one world and it's not this one and if it hadn't been for me she'd still only know that world. Please…help."

They were all too stunned to say anything and felt too awkward to speak. There was nothing they could say because for the first time since arriving down here they had real hope of escaping this world and without this pleading individual they would still have been hiding underground with the photos of the 'lost' for company.

"What do you want us to do?" Faon finally broke the silence. "You've given us our pride back and the same people who took that away from us will most likely have your friend. They've had things their way for too long. It's time somebody tried to make things harder for them: maybe that's us." The awkwardness dissolved. Faon realised she had just sounded a rallying call of sorts. It may not have been to hundreds or thousands but beating a tightened fist on the underside of their craft she felt empowered. It was a good feeling. She looked down to see just three pairs of eyes fixed on her. Embarrassed, she turned to walk up the ramp unaware that the two largest landing lights had cast a heroic, maybe angelic, glow around her. The atmosphere changed and instead of nervousness it was one of determination. Leaping up, Sted could only think to cry:

"Come on!"

His moment of heroic action was ended swiftly by the sound of his head hitting the Predavator hull. He staggered back, landing in a particularly awkward-looking heap on the metal floor.

Carrying him up the ramp the other two simply compounded matters by crashing his head once again on their underside of the craft. Easing him into one of the bucket seats, Faon found inside the medical kit, a plastic bag that became cold when it was shaken. She placed it on his wound, placed his hand to keep it in place then disappeared into the narrow cockpit.

Emerging into the cockpit, Reznor found her studying an on-screen map – he joined her immediately, pointing up at various points as they made agreeing noises. Albie looked at it and could only see lines and squiggles; with the odd image here and there. Nevertheless, he studied it along with the others, trying to mimic the noises they made, pointing when they did and nodding in unison. He felt involved. It was only when Faon and Reznor disagreed that they turned to Albie for his opinion.

"…what do you reckon?" all eyes turned to him but Albie was too busy nodding to notice. He had convinced himself that he knew what he was looking at and had drifted away from the discussion, getting carried away in the process: pointing at various spots on the map while muttering inaudibly.

"…Albie?" Sted repeated himself, still trying to sooth his head with his cold compress.

"What do you reckon we should do…?"

Albie looked quizzically at him

"…where should we get in…?"

Albie still gazed blankly.

"…into the camp?"

He tapped the screen, drawing Albie's eyes onto the map. He just shrugged and with a complete absence of expression confessed:

"Haven't got a clue – what is this anyway?"

"It's a map, a kind of picture, of the part of the camp we think your friend will be in because she's one of the youngest. They only keep her there briefly until she is strong enough to do more physical work elsewhere: it's a sort of halfway camp. They are better fed and have shorter shifts. But there is only one purpose: to eventually allow new entrants to work full shifts in the mines or the factories. After a day or so, their drugs will have kicked in so the shifts will become longer. She might be lucky and still be above ground but this is where they condition you to do what they want. This is where your spirit is broken by the cocktail of mind and pain control drugs: once that's gone you'll do anything they want you to. It's brutal but at least she'll probably be alive."

"It's in the middle of the other camps – to discourage escape," continued Sted grimly, his eyes glazing over as he continued, "they march you through the other camps just so you can see what awaits you. Pride is taken in showing you how pointless thoughts of escape are – the Predavators above, the gun towers, the SPDRS, minefields, not to mention the down-beaten looks around you and the dismal conditions…" he began to remember and back came the Sted Albie had first met. This time Faon was comforting him; reassuring him as he sat down holding his head in his hands.

"Let's just fly there and take it from there. This craft's one of theirs, the uniforms the same … We'll try to blend in with the crowd," suggested Albie, "It's about the best I can think of. Let's get some food and rest now, to make sure we are in a better state to fight and then head off." He considered the still-dazed Sted, who was still holding his compress and rubbing his head then began searching the lockers in the hold for food.

After handing out energy and recuperation bars she had found, Faon sat back down in the pilot's chair.

They all marvelled at the effect of the food bars they had eaten. From the first bite they felt its effects surge through their bodies: like healing waves repairing their battered bodies. Even though Sted and Faon had been in an emaciated state when Albie had found them, they had almost made a complete recovery from their months of depravation. Although their faces still looked drawn, their muscles no longer ached with every step and action. They felt alive. By the time Albie had decided they had had enough rest, they were ready to don their borrowed uniforms.

Faon checked through the flight instruments while Albie handed them all domitors that he had found stashed away in a separate compartment in the hold. Albie gave them a quick explanation of how to use them. A satisfying test fire into the dark spray that lashed outside followed. Finally, they boarded the Predavator to join Faon in the cockpit.

"We'll have to remember that spot," Faon announced as she gently flicked the switches around her.

"What is it? Why have a big slab of metal drifting in the middle of nowhere?" asked Sted.

"There are about a hundred of them all dotted

around the underworld, just in case the Predavator pilots needed a spot to land. Some are bigger than others and below deck are living quarters, hangers, kitchens…everything pilots and their crews could need in an emergency." Faon's matter-of-fact manner made Sted, who had taken the spot next to his partner, look twice at her once again. What other surprises did she have up her sleeve? Shaking his head, he began to doubt she had ever spent those months rotting away with him in the tunnel.

In the hold the others all drifted into their own worlds as the engines started with a slow whoop – whoop – whoop. This became faster and faster, louder and louder until it blotted out all hope of quiet and private contemplation with the familiar, nerve-shredding rippa-rippa of the pred's engines. Reaching a peak, they lifted off gently from the slab that had given them a chance to recover and plan.

They were blindly charging back into the lion's den but at least they all knew why. Although, knowing why they were risking their lives only made it slightly easier.

As they approached the camp they could see that it wasn't going to be easy. News of the loss of two Predavators had stirred up a hornet's nest. The dark air above the camp was filled with dots of light that they all knew were craft similar to their own. Even above their own din they could hear the sound of a thousand ripping, angry engines – buzzing and probing every spot. Searchlights scanned the water and the land either side of it frothed with the non-stop searching of jet-ski lights. Not one spot was being left untouched by the search; certainly, they were not going to sneak back unnoticed anywhere.

The figures in the cockpit stared at the busy scene before them, each lost in their thoughts and plans. An ominous silence descended upon the cockpit. At that moment four craft peeled away from the search and headed steadily towards them.

"Suggestions please and quickly!" urged Faon, her hands tightening her grip on the joystick: the whiteness of her wiry fingers betraying her fragile state. She glanced at the fire button but instantly looked away. Another glance confirmed the delicacy of their situation: one blast of fire and she knew there'd be more than four to deal with. She still found herself being drawn to it and had to fight the urge to shoot.

Next to her, Sted was eyeing it as well: the same thoughts running through his mind. He eventually cut through the silence.

"Are we in communication contact with them?" he mused.

"What do I say if they ask where we've been?"

"Tell them…" they all waited to hear his fantastic idea; wide-eyed and praying for inspiration on Sted's behalf. "How about…" they were hanging on his every word now and he knew it, sweat began to build on his forehead: he was wide-eyed, wishing he'd kept his mouth shut as usual. It was then that it flashed before him: "It's not brilliant...but...Tell them we intercepted an illegal craft heading for the complex...and..." The others tried to help him out but could only eye the weapons console. The dots drew nearer, searchlights aimed at them making it harder to see anything else. Faon switched on the communicator and prepared her explanation. Running it through her head she could see the way the discussion would head:

"Why are you so far from base without authorisation...? Why didn't you request support? Who are you? What's your operating code?"

These would probably be followed by the inevitable "Maintain this course," and "Do not deviate," before landing in the middle of the complex to be welcomed by a large and armed welcoming committee.

"Albie, Reznor get to the side windows, find any weapons you can but stay out of sight until I say! Sted, are you ready with the forward battery?" she ordered, death was a better option to a return to slavery – neither would help Tissa but then at least they'll have done their bit to slightly dent the powers-that-be.

Still skimming above the inky water, the landing lights shimmered as they headed towards their welcome. The communicator crackled into life:

"Predavator 31-33, explain your deviation from assigned duties." There was a still silence as Faon wrestled with Sted's idea but even he didn't look too convinced by it. She wracked her brain as the question was repeated, this time an abruptness gave an indication all was not well.

"S...sorry, control, having directional difficulties...circuit overload...only managed to regain manual control and communication systems..." Sted looked at her, obviously impressed. Seconds later their communicator crackled once more:

"Maintain present course...inform us of any difficulties and prepare to submit to our guided autopilot."

"Confirm, control...31-33 responding." She wasn't sure whether this was a good course of action to follow or not but if nothing else it bought them a bit of time. Albie emerged carrying weapons for them both, a reluctant expression telling them of his idea. Faon and Sted took them hesitantly before returning to the controls. The four craft had formed an escort troop around them – two in front and two behind as they were guided toward a smog-covered island. A complex of large factory buildings, smaller accommodation huts and landing pads grew ahead of them. Faon jumped as the joystick forced itself out of her control. They were heading under guided control to wherever the other preds wanted them to go. Next the weaponry panel switched itself off: its panels sinking into an inky blackness.

"Guess we won't be able to fight our way out, then." Muttered Sted as he grudgingly released the fire button and guiding panel. Instead he stroked the weapon he had now stuck inside his belt. As he did so, Reznor popped his head through the door, announcing 'I've got an idea..." No longer needed to pilot the craft any more, Faon followed Sted into the main hold where Albie was squeezing himself inside what could only be described as a large transparent ball.

12

Approaching the shoreline of the complex, they could make out an array of colours and lights. The Predavators were now barely ten metres from the surface of the water and slowing rapidly. The middle Predavator that was being escorted by the other four vanished into the gloom as all its lights suddenly blinked before being snuffed out.

The third last thing the Predavators behind did was immediately focus their searchlights on it.

The second last thing they saw was its crew abandoning 'ship' via its lowered ramp using life support bubbles.

The last thing either ship saw was that same crew; as they abandoned ship, take aim at their rotor blades with what looked like rocket launchers. The two tail ships were instantly rocked by the initial strike that blew away their engines, before the fuel lines that supplied them also erupted, ending any chance that they could report the disappearing crew.

Sted and Reznor safely away, Faon watched with great satisfaction as the two escorting craft were engulfed in flames. An instant of panic struck her as she watched the wreckage drop perilously close to the escapees from her craft but a reassuring shove from behind forced her back to her own predicament – any second now the remaining escorts would come to investigate, and most likely spot the others floating to shore.

Gingerly she stepped into the final bubble and walked herself towards the end of the ramp. She wondered whether this really was completely necessary as she stared into the nothingness below.

Stealing herself inside the bubble she took a deep breath…then another.

This wasn't easy.

She couldn't do it.

Her whole body longed to be back in the cockpit.

Filling her lungs once more to waste a few more seconds, she felt herself suddenly moving as a flying Albie leapt onto the back of her bubble sending both of them tumbling forwards and out as their hijacked vehicle exploded in a ball of sparks and flame. The area around them was lit up momentarily as the remains of the ship quickly struck the water.

Albie scrambled to climb on top of Faon's bubble as it skipped across the waves. The wreckage in front of them zipped by as the struck the water's surface.

The bubble began to slow down as his grip began to slip; water and sweat loosening his hold. Unable to stop himself, he slid into the water, a familiar icy bite gnawing at his legs, making him clench his teeth ready for the inevitable.

He had steeled himself but as his chest hit the water and Faon's bubble slid away from him, it wasn't the sensation of freezing water he felt but the pain of hard rocks below the surface. His body screamed at him as it hurtled forward, throwing him from the icy clutches of the water onto the merciless, jagged outcrops of the shoreline. At last he stopped and lay still; waiting for the numerous cuts and scrapes to begin complaining once the shock had worn off. He daren't move for fear of finding he'd broken ribs, arms or legs. However, although he felt every muscle and limb calling out in protest, he realised he could still move his legs and arms. Scouring his skull, he couldn't feel any blood seeping out: miraculously, he was intact!

Lifting his head up, he caught sight of the others emerging unscathed from their bubbles that had survived bounding up the rocks, coming to rest at the foot of a small but steep mud cliff.

The waters behind him would soon be vigorously

scoured as lights crisscrossed towards them. He realised it would only be a question of time before the search took them to the shore he was now trying to summon up the strength to climb. Whipped up spray told him the search was getting closer.

The others were safely tucked between boulders that formed the base of the precipice but try as he might he was too tired to walk, he just wanted to lie here and wait; it wasn't that cold any more. He could barely feel his knees and elbows. They had taken most of the impact, despite the protection of the pads that now lay ripped at his side. The waters lapped about him more vigorously and he could faintly hear words of encouragement but he felt so sleepy and was so tired. Lights swept nearer his feet, sweeping from left to right and with each sweep they inched closer. He just needed to rest and that was the last he remembered as the pain overcame him and he blacked out.

Waves battered Albie's body now and still he couldn't or wouldn't move.

"Move, Albie, move…" Sted muttered but his friend just remained motionless, except for the lashing of the waves that was now becoming more frequent and vigorous. His head was resting serenely on a rock, lolling occasionally in the odd wave that splashed it. Albie displayed none of the panic at the activity that was growing around the foot of the cliff.

"We've got to get him – he doesn't look like he

can help himself," decided Reznor "another sweep and they'll spot him." With that he leapt out from cover and raced across the rocks to the spot where Albie lay, half submerged.

Turning around Reznor was relieved to see that Sted had followed behind him. Grabbing a limp arm each they dragged Albie's body away from the pursuing lights, a faint groan all the encouragement they needed. Reaching Faon they retreated further under the cliff face until they crouched on top of the escape bubbles they had deflated and buried as best they could in the mud. Hidden from view by two large boulders either side of them and a third that sat above them the dark figures recovered their breath.

Under this they watched and waited, as the lights grew closer. The ominous ripping filled the air – soon there'd be more along with an extensive land search. They were safe for now but would have to move very soon. But where to?

For the time being they weren't moving anywhere. Albie would have to regain consciousness first. Faon once more tried to work a miracle. Albie remained still: he was not stirring. She had nothing to work with; no medical tools or tablets to give him so she sat, rocking him with his head in her lap. Despite the fury of the search and the waters that lapped quicker and further onto the rock shore, she started to hum. It was a tune she'd not thought about since being a tiny child on her mother's knee and it comforted her. She was delighted to feel a slight cough. Before she knew it, Albie was leaning over, coughing water onto the rocks, shaking as he did so. A warm sense of relief filled her as the waters began to lap at her shoes.

"Now we can move…" Reznor urged as both Faon and Sted surveyed him incredulously, refusing to move. Reznor turned around to take hold of one of Albie's arms and stopped dead as he saw their looks of defiance. "This area will be crawling with uniforms soon; we'll be discovered for sure…" They seemed to accept this and as Sted took an arm, Faon grabbed hold of his legs. They scrambled out of their hiding place, taking a moment to watch the continuing search further along the shoreline. By now another three more Predavators had added their searchlights to the hunt. The friends struggled along ducking behind boulders to catch their breath whenever they could. Gradually they managed to put distance between themselves and the sweeping lights that seemed to be scouring in the opposite direction for now.

After exploring the shore, they realised that there was going to be no easy way off the beach: they would have to tackle the cliff.

Even though he was relatively slim, carrying Albie was still a great effort. First Sted and Reznor would climb up a rock while Faon struggled to hold both herself and a still-coughing Albie. The others would then haul him up as Faon struggled on behind them.

The sounds of more intense searching were

growing more distant but it would only take one craft to stray too far and they would be the centre of attention once again. Progress was slow; Albie's return to consciousness was gaining speed, aided by the buffeting he took every time he was dragged up and over, and Faon's ability to keep themselves both upright was dropping by the minute. The occasional groan at least reassured them that he was in some living state.

Activity began to move towards their section of the beach, this time aided by the appearance of troops on the ground; they could just hear the crackles of their radios as they followed the guiding lights. Occasional instructions echoed from the Predavators and the search was growing in intensity and size. For the first time, the fugitives were glad of the dark – even if it meant they were stumbling into unexpected outcrops with painful consequences. The glare they were escaping, helped them to avoid the jagged rocks looming out of the darkness. It was a help they willingly would have done without. A few bumps and scrapes would have been preferable to the unease they felt at being so close to the hunt. Every time a light flashed in their direction they froze - fear pinning them to the spot: their bodies just refusing to move. Trying to merge with the rocks soon became their own only protection…but for now, thankfully it was working!

Despite the threat the searchers posed, they felt comforted working together and relying on each other: something positive had come from their years of misery. Pulling Albie over the last outcrop, they were able to recover in a small valley with the rocks and the water behind them and a steep muddy bank ahead.

It hardly seemed a minute that they had sat there, panting before Albie came to. He muttered some unrecognisable words and managed to steady himself enough to sit up. He mumbled a drawn out "Thanks" before joining them, silently, as they watched the activity below. Odd flashes of light illuminated the area around them as the searching beams continued to stroke the earth. On the occasions that they could make out each other's faces there was only grim determination on offer; smiles were absent and hard to form.

As a light brushed past them, Faon, using handholds provided by the rock sheltering her, hauled herself up, encouraging the others to follow suit. With more discontented grumblings they managed it, Albie able to stand with help, before setting off up the slope.

This part of their journey proved to be more difficult, however. The mud clung to their feet and in doing so made them slip more. Lifting slabs of sludge with each step sapped their energy quicker than the rocks had: but they had to keep going. Albie's return to the living had come too soon as he stubbornly refused help. His companions were forced to struggle around him to stop him falling and becoming a permanent part of the sludge. Every time he stumbled there was a helping hand to return him back to a relatively upright position. If his body language was anything to go by, it was help that was not appreciated: it was a good job that the gloom covered his expression each time he stubbornly pushed away their supporting hands. His unsteady nature made it even slower – dragging him unconscious would have been so much easier. It was hard for them to be glad that he had returned to them at this particular moment.

Nevertheless, in spite of wading through increasingly more sticky sludge and having to pause each step to pull increasingly larger chunks of sticky ooze from their feet, they managed to progress. The rocks still lit up occasionally but the dirt above it was being ignored and they were able to progress unnoticed and reached the top safely: if not on speaking terms with Albie for the time being.

Perched at the top of the ridge, they were able to pause, peel off more layers of mud from their shoes and watch, with some amusement, the frantic efforts below. For the time being they felt safely out of range. It wouldn't be long before the search was widened and they had no idea how much of their path was showing in the sludge.

Reznor studied Albie, about to ask him how he felt but a look at the determination on the youngster's face made him think twice. There was a chance that Albie might still be injured but now he was on the same piece of land as Tissa, nothing was going to stop him reaching her. His trademark smile still hadn't returned and every so often he kept pausing to look at the glow from the camp ahead.

They were still sitting silently when a sound of movement made them jump. People were starting to emerge from the camp; just shapes in the distance but it forced the fugitives into action. Albie showed surprising agility, pulling out the domitor that was stuck into his belt. The others gaped at him – was this the same person who had struggled through the mud and slime? He sensed their looks and turned on them:

"Come on, we're on a rescue mission!" More delighted than anything else, they jumped up. With rather less energy they followed obediently behind him. It was Reznor who echoed their thoughts:

"To think we've carried him all this way and not a word of thanks!" he muttered. Albie instantly froze before slowly and deliberately turning his head until they could see his serious expression reflected in the camp's glow. They considered each other. Albie's expression changed and a familiar smile replaced his grim expression.

"You're right, Rez – thanks… all of you," Looking back they were sure a tear had rolled down his cheek at that point; a detail Albie vigorously denied. The instant disappeared as soon as it had emerged.   Albie barked out his orders: "Now, come on!"

"…And it's Reznor." Reznor added sulkily, deciding that Albie's change in character was not quite to his liking.

The company trooped forward, keeping low to the ground – each of them armed now with the weapons stolen from the Predavator.

They stayed out of sight of the uniforms emerging in increasing numbers from the camp. Inevitably, they closed in on an enormous concrete wall that circled the camp. There was only one way in and that was through a 3-metre high metal door that had just clanged shut. It looked far too thick to be dented with the weaponry they were carrying: even the large rocket launcher that Reznor had gleefully acquired. The wall must have been twice as high and almost completely smooth – it seemed to shine as if it was metallic. Either way – they weren't blasting their way in or climbing over. Faon spoke first.

"Looks like we'll have to knock, then…" A look of ridicule told her what the others thought of this suggestion but she continued; "Look at us…apart from Albie that is." They did so and for the first time they realised they were still dressed in the black uniforms they had 'borrowed'. There was a large amount of mud on them but apart from that, and the lack of helmet, they looked the part.

"We look as if we've just been dragged through a slimy bog…" Sted put in as they stood in the towering shadow of the wall.

"…Or survived a mid-air explosion?" Faon replied. She looked a bit too smug for Sted's liking and he was sorely tempted to cover her face with mud so that she could look even more the part. However, he resisted, feigning calmness.

They had to admit it – she was right. Anyone could lose a helmet: especially in a crash.

"What shall we do about Albie?" Reznor mused, taking in the scarred figure before him.

"Albie, give me your weapon…" A look of disgust filled his features as he edged back. "Listen, it's an old plan – but I've seen it work on a videodisc: trust me." With a sigh he handed it over and with Faon now leading the way, they advanced towards the metal door: the three trying to look authoritative and Albie trying to look beaten and not disgusted at the loss of his favourite 'toy'.

13

Standing at the foot of the immense wall, it was hard to look at it in anything but awe: the size of it and the fear of what lay inside. There was no doubt getting in was the easy part, getting out would require a lot more thought and a lot more luck.

Faon studied the door, which was tightly sealed shut with no sign of a button or a black pad to open it. The four studied every corner of both door and wall without success and any attempt at a confident swagger quickly disappeared. With each passing second, they looked more and more uncomfortable.

Albie was ready to grab a weapon and start blasting when the door slid open to reveal two curious bodies. The two groups studied each other before Faon took the initiative:

"Prisoner retrieved from the crash site…" Then added: "…for processing." Maybe it was the added information, or the way she tried to sound gruff, but the bodies in front of them weren't convinced.

"Really?" one replied, studying Albie with disgust. His colleague started tapping the domitor in his hand, mirroring his colleague's air of distrust. "Where are your helmets?"

"Lost them capturing this one, he's a toughie…" Faon replied and was about to continue when she was cut short.

"Doesn't look like much, better get some clarification on this…" this was too much for Albie and he leapt at the trooper just as Faon shouted for him to stop. The second trooper immediately took aim but was unable to finish as Sted, who was standing closest to him, brought his weapon down on the back of his neck. Caught off balance, he tumbled back against the wall where Reznor aimed a kick straight at his chest; silencing him.

After exchanging satisfied glances with Albie, who had disposed of the other trooper with the help of a kick from a smug-looking Faon's boot, they began to strip the troopers of their uniforms.

Faon and Sted removed the helmets from the unconscious troopers and headed straight to the computer screen and keyboard in one corner of the gateway. Albie and Reznor dragged the two troopers out through the door and, following the line of the wall, dropped them out of sight at the foot of the wall. Once they had returned, Albie was finally able to put domitor to pad and the outer door slid shut.

They were in a hallway as high as the gates with a pair of similar-sized doors opposite. Two smaller doors led either side. Apart from the computer, the hall was bare and metallic. Faon and Sted, at the computer, were studying the screen as Albie joined them.

"Busy looking for your friend but there are no names on this list – only numbers; the camp supervisor will have names."

"How about checking new entrants?" suggested Sted; "there are pictures of them here if you can think roughly when she came in…" the three were so intently studying the screen that they were completely oblivious to anything else.

Reznor however had entered one of the smaller doors, having used his domitor as a key. He found himself in an equally bare and dull metallic room with an identical door at the opposite end. The only object in there was a screen in the wall linked to a camera that must have been positioned high above the wall. It looked out onto the area outside the gates and so there was no wonder their story hadn't been believed. It was also a stroke of luck that there weren't more troopers at the gate – the search had done a good job of drawing them away. He watched an infra-red picture of the barren, flat stretch of land that lead to the mud slope and the water and, breathing a sigh of relief, he was pleased to see the area was clear.

It was then that he noticed four pads underneath the screen, positioned so that they made a diamond shape. Pressing the left-most button, the picture moved and he could make out the spot where they had laid the two troopers. Pressing the top pad, he was able to zoom and could make out the pair, still 'sleeping' soundly. Chuckling to himself he pressed the bottom pad and the troopers became smaller. Touching the right pad, the view moved once more and this time, he wasn't quite so pleased. From the opposite side of the wall, three uniforms were heading towards the doors.

Rushing back to the others he warned them:

"Time to go…incoming visitors." However, they were all engrossed in the search for Tissa and hardly heard him.

"Come on, company's on its way!"

"Nearly there…" replied Faon as faces whizzed past the screen, with Albie shaking his head furiously and looking despondent.

Rushing back to the camera screen, Reznor saw the uniforms were close to the door and quickly returned to the others, just as Albie screamed "It's her, it's Tissa…find her number…how long's she been here…is she still …" his voice tailed away when the door started unlocking. Faon and Sted dragged him into the room Reznor had found, just as the three arrivals entered the room.

There was no time for any questions as Reznor urged them through the door opposite. Behind them the screen was focused on the last of the uniforms as they entered. There was no way of telling if they had been suspicious of the lack of bodies in the hallway or noticed that the computer currently displayed Tissa's image.

"Stop, I've got to go back," announced Faon as they emerged into a large open yard, with the perimeter wall looming behind them. "The computer needs to be switched off – or put onto a different prisoner or they'll know who we're after!" They huddled between the wall and a handily placed hover vehicle so that they could think of the options. "If I don't go now then more searchers will return and the position will be worse."

They had to agree that she was right. They certainly didn't want anyone to know who they were trying to rescue.

"Put this helmet on and I'll come with you. You two…" decided Reznor before looking at Sted and Albie, "…stay behind this and don't touch anything."

He missed both an angelic look from Sted and a glower from Albie as he and Faon slunk back into the building they'd just left.

They tried to look calm and casual as they re-traced their steps but as the door slid effortlessly open to the screen room, Faon couldn't help jumping at the sight of two uniforms studying the view outside the wall. They turned to face them as Reznor stepped through the door.

"Where have you two been? There was nobody on duty and…" taking one look at the still mud-covered pair the more senior trooper stopped, taking in the state of their uniforms. He then stood up to his full height but found he could only peer down on Faon; which made him even angrier. "You two are a disgrace – what are your numbers?" he demanded, just as Reznor let off a quick shot. The blast sent him spinning against the screen and he slumped down in the corner. The moment Reznor had opened fire the other uniform headed for the doorway but Faon's trip had sent him crashing against it where Reznor finished him off.

"Well, it wasn't going to take long for them to find the other sleeping beauties was it?" Even though he couldn't see her eyes he knew Faon wasn't impressed. Bursting through the door into the hallway, she was equally unimpressed with his choice of blasting first the third member of the group and then the computer.

"Ever heard of a power switch or is that too much for your tiny brain?" she asked sarcastically; but he was unrepentant:

"Sure, but it's not half as much fun. Come on let's go. Even my tiny brain can work out it's going to get busy soon." With that he charged out, leaving his partner staring at the ceiling in a vain search for inspiration.

His further encouragement forced her to move and they were soon huddled behind the vehicle with the others, Faon still arguing as she removed her helmet.

"…And we must find out what uniform numbers we are – can't go around blasting everyone who asks!" The complete lack of interest on Reznor's behalf added to her frustration so she just gave up, preferring to study the helmet she was cradling in her arms.

Despite the firing, there was still an eerie silence in the yard as the group broke cover. Putting on his borrowed uniform, Albie raced to catch up. Nobody asked Faon where she was leading them but she assumed control once more. Row upon row of squalid metal boxes appeared in the distance: featureless and miserable in their uniformity. In the distance an increasingly frantic and fruitless search continued on the dirty shores that surrounded the walls of the camp, yet here an uneasy calm had descended. There was too much open space to cover for their liking. They crouched, waiting for uniforms to come pouring towards them, but nothing stirred anywhere. Either side of them was the same dark emptiness – a no-man's land between camp and wall aimed presumably at discouraging anybody thinking of breaking out (or in). All signs of the search outside suddenly stopped: this only put them further on edge and quickened their pace across the unnervingly flat earth.

Reaching the halfway point, Reznor felt a slight tug at his foot. Freezing, he dared to look down and found himself caught by a thin wire that had wrapped itself around him. Instinctively pulling himself away, he felt a sharp burst of electricity surge up his body. He slumped forward, thudding into the ground.

"Don't struggle," warned Sted "the more you do, the worse it gets." Reznor lay motionless, trusting his friend's advice and preferring not to experience the effects of the charge that had just knocked him flat. He switched off from the shooting pains and Sted's frantic actions as he stared straight ahead into the black sky. He tried to think of anything he could to distract him from the pain that accompanied the slightest movement of his leg. Clenching his teeth tightly together, he felt the pulses of electricity as they shot up his leg making his head buzz.

His body arched involuntarily, as a bolt of energy whizzed narrowly above his head. More bolts flashed past him. Reznor fought to remain still but his body was becoming racked by the pulses that accompanied every tiny movement. Sted continued to work feverishly: now with his head barely off the ground. Reznor could hear Albie and Faon taking aim in the direction they had come.

"They are coming from the walls, aim for the antennas!" cried Albie as the shapes of two robot SPDRS emerged: their familiar red eyes glaring through the gloom with reaching and snapping pincers despite the fact that they were still some way off.

The metallic insects scuttled steadily closer and Sted was still unable to release his partner, his fingers feverishly scrabbling in the dirt, gradually exposing more and more of the wire.

"Almost there," he muttered, hoping to reassure them but the panicked edge to his voice was unnerving for the stranded Reznor. The bolts zipped ever closer: he had no other choice but to wait.

Faon, lying flat on the ground, took aim and gave silent thanks when one of the SPDRS exploded. This seemed to enrage the other as it unleashed shot after shot at her, forcing her to bury her head in her outstretched arms. Albie took his chance while he was being ignored; he took aim at the SPDR's head. An immense feeling of satisfaction and relief filled him as it too was engulfed in flames.

With the second explosion, Sted was able to lift his head and immediately uncovered a black box in the ground that was connected to the wire. Pointing his domitor at it, he let off a single blast. The remains of the scorched box lay strewn at his feet. Reznor was finally able to throw away the charred remains of the snare. He stared uncomfortably at Sted. Noticing his friend's quizzical look, he seemed about to explain but the sounds of movement urged him otherwise.

"I'll explain later…" he promised as all four dashed towards the rows of featureless boxes ahead of them. More SPDRS were appearing from various stages of the wall and were scurrying towards the spot where their fallen comrades' parts lay.

They were tempted to throw caution to the wind but it was Sted who urged prudence, ordering them to follow his careful steps whilst using the weapon in his hand to scrape the dirt ahead of them in search of more snares. It was only after they had reached the metal box-buildings that they dared a peek behind them. The SPDRS were scurrying around the open space unable to 'pick up the scent' of their quarry.

"They only have short range sensors when they are outside and away from the city – we'll be moderately safer here." Sted told them as they lay, panting for breath. "They used the snare as an extra antenna but even then, they only had a rough fix on us: bad design. They were an early model, though." Three pairs of eyes were fixed on him as he studied the insects scuttling about: still the only movement they could make out. With the detached air of a fascinated scientist, he was blissfully unaware of their interest.

"And just how do you know so much about them?" asked Reznor, who was becoming increasingly bemused by the secrets that his two companions had failed to mention to him throughout their time trapped underground together. Sted turned around: his face filled with renewed pride. This instantly disappeared with an embarrassed cough, as Reznor's expression changed to one of understanding. "You helped design them, didn't you? Those things that were trying to get us – you…" His voice tailed away as the anger boiled up. This time he studied Faon. "If there are any more confessions from you two then I…" Reznor's words dried up as he marvelled at the pair he had selflessly spent so long protecting.

He turned towards Albie, "Did you have a part in designing that city up there?"

Albie gave a lingering stare, narrowing his eyes slightly trying to look cross but with a wink he replied "No, but I re-designed some of the sewers."

Turning his back, before Reznor could react, he headed to the corner of the box they were sheltering behind. With a quick glance about him, he slipped around the corner and it was there that Faon found him studying a door at the top of three metal steps.

"These are where the poor souls rest," she told him. "There's hardly anything for them – no windows; barely any light, not that they do anything else there. They eat where they work…and die there. They only come out to sleep and the only reason for that is so that another group of wretches can take over their workstation!" While she spoke, he was feeling the frame of the door…trying to find any trace of the unfortunates who were herded into it each night but there was nothing but an inhuman coldness about the building: smooth and characterless. He tried to blot out the thought of Tissa in one of these boxes but he couldn't. His eyes swelled with tears but he fought them back, wiping furiously with his muddied arm, leaving smears of dirt across his face. He beat the door in frustration as the others joined them. "You did find her, didn't you? Tell me she's still alive. Where is she?"

Faon nodded sympathetically to his relief "Our mission still has a purpose – she's still alive…and working in the underground factory at the moment…follow me." She pointed towards the steps with a wary finger.

14

Looking at the lift entrance there was nothing to suggest the toil that was underway below their feet. There were no sounds of unceasing machinery or any life whatsoever. Floodlights beamed down on the camp and the friends stood at what seemed the brightest part – thanks to the open space that separated them from the surrounding boxes. The lack of shadows made them an easy target.

Faon tapped the pad by the doors and they instantly opened to reveal the inside: another dull, metal box large enough for them all to fit inside with plenty of room to spare. Cautious looks exchanged and weapons at the ready, the four stepped in. A single panel to the left of the doors contained four buttons with digits on each.

"May as well go all the way…" Sted decided, taking the initiative as the others looked for inspiration, "If I was going to put the prisoners somewhere I'd put them down there – further for them to escape to the surface and the wall." A wry smile from Reznor disappeared as the doors shut silently and effortlessly behind them. It hardly seemed as if they were moving but their stomachs were a good way above them as they plummeted. As quickly as the lift had dropped, they stopped. There wasn't a chance to recover before the doors swished open and they were hit by a cacophony of noise from hundreds of machines that stretched away into the gloom. Steam rose incessantly from hundreds of toiling bodies seated in rows; all of them dressed in white outfits – identical to the ones worn by Sted and Faon when they had first met Albie. The steam rose up to a rocky ceiling where it hung, forming a fog where Albie's group stood. Out of the fog enormous white banners with imperious red trims hung from the rocky ceilings.

"Keep Tenebria strong and stable!"

"Recycle to renew!"

"Every worker counts!"

"You are our team!"

Faon shuddered as these phrases reverberated around her head. These self-same tired and worn-out phrases had been repeated robotically and inhumanely to her, and all the workers, every day of their imprisoned life and had made no difference to their work output but had only served to reinforce the feeling that their sole purpose in life was to serve the privileged Elite of Tenebria.

The group stood studying the scene from a metal gantry that formed a balcony along the perimeter of the walls. A series of walkways stretched between the parallel sides and series of metal steps led down. Apart from the workers there appeared to be no other human life. Out of the blue they heard a loud buzz and were immediately expecting to find out they had been spotted but they remained undetected. The only activity was below them, as all work stopped momentarily and pale-coloured objects were passed from column to column.

"Let's go and meet the workers then…" announced Faon as she jogged along the gangway before turning around to snap back at them: "And don't forget your serial numbers!"

"I'll go with Faon – you two head to the far side; we'll be quicker if we split up." shouted Reznor, struggling to be heard over the frantic din of machinery below them as he jogged after Faon. Albie and Sted set off in the opposite direction and as they drew closer to the workers it became clear that the poor wretches had not been left alone. Along every row a robot SPDR patrolled, while another machine hovered overhead, constantly scanning the workforce. It had the general shape of a human sitting on a kind of dish but in place of hands it had a laser-whip and a domitor. As they hovered, two red lights in what would have been their head, beamed out in a sinister manner: unblinking and staring. The dome-shaped heads swivelled to take in the struggling souls below them.

Albie stood at the top of the steps, staring at the robot guards' ceaseless scanning and patrolling. One of the white-clad workers slumped forward. Albie tried to see if it was Tissa: she was a girl but looked a good ten years older than Tissa and a lot thinner than Albie had remembered his friend to be. She rested her head on a pastel-coloured bench. Albie exchanged glances with Sted as one of the mechanical SPDRS closed in.

Instinctively fearing for another human being's safety, Albie and Sted started to hurry, their boots clanging on the steps, readying their weapons as they stepped off the last step.

For the first time they were able to see what the workers were doing. Each column was a part of a production line with its own particular job to do; cutting out the same coloured cloth, stitching first one side then the other, adding buttons…the tasks stretched across the factory with cloth being passed on with military precision at the sound of the buzzer, no time to recover before another piece passed across. Steam rose from perspiring heads as each of them worked furiously to keep up. Yet each worker displayed the same expression. Focussed on the task at hand they were unaware of anything else and their eyes even seemed to be glazed over as if they were barely awake and had completed their task so often that they could have completed it with their eyes shut. Their machines pounded non-stop.

Turning their attention to the collapsed girl, Albie and Sted saw a SPDR lifting a single front leg towards her. As if suddenly sensing the creature next to her, her body shot bolt upright and she screamed, shocked, before furiously re-starting work. A minute later, the buzzer rang out but this time there was another buzz straight after. As the pair approached they could hear the girl sobbing:

"No…no, please. I was tired, that's all, it won't happen again…" She continued to work; desperate to catch up as the SPDR returned to her, she was still stitching; vigorously working her machine.

The SPDR lifted its other front leg whilst inching its way towards her. Another worker, a young boy was inching his way towards her with a SPDR scuttling behind him: not daring to approach but trying to keep ahead of the robot prodding him on.

Before Albie could reach them, the girl had been pulled from her seat by the thin coil of an electro whip which stunned her. She now lay still in the aisle. She was led away from the workstation by the SPDR and the floating guardian. The young boy took her place and seconds later he was handing the cloth he had just finished over to the next row. The moment he did so the buzzer rang out again and the work and the noise immediately re-started as if nothing had happened. The girl was now meekly allowing herself to be shepherded away. None of the workers she passed dared look up from their work and she couldn't lift her eyes from the floor.

Albie could see the pair making their way towards him and ushered Sted to keep moving back to the steps they had come from. Up to this point neither robots nor workers had taken any notice of them. On the far side of the factory he watched Reznor and Faon wandering unnoticed up and down the rows but he still had no idea where to look for Tissa: there were hundreds of workers in white - where to start?

The girl stumbled, sobbing quietly, past the steps that Albie and Sted had climbed back up, swiftly followed by her floating guardian. Both ignored them as they stood aside to allow the metallic creature and its prisoner to pass. Nonchalantly pointing his weapon at the rear of the robot's head, he smiled as it fizzed before slumping forward. The smoke that rose from it was swiftly lost in the general fog that covered the factory. Sted ran after the girl who had carried on walking. Grabbing hold of her wrist he found himself being pulled over as she headed towards a plain, metallic door. Her determination took him by surprise; she didn't even look at him but became more frantic and desperate to get away and through the door. Pulling with both hands, he held onto her wrist yet still she fought. For the first time she turned around and he was reminded of the terrified, haunted look, both he and Faon had once had. Her fragile body hid the strength that desperation to obey had given her and Sted couldn't stop himself from letting go.

Albie had no intention of seeing what was beyond the entrance and turning his weapon to the lightest shade he aimed a bolt that whizzed over his partner's head before knocking the girl over.

Turning around he expected to be engulfed by all manner of mechanical objects but nothing had changed. The workers were still fixed to their tasks and their desks. None of the flyers seemed to have noticed, after all no work had been interrupted. Sted approached Albie, who was crouching over the girl's sleeping body.

"They are only programmed to keep production going – not to watch out for intruders – and remember we still look like troopers – of a sort," he murmured, as he looked Albie up and down. "They probably haven't been programmed to recognise intruders – after all who could make it down here or for that matter would want to come down here?"

With that he joined Albie who was staring downwards.

"It's not her is it?" Sted asked hesitantly but Albie just shook his head. Caressing her cheek, he found he could not take his eyes off her thinness, the way her skin clung to her cheekbones…thoughts of Tissa filled him. A mark caught his eye to one side of her neck: a series of thick and thin lines with symbols above it. Studying it, he turned his attention to his companion.

In reply, Sted rolled back the uniform that covered his neck to reveal a similar mark and Albie realised that he had never seen the necks of his companions – they had always been covered.

"It's a code: to show you are a worker: their property, to do with as they want. Come on, we'll leave her on the steps and come back for her. Let's…" Sted's voice tailed off as he spotted a flying guardian gliding along the aisle towards them. They froze, somehow hoping that they could blend in or that it hadn't noticed them, but it had. It stopped in front of Sted, a keyboard and screen dropped down at the front of it and waited perfectly still apart from a blue dot that moved from side to side in what they thought was its head.

They stood just as still, holding their breath, studying it for any sign of a threat but none came. They fully expected it to instantly attack but it didn't.

Sted shuffled a step closer.

Still nothing.

The blue dot just continued moving to and fro. It was waiting for them. Another step brought no reaction so they moved slightly more confidently to study the screen.

"It wants a serial number..." Sted announced as Albie released his tight grip on the weapon in his hand. Quickly glancing at his uniform, he found a number and, praying it was the right one, began typing it onto the keyboard. The 'eye' blinked, turned green then returned to blue again as a series of instructions appeared.

"Here," he announced cheerfully, "Prisoner location..." He typed in 1...8...8...6...9. The moment he typed in the final digit it rose into the air and headed across the factory.

This took them both by surprise. Albie reacted quickly, racing after it, leaping around workers and tables: not once did any of them turn away from their work or miss a stitch as he flew past them. His heart was racing as it stopped next to a young girl slaving furiously with a hand held sewing machine. He stopped a few rows away and stared: it was Tissa.

Gone were the stylish clothes and the immaculate hair: once a finely balanced tower, it now looked ragged and clung to her neck in great clumps. Dirt and sweat mixed together in streaks that ran down her arms and probably her face too but Albie was unable to get a look at that because she was bent over the cloth in her hands, desperately trying to keep up with the others before the bell rang.

He stood there waiting, he had found her at last but couldn't believe the changed figure before him: all in such a relatively short space of time. Crouching down to get a better look at her face, he was interrupted by the sound of the buzzer. She had a brief moment to take a sip on a blue drink on her desk then handed on her work and another piece arrived. It gave him the opportunity to see her face, a sight that pleased him even less. The Tissa he had known just days… hours… earlier had had a rounded face finished off with a welcoming smile. Now gaunt features had replaced these, along with two black holes that her eyes sank into. He tried to attract her attention but Albie was still unable to distract her from her resumed efforts. He wasn't sure but the more he looked at her, the more determined she seemed to be not to look up and allow herself to be distracted from her work. However, he dared not shock her by touching her, preferring to wait for her to notice.

The flying guardian hovered motionless above, ignoring Albie, occasionally letting out a series of long and short beeps before falling silent again. Finally, the buzzer sounded for the work to be handed on and she turned to face Albie for the first time. With outstretched hand she began to reach out to hand her work over when she stopped and briefly he caught her eye. She refused to recognise her friend. Instead she looked straight through him. Albie was still stunned at the change in her that he couldn't break the silence between them. Touching her shoulder gently their eyes met: she momentarily glanced at him before resuming working. A flicker of recognition rapidly disappeared. Her expression changed once more and this time the tiny flicker returned: she did know him! That very moment the buzzer sounded once more and it vanished.

Immediately, she grabbed her next assignment and was about to set to work when Albie pulled her arm away. She let out a scream that was drowned out by the noise around them as she tried to pull her arm back.

"It's me, Albie…" She continued to struggle but he held tight hold. There was the same fear that he had seen in the girl who had run. As her efforts became more frantic the guardian above started to click and whirr with increasing regularity. Albie grabbed her other hand and she screamed once more, this time the robot above them started moving towards them, upset that her work was being interrupted. Scuttling feet from either end of the row approached the two fighting figures but neither was aware of this fact: Tissa desperate to work and Albie desperate for her to stop and recognise him. He hardly felt the electric shock that surged through his body, knocking him flat as Tissa jumped eagerly back into her seat and began to work feverishly to catch up. Albie slumped onto the solid concrete floor and there he lay, motionless.

Reznor and Faon had started searching row after row of bowed heads without success. Not one gave them so much as a glance, in fact it was as if they had been programmed to do nothing but work: as mindless as the robots that guarded them.

They had lost sight of the others the moment they had set foot on the ground floor and there was no way they could be heard over the din of machines.

Suddenly they spotted Albie's racing head as it bobbed through the crowds of workers following a guardian. They watched as it hovered at the spot they thought Albie had stopped at and became worried as more guardians closed in on the same spot. They began quickly climbing over uniformed rows of desks hoping they were in time to help.

Sted examined Albie's sleeping girl, after hauling her up the steps. It was from above that he watched Albie's struggle with Tissa, his collapse upon the floor and Reznor and Faon's rescue charge. His first impulse was to run and join them but he quickly realised that his was the only route out. He remained there, making sure they were going to be able to escape as well as protect the young girl.

Albie's unconscious form was soon being dragged towards the very door that the girl he had knocked out had been running towards.

A SPDR had tight hold of his leg and was scuttling effortlessly away while two others brought up the rear, acting as escorts.

"We can't let them take him through that door," said Faon as they raced along a parallel row, "There's no telling what's waiting on the other side…"

"Well if you weren't so slow," muttered Reznor as he started to speed up. Their charge was suddenly halted as the SPDR patrolling their row appeared menacingly in front of them. Reznor ground to a halt and in one motion took aim at the SPDR. Just as he was about to shoot, he felt Faon's collision with his back. A bolt shot over their heads from his weapon as they dropped to the floor. As the bolt harmlessly struck the rocky wall, the SPDR was upon them and was poised to strike with one if its pincers when a bolt from above ripped through it, covering the pair of them with shards of metal.

"Nice shot!" complimented Faon as she glanced up at the jubilantly waving Sted. Reznor continued on to the door and reached it just as the SPDRS and Albie disappeared though it. It closed before he could reach it. Beating the wall with his fist in frustration, he remembered the domitor in his hand. He spotted the panel to open the door, tapped it and after stepping through was consumed by a blinding white light.

Faon was about to follow when she caught sight of Sted standing and motioning towards Tissa. They had come through all this to rescue her so they might as well make sure that they accomplished one thing: after all, Reznor was ugly enough to look after himself she decided.

Making a real attempt to walk calmly back up the row, she stopped at the row where Tissa was still beavering away. The guardian had resumed its duties and once the SPDRS had taken Albie away it had hovered further along the row, scanning for any other break in production. Thanks to all the scuffles that had gone on, her row was temporarily unguarded so without any ceremony Faon knocked Tissa out with her domitor and started to drag her away from her workstation. The moment she did this a red light started to flash that pierced the mist. Within seconds a pair of guardians was on its way, heading from opposite ends of the hall.

She realised she might have bitten off more than she could chew. Despite Tissa's skinny figure, she found she was unable to drag her more than a few metres, still well away from a set of steps. Dropping the limp form with a sickening thud she apologised to Tissa then watched the guardians gliding towards her. Heart pounding as she struggled to catch her breath she tried to take aim. Her shot streaked past the nearest one before disappearing. The whip zipped past her ear as the creature tried to ensnare her. Out of the mist a bolt struck the nearest one. Relieved to have escaped for the moment, she tried once more to drag Tissa. Grabbing her arms, she suddenly felt a great urge to fall flat on top of the body. As she did so another whip lashed across her back just before its owner was sent flying across rows of workers. The desk-bound workers merely ducked as it flew past before continuing with their work. Not a stitch was missed.

Daring to glance up, Faon was pleased to make out Sted's form as he ran towards her. Putting her back up on her feet, he grabbed hold of Tissa's wrists and managed only slightly better than Faon before he too was forced to admit defeat and together they pulled her to the steps.

Taking a quick break, they noticed the number of guardians scanning the area around Tissa's station. They lifted her up onto their shoulders and after a combination of stumbles and staggers reached the landing where he had left the other body.

"We need some help with these two. If we can get them to the top landing, we can keep out of sight and hope the fuss dies down."

"I've a feeling they aren't going to like losing all these robots so the sooner we can get up there the better." They began to drag the two girls' bodies, one at a time, up the stairs. With each step the feet of the limp bodies clanged onto the metal but the workers below paid no attention to them. The confusion below drew all the circling guardians towards it, enabling them to slip away before they were spotted.

By the time they had propped them both on the walkway that led to the lift, the activity below had become frantic. Faon crumpled against the rock wall and gasped for breath. Sted did likewise. There they lay, muscles and lungs aching from all the unaccustomed lifting and running.

It was a casual glance at the lift that warned them as an indicator light started to blink. Something or somebody was coming down from the surface.

15

Reznor was forced to shield his eyes from the glare as he stepped through the door. He found himself in a small chamber with a large glass window on the far wall and computers dotted along the others. The only other way out was a single arch to his left. Recovering his composure, he decided it wasn't such a good idea to continue charging about and decided to catch his breath whilst taking stock of the situation. Peering through the glass he saw row upon row of narrow tanks, filled with a blue, watery liquid. Looking closer, it didn't surprise him to see each contained a serenely floating human body. Wires ran from their heads to a set of circuits built into the glass tanks that flashed green and blue.

Each body lay just under the surface with a pipe attached to their mouth, they seemed perfectly relaxed. Albie's body came into view as it was dragged behind two scuttling SPDRS. On arriving at an empty tank, they dropped him and without a second look hurried off.

Reznor followed their progress as they emerged through the archway before disappearing back into the factory. He rushed in the direction of his friend and could soon make out Albie's shape being lifted upwards on a metallic stretcher. Two flying guardians, this time equipped with arms in the place of any weapons, were attaching electrodes and the pipe when Reznor reached him. Albie was completely still throughout the operation and was showing no signs of moving. Reznor began pulling everything that had been attached to his friend's body but as fast as he pulled them out he found them being replaced with increasing speed by the two robots. Giving up his fight, he resorted to violence and with two quick domitor blasts had neutralised his opponents. In their place floated two smoking bases. This proved to be the worst possible thing he could have done as the moment the second machine had exploded, alarms sounded everywhere in the room: the sedate lighting was replaced by a red flashing glare. Taking this to be a bad sign Reznor threw Albie over his back and hurried up the rows between the tanks; whose occupants were still blissfully sleeping unaware of the excitement outside.

Emerging through the arch, only the flashing lights behind seemed out of the ordinary; that was until he glanced at the doorway to the factory from which SPDRS and guardians were now pouring through. Dropping Albie carelessly behind him, Reznor easily dealt with the first SPDR…and the next two went the same way: smoking and charred. However, it became abundantly clear to him that there were plenty more where they came from.

"Looks like I shouldn't have done that," he muttered to himself. Dragging Albie by one arm he pulled him back into the tank room; exchanging shots as he withdrew. "Why do I feel like a trapped rat?" Reznor mused as he disappeared down the nearest row.

Faon and Sted slowly and painfully dragged the two bodies back along the walkway, away from the lift which was about to open at any moment. Spotting a gap in the rock they tried to push themselves out of sight as the doors slid open. Before they knew it, uniforms had swarmed out and were hurrying down the stairs. They realised that whatever was through the door, was pretty important to have got the place so busy. There were now no SPDRS or guardians patrolling the rows of workers. Instead, there was a great scrum to get through the door.

The lift doors shut once more and a light once more showed that the lift was rising back up to the surface. Faon and Sted exchanged glances and even though they were still wearing their guards' uniforms they lacked the confidence to try faking their way past anybody. So, they sat and waited, praying they could remain unnoticed. They would have stayed hidden if one of their bodies hadn't chosen the exact moment when another set of uniforms left the lift to make a break for it. She leapt up taking her captors by surprise and was dashing towards the lift as Faon emerged from the shadows.

Faon took the initiative, calling for the new arrivals to restrain her and by the time she had arrived two of them had tight hold.

"This lot will do anything for a bit of rest and re-programming," they were joking as Faon arrived.

"Work shy that's all they are," muttered another: with their visors and helmets on, their jokes lacked any humour and seemed threatening more than anything else. She just nodded.

"Is this one yours then? Where are you taking her?" Faon panicked, she had no idea where she was taking her, she didn't know where anything was; except outside of the walls and she didn't think announcing that would go down too well. She could feel herself stuttering and mumbling but was saved by Sted's appearance over her shoulder.

"We were taking it for treatment when it ran. She must have been heading for the lift when we caught her." He sounded so confident that Faon couldn't help but be impressed. Sted was pleased himself and was beginning to feel as confident as he sounded when he was brought back down to Earth with a thud.

"We'll give you a hand then…"

"N…n…n…o need for that, anyway…" he could

feel inspiration once more bubbling up inside him, "…anyway," the confident swagger returned, "there's a bit of a problem down there, best lock her in her quarters."

The troopers missed Faon's amazement at the unconvincing pack of lies Sted had told and they headed off down the stairs none the wiser.

At the top of the steps Sted and Faon, holding their 'rescued' girl, tightly breathed a sigh of relief. Her struggles were ended by a quick jab of Faon's weapon and she slumped to the floor. Between them they dragged the sleeping bodies into the lift. The doors closed with Tissa and the unknown girl safely inside so Faon allowed herself a smile and a sigh. Their bodies lurched as the lift shot effortlessly upwards.

"I don't know where the others are or what's been done to these two but we need somewhere to lay low while we think. Reznor and Albie will have to look after themselves" decided Faon. Sted simply agreed with a nod and collapsed onto the floor. It had all been too much really: all this rushing about just wasn't his idea of fun.

Still feeling like a rat with an extremely large piece of cheese (a smelly one at that) Reznor had retreated further into the tank room. Discarding his helmet, he was able to get a better view around him. Although he couldn't see through the window that looked into the room he had just left he sensed that there was an awful lot of SPDRS on the other side about to pour through the arch. Occasionally he would slap Albie's face and urge him to wake up but any awakening looked a remote possibility. He carried on dragging and had decided that maybe this piece of cheese wasn't quite worth the effort when he collapsed, exhausted behind the furthest row of tanks.

He had been trying so hard to pull Albie behind him that he had failed to spot that the SPDRS, despite their probably overwhelming numbers, and the flying guardians weren't following him into the room. He sat catching his breath, studying the empty doorway and the scuttling shadows confirmed his fears – there were a lot of them but they weren't coming in. "Why not?" He wondered. Leaning against one of the tanks, it came to him. "They don't seem to want to lose any of the workers, yet they've got plenty…" Peering, he watched the shadows as they shifted on the wall but they were still not moving. "It's the tanks…they don't want them damaged, must be how they get the workers fit when they can't work anymore." Daring to stand up he looked at the nearby tanks, although their occupants looked quite peaceful, they looked tired, drawn and in need of major rest. "You can't do without these tanks, can you?" he began to laugh and was half tempted to start shooting a few just to annoy the SPDRS. He pretended to take aim then imitated the sound of a blast. Exhaustion and euphoria made him feel giddy and ever so slightly manic as hysteria began to take hold.

A groan next to his feet brought him back to reality: 'the big cheese' was waking up. Dropping to the floor Reznor helped Albie sit up and waited for him to open his eyes and speak. Eventually he did both.

"I feel like…" He groaned but Reznor interrupted him.

"I know, you're going to feel worse when you find out what's been going on."

"Tissa…" he mumbled, "She…"

"She's not herself, none of them are. They're doing stuff to them – don't know what…but we've got to get out of here…" His voice tailed off as the shadows changed – human shadows had appeared – It occurred to Reznor that the troopers might not be so bothered about risking a fight in here. The shadows started moving as Albie, who had managed to raise his head off the floor, joined Reznor. The pair now peered over a tank in which the floating occupant was blissfully unaware of the tense standoff that was about to take place.

There now seemed to be a distinct lack of movement outside and after a few nervous minutes the pair were starting to exchange anxious looks. A quick glance round the room told them that there was only one other exit so after a swift peek at the arch they slowly made their way towards it with Reznor half-dragging Albie.

Keeping low, they realised that the scuttling sound was close. Glancing under the table they waited but nothing appeared, the shadows of their pursuers were remaining around the corner. Something was moving. But what?

The floor was solid enough Reznor decided, after a quick couple of stamps, so the scuttling was not coming from below. He continued his search for the source of the noise. It felt very close but with both sets of eyes darting from floor to door to wall there were still no sightings. However, it was also clear that their progress had slowed down dramatically.

"Come on, come on," Reznor started muttering as he nervously bounced his leg up and down. Albie's eyes, meanwhile, rolled around the room: he still hadn't fully recovered. This just adding to his partner's sense of anxiety. The door in front of them was just like all the others they had passed: metallic and featureless but this one gave Reznor a greater feeling of unease the closer he got to it, there was something he didn't want to find behind it and he certainly felt sure it wasn't a way out of this mess. The scuttling was now rattling every part of him.

"Where are you? Show yourself you metal..." laying Albie against a tank, Reznor suddenly realised. Staring at the ceiling it started to make sense. "Oh no, that's not fair..."

Grabbing Albie's weapon, he started blowing holes in the roof. Albie looked blankly at him but as chunks of plaster rained down on them it dawned on him what his partner had realised a few moments before. There on top of the ducts that ran above their heads were row upon row of SPDRS scuttled one behind the other: a miniature metal army. They began dropping as they reached the stricken pair. Reznor started blasting as they fell but felt like he was fighting a losing battle; he had no time to look at Albie as both his weapons continued tearing chunks out of machines, ceiling and machinery. Charred fragments of SPDR littered the floor around them: a mass of spitting sparks and fizzing, twitching electric wires. One SPDR landed on Albie's shoulder, giving him a sudden jolt as he felt its heat. His once-bleary eyes shot open and he instantly began taking in where he was.

Just as he thought the aerial attack was under control, out of the corner of his eye, he spotted uniforms pouring through the arch and dispersing amongst the rows of sleeping bodies. Turning to help up Albie, he only had time to flinch as he realised he had gone. More figures swarmed into the room. He carried on firing. However, this time he took aim across the room at the new intruders that were swarming towards him. Turning to run towards the still closed door, Reznor suddenly dropped as it slid open and more uniforms emerged. He couldn't afford to think of Albie now. Instead, he took it in turns to shoot at whichever group was closest but he knew it could only be a matter of seconds before they reached him. Every exit from the room seemed to be spewing more and more bodies pushing to get to him. Escape was no longer an option for him.

16

The lift rose to the surface slowly. Its arrival was signalled by an ominous chime before the doors effortlessly slid open. The uniforms gathered outside looked curiously in. At first, nobody emerged. However, as uniforms began pouring into the lift they were soon being pushed back as two troopers struggled through the crowd and out of the lift, slowly dragging two unconscious workers. They appeared the scrawniest of troopers with badly fitting equipment. To the curious observers they seemed to be making a bit of a meal of carrying out two wretches. Silence settled upon the gathered crowd as it watched. They parted to allow the duo through but behind their visors, suspicious eyes studied every stumble and pause until a single metallic voice brought the stumbling group to a standstill:

"Let us help you with them…" A sinister tone made the two small figures freeze: not daring to refuse. With that, pairs of strong hands took each of the unconscious workers. A further pair arrived to 'guide' the two feeble troopers in the direction of a nearby hut, followed by the voice that had first offered 'help'. The other bystanders began to bundle into the empty lift once again and by the time the doors shut both groups had moved away and the camp was once again eerily still.

Reznor continued to shoot at the hordes on either side of the room. No matter how many he managed to pick off, the tide of bodies never seemed to ebb. Cursing Albie for his disappearing act he carried on shooting at whatever object moved closest: he really wasn't picky what or who he wiped out.

He was so intent on destroying men and machines that he failed to spot the thick, knotted cable that dangled in front of him. The cable swung back and forth, spoiling both his concentration and aim. Each time he swatted at it, it quickly returned. Annoyed, he scanned up the cable and aimed his domitor skywards. Just as he was about to take aim, he froze. There amongst all the burning wires and exposed air ducts was an ecstatic Albie.

"Where the…" Reznor was about to shower him with questions but the troopers inching closer made him decide to just follow his friend. Slinging his domitor over his shoulder, he began climbing.

Bolts crisscrossed around him as the troopers doubled their efforts to shoot Reznor back down to earth but the quicker they shot, the less accurate they became.

As Reznor climbed, Albie blasted away at anything that raised its head above the tanks. Reznor was soon able to see how close the uniforms had got and that not one of the tanks had been damaged: was it the workers or the equipment they couldn't afford to lose?

Finally reaching the top, he felt Albie tugging him into a duct that sloped upwards. Reznor's aching arms relaxed as he grabbed hold of Albie's with both hands and felt himself being pulled into the duct. The blasts grew closer and closer and he felt their heat as his legs rose to safety. Finally, Reznor could catch his breath.

Whistling in relief, he turned to thank his friend but Albie was swaying; struggling to stay upright. Albie jerked back, stumbled then fell forward: out of the duct.

The cable slapped his face so he instinctively flung his hands out towards it. He felt his arms being wrenched by his body as it momentarily continued its descent. He fought to cling onto the cable his friend had just scrambled up. Breathing heavily once more, he looked down. Something metal had hold of his leg…no, both his legs. He furiously tried to move them but at the end of each dangled a robot SPDR. He couldn't shake them off; no matter how hard he tried to kick out. His fingers struggled to maintain their grip and they burnt as he slipped further. Once again, he just managed to cling on but he could feel his strength sapping quickly.

The two robotic cling-ons shot tiny metallic threads of their own towards even more SPDRS scuttling along the pipes. More and more SPDRS swung from the pipes to dangle below his feet and Albie felt his body straining as more robotic arachnids clambered up towards his feet. There was nothing Reznor could do except swing, each time gathering momentum, but the SPDRS still clung on.

"Albie," called out Reznor. "Grab my hand!" Albie swung out a hand but it missed and his body was yanked further down the cable. One of the knots he had put in earlier stopped him slipping too far. He made a mental note to congratulate himself later: if he was able to. He grunted with the increasing weight hanging from him and the myriad of beeping machines only served to antagonise his senses further.

Reznor beat the duct in frustration. As if in reply, the uniforms that surrounded them opened fire on his dangling friend.

"As if it wasn't bad enough already!" he muttered. After returning fire to random parts of the room, he turned his attention back to Albie. The first SPDRS were nearly at his feet.

Holding his domitor with one hand, Reznor sank to his knees and lowered himself down the cable Albie was clinging to. Finally, he was within touching distance of his friend.

He gripped Albie's arm tightly and tried to pull him up in this position, there was no way he was going anywhere but down carrying this lot. If anything, the SPDRS scrambling up Albie's feet were getting a much better hold. Sensing too that this escape plan wasn't going to work, Albie reluctantly let go and clung once more to his swinging cable.

He scanned the room hoping against hope for a way out of his predicament but could only focus on the uniforms taking aim to finish him off. He gripped even tighter to the cable but in the heat of the room was finding it hard to stop his sweaty hand slipping. In a final desperate act of defiance, he managed to clasp the cable once more even though he could feel like he was slowly sinking downwards with the extra unbearable weight. Five or six more SPDRS were now clambering up him.

"What a way to go…" he muttered, "Caught like vermin in a trap." More blasts shot past him, singeing his clothes. His legs flapped furiously but the SPDRs kept coming. By now he felt a metre taller… He could see Reznor had wedged his feet into the duct and both his hands were tightly gripped around the cable. However, Albie was fighting a losing battle. His friend was sinking lower and lower. He reached for the cabling and pulled: hand over fist. Reznor slowly began to rise.

A bolt zipped past Albie's cheek but he barely noticed the cut that it had opened up. He managed to slam his legs together: one SPDR slipped off, caught unawares. Albie gave the vaguest hint of a smile as it slammed onto a guard: the pair lay sprawled on the floor.

"Keep going!" he shouted up and Reznor pulled even harder, his whole body shaking with the effort. Albie slipped between the jagged and charred remains of the ceiling panels and as he did so, managed to release the cable as he clambered onto the metal supports that crisscrossed the ceiling. The instant he did this he began furiously swiping at the SPDRS that were still climbing up him. Coming to his friend's aid, Reznor took aim at the SPDRS clinging to Albie's legs. The first one fizzed then fell away, taking with it three of its 'buddies'.

"Watch my legs…a bit lower…" screamed Albie as Reznor took aim a second time.

"Don't tell me how to do my job!" cried Reznor. To Albie's relief, his aim was true and at last Albie was free of the metal arachnids.

"Never even doubted you!" he replied, studying the burn marks on his clothes.

It took a bolt zipping between his legs, igniting a nearby control switch, to make Albie climb into the duct. Instead of climbing up to join Reznor, though, he unclipped his weapon and started picking off the guards below him. Now it was their turn to scramble for cover. Only when Reznor's calls to move combined with his own thoughts of Tissa, Faon and Sted did he reluctantly tear himself away from his sport; clambering quickly into the darkness and out of sight.

The second they had stepped out of the lift, Faon and Sted knew things weren't going well. The menace in the voice they had heard as they struggled out of the lift had set their nerves on edge. Every muscle in her body had urged Faon just to run but she couldn't summon up the energy. The moment her load had been taken away from her she had started to shake. She fought to carry on acting out the part but every part of her body was screaming for her to run: anything was better than being a prisoner again: the never-ending shifts along with the drugs to give her energy and to dull the pain.

Sted wanted to touch Faon, reassure her, as they were marched off but she was bundled away too quickly and ahead of him. His arm stretched out to her pathetically before it too was grabbed and led forward. He let out a sigh of relief as they were both led towards the same hut but his body ached as they were kept apart. She stoically held her gaze, staring straight ahead, and he felt lost and alone. His strength and resistance began to fade. Finding themselves heading back into one of those depressingly featureless huts, once again, sucked hope from them. He knew how hard this had been for her, how she'd suffered and he wondered what had stopped her from blindly sprinting off. In his mind, he could feel the fear she felt but he also sensed determination in her pale features. He fought the urge to think that their freedom had been snatched from their grasp.

The dull glow of the camp outside disappeared as automatic strips of lights exploded into life, filling the bare room they had entered. Tissa and her friend, who were slowly coming to, lay against the far wall, tied to hooks that hung from the black metal wall opposite: like animals. Faon and Sted hardly noticed the doors had slid shut behind them before their helmets were ripped from their heads. They were grabbed from behind and thrown onto the floor with the others as three pairs of eyes stared at them from behind darkened visors.

Silence fell upon the room. One of the uniforms approached Faon, who maintained her cold stare as it drew closer. A gloved hand gripped the collar of her uniform but she refused to flinch. Sted could see her defiance and he felt a rush of pride, hope even, run though him and a single tear rolled down his cheek as he struggled to control his own fears.

Faon's collar was ripped away to reveal her prisoner's bar code on her neck. She stood still without a flicker of emotion, save a cold hateful stare.

"A returnee?" Sneered the voice. "Did you miss us?" Its attention turned to Sted who couldn't stop himself from shrinking back.

"And what about you…?" Sted tried to steel himself, mimicking Faon's stare but he only succeeded in twisting his face as if he was going to be sick. Faon coughed and he was saved for the moment as they returned their attention towards her. The lead figure angrily beat his weapon into his free hand as he made it quite obvious that he found the idea of any prisoners daring to wear a guard's uniform a great personal insult.

"How did you scum think you could rescue these…and why?" He hissed as he pointed at the sleeping figures that had barely moved since they had been left to dangle. He paused as his mind ran through the possibilities: slowly. Approaching him, the trooper grabbed hold of Sted's ill-fitting uniform before pulling his chin up to his visor. Sted, unwilling to look at his own gaunt reflection, screwed his eyes shut. A single utterance of disgust was followed by a rushing sound as Sted's flimsy form was hurled against a wall. He managed to remain silent despite the cracking sound his skull made as it crashed against the metal.

The lead uniform tapped a finger, more casually this time, on his weapon. He mused the reasons behind their failed rescue attempt.

"One of you was the pilot of that craft that crashed. Which one of you?" He hissed and was about to raise his stick when he suddenly stopped as a thought crossed his mind. "You couldn't have dragged two troopers anywhere, let alone manage to knock them out. There are more of you…" his voice tailed off as a plan began to form. "I think I'd like to meet your friends…" once again his voice dropped unnervingly and with that he marched towards the doors barking out orders as he left:

"Nobody comes in but me – and take those disgusting things out of our uniforms. Have them fumigated!"

It hadn't taken Albie and Reznor long to find an escape tunnel with a vertical ladder ascending above them. However, reaching the end of their seemingly endless climb through the dark, damp (and draughty) tunnel was another matter. Finally, Albie and Reznor were relieved to breathe air that hadn't been pumped around a factory a few dozen times. At least the air on the surface was only stale and polluted and didn't contain the smell of hundreds of sweaty workers. Both of them took a deep breath then coughed once they had hauled themselves out of the hole. After all it had been quite a climb (most of it vertical) and very damp (especially for Reznor who was questioning the wisdom of keeping his uniform on). They replaced the grille that had sat over the hole they had climbed through and scoured their surroundings.

Nothing seemed to have changed – the camp was still deserted, the lift doors still shut and there was nothing to suggest anything was happening or had happened down below: it was unnerving, almost as if the camp had a surprise waiting for the pair: and it wouldn't be a party that's for sure.

It was the swish of a door opening that sent them diving behind a nearby hut. A large, uniformed trooper strode across the mud strip towards the lift doors.

Albie felt there was something familiar about this trooper: a familiarly arrogant air about him, as if he only had to click his fingers and his wish would be granted immediately. Just as he reached the lift, there was the swish of opening lift doors and four troopers appeared. They flinched as they saw him, obviously afraid. From the way he was standing, Albie and Reznor could see he was irate. They were too far away to hear the whole conversation but managed to hear the odd snippet whenever he raised his voice. They heard "...the others...", "...trying to rescue two workers...", "...escapees..." and "...find them or it will be you working the machines."

The angry one watched the others as they disappeared behind a hut then he too stormed off in the opposite direction. Reznor was about to step out when Albie pulled him back.

"It doesn't feel safe yet," He mumbled as he scanned the compound. The lift doors opened once again and a number of troopers appeared, this lot had obviously been involved in the battle below and looked dirty from the action and subsequent search. They moved off to continue their search around the camp and the watching pair began their own search.

The two 'rescued' prisoners barely lifted their heads from the floor, let alone dare to move. They certainly had no thoughts of thanking Faon and Sted for their efforts. Faon, on the other hand, had no thoughts of accepting defeat. Her body felt weak but her mind was still strong and searching for a way to hit back.

Unfortunately, there was only one way in or out and that was through the door that two static troopers stood in front of. Since their leader had left they had remained motionless by the door, their prisoners' every move watched from behind darkened visors. This fact didn't stop Faon's brain from racing.

Sted sat forlornly on the cold steel floor, head leaning onto the knees he had pulled up into his body. Escape was not an option for him – his hope was fading rapidly and he was preparing himself for a return to life in the factory.

He slipped from consciousness and fell into his memories: a time far removed from the troubles of the present. He was a boy: a boy with a secret. He would spend furtive moments hidden wherever, and whenever, he could: scouring his prized possession. It was called a 'book': there was no need for such things now because everything came from a screen, but at one time people would read bits of paper stuck together on one side. Finding one of these 'books' amongst his dad's old things, he was amazed to find pictures of places where there were no buildings and hardly any people…and strange creatures called 'animals' wandered around freely. There had been no screens flashing at him, no orders he had to follow, no lifestyle based on what he had to wear or way he had to look …his idea of paradise. Of course, he had never told anybody, that he had had the 'book': not even his brother…his brother, with whom he shared everything…nearly everything. Only his dad knew. It had been his; and his father's before that. On the furtive visits his dad had made, he had told him that he had managed to keep it a secret, as had his dad, and like him they too had longed to touch this impossible paradise.

Maybe that was why they had taken his dad away: "for unhealthy ideas" his mum had called it. But from that day on: Sted had never dared open the book again. A chance discovery of the book by a friend (some friend) had led to Sted's own arrest and his life at the factory. There had been no ceremony when he had been arrested. The hood had been fixed over his head, arms taped behind his back and he had felt himself being dragged to the service lift: not even the front entrance. He had smelt the mixture of fresh air and the fumes of the Predavator when he had arrived on his living block's take-off pad. That was his last memory of the city as the next sensation he had felt was a sharp prick before he had blacked out, waking up in the factory.

This painful memory brought him back to reality. His eyes briefly blinked open, just long enough to scan the room: Faon was still scowling at the guards, she was tough inside: there was no doubt about that, while the other two were slumped motionless in their chains. The situation was still hopeless so he closed his eyes once more, trying to drift away but his mind wouldn't do that anymore; thoughts of the family he had lost sank from his thoughts.

His mother.

His brother.

His dad.

They were all disappearing from his mind, no matter how hard he tried to keep them there. The more he tried, the more he thought of the here and now. What had happened to them? Where were they now?

Then it was: where were Albie and Reznor? His heart sank once more; the chances of them escaping the troopers were slim indeed: no use getting his hopes up.

Four pairs of eyes stared at the door as it slid back, a moment's hope of rescue instantly quashed as they saw the figure enter. The two uniforms straightened up and stared stiffly ahead; knowing exactly who had returned by the purposeful stamp of his boots and the sound of weapon beating against hand.

"A pilot, eh?" he started as he tapped Faon on the shoulder "…and a drifter." He turned his attention to Sted, "been dreaming of open spaces, have you? When will you fools wake up…it was the chaos of the wilderness that caused all our problems. We now have order and structure: stability and strength! It is foolish to think otherwise." With that he slammed his weapon against his leg. He was the only person in the room who didn't flinch.

He turned to Faon now, seeming even angrier, "You had it all, respected job, good pay and life then threw it all away…for what, a dream?" He circled her like a vulture, Sted already completely dismissed as worthless.

His ranting continued but Faon stubbornly refused to look at him; preferring to stare straight ahead at the door. It was only when his stick crashed upon her shoulders that her determination was broken. She lay motionless at his feet. He broke off his attack, preferring to roll her body over with his feet: she wasn't going to answer any of his questions now.

Angrily, he turned his attention to Sted who was fighting a losing battle to stop himself from shaking. Lifting Sted's flimsy figure with one hand, he pulled Sted's face to his own cold, emotionless visor. Sted shuddered from the touch and was even more shocked when his feet dangled in the air. "Where are the others, dreamer?"

Sted wished he could stay defiant but it was no use. He was about to give in when his own weak body took over once again. He blanked out and he found himself drifting away…from the room…the guards…and most of all…him. He was floating away from everything and he never felt a thing as he collided with the wall, before crumpling into a heap against the door.

17

The tall, domineering figure left the featureless interrogation room, ordering more troopers to surround the block. He was unaware of the two figures hiding outside: close by.

Albie and Reznor could briefly make out Sted's slumped body in the hut before the door slid shut. They hoped for a sign, anything, to confirm that at least one of them was still alive and putting up some kind of resistance: however small. But the starkness of the closing door denied them this. Their hearts sank when the hut was surrounded by troopers and every nearby searchlight seemed to be trained on it. It was a good sign at least because they wouldn't have devoted all those troopers for a couple of dead bodies.

The glare was so intense that they were forced to find themselves a shadier spot to watch the comings and goings and an enormous column that reached up into that blackness provided just that.

Leaning against the smooth surface the pair studied the scene, struggling furiously for a way to get into the hut but nothing came to mind short of burying under it – and they had nothing but their hands to manage that: so, they continued watching hoping for either inspiration or good fortune.

After an age, the troopers around the hut moved, left their posts and seemed to be forming two lines; one guarding either side of the factory lift entrance: the whole site was still lit up. The uniforms snaked away, forming a corridor to the nearest hut. The lift doors slid open and a group of around fifty workers shambled between the two lines. They barely seemed aware of their surroundings, exhausted from their efforts underground it was the most they could do to put one foot in front of the other.

From the dark, Albie watched the trooper who had emerged from the hut that held Sted. He was still tapping his leg with his domitor but it was clear that he hardly noticed the exhausted bodies that paraded before him: his gaze fixed straight over their heads, bored with the sight of them. Occasionally, and without warning he would beat any that got too close: his disdain obvious. The poor souls would crumble in an exhausted heap only to somehow find the energy to haul themselves up again. The threat of more pain at the other guards' hands a great incentive. Albie felt his grip tighten on his weapon: he wanted to shoot him now but knew that there were people relying on him: that one would keep. He studied him instead, making sure he could recognise him next time: no other troopers stood as straight as him or held their head as arrogantly high as him; he was so full of himself.

"What have you done to the others?" Albie mused. "If you've hurt them…" He wasn't sure what he'd do but he knew he'd have no trouble recognising that trooper: the red and gold lapels on his shoulder, the immaculate uniform; surely a bad sign if ever there was one.

It was Reznor who broke his stare with a nudge. The lift doors had slammed shut and the last of the white clad workers had been pushed into the first hut.

"Look, they're changing…" he pointed at the two lines that were now shuffling with uniform precision so that they formed another channel to the next hut. Another procession of poor souls filed slowly by: not one having the courage or energy to dare turn around to study their guards or even lift their eyes from the dirt that they traipsed through.

The procession passed, Albie and Reznor sensed their chance. The hut with their friends in was momentarily being guarded by just two troopers. The lights still beamed down and there wasn't much chance of reaching the hut without being spotted. Skirting around the outside of the circle of huts that surrounded the factory entrance they managed to get closer but the hut they wanted was set slightly away from the others and as they got closer looked to be made of a stronger metal. There were no gaps between the walls and it looked as if could withstand a good battering.

Pressed against the side of the nearest hut, Reznor was beginning to despair. Looking skywards for inspiration his eyes jumped from light to light: four in all. Nothing clicked in his mind as he dropped his gaze to the scene below but that was when he noticed the dry dusty ground. As the workers filed into their huts a cloud of dust was being kicked up: years of polluted filth and rubbish, disturbed by the shuffling feet, was rising up. The troopers' heads watched: not one moved; polluted mist swirling around their ankles, rising with all the comings and goings. Reznor jolted Albie and pointed in turn at two of the enormous lamps then pulled out the domitor shoved into his belt; his friend nodded and did the same. Reznor then indicated the target hut; again, Albie nodded and smiled a nearly toothless smile.

Both took aim then looked at each other and mouthed:

"...3...2..." On reaching "1", two dark blue bolts streaked up. Not waiting to see if they had hit their targets the pair instantly took aim at their second targets and once more released their bolts. Four explosions above them were followed by a rain of sparks. The air was filled with filth and dirt kicked up by the panicking workers as sparks rained down upon them. Not waiting to look at the effect on the other occupants of the clearing the pair bolted from their hideaway. Swirls of dust followed them as they scurried to within touching distance of the troopers.

By the time they had been spotted it was too late: two swiftly aimed kicks had been launched and the troopers lay writhing on the ground, an extra blow sending the troopers to 'sleep'.

Placing his stick on the door, Albie waited for the now familiar swishing sound but it didn't happen: the door remained shut. He was beginning to panic. The workers were scurrying quickly into their hut, encouraged by the troopers with beatings and metallic shouts. All this movement was kicking up even more dust; making it harder to spot Albie and Reznor unsuccessfully trying to force their way into the hut. Giving up, they turned their attentions to the bodies that lay at their feet but frantic searching revealed nothing that might open the door. Glancing up they could see that all the workers were nearly safely stowed into their hut and the troopers had split into three groups: one guarding the huts, one the factory entrance and the third was heading back towards the dust that was doing its best to hide the frantic pair.

Admitting defeat with the door, Albie grabbed hold of one of the unconscious trooper's helmets.

"Put this on then hit me and make it good…" There wasn't any time for Reznor to react as the helmet was pushed into his midriff. Putting it on he could just make out the rapidly approaching troopers through the dust that was still swirling about. Albie took a swing at him but made sure Reznor managed to avoid the lunge. Without thinking Reznor jabbed his friend in the chest and was surprised to see him collapse just as the troopers arrived. The helmet wobbled as he stood up but thankfully stayed on his head: if a touch lop-sided. Daring to take in Albie's body at his feet, he was annoyed to see him mouthing instructions. Reznor had no idea what he was saying but thought it might be a good idea if he put his foot on his friend's head before pointing his weapon at him. The approaching troopers slowed down when they saw this and luckily didn't see Albie's relieved expression as Reznor finally realised the plan.

"Go get Lord Abus." Barked one of the troopers as he approached: Albie couldn't help giving out a shiver as he realised who it was making his way towards them. The uniforms in front eyed Reznor's dishevelled uniform suspiciously, slowing down but that all changed when he aimed a kick at Albie's still figure.

"Good act," he thought as he took his foot away from Albie's stomach.

Taking a deep breath, he prepared for the grilling he was about to take: Albie's part as the unconscious body had been extremely convincing but Reznor wasn't sure that he could match this performance.

Reznor remained still and soon felt a wave of panic surge through as Bara Abus appeared. He seemed uncharacteristically eager to see the scene for himself. The closer the tall, stiff figure got the more uncomfortable and jittery Reznor became.

"This trooper managed to capture…" began a trooper next to him but the explanation was cut short by a single wave of Bara Abus's domitor: he had no time for congratulations. Instead he seemed to be studying Albie's form:

"Good. Good. I've been looking for this one for some time…" he appeared to be talking out loud: almost purring. "Always one step ahead of us. I wonder how!" He mused. Four troopers gathered silently around him: "Bring him inside…then find his accomplice…oh, and get these two some factory clothes, pointing at the troopers still sprawled on the ground, it's about all they are going to be good for." Opening the door to the hut with a wave of his domitor he stepped through without a second thought for the two souls he had just condemned. Reznor took one of Albie's arms and with the help of another trooper lifted him into the hut dropping him unceremoniously next to Faon whose face dropped as he fell onto her.

"Leave us…and get me some serum for this lot, I want some answers." Reznor held back, remaining in the room, allowing the door to slide shut behind him.

Bara Abus was so intently studying the bodies before him that he ignored the others around him, absentmindedly tapping his still polished boot. Reznor daren't move, instead he waited for the right moment to strike - a shot was out of the question: too noisy. It would have to be a well-timed blow on the back of the neck. Just when he thought he had the perfect opportunity, the upright figure would move.

Keeping out of reach of Albie as well, he began to talk: as if he knew Albie was listening:

"...found your mother: she got careless in the end..." Albie was desperate to hear more...he was being taunted...yes, there was definite enjoyment there...yes, he was definitely taunting Albie. The way he was talking, his whole manner suggested he knew a lot about Albie and his family. Was he hoping he'd give him an excuse to shoot? Albie didn't think so despite all the venom in the large man's voice. Bara Abus continued. "...thought we'd got you when we found that hole you squatted in..." The tap, tap, tap continuing as he wandered backwards and forwards. He was talking to Albie's back, not even bothering to see if his captive was listening to his gloat. Albie was, of course, and it was becoming harder and harder for him not to lash out but he had an idea that his first lunge would be a big mistake. Instead he had to wait for Reznor to make his move...if he was in the room with them...surely, he hadn't left them here with this maniac? He knew though that this was the first time he had heard his family mentioned and wanted to hear more from this bitter, ranting individual.

Bara Abus had now slowed down his pacing but his speech continued, "...Why your father had to get involved with you. Have you ever heard of anything so sick? Males showing affection towards their offspring! He was a brilliant mind: one of the elite! I trusted him, gave him the chance of greatness...he had everything then threw it all away. For what? A child. Children are for the women. He pathetically got attached... had to see you. Instead of making the greatness we had always planned for, he started skulking about…meeting you and your mother: it just wasn't natural. Then he met that pathetic group: who wanted to put themselves before the city. He abused his position, that's what he did…"

He paused to reflect and Albie realised this man was the one person who knew who he really was: had he once liked his father? Why was he so bitter? The moment was fleeting and was quickly replaced by the sarcastic tone that had dominated. "Oh no, he had to try and help: help them when they discovered, helped so many escape: like rats escaping to the sewers of the Underworld. Families' they called themselves: freaks, more like. It was bad enough he wanted to see you so much, we could cover that up…but he went too far, tried to leave the city. I couldn't allow that. We…"

The next thing Albie heard was a rapid series of thuds and the sound of bodies hitting the metal floor. Opening his eyes, he saw Reznor standing smugly with a broad grin on his face and his domitor lightly tapping an open hand.

"Not bad; eh?" Albie's reaction was not the one Reznor had expected, instead of the congratulations he had expected, Albie pushed him aside, grabbing Bara Abus's body. "What?" Reznor burst out; annoyed his best moves had been greeted with such disdain.

Ignoring Albie, he turned his attention to Faon and Sted who were slowly coming to and were trying to smile at him.

"At least you're pleased to see me…no pleasing some people." He added, releasing her hands and feet from their ties. Dropping into his arms she couldn't help herself sliding down as her legs and feet refused to work…a sudden rush of blood making toes and fingers throb. Unable to talk, she gave him a hint of a smile as he lowered her to the floor where she rubbed her feet and wrists.

Albie was now furiously searching Bara Abus while Reznor continued to release the others: this time it was Sted's turn to collapse: he too made an attempt at a smile which was a comfort to Reznor; who was feeling slightly underwhelmed by Albie's current attitude. He was just about to release Tissa when he stopped, studying her, and remembered their last attempted rescue.

She was alive but covered in sweat as if fever had taken hold of her. All colour had left her face leaving big dark patches under sunken eyes. Her eyes were half open but she had no idea where she was. Her companion was in a worse state, completely unconscious, her damp outfit clinging to her body.

"Drugged," announced Sted when he was able to speak "They are going through withdrawal…they'll not be running away…even if they were able to!" Faon nodded, remembering a part of her life she had tried to forget.

"We…we went like this before you found us," she turned to Reznor, "They'll need to keep warm," she advised, managing to pull herself up so that she could release Tissa while Reznor did the same to the other girl. Sted scoured the room but there was nothing to wrap the figures with.

"We've got to get out of here – they'll get hypothermia if we don't." Faon continued nursing Tissa and trying to ignore the damp clothes that now clung to them both but Albie wasn't listening, so intent was he on searching the figure who knew more about his past than he did.

"Nothing, nothing…" he ranted, oblivious to everybody else's worries. He turned to Reznor who was now wrapping his borrowed uniform around the shivering, unconscious figure that lay in his arms. "He was going to tell me about my mother…"

"Albie!" gasped Faon, "We've got to get them out of here…there are ways to find out about your family but not…" She broke off abruptly as the door slid and a trooper stepped in carrying a flat box. He barely had time to gasp before Reznor pulled him through the door, Sted inadvertently tripping him up in the process. The new arrival flew forward landing next to Albie who gave him a swift blow to the back of his neck.

The others waited for the grin but there was none. Albie held Faon in a cold, icy stare. She wanted to shy away from his stare, focus on anything else but his expression: but she couldn't. There was no way they could carry Bara Abus's body and even if they could, the chances that he would tell Albie who his parents were and where they had gone seemed remote to everybody else but the distraught Albie.

On his own he had just accepted his lot; his lonely life. Now he had become quite reliant upon these friends of his. Seeing his mother's picture in the cave had unlocked a part of him that he had forgotten existed: feelings that were now getting out of control and he had no way of stopping them. He considered the still body that lay at his feet – did it really know anything or was he just playing with him? He had to know…how did this man know about his father…his mother? Had they really been searching for him? His mind spun with unanswered questions; his own Pandora's Box: now that it had been opened he couldn't shut out the emotions he now felt: emotions he had long ago buried. But was this man the key to them all?

Faon's gentle touch on his shoulder brought him partially back to the present day.

"We've got to get them out of here or they'll die. The lift…we'll get you answers, but not now…please help us." It was her turn to hold his gaze and as she did so he realised she was right. Looking past her at Tissa he could make out the girl he had come to rescue…and she needed him now. He looked once more at Faon but he didn't need to say anything: they knew how much they were asking of him. His friends watched him pick up Bara Abus's fallen domitor, before glancing over at the two huddled figures.

"Okay, time to leave…but…" he stopped and they simply nodded.

"The lift it is…and you better be right, 'cause if you're not I'm coming back for him."

Was there a slight smirk as he turned to slowly lift Tissa? If there was, nobody dared mention it as he led them silently into the gloom. They skirted around the outside of the ring of huts. Nothing stirred as the search for Albie's accomplice continued in the distance.

Reaching the lift to the city above, they found it deserted. Faon tapped the panel with Bara Abus's domitor and they were in: simple. Clutching Tissa closely, Albie turned to take one more look. All the effort they had had to get in and now they were just walking out. Far from being happy, though, there was only emptiness. A fight would have been easier…the relative stillness made him think and feel. The cold metal hut and the secrets within were like magnets drawing him back: goading him. He thought he heard Tissa groan and that made his mind up. Taking a breath, he stepped over the threshold and the doors slid shut. The cold damp outside was immediately replaced by a blast of warm air as they felt themselves rising, slowly at first but gradually gathering speed.

For now, *they* were Albie's family: Faon who had constantly surprised them, her devoted Sted and Reznor: the strength of the group, then there was Tissa and the girl they had forced to join them: who knows what her story was. All that mattered was that they needed him and...yes, he needed them, who'd have thought that?

18

It was the deluxe of lifts and obviously not for the ordinary citizens or even for the ordinary trooper. From the rich, red carpet, which made the lift darker, to the glittering panels, it was designed for the elite. It certainly wasn't the homely deep carpet that Albie had rolled about happily in Tissa's home block. Even the walls boasted carpet, walls disguising welcoming seats that swung down. Above them rows of lights shone down making the redness richer but as they continued their ascent the red softened, approaching pink and the mood appeared to lift somewhat as everything became that much brighter.

The only piece of bare metal they could see was the control panel to one side of the mirrored doors. It was a shock for all of them to gaze upon their dishevelled reflections: they could hardly see any skin colours behind the layers of caked dirt. Tissa's white factory uniform was now caked grey with a hint of black, and any gleam from the 'borrowed' armour had dulled.

Glad to be free of it Reznor threw his borrowed trooper's helmet down into an empty corner and studied himself. Scratches covered his face and he was squinting under the unfamiliar glare of the lift: so accustomed had he been to the dark world below. He ran his fingers over each scratch, remembering how he had got every one of them and his anger grew. A sick sensation in his stomach brought him back to the present.

They hardly knew they were moving: the occasional stutter of the lift was the only way they could have known. Each of them had picked their own spot of floor to reflect on their ordeal. Albie lay holding the soundly sleeping Tissa: still unaware of what had happened. She wasn't sweating or shivering as much as she had been, helped by the warmth of the lift which drifted down upon them from the rows of strip lights above. The other girl was making similar progress but Reznor had preferred not to have her draped against him; choosing to cover her with part of his requisitioned uniform instead. He now sat to the side of her keeping an eye over the girl they had become responsible for but knew nothing about. The first thing he noticed was her striking beauty. Despite her gauntness, Reznor was struck by her skin which was a much darker colour to his own: a deep, earthy brown: he couldn't believe he hadn't noticed this. Her hair was a tightly curled collection that approached the top of her ears and eyebrows. She looked much older than Tissa, extra years in the factory having taken their toll: from her sunken eyes to her wasted limbs. Reznor wondered how she had managed to survive so long working for hours in the factory's heat and suffocating atmosphere. He realised, however that he had no idea what she had looked like when she had been brought in. At least Tissa looked as if she had known some life. The endless rounds of work and exhausted sleep, pepped up by whatever drugs they had given her to keep her meant Tissa had been lucky in comparison.

They had now been in the lift enough time to realise the light from above was also giving them energy, recharging them...like batteries. Cuts and scrapes didn't hurt as much and aches were soothed. The two escapees showed signs that their shivering and sweating was over and for the first time, Tissa was able to sit up on her own, still dazed.

The hum of the lift changed and brought them to their senses: they were slowing down and by now the lights were nearly white, making things look positively sterile – even the dirt on their faces looked clean.

Exchanging glances, they busied themselves: weapons were readied and the two bewildered new arrivals were pushed away from the mirrored doors without a word of explanation. Albie and Reznor stood in front of the doors while the others pushed themselves against the cylindrical walls. With a domitor in each hand Albie thought he looked quite heroic. His posing stopped as he caught Reznor laughing at him. Embarrassed, he toned it down by lowering them.

There wasn't even a jerk but they knew they had arrived. Where? They had no way of knowing.

The mirrored doors slowly parted and bright light blazed through the widening gap, forcing them to shield their eyes as they staggered back. Not being accustomed to the glare they couldn't bring themselves to do anything but cower. Reznor fumbled on the ground for his helmet then pulled it on so that the visor protected his eyes. He looked out on a scene he had heard tales of but had doubted really existed.

Light poured down from the sky picking out objects that he, once again, could only wonder at: immense buildings that shimmered in the heat with electronic screens on them that flashed and screamed at him, painful at first but it didn't take long for his visor to darken so that he could marvel at his first glimpse of the surface for well over a year.

Ignoring the figures behind him he stumbled forward, emerging into a plaza surrounded by slender trees with leaves that somehow sparkled as they waved in front of the sun. He spun around trying to take everything in, failing to notice the looks of the mystified onlookers who had withdrawn to the steps on the outskirts of the plaza to study the new arrival. Reznor's eyes were firmly fixed above and took no notice of their murmurs.

Inside the lift Albie realised Reznor had left and decided it was up to him to haul the others out.

"Come on, time to brave the outside…if we're not careful we'll be on our way back before we known it," he announced. Faon and Sted gave the unknown girl a shoulder each, shielding their eyes with their free hand. Behind them, in the lift, Albie watched their silhouetted bodies stepping into the daylight then he bent down to help Tissa to her feet. As he did so he heard a click and the mirrored doors began to slide shut in front of them.

Hurling the pair of them forward, Albie managed to jam his commandeered domitor in the way. Immediately alarm bells screamed out from the lift and the others turned around, still squinting, to see Albie pushing Tissa through the door. The wedged domitor began to buckle as Albie squeezed under it, finally rolling out as the doors snapped shut silencing the ringing. Breathing a sigh of relief, Albie looked down upon the shattered remains of the stolen weapon.

"That would have been useful…" he began to mutter but was interrupted by a new sound as a ripping filled the air. "Reznor…" he shouted as the unwelcome sound filled the air.

Reznor's eyes dropped and for the first time he noticed the crowds around him: bemused, silent and static. It seemed to be a bank of shades of green, reflecting the sunlight. Every one of them studying him: disbelieving. Some began pointing angrily at him, muttering.

"How could these things get into our city?"

"Sound the alarm."

"How dare they come here bringing down our block's reputation!" commented another but not one voice rose out of the crowd: not one wanted to stand out and become a possible target. Every voice was a murmur.

As soon as Reznor moved to run back to the others there was a moment of panic as perfectly shaped bodies and styled hair feared he was going to get close to them. Those nearest pushed back, terrified, but those at the back wouldn't budge, happy to have somebody between them and the intruder. In between the smug and the frightened a scrum resulted as the unfortunate people in the middle were jostled and squashed. Their fear spread quickly and the mood changed as the crowd became a mob, desperate to stay upright and avoid being trampled under fashionable heels.

Everything ended abruptly as the air was split by the sound of approaching Predavators. The people at the back, who had been so determined to stand their ground despite the anguish below them, quickly disappeared into the safety of the surrounding buildings. Those left behind stumbled backwards and a mass of bodies once again fought to escape becoming involved with these intruders.

At the same time as his audience was trying to flee into the surrounding buildings, Reznor ran towards the group gathered outside the lift doors, wind whipping around him as the craft closed in. The lift doors had closed as he reached them and his ears filled with the beat of the engines.

"Stay where you are…" boomed a voice from the craft. By now they were alone in the square, just a few pieces of discarded clothing: coats, shoes, bags…all dropped in the scramble. The lighter objects whirled about them: scarves, gloves, throws... The Predavator hovered overhead forcing them to stand still. There was no way they could move in the hurricane whipping around the square: try as they might.

The cockpit followed Reznor as he tried to draw its attention away from the others. It was just a featureless metal front, but Reznor knew the screens inside would all be relaying his every movement. Lifting his arm to take aim with his domitor he felt an intense pain shoot up his arm as a laser blast scattered pieces of the weapon about him. Screaming, he clutched his hand and the same dull voice boomed out once more:

"Do not move…any further actions will result in your instant elimination." Reznor looked down at his hand as he crouched on the concrete, there wasn't a mark to show but the force of the blast had probably broken something because although he wouldn't admit it; it hurt like…

His mind drifted away from the tempest lashing at him and the crowd that was even now watching him from the comfort of their homes. Even the guns that had inflicted this pain on him slipped away. He remembered just minutes earlier; the feeling of the sun's warmth, smelling air that hadn't been relentlessly polluted. He had seen the sky once again. He'd never thought he'd make it out of the underworld and if it was going to end now at least he had achieved something…There was still light after all that darkness and…there was hope. They were away and if nothing else he'd bought the others some time. They weren't going to get him without a fight.

He steeled himself as his head began to spin; his hair dancing madly upwards, spine tingling, hairs on his back standing on end…any minute now he would grab hold of the first trooper to touch him. His last stand before they finally managed to catch him…

But nobody touched him, the next thing he knew an explosion ripped the sky above him and he was sent flying, an intense pain ripped through one side of him as he landed. He winced as he felt the effects of sliding across the rough concrete, scraping the skin off one side as he skidded to a halt at the foot of an immense pillar. He shielded his face as the predator crashed into the building they sheltered under before exploding.

Debris rained around him. However there a few metres away from him, leaning casually against one of the pillars, was Albie: smoking weapon in hand. Reznor didn't know whether to hug him or hit him. In the end he did neither, hauling himself onto his feet he limped over to his smug companion.

"This way…" announced Albie as he led him in between two of the concrete buildings where the others lay. Half dragging Tissa, he led the ragtag group away from the square.

"I know a way out but you are not going to like it." There was something about Albie's expression that told them they *really* weren't going to like it.

Hurrying away from the scene, they soon appeared at a small metal grille in the ground, big enough to fit one body through. Albie touched the panel with his domitor and it slid open. They could hear reinforcements arriving in the plaza but luckily the smoke from the downed Predavator hid them. Reznor stopped at the hole before looking hopefully at his partner as the others passed by him before disappearing.

"Not down there…please. I'm just getting too used to the light…and we've spent so long trying to get out of there…" By this time there was only the two of them left. Albie ignored his plea and bounded into the darkness.

"Come on!" he shouted but still Reznor didn't budge as the smell of the sewers hit his nostrils. "Trust me. You'd rather be down here alive than take your chances up there…" the voice was softer but starting to grow fainter. "…Come on, you big lump. The grille will be shutting in a minute: NOW JUMP!"

The final force of Albie's voice and his receding steps in the watery tunnel convinced him to take the plunge: as did the sound of Predavators landing in the square. Smoke and ash billowed towards him. He nervously jumped, holding his nose with one hand as the grille started slowly closing, threatening to separate him from the others.

Reznor's fall was a particularly hard one because he hadn't been expecting to hit the ground so soon: expecting to plummet back into the underworld they had escaped from. He staggered in the water that ran around his boots: the light from the grille crisscrossed his face and he summoned up the courage to let go of his nose. He had steadied himself as his knees took his full weight; his face changing from stunned surprise to…relief. The others were waiting impatiently at the entrance to one of the many tunnels that led back into the dark so he coughed and composed himself; trying to regain his cool. He realised the two factory workers were staring at him.

"I'm good…. not as far down as I was expecting…name's Reznor…" He introduced himself.

"Tissa…and this is Ordenne." The two girls flashed quick smiles as they were helped to their feet. Returning the compliment, he tried to hide his embarrassment by adjusting his clothing.

"…where…?" he continued but stopped as he realised they hadn't time for an explanation and were stumbling away: Albie leading the way, helping Tissa, Sted and Faon helping Ordenne, who was able to walk with some assistance and had even managed to give him one last smile. Tagging meekly behind, Reznor kept glancing back still not able to believe he wasn't fighting to stay afloat in the murky waters far below: why hadn't anybody told him it was such a short drop?

"Would you believe it?" he murmured as they plodded on. "Quite a stroke of luck really – never was keen on swimming. The air down here isn't nearly as bad…!" Fearing he'd lose sight of the others he hurried after them, splashing as he stumbled after them.

They waded through varying depths of murkiness, feeling their way along the dripping walls and occasionally touching something that either wriggled away, giving them a start, or something that they wished they hadn't touched. Water was making their boots heavier and Tissa and Ordenne soon had to be carried on people's backs as they toiled.

Neither girl carried much weight after their time in captivity so despite their extra loads Albie and

Reznor found they were able to force a quicker pace. They plodded on in silence; lost in their own thoughts but with a gentle squeeze of Albie's neck Tissa broke the quiet.

"Thanks for coming to get me…a part of me knew you would. Even when I was in the factory I kept believing…but I was lucky: Ordy's been there for years. I'm sorry for running: it wasn't me it was…" She'd had so much to tell him and found it hard not to ramble and blurt out everything but Albie's quick squeeze of her ankles brought her to a stop. He smiled as he remembered this was just how she had been when they first met.

"It's okay," Albie replied, "You're safe for the moment, this is my territory." Tissa relaxed and rested her head on his shoulder, pleased that she had broken the awkwardness between them.

"How come you know where you're going, Albie?" Faon wondered after she had managed to catch up with him: the extra weight beginning to slow him down.

"This is where I grew up, it's virtually the only place I remember…troopers have chased me around these tunnels for years and never caught me. They didn't live here, know the place inside out and they were never keen to stray too far from the grilles in case they got lost…some nasty things down here and it's not just the smell. Although the smell never bothered me for some strange reason…I've smelt worse." The others had to confess that after experiencing the underworld, with its stale, polluted smog, the sewers were comparatively fresh.

Despite Albie's relative happiness to be in familiar surroundings, the others were finding it hard to share his upbeat mood. They had escaped one torrid subterranean world only to find themselves in another: almost as unpleasant because they didn't know what it was they were standing in and know for definite why everything they touched was so slimy. The cold water swimming about them and the extended march had given them an uncomfortable combination of numb but blistering feet.

"Ah! Here we are." Albie called as they stopped abruptly with seemingly nowhere to go. The tunnel sloped off ahead and behind them but he had stopped in front of a solid brick wall.

"Where are we?" asked Faon as they looked about them, searching for something that didn't look like another endless tunnel wall. She was cold and hungry and in desperate need of rest and nourishment. She did not feel like playing any guessing games.

"Where are we, Albie…? Is it food…? Is it a bed?"

Albie was a bit put out they didn't want to play but looking at Sted's subdued features, Faon's folded arms and worn out expression and more importantly his aching arms from carrying Tissa he decided to reveal all.

Handing Tissa to Faon and Sted he set about pushing the bricks so that they disappeared with the sound of stone on metal. Before long he had removed a hole big enough for a person to clamber through but high enough above the water line to allow their feet to come back to life. As they stepped through they were welcomed by a waft of warm air that immediately turned the mood back in Albie's favour.

The best was yet to come as they were lead into a room that Albie lit with his domitor. Beyond the light of the domitor lay a cluttered room. It was large enough for them all to sleep comfortably in their own space and more importantly was piled high with old chairs, mattresses and other objects that had once filled the fashionable homes above. Tissa moved from object to object making the same comments she might have made seeing a collection of vintage clothes. Reznor laid Ordenne into a large plastic armchair before he too collapsed onto a particularly thick mattress that he had pulled from the pile. Albie wedged his domitor between the wall and a handily placed plastic chair so that it cast a faint glow across to the far, crumbling wall. All the walls were made of crumbling stone but looked solid enough while the shapes of the furniture about them cast lengthy shadows that decorated the bare bricks.

As they explored, Albie set about reconstructing the wall until there was no sign that there had been anything but stone wall. All thoughts of the dampness beyond began to evaporate in the warmth of the room. Albie recovered some brightly coloured packets from a box, passing them around to his bemused but delighted friends.

"It is amazing what you can find down here and what the world above throws away. This is one of my little holes that I use to hide things away." A respectful hush followed as they studied the packets they had been given. Finally, they tucked in: the others following Albie's lead. He was able to keep them supplied as the hunger they had managed to ignore until now was gradually satisfied with a range of fruity and cereal snacks. The exotically decorated, but drastically faded, packets soon littered the floor. Albie was next able to provide them with a range of similarly decorated drinks. They could have been eating anything and it wouldn't have mattered: they were eating and that was all that counted.

Finally, exhaustion overcame them and it wasn't long before sleep took each of them.

Allowing himself a brief moment to congratulate himself on his choice of hiding place, he looked around at his sleeping 'gang'. For the first time in years, he felt a strange warmth that he hadn't known since…he struggled to remember when. Contented that they were all sleeping he lay down next to the 'door' and promptly fell asleep. "It's good to be back," he muttered to himself.

19

It was the best sleep they could remember having; relaxed by the feeling of warmth and a chemical-free air. Even the smell outside couldn't penetrate… or was it that they had just become accustomed to it?

Albie crept away from his sleeping friends,

climbed a metal ladder tied to the wall before emerging through a hole in the roof that had been covered by a sheet of light metal. He slid silently down the sides of another steel ladder that dropped down to the floor of a platform suspended above an inky blackness.

Nothing stirred so he sat listening to the constant trickle of water outside. The distant hum of the city above, the faint sound of relaxed breathing blended with rumbling snores to make Albie's perfect morning soundtrack. He was at peace with his surroundings. This was his domain.

After an age, he was startled by a figure that moved behind him. It was Tissa, an unkempt and tired Tissa, but a welcome sight as she moved from the shadows. He motioned her to sit next to him, their legs dangling over an abyss.

The humming started to grow louder as they sat. She sat, confused and uncertain. Albie put his finger to his lips and pointed below them.

"Where....?" she began sluggishly but he just returned his gaze downwards. Finally, pinpricks of light grew like a field of stars. Gradually Tissa could make out that they were in the corner of an enormous open space: the size of a factory. Below them, piled high, were assorted pieces of rubbish – similar to the pieces of furniture that littered Albie's hideaway. Albie swung around so that he lay on the floor with his head sticking out over the side. He motioned Tissa to do the same.

"These are all relatively new," Whispered

Tissa. "We have them in our flat…" Then she paused, realising what she'd said and how her life had changed. Her voice began to tail off as she thought of her mother. "Least, we used to." Albie smiled sympathetically and she shrugged. They sat silently scanning the debris.

"This is the best way to watch," He informed her.

"Watch what…?" she began but was stopped in mid-sentence by the sounds of machinery. The orange glow around them changed to flashing red and all Tissa could make out was the reflected glow of Albie's eyes and reassuring toothy smile.

The humming grew louder until a loud clang broke the relative calm, making her jump. His reassuring hand told her she was quite safe so she remained still but unsettled. Another clang followed, echoing around them and this time the rubbish moved slightly, chairs, beds, tables jostling with each other as they dropped suddenly through a long crack that had materialized in the floor. Everything rained down and away from them. Tissa recognised the stench of the musty, polluted air of the underworld. The objects fell in slow motion, jostling with each other as they fell.

Underneath the rain of rubbish, lights flickered then blinked on; illuminating everything that was falling. Tissa looked at Albie for an explanation. He just shrugged. Although he'd seen this happen countless times he still knew little about it.

"All the rubbish falls onto that floating slab-thing then disappears inside it." He tried to sound like an expert but was failing miserably. "Then the lights go off and the doors shut."

"It is taken to be recycled," The voice behind them made them jump and they instantly pulled themselves away from the edge to confront the intruder. Ordenne stood there with Reznor's coat still wrapped around her. She leaned unsteadily against a railing: still looking extremely fragile. "Didn't mean to startle you, sorry." She backed off but as Tissa held out her hand for her to join them she was able to relax and nodded accordingly.

"Where does it go then?" asked Tissa.

"It's all taken to the factories. The plastic is remoulded and coloured according to the latest fashions and everything else is changed to whatever is the vogue. Some things only last a few weeks and they are thrown out because they aren't cool any more – it's such a waste. We were just the poor wretches who had to half-kill ourselves to keep up with the never-ending demand." She looked down at herself, at her spindly arms and legs, the marks caused by the drugs that she had been given to keep her working quick enough. "I used to think I was quite chubby…once. Healthy I called it." Ordenne realised the pair were staring at her and stopped.   She turned away and stood up to leave but suddenly lurched forward. Albie just caught her in time before she tumbled over the edge. She glowed even more as he gently took hold of her.

"I'm okay, thanks."

"Breakfast!" Albie decided and guided the young girl back into the warmth with the others; the cold, damp air from the Underworld still blew up through the open doors below them. As they helped Ordenne down to the others, who had by now been woken by the rubbish disposal, the clanging restarted and the doors gradually closed. The humming softened once more and returned to the background.

After rummaging through a pile of 'debris' in the corner of the room there was great delight when Albie pulled out a wider range of packets and bottles.

"There's another dump on the other side – some people chuck away food without even opening it – which is good news for us." he told them as he studied their amazed faces, "It is all unopened stuff."

At first, he failed to notice Tissa had gone quiet as Ordenne had been telling them about the recycling factories. She remained completely still, head bowed. The others tucked into processed pieces of meat and fruit but still she refused to join them, turning a processed food packet over in her hands before retiring to the bed she had taken in a darkened corner. Albie came across and sat down next to her.

"Go on, have some. You look like you need it. I only got unopened stuff, honest!" but she ignored him.

"I can't…If it weren't for people like me, throwing things away all the time, there wouldn't be any need for the factories and Ordenne and the others wouldn't have had to suffer…"

"…And you," He reminded her. "You were in there too…look at what happened to you. You can't live your life regretting what you've done but you can make sure you try to change the things you do in the future. Faon: she lived just like you, so did Sted and Ordenne but they changed and so did you. Reznor…well who knows about him but we are going to stick together and try to make a difference."

"He's right, you know youngster," butted in Reznor who had heard the conversation. "Remember the past so that you can mould the future…" He stopped abruptly as he realised they were all looking at him, smiling at his rare attempt at being intelligent. The smiles turned to grins then laughter filled the room and the serious mood had disappeared.

"Wise words, master Rez…" Sted laughed, bowing theatrically and slapping Reznor on the back with a strength he didn't realise he still possessed.

"Fine…" commented Reznor, turning his back in a mock show of anger.

It had the desired affect and Tissa joined them in eating and for the first time felt part of a group that she knew actually cared for her. She had had plenty of 'friends' in the city but would they still have liked her if she hadn't tried so hard to wear the right clothes, listen to the right tunes or just been like all the rest. She'd never known misfits such as these but if she hadn't tried to help Albie, a misfit in trouble, she wouldn't have felt it possible to be so close to anybody other than her mother. She had now found friends who would stick their necks out or risk their lives for her: she felt privileged to be here. Would she have traded all her objects for friends like these if her hand hadn't been forced?

As one of the newest members of the group, Tissa began to feel more and more welcome, her old life in the city had been one of keeping up with appearances. This new group couldn't allow themselves the luxury of giving a second thought to fashion, appearance or position in society. She watched them as they laughed but for now couldn't help herself from wanting to remain slightly detached; she laughed but part of her knew it would take time for her guilt to disappear. She had learnt to fit in, a skill that had served her well in the city and avoided offending people or making enemies. These people were different. There was no need to change herself to fit in. However, she still knew she couldn't be as open with them as she wanted to. She still didn't feel confident enough to open up to anyone so she sat quietly and listened. Tissa watched as the attention turned towards the other new recruit.

Ordenne looked up as she realised they were all watching her expectantly.

"Ordenne…" asked Faon.

"Ordenne…" she repeated and finally the young girl looked up.

"How come you ended up at the factory?" Faon asked with a reassuring look. Ordenne look at her cagily, not wanting to give anything away and Faon seemed to pick up on this. "If you'd rather not say it's okay."

Being given the option set her at ease and Ordenne studied Faon before nodding.

"It's okay, there's not much to say. I've been in the factory longer than I care remember." She paused to look at her fingers, turning them over to examine them: the scratches and bruises that covered them, the thinness… "It all started because I was clever. My mum always pushed me to do my best; I was just doing what came naturally to me. I had learned everything the schools were allowed to teach me by the time I was ten. So, they put me to work programming computers…then designing them. At first, I was a novelty: the Compu-kid they called me but it was hard having no-one of my own age to talk to so I began to lock myself away. I studied instead of going out and meeting people. I read everything I could on the city's compu-net and wasn't too bothered about how I looked. I was no longer bothered about keeping up-to-date. I didn't use the latest make-up colours or wear my hair the right way, those friends I had at home started talking behind my back then officers from the ruling council took an interest. They started watching me, saying nothing; not asking me if I was happy the way I was. Everything was assumed. Then the gossiping behind my back grew out of control and I found myself on my own. Don't get me wrong, I was presentable and clean, but it wasn't enough.

Eventually I was labelled anti-social and had to attend 'Self-correction' sessions: they just made me angrier and more determined to remain the same. There was nothing wrong with me – it was them who had the problem I kept telling myself. I kept myself busy when I wasn't at work – reading, walking around the city and I kept diaries: someone to talk to. Suddenly I was a problem, the final act was when my diaries were discovered and I was charged with having 'Anti-social thoughts'…" As she said this Faon sighed, nodding in agreement, "The next thing I knew they were taking me away. I remember my mum crying and being told it was "For everyone's good.""

"In the back of the Pred, I was tied to the seat…" Ordenne stopped abruptly as she began shaking and tears streamed down both cheeks. Faon moved across towards her, settling herself down on the stained mattress Ordenne was perched upon, and put her arm around her shoulder.

"You've just described a hundred different cases…every one of them when people have been arrested for just being themselves." Faon carefully lifted Ordenne's emaciated face so that their eyes met: and Ordenne's quaking slowed. "That city up there looks fantastic and bright but its core is rotten. You are okay if you toe the line, do what you are expected to do – think about little more than looking like everybody else…following whatever is decided is the way to be…" This time she shrugged before adding, "That's all in the past now…we all need to put our pasts behind us. What we need to do is decide where we go from here."

"We've got to get ourselves new identities and kill off our old ones," replied Ordenne through the tears. Sted gave a cough of disbelief, half choking on a spongy brown bar wrapped in a shiny packet.

"Just like that…walk up to the nearest compu-terminal and ask for a new identity?" Reznor, Tissa and Albie turned to warn him about his lack of sensitivity but Ordenne, and surprisingly Faon never batted an eye lid. The former scowling unhappily with her arms folded across her chest that her idea should be laughed at so out of hand. Sted coughed before apologising.

"I'm sorry, it's just I have no idea how…"

Ordenne sat there a moment composing herself, wiping her tears away before studying them.

"Actually, it's not too hard to do." Ordenne's embarrassment and tears were replaced by a knowledgeable expression. It was her turn to cough but this time it was apologetically as she continued, "When I found myself isolated I started to spend a lot of time fiddling with the computers late at night at work – I had nothing else to do, after all, but walk around, exploring both city…and the net." She studied her feet again and the rubble on the concreted floor to avoid everyone's expectant gazes. Even Faon had turned to look at her, pleased to have her support but intrigued to find out what their new recruit had to say for herself.

"Go on," She prompted, encouraging Ordenne.

"Well…" She had felt warm inside having people caring about how she felt and trying to make her feel better. However, she was still not confident that her friends would feel the same way if they didn't approve of something she had done. Would they think she was as shallow as those people that had snubbed

her? Would this be the end of her part of the group?
"…Well, I started exploring the computer system,
using the codes I used at work…I suppose I abused my
position but…I started creating these people…they
were just files but…I don't think anyone found out
about them because nothing was mentioned when I
was taken. It was just a way of passing the time, that's
all."

"How many did you create?" wondered Sted.
"Two…? Three…? Ten…?" Each time she shook her
head wearily, she didn't think this was going well. He
paused before whispering "More?" She mumbled
something back but her head was buried into the coat
she had been lent so they couldn't make out a word.
Albie and Reznor were looking bemused but Sted and
Faon were perched on their knees in the dust, waiting
expectantly. Ordenne lifted her head just enough so
that could hear her.

"…About...a hundred…boys as well as girls…I
used to write to them on to my computer-diary, some
more than others…if anybody had known they would
have thought I was extremely peculiar. They did find
out I was peculiar…but that's a different story." Sted's
roaring laughter brought her back to the present. If that
wasn't bad enough he then grabbed Faon and started
half dragging half dancing her around the room,
sending dust flying over everyone. Their coughing,
combined with the racket he was making, would have
woken up the underworld and it took the joint efforts
of Albie and Reznor to force him to the ground and to
be still.

"You'll have the whole city here in a minute if you don't stop. What's got into you?"

He still wore a broad grin across his face as he regained his composure. "Don't you realise? Ordy's created these people that don't exist – they have identities of their own, we can take their places. Me, Faon Ordy and Tissa are designated as factory workers but she can tap into the city's computer systems and delete us – the troopers won't be looking for us anymore. She can do the same for you as well. We can get new identities so we can move freely above ground: might need some clothes and a wash…haircut definitely…personality bypass for Albie…" Albie's hand shot over his mouth but instead of pretending to be angry, Albie wore a deadly serious expression on his face and froze. He had heard something.

20

They could only hear the steady trickle of water outside. Fingers on his lips, Albie motioned the others up the metal ladders and out into the platform above the recycling plant.

They crept slowly to the steps, Ordenne and Tissa being ushered up first, followed by Faon, Sted and finally Reznor. Albie crept closer to investigate the tunnel they had left the night before.

On the other side of Albie's carefully bricked up wall, the water still ran freely but sounded as if it had to flow around many obstacles. There were people in the tunnel. Years of paying attention to the sounds of the sewers had helped Albie to stay focussed and alive. In the distance he heard the splashing of wading bodies but that stopped as it got closer to the hole he had filled the previous night.

By now Ordenne had climbed the ladder and was easing herself out through the hole in the roof, her body just a silhouette against the dull orangey glow, Tissa was just behind her with the others crowded around the base of the ladders, waiting silently and expectantly. As they waited they studied the bricks that Albie had painstakingly replaced and most had thought, in the back of their minds, had been unnecessary. How wrong they had been. Still crouched behind a plastic chair, he urged them up as Tissa disappeared from his sight. Without realising it he breathed a sigh of relief that she was out of immediate danger. In the dark he picked up one of the many bags that he kept in his hideaways, filled with the bits of junk that usually came in handy: he'd felt quite naked without one, recently.

Only Reznor remained at the foot of the ladders when a scraping sound made them both spin to face the wall: a brick had moved slightly. His feet refused to move, Albie had eased his way towards him, half crawling, half stumbling through the dusty rubble and all the time the bricks continued to be eased out but not one had fallen. Albie motioned to Reznor who hadn't noticed that Albie had turned off his 'torch'. As he did so the room was plunged into darkness with an orange circular glow above them the only source for them to head towards.

"Go…" muttered Albie to his friend but Reznor couldn't find the ladder, his hands feeling the dark. Just as a relieved hand touched metal the first brick clattered to the ground, rolling twice before it came to rest. The fate of the brick (and the others that swiftly followed it were largely ignored by the occupants of the room as numerous torches scoured the room. The shadows of discarded furniture that stretched across the filthy walls managed to distract the newcomers long enough for Reznor to dash up the rungs, paying little attention to the clangs of boot on metal that reverberated around them. Thankfully for him the sound of bricks falling to the floor and a body struggling to climb into the hideaway masked his escape.

While Reznor's feet disappeared through the hole, Albie found his escape blocked by a light that focussed on the ladder. Pushing himself further into the darkness, he waited as the familiar chattering of radios grew closer. A single trooper was creeping towards the ladder while the rest of his troop eased through the hole. Sensing his chance, he took aim and blasted the intruder, grabbing his domitor before it fell. Albie's figure was immediately picked out by one of the torches and a shot zipped past him, nicking the padding on his shoulder. In spite of escaping injury, the whole idea of being shot at did not please Albie and he swiftly returned the compliment, the torch's owner fairing considerably worse than the annoyed youth. Albie dashed for the ladder as uniforms poured through the hole. Albie hauled himself out before the room was filled with torchlight and laser fire. He dragged the metal sheet as quickly as he could over the hole and then turned to assess the situation.

The others were studying the rubbish dump before them. Small bits of furniture were dotted below them.

"There are some steps over there – we can get out there," Albie was pointing across the area that had only recently swung open to allow tonnes of furniture to drop hundreds of metres below. "It's safe enough – the doors won't be opening for days now – they don't open until it is full…and we can't stay here: it's not going to take them long to work out where we've gone."

"Please, isn't there another way? I'm not going over there!" pleaded Tissa, remembering the distance the rubbish had fallen.

"Look, the ladder will be discovered very soon…" Albie began but as he did so the metal cover was catapulted into the air. Before the first trooper's head had appeared half the group were scrambling down the rungs set into the metalwork to the floor far below. Reznor and Albie trained their guns waiting for the new arrivals. They quickly arrived. Shots flew from their weapons knocking the trooper back down the hole and as he did so they heard the crumple of several bodies tumbling down, colliding with the rungs as they did so.

Seizing their opportunity, they followed the others down into the v-shaped dip that the two huge, closed doors formed. It was fairly easy to slide down to the middle of the huge dump but once they reached the middle, it was a slow upward climb up the other side. Every so often there was a rung to hold onto but these were few and far between. For every few steps the group managed up the slope one of them would lose their grip, their balance or both and collide with the person behind them. All the time Tissa couldn't help feeling that any moment she would hear the vibrations then hum of the doors warming up to open and plunge them into the waters below. This recent, vivid memory was praying more and more on her mind.

Just behind Ordenne in the queue climbing up to the safety of the far ladders, Tissa suddenly froze as a laser blast pinged off the ring ahead of her. A number of troopers had now appeared at the top of the ladders behind her and were taking aim. Shots whizzed past, melting nearby plastic chairs and tables with the heat of the blasts.

"We've got to keep moving Tissa; we're an easy target," Urged Faon but Tissa simply froze.

"I can't move...my legs: they just won't." Faon took her arm and starting tugging at her arm.

"We've got to move, it's hard enough to keep going without having to pull you up too...please!" The urgency in her voice still didn't move Tissa. A shot zipped in front of them; striking the rung she clung to. The heat caused Tissa to let go and she lost her footing on the slope. With a scream she slipped, slamming into Faon as she slid down the ominous, metal recycling doors.

They rolled back down the slope making the others scatter or cling to any available rung. Shots continued to fly around them. Faon grabbed instinctively for a handhold as she slid and was grateful to stop herself from falling any further. She jerked to a stop giving her arm a wrench as she did so. Her body swung back and forth like a pendulum: her already-overloaded fingers threatened to dislocate. She winced as she forced her fingers to keep hold, eventually managing to grip on with both hands. The next thing she knew Tissa's body had collided with her, threatening to dislodge her but she clung on, more through grim determination than any strength she might have left. Tissa screamed at the same time but the collision managed to halt her descent allowing her a moment to cling onto Faon's frail figure.

Once more, Faon felt herself slipping, it was bad enough having halted her own slide but now she had an extra weight to bear: a weight that was now frantically trying to claw its way up her emaciated body. Her fingers began to slip with the cold sweat that was now covering her hands. It was only a matter of seconds before they both continued their downwards path and Faon closed her eyes in a vain attempt at focusing her energies on staying put.

Suddenly the screaming load she was carrying was gone. At first there was relief that she wasn't falling but this was soon replaced by the Realisation that Tissa wasn't with her any more. Remembering her eyes were shut, she gingerly opened them, just in time to see shards of plastic fly past from another blast.

Tissa had gone. Faon let her head fall back against the steel, not daring to look down, the rounds erupting around her forced to think of moving.

The others edged their way up the slope and soon reached the far wall. Desperate to escape the line of fire the first pair hauled themselves to safety: Ordenne leading the way, followed by Reznor. Sted looked back to see Faon lifting herself onto her feet and began clambering down to help his bruised friend.

"Tissa!" called out Albie as she slid past him. He threw out a hand but she sped past him before he could get a grip on her. He immediately rolled onto his back and followed her down. The air whistled past him as he dodged the few bits of furniture that had been discarded by the citizens of Tenebria. Finally, he slid to a halt next to Tissa. He grabbed hold of her and held on as she slowly calmed her panicked clawing of the smooth metal giant hatch.

Faon braved a look behind and was relieved to see Albie picking Tissa up as she clung onto one of the lowest rungs, still terrified and refusing to move. She smiled as the shots about them eased, thanks to Reznor returning fire from his new vantage point above. She felt Sted's hand on her shoulder and gave it a quick squeeze, relaxing momentarily as the pair below her began making their way towards them, Albie's arm around Tissa giving her the confidence to re-start the ascent. The laser fire concentrated above them was now simply an irritating backdrop.

Without the extra distraction, they were able to make good progress and Faon was relieved to touch the bottom rung of the ladder up the side of the 'rubbish pit' they had just crossed. Glancing over her shoulder she saw Reznor, who at least, had had some success, as another trooper cried out before tumbling into the pit. Steeling herself she took a deep breath, coughing as she inhaled the stench of the pit, before scaling the wall. Reaching the top, she felt a shudder and her foot slipped before being caught by Sted's shoulder just below, steadying her. They both breathed a sigh of relief, pleased to be able to cling on. The laser fire instantly stopped as the lights changed to red and they became aware of a humming that they hadn't noticed building.

Albie braced himself as the tell-tale shudder of the opening doors registered. He pulled Tissa towards him as they both crashed onto the metal floor at the same time as the shuddering grew. Ignoring the vibrations, his hand scrambled for a hand hold. Hooking himself onto a rung to his right he caught a momentary breath only to wince a second later as the full weight of both bodies yanked his arm. He squeezed her as she shook. Her screaming in his ear had carried on for a while but even that died down to tiny sobs by the time he pulled them both uncertainly up on to their feet.

His arm wrapped itself firmly around her waist and, using all of his determination to keep them both upright and moving, he was able to make slow progress from rung to rung. Tissa began shaking and gasping for breath, not even Albie's arm provided enough comfort and he found it more and more difficult to hold on to her.

"We're nearly there; just hang on," he reassured.

Panicking, Tissa wriggled out of his grip and tumbled onto the metal. The force of the fall made her come back to her senses and she finally was able to think more clearly. Shooting out an instinctive hand she grabbed hold of a rung and clung on for dear life. Unbalanced, Albie could only cling onto the rung with her.

"Not again, please no…not again…" She pleaded, oblivious to all of his support: hope of avoiding the drop fading rapidly.

"You're alright, we are going to make it," he comforted, "But we've got to climb now!" He was shouting to make himself heard but she wasn't paying any attention. The rumble of machinery had grown louder than the humming and now the metal they were clinging to had started moving. Tissa began thrashing about for a handhold once again.

"Climb or we'll be back where we started!" Albie roared but she was beyond listening. In her mind they were going to fall back into the Underworld. If they survived the fall, she convinced herself then they would both be picked up and returned to the factory. Finally, she fainted. Just as she lost consciousness, her grip on the metal rung ended.

Albie hadn't planned for this but he instinctively grabbed her, wrapping both his legs around her waist as she began to slither down towards the widening gap. With Tissa now immobile, Albie turned his attention to his bag and a desperate search for inspiration.

He was relieved when all the hours he had spent scouring the city's rubbish dumps turned out to have not been in vain; pulling a coiled loop of rope from his bag. Working one-handed, he looped one end of the rope around Tissa, just below her arms before tying his best knot in it. He coiled it twice around the rung while the other end he tied around his own waist.

He then let go. He said a silent prayer to whoever might be listening as he dropped.

The gap between the doors was now widening rapidly, the earlier shuddering doors now swung smoothly open. As the gap between the giant hatch doors widened, their legs lost contact with the floor until Tissa and Albie dangled above the Underworld. Their weight was taken up entirely by the rope and the rung they had initially clung to: the only things that separated them from the yawning blackness below. There they swung to and fro, buffeted against the metal door at their side by the wind whipped around below them.

"At least she isn't struggling anymore," muttered Albie as he watched the small number of chairs, tables and household debris slide relentlessly downwards before disappearing. Above him the light was still flashing and any heat there had been in the pit had been lost. He couldn't see a way out. The rung above was too far to reach as was the rung below. He checked Tissa, she was out cold. At least one thing's going for us he thought. It was scant consolation because he didn't know how long the rope would last and, if they wanted to, the troopers could just keep the doors open until the rope snapped. The more he pulled the less his arms responded.   Just then, a chair appeared above him, glancing across his head as he too slumped into unconsciousness; the pair dangling from the single creaking rope.

21

Far above them, Faon, Tissa, Sted and Ordenne watched helplessly as the ground dropped from beneath their friends but were relieved to see the rope that had been coiled around the rung they had been hanging on to.

"Where are we?" Faon demanded as she searched for a way to help.

"This is a rubbish dump for one of the city blocks, each block has four – one for plastics and metal, one for food products, one for cloth and one for…" replied Ordenne.

"Get the picture." Faon answered, not wanting to entertain the idea of the fourth dump. "Where are they controlled?" She looked straight at Ordenne who was quickly turning out to be a most useful recruit.

"I think there is a control level that deals with each dump but I'm not sure where it is." Faon's head dropped slightly; perhaps she'd been expecting too much of Ordenne but it was Sted who brightened her mood by calling out:

"Could that be it?" They looked where he was pointing to one corner and sure enough there was a long row of windows virtually hanging from the ceiling, the only source of light that didn't flash unnervingly. Faon smiled briefly but once again that disappeared as she realised they didn't know how to get up. Instinctively she once more turned to Sted who had taken hold of the bottom rung of another ladder. Their eyes followed it skywards where it eventually joined a walkway. Despite the flashing light they could see it lead to what looked like a door in the side of the control room. Faon nodded her approval at his sharp eyes and turned to Ordenne.

"If we can get you in there could you close the doors?" She didn't even wait for Ordenne's nod but lead the way, taking Reznor's domitor as she started the ascent, climbing through the first of a series of circular metal rings that repeated every metre or so up the ladder, big enough for one person to climb through.

"As soon as we get the doors shut, climb down and get them…" she ordered to Reznor and Sted. She was about ten metres up when she stopped suddenly before calling down, "…And be careful."

With that she was gone and the two men turned their thoughts to their friends below: now obscured by the swirling smoke and shadows below. The only good piece of news was that they could just make out the taut rope dangling either side of the rung. They could only pray that Albie and Tissa were on each end and were still alive.

Fleet of foot and adrenaline pumping, the two girls were soon racing along the gantry, Faon prepared for anybody appearing through the door ahead. They reached the door unhindered and took a quick moment to catch their breaths. Ordenne leaned against the protective rail that ran either side of the walkway and peered down upon the figures they had left just a few minutes ago. Narrowing her eyes, she could just make out two shapes still dangling, it had to be them. She turned to let Faon know but she was at the door, pressing the domitor against the panel at the side of the door. It slid open and they slipped in.

The two occupants of the room jumped; surprised at the new arrivals but that was all they were able to do as Faon waved her domitor to indicate it would be a bad idea to do anything but sit still.

"On the floor! Now!" She enjoyed adding the last bit as it gave her a sense of power she hadn't enjoyed before. Being in charge was good fun, she decided, as the two poor individuals, clad in orange overalls and obviously not familiar with anything but disposing of rubbish, did as they were told. They certainly looked extremely unlikely to put up any sort of fight.

"Which computer closes the doors?" she demanded. "Our friends are down there so you better hope that nothing happens to them…" Faon's sudden cut off achieved the right element of threat and both immediately pointed Ordenne in the right direction.

The room was circular and contained a ring of computers spread around the outer rim while in the centre stood a closed pair of doors set into a cylinder-shaped wall. They looked amazingly like the circular body of a lift. Ordenne sat down on a black swivel chair that she could push along from panel to panel. Faon watched her examining the computers and wondered whether she knew what she was doing.

The two men, still spread on the floor, were watching too as Ordenne's fingers soon began gliding across the keyboard and dials virtually without touching them, and all three voyeurs waited to see if she could in fact close the doors.

Ordenne's fingers started typing slowly, gathering speed before they finally relaxed. With a shudder the bay doors started swinging shut and Faon smiled, turning to look at the men who were as relieved as she was so they returned the compliment. She realised she was being too friendly and immediately frowned angrily at them, waving her domitor aggressively. This did the trick as they buried their heads into their outstretched arms and remained motionless.

The red flashing light stopped and orange returned. Reznor slipped down towards Tissa and Albie who were still lying ensnared in the rope: oblivious to their imminent rescue. He shook the bigger one.

"Come on Albie, you big lump, that's enough hanging around for you." When there was no response he shook him again. This time there was a slight groan and Reznor let out the breath he had been holding. As Albie's eyes opened he couldn't quite believe he was still alive.

"Well I can't be dead because if I was you would

have to be the ugliest angel I have ever seen."

"You will be in a moment," Sted replied as he joined Reznor and began untangling them. "We've got visitors." Tilting his head, he indicated the troopers gathering above them on the side they had originally escaped from.

The next moment they were subjected to a bombardment as shots zipped everywhere around them.

"Thank goodness nobody taught them how to shoot." Reznor laughed pulling Albie onto his feet. The pair of them took hold of the still peaceful Tissa while Sted brought up the rear, armed with Albie's domitor.

"Don't forgot the rope – useful stuff that is!" Albie ordered Sted, who wasn't too pleased about having to get nearer to the edge of the bay doors. Even so he wasn't going to argue with Albie.

Help arrived from above as Faon showed her own skill picking off troopers at will from her vantage point on the walkway. The fire fight that ensued allowed them to make their way up to the control room with Tissa, tied to Reznor's back with the recovered rope. She barely registered the odd bashes on her head from the ladder's protective hoops.

"Where to next?" asked Sted as they emerged into the control room, stepping over the two forms on the floor who had long since stopped doing anything but lying still.

"The lift?" suggested Ordenne as she stood leaning matter-of-factly at the centre of the room.

"Good thinking" chorused the others as they headed over to join her. As soon as domitor met panel the doors slid open. Faon was just about to step in when she paused and turned to the two on the floor.

"Where does this go?" She asked, still maintaining her air of authority with them. They shuffled around to face her; still lying flat.

"From h…h…here to the locker rooms and showers, that's all, another lift takes you up to the ground floor."

Sted ushered Faon inside then he too stopped, studying the computer banks around them. As he did so the pair on the floor quickly dropped their heads to the floor, tensing up once more.

"Couldn't we use these to get our new identities…?" Ordenne was quick to halt him with a shake of the head.

"Not connected to the central computer, need to get to one of the living blocks – some of those computers will be connected." With that the lift doors slid shut and finally their two prisoners were able to relax.

"Thank goodness she's gone…bit pushy, wasn't she?" One decided.

"I don't know," replied the other "She certainly knows how to get her own way; she'll go far that one!"

"Yep, all the way to the locker room." They both agreed this was the funniest joke they'd heard for years as hysteria set in and remained on the floor, giggling, right until the room was filled with irate and humourless troopers.

It was unusual to see any technicians during the day outside of their workplace so it was quite a shock to see six emerge from a lift into the plush lobby of block 2904. The lobby was filled with the young people of the city enjoying an evening drink, all gathered around the brightly lit drinking points in the block's recreation level. Musical beats boomed out of every side while various shades of the same - coloured lights flashed in time.

These had to be the weirdest, unkempt and smelliest technicians the city had ever employed thought many of the residents of the block as the workers emerged from the service lift, not that anybody had ever seen any technicians before. There was also the feeling that giving jobs to those sorts of people perhaps wasn't very hygienic and why had they come out when normal people were enjoying themselves: why did it have to be in their block? It was disgraceful!

Of course, it made no difference to Albie and co. who casually climbed up the plush carpeted stairs that led up either side of the entrance to the shopping zone and its flashing display windows.

The out-of-place group left the revellers below without a word but if anybody had taken the time to study their faces, before shielding their eyes from the disgusting sight, they'd have noticed a distinct air of satisfaction that such lowly workers should never have experienced.

Once out of sight, the group quickly scurried up the stairs, finally emerging onto a functional foyer. The carpet was still plush but the walls were bare except for a row of screens that featured pastel patterns floating from one screen to another across the foyer as if the patterns were all joined. As they twisted they gradually changed shape: calming and somewhat mesmerising. Downstairs, everything seemed brighter from the glittery walls to the artificial plants that gradually changed colour: giving the impression of flowers without the need for the unpleasant smells that natural objects had.

Tissa had always liked the smells they gave the plants in her old block – always the latest scents. On her return to her former world she hardly gave them a thought. She was too intent on leading the rag tag crew to the nearest computer without attracting too much attention. She was under no illusion: their entrance would be reported, someone would have complained the second the lift doors opened?

"The Edu-suite!" she announced as they eyed up each of the lift doors that opened out onto the hallway. "There are so many computers there…"

"They're all connected to the city computer so that the council can keep an eye on the youth… and the teachers: telling them what they should be teaching,"

Ordenne interrupted her, annoying Tissa. "Just to make sure neither were getting any strange ideas."

"Which way, then…?" asked Faon, trying to

hurry Tissa along.

"Not one hundred percent sure but if it's the same layout as my block then…" she stopped as she realised for the first time that it was no longer her block. Her flat, the one she had shared with her mother, would probably be repaired and somebody else be moved in; they wouldn't have a clue what had happened to the previous residents, or care. After all, why should they? Tissa and her mother never knew who had lived there before them. Had those before her been taken away for not fitting in or talking to the wrong people?

"Well…?" Faon's tone was gradually changing as she became more anxious: the urgency in her voice jolting Tissa back to reality. They were standing at a crossroads with a choice of three destinations: each identically decorated with calming pale blue walls and carpets. The glare of the strip lights embedded into the ceiling meant there were no shadows to hide in and the picture frames on the wall were now screening live views of the city to remind them that numerous hidden cameras would be watching their progress.

Tissa nodded to indicate a left turn and they followed her. Albie was suspiciously studying the corridor lights above them; not comfortable at the way they switched off and on as they made their way.

They soon stopped in front of a door, identical to all the others but with a small square pane of darkened glass in it. Albie was about to tap the plate by the side with his domitor but Ordenne stopped him. "Use those to open the door and they'll know for sure where we are: they have probably got alarms set for our weapons…"

Huddling around the door, they waited as Ordenne began tapping codes into the control panel. The longer she typed the more anxious she became. Everyone waited expectantly but the door remained shut. Faon resisted the urge to remind Ordenne of the need for urgency: she needed no reminding and it was with frustration that she had to admit defeat, slumping to the floor.

"Those are all the codes I know, unless anybody's got any bright ideas?" Her head dropped into her hands as she racked her brain for ideas without success. "Must have specific education codes…" her voice tailed away, their scheme was in danger of falling apart.

The others looked around the corridor for inspiration but there didn't seem to be any way in until Sted felt a tap on his shoulder. He turned around to see Albie studying an insignificant-looking panel in the ceiling. Sted nodded before cupping his hands together to make a foot-hold. Albie stepped into Sted's hands but he couldn't support the younger man's weight so promptly dropped him to the floor. Albie collapsed onto the prostrate Sted who, despite looking distinctly embarrassed, was muttering something about "boys these days" being "heavier than they looked" and how "If his hands hadn't been so sweaty."

It was Tissa who reacted quickest, making Sted look even weaker. Leaning against the wall she cupped her hands together on top of a bent knee. She called for

Albie. He swiftly obliged and in one motion was able to quickly push the panel up before pulling himself into the darkness: much to Tissa's relief. A hand dropped down as he reached out for Ordenne.

"Come on, we'll take the back door." He called down. Gripping hold of Albie's wrist, she braced herself as he lifted her up; with the help of a couple of hands pushing from below that didn't exactly meet with her approval.

"I could have done it on my own!" she called back indignantly. The sounds of feet banging against the thin metal walls of the shaft alerted them to the possibility of discovery. It was Faon who spoke first:

"We're going to close the panel…find out what you can and we'll meet you back here."

With that, Tissa placed her back against one wall before bracing her feet against the other. Gradually she inched her back up one wall and feet up the opposite one until she was able to reach the opening in the ceiling. Watching spellbound the others held their breaths as her fingers felt for the panel inside the duct. With a slight grunt she was able to slide it shut, muffling the sounds of the pair of climbers above. Returning back to the floor, she stood up and dusted her overalls down: more through force of habit than anything else and was surprised to see the others watching her.

"I used to do it all the time when no-one was watching…it's the only way to travel." She shrugged as they listened to the sound of Albie and Ordenne making their way up the metre-square metal ventilation chute. That was, of course, except Sted who was sitting on the floor staring at his hands and arms.

"Well, it might buy them a bit of time!" decided Reznor but any further conversation was interrupted by Sted's alert:

"We've got company…" he called as the door slid open to reveal a couple of annoyed residents and two troopers. A smartly-dressed young man stood there in perfectly pressed and dazzlingly shiny green trousers, shirt and matching hair pointing at them.

"They walked up through our lobby, bold as you like, during daylight, just like that...we'll never live this down if the other blocks find out about this." As he spoke he gestured with a brightly coloured drink in his hand. "Could have ruined my afternoon…"

"What sort of a worker allows himself to be seen by his superiors?" added a similarly attired girl (with matching hair and drink). She seemed more annoyed that she had been dragged away from the merriment than anything else. "If you ask me…" she continued but the troopers were taking no notice of her, simply pushing the pair out of the way. "Hey, watch the outfit." She cried, grabbing the nearest trooper and spilling her drink as she did so. The trooper turned quickly round which made her stagger back.

"Delaying a trooper and defacing his uniform is an offence, citizen…go back downstairs…you have done your duty!" As he warned her, he wiped drink from his shoulder and drew his domitor. The door swished open and the pair of informers had disappeared through it, relieved to return to their friends.

They moved to the far end of the corridor where the four technicians were: one lying on the floor.

"Tell Bara Abus we have them in sight, only four it seems…send the capture wagons immediately." The lead trooper's radio crackled in agreement and the pair stood studying their prey; weapons trained.

"There is no escape, place your weapons on the floor…" the motley group didn't move. "Place your weapons on the floor, you are not permitted above ground, if you co-operate now you will make things easier for yourself." But the four didn't lay down their weapons or make a move.

More radios crackled above the beats booming out below them. Reznor glanced down at Sted still sitting on the floor then took in the troopers at the far end; they were nodding and he guessed it meant more uniforms would soon be arriving. Whatever happened they had to draw the troopers away from the pair clambering above them. They wanted him to lower his weapon so that's exactly what he did. Raising one hand above his head, surprising his friends as he did so, he slowly lowered his weapon towards the floor and onto Sted's outstretched hand. The moment Sted felt the metal handle rest in his hand, a bolt zipped along the floor towards the uniforms, striking one on the foot. This took both troopers by surprise and as he stumbled, he knocked the other. As the pair fell, a single blast struck the ceiling covering them in a shower of lighting, wiring, panelling and masonry. The thud of the heavier chunks of ceiling was bad enough but as they emerged from beneath the debris they were greeted by spitting, snaking wires dangling down.

Faon suddenly brought their audience to an end. "We'll need some transport when we're ready to get out of here so if Sted and I go for a wander to see what we can find, how about you two find another way out of here. Can't see them letting us leave the way we came in. what do you reckon…?" she turned to look at Tissa who was quite flattered by being asked and blushed, "…After all this is your home."

"There's only one way out that I'd like to use, but we'll have a look anyway." replied Tissa. "I don't like all this hanging around and we're a bit conspicuous as we are dressed so may as well keep moving."

"Seems fair enough," Piped up Reznor who was a bit put out he hadn't been consulted but then he had no idea about this world so it was probably just as well nobody asked him. With that they all set off along the corridor, leaving Sted standing alone and he too was put out that nobody had asked him either or even noticed that he was not following.

"Me too," He muttered to himself but a shout from Faon telling him to hurry up made him feel better. He started trotting slowly after them when he heard the sounds of movement behind him and his pace instantly quickened into a sprint.

By the time the two troopers had recovered, their quarry had vanished. The one whose foot had been scorched by Sted's shot sat upon the rubble, sprayed inside his boot and breathed a sigh of relief. Behind him his companion was pulling his weapon out of the rubble and brushing himself down and adjusting his helmet.

"We'd better find them quickly or there will be trouble. You can kiss goodbye to the idea of visiting any drinking points…we'll be working down in the factories tonight if we don't find them. So, come on." His foot no longer hampering him as much, the other pulled himself to his feet and headed gingerly behind his colleague. There was no way he was going to risk ending in a labour camp; it was bad enough guarding the no-hopers, never mind being one.

The corridor was empty when the unmistakeably commanding figure of Bara Abus stepped through the door and he simply glanced at the rubble as he glided up the corridor. He was drawn to a marked line that led along the carpet from the rubble and abruptly stopped. His eyes darted up and down the corridor as he searched for more evidence of battle but was disappointed to find there were none…someone would pay for this: not one shot fired by his troopers! The beats from downstairs still thumped out which seemed to irritate him even more.

"Where are the troopers who responded?" he asked the lead uniform following, who promptly pulled out a tablet shaped black computer. Tapping on the screen, uncannily at the same rate as the beats below, he was able to pinpoint the two officers, "They are just leaving the level: they seem to be in pursuit of four targets. There's something else…interference coming from somewhere…" He slowly scanned the area around them but Bara Abus was thinking ahead of him.

Studying the end of the burn he stroked the carpet then tapped the wall, his eyes walking steadily up them then above him and he found himself being drawn to the panel directly above him. There was something not right about it; was it shadow or dirt he could see?

"The panel…" he ordered and the trooper slowly pointed his scanning device up into the dark. Urgency getting the better of him, Bara Abus dislodged the panel with his domitor and it tumbled down to land at his feet. He barely batted an eyelid but concentrated on the darkness. The air pumping through the duct blew past him but Bara Abus stayed abnormally still: an icy stare studying the area lit by the light of his torch. A cold smile spread across his face. "How many?" he turned his gaze to the trooper's computer who shook slightly under the pressure, he was also feeling extremely nervous and warm.

"T…two…they are in the ducts" he managed to blurt out and the cruel smile on Bara Abus' face broadened.

"I've got you now…" he crowed quietly.

"Shall we follow?" asked the trooper, relieved to escape Bara Abus's stare.

"No," his lips curled around the word, pleased with his discovery "Activate the SPDRS."

22

The moment the panel slid shut plunging the pair into near darkness, Ordenne's bravery slipped somewhat.

"I can't do this," she announced. Albie stopped climbing and could just hear Ordenne gasping for breath above the eternal thumping. "We've got to get out; we're just sitting targets in here!"

She started scrabbling, trying to find the way out. Albie dropped down shining his torch on her. Her face was now soaked in tears and she looked exactly the same as she had when they had tried to help her at the factory: in fear for her life. She edged back against the wall of the tunnel. Albie gently took hold of her shoulders and she looked up, took a deep breath and managed to calm herself.

"We've got to do this, otherwise our faces will appear as those of fugitives on every computer and we'll be hunted down and when they catch us…there'll be a worse fate than the factory. You and Tissa deserve better." She managed an attempt at a smile and he smiled back.

"She's a lucky girl…" She started saying but suddenly stopped, realising she had said too much.

"Who is?" Albie had no idea what she meant.

"Tissa, she knew you'd come for her, kept telling me you'd come …" she cut off once again and was surprised to see he had absolutely no idea what she was talking about. Ordenne paused to think through his reaction then smiled. Thankful to have regained her composure again she pushed her back and feet against opposite sides of the chute above them and began easing her way up.

"Come on then." She told him, breathing slowly. Albie watched as she climbed before following, holding the domitor to light the way ahead.

By the time they reached the top and she could see a vent stretching in front and behind them, Ordenne's fears had been pushed to the back of her mind. She was now focussed on the task at hand.

For his part, Albie was trying not to think about finding out about his parents yet he was still wondering what had been so wrong about his father wanting to see him? He didn't hear the crash of the panel opening once again below them and that the one man who held the answers to all of his questions stood close by.

Bara Abus knew Albie was there. He felt only hatred towards this boy: a boy whose family had caused him the worst embarrassment he had ever felt. Never again! He would enjoy it when the SPDRS brought him down: it would be a moment to savour.

It was a strangely familiar feeling for Albie as they looked through the grille and down onto the empty school room. The room had the same dome shape and everything from the screens on the walls to the chairs sitting idly below them was the same as the place Tissa had brought him to. It seemed like another life time. How his life had changed – he now had friends and thoughts of his parents had returned: once they had just been a distant and painful memory that he had managed to ignore. Now, they were a source of hope.

It was easier to force the grille from inside the tunnel and after a quick rummage in his trusty and ever-present utility bag he was able to pull out his rope, just long enough to reach the floor.   For some reason he looked at the bag and decided it added a certain something to his orange technician's overalls: he could just hear Tissa's voice commenting about the colour combination and that got him thinking once more about Ordenne's earlier comment about Tissa, what was that girl doing to his head? She was suddenly, the most important thing in his life. He thought about her: but not in the same way he thought about the others. He was feeling mixed up; unlike anything he had felt before.

He returned to the rope in his hand and began the simpler task of tying it to the hinge of the grille.

He slowly lowered himself down the rope and was about half way down when he had to stop and take a breath. Following the rope up, he watched Ordenne uneasily following him down when he thought he heard a scuttling sound from the chute. Convincing himself it was just his imagination he looked once more at Ordenne who was by now nervously spinning, desperately clinging onto the rope with her eyes shut. Albie's faced dropped when he saw a SPDR scuttling out of the chute, its tentacles wandering around the room: searching. More and more of them appeared and as they did so the silence of the empty schoolroom was replaced by the growing sound of beeping as they all chattered away excitedly to each other.

Losing his concentration briefly, Albie plunged headlong, squealing as he did so, legs and arms frantically flailing to grab the rope. Managing to wrap his legs and arms around the rope he used his feet to slow himself down. His squealing changed to a muted scream of pain as his hands slid down the rope: the friction burning. Everything was happening in slow motion: the dive, plunge and burning. Albie could only think of gripping on tighter and when he crunched into the floor even the softness in the carpet couldn't dull the pain. He hardly had time to reflect on his lucky escape when there was a crunch next to him as the metal body of a SPDR landed, its antenna twitching as it readied itself to strike at the stunned figure of Albie.

Above, the dome was filled with more and more silver objects, spewing out from the chute in every direction, eventually covering the whole of the dome as the sound of hundreds of scuttling legs filled the room. Concentrating on not plunging down the rope, Ordenne was oblivious to both the creeping robots spreading out around the walls and the disorientated Albie. Making a mental note to lecture Albie about her fear of heights, she took a quick peek and instinctively screamed a warning to Albie.

The shrillness of her warning brought Albie back to his senses just as a metal clamp shot towards him from the SPDR. Throwing himself to one side he winced as it smashed against his shin. A second later another clamp brushed past his head. As the SPDR prepared itself for another strike, Albie leapt at it and in one motion managed to pick it up before hurling it at one of the windows that ran along his left.

As it bounced off the reinforced window, the SPDR's beeping turned into an angry clicking. Ignoring Ordenne, who had lowered herself tentatively to the floor, the other SPDRS swarmed towards Albie as they imitated their wounded comrade's call. The walls were now covered by a stream of silver bodies angrily bearing down on Albie; who was running out of floor space and was taking shots at as many of the leading pack as he could. He was completely surrounded and hopelessly outnumbered. Climbing onto one of the flying chairs he tried to remember how to switch it on with one hand, as he fired his domitor with the other, but was having little success with either. Giving up his attempts to work it he climbed onto the back of the chair, hoping to buy himself some time to think but instead found himself being tipped back as it fell onto the floor scattering SPDRS as it crashed. As the chair did so, Albie felt the domitor fly out of his hand. Lying sprawled on the floor once more, he found himself staring into the burning eyes of a SPDR readying itself to lunge. Unable to move he braced himself for its attack.

The strike never materialised as the metal arachnid froze. All around him the SPDRS that had been intent on his capture were now meekly scurrying back up the wall. The floor was soon cleared as they made their way back into the chute. Preparing himself for some other form of attack he pulled himself from behind the overturned chair and thought of Ordenne. Hunched over a computer terminal, she was furiously typing without a second glance at the retreating bodies.

A relieved Albie stared at Ordenne.

"SPDRS in search of a fugitive once attacked a class of students. There was such an outburst from the residents that the ruling council programmed the schoolrooms with an override." She calmly informed him. "It will buy us some time but we'll have to work fast." Shaking his head in disbelief and still reeling from his fall, he checked his arms and legs and was reassured to find out that they were still working.

"That's a useful tip to know," he replied coolly and sat down, staring at the chute into which the army of SPDRS had just retreated.

Ordenne didn't even giving Albie a second glance. Instead she was settling herself down once more at the main computer for the schoolroom. She paid him no attention as he wandered over then hovered behind her, shifting from one foot to the other nervously. He wondered whether to ask her about his parents now or leave it until she had finished giving them all new identities: just in case he put her off. He froze as she stopped typing, appearing irritated, and looked at him.

"Why don't you see if there is another way out of here or something we could use to help: I've overridden the door controls so I'll be safe."

"Okay, just holler if you need anything…" he started but she was engrossed in the screen once more.

Glancing about him he noticed a door that wasn't the door to the corridor and tiptoed gently towards it, resisting the urge to curse as he tripped over a trailing wire from a pair of head phones. He never noticed Ordenne's chuckle at his lack of stealth or her sigh of relief as he disappeared into the other room.

He never thought he would emerge into a room as big as the one he found himself in. Such an insignificant door shouldn't have led to this vast hall. On either side of him and opposite were rows of banked seats with tall see-through panels in front of them, separating the seats from a curved floor that banked around the edges. Two of the panels made a door to the main floor of the hall. The floor itself was smooth, white and covered in scratches. At each end of the hall stood two waist-height rectangular boxes with what looked like metal nets around them. Albie's feet echoed as he stepped from the tunnel that was made by the seats above and either side of him. Directly opposite was a similar tunnel with similar doors, also open.

A huge box hung down from the ceiling with what looked like screens on each face. Either side of the box bright banners hung down. There were funny squiggles on them but his crash education course only taught him how to talk to and understand other people: understanding these squiggles was a different matter. At the very top of the opposite bank of seats was a row of transparent panels.

He felt uncomfortable with all this space and

couldn't shake the feeling that he was being watched. He glanced up at the panels opposite: had he seen a shadow move? Dismissing it as his imagination he set off for one of the boxes with nets at the ends of the room. Every step boomed out, he just couldn't find a way to move quietly, every few steps he glanced up above him but still couldn't make anything out. He felt the tiniest breeze sweep past his neck, immediately he spun around to see the banners flutter slightly. Studying them, he decided they definitely hadn't been moving before. Abandoning his decision to investigate one of the net structures, he set off back towards the tunnel. Just as he was about to step through the open doors, the screens on the box above lit up and he could hear cheering, although the seats remained eerily empty. The noise from the haunted seats was joined by that of a trumpet announcing something: but what? The doors swung effortlessly closed in front of him. Pushing them he started to panic as he realised he couldn't get them open.

Reaching inside his bag he realised his domitor wasn't there, he must have dropped it in the school room. The panic spread and he tried jumping up at the panels but he couldn't reach the top, all he managed to do was get half way before sliding back down.

Glancing above him he could see moving pictures of a cheering crowd and he recognised they were in the same hall he was in: with the same net things at the ends. The opposite tunnel doors were open but he decided he definitely didn't fancy going that way.

Searching for a foothold to help him over the doors, he kept on sliding down as the crowd bayed in the back ground, the louder they grew the more anxious he became. His fingers clawed wildly and he felt trapped in a transparent prison. With one last effort he leapt against the panel, failing miserably and once more slid down onto the white floor. That was when the sounds of the crowd suddenly cut out leaving the only sound, that of an out-of-breath Albie gasping for air.

It was then that he heard a tap – tap – tap – tap coming from the tunnel opposite. Holding his breathe he tried to make out what could be making the noise but he had no idea. Through the opposite doors he could make out two red spots of light shining at him through the dark. They were getting closer.

Tissa and Reznor charged along corridor after corridor, passing numerous identical doors. After passing through the fourth identical passageway, Reznor noticed that the moving images on the walls were the same: from the scenes they showed to the order they appeared: there were the shots of the building: the plaza at the front of the block moving clockwise around the building then onto some obviously important super block, probably in the middle of the city, followed by the rooftop view across the city. Hydroponic farms completed each city block; feeding residents that had no idea where their food came from.

He suddenly ground to a halt and stared at the

image on the wall of ranked masses of Predavators in hangers underneath the farms near the summits of each tower block. Tissa was about to turn the corner when she noticed Reznor had slipped behind her.

"Look, I said I'm sorry, but I just can't remember much about the block I lived in, must have been the stuff they were pumping into us in the factory. In fact…" She paused, half thinking about her old life and why she couldn't remember much before Albie appeared. Turning to look at him she began to wonder why Reznor was staring at the picture of a brick wall. "…Come on, we've got to keep moving." She urged, trotting back to him. Looking at the picture she realised why he had been so fascinated by it.

"Our way out…if we can get up there! We could easily steal a Predavator…" Reznor paused: disappointed that she didn't seem so convinced by his plan. Best not discuss it with her now, he decided: act now, explain later. "Now all we've got to do is stop running around in circles and find the way up there."

Tissa looked about her; there was nothing they had passed that suggested there was anything to this block, just like all blocks, but endless doors: no difference in the colours or designs: uniformity ruled. Looking for inspiration, her mind was cast back to the monthly elections that would hold everyone's attention and be a great source of debate: even amongst the young. It all seemed so shallow looking back.

What made everybody so animated? Block identity and appearance. She now felt sick thinking that anybody could get themselves so worked up about the colour of the walls and the clothes they wore when there were so many below ground being flogged and drugged to satisfy the whims of those people above ground who would never know or care: unless they found themselves joining them. Just as she had.

She remembered how people who had never said a word to another soul suddenly wanted everyone to vote for their favourite scheme or idea. There was never really much to choose between the styles and pastel shades on offer but once the block residents had voted, the colours would instantly change: the walls, carpets even people's clothes. It gave people something to do and they thought they had control over the running of their own block. But the word that stuck in her mind was the word 'control' They let you choose the small things but everything else was decided and imposed upon you. If you thought about something more than "What outfit am I going to wear?" What happened? She'd now seen it all first hand. Her mother, what had she done wrong? Ordenne? She'd only dared to think differently and wasn't it everybody else that had pushed her into this: by ostracising her?

The people who met in the foyer to chat at the various drinking points followed the same routine each weekend: chatted, admired each other or simply stared into space, wrapped up in their own micro-world. Their whole week spent preparing themselves for just two nights: what were they going to wear? Who would they meet? How would they escape from themselves? Was that living?

When they were there, Tissa had seen them casually looking around, comparing themselves to everyone else, checking they had dressed appropriately. She looked at Reznor. Despite all he'd endured, just to survive, she envied his lack of dependence on anybody: his self-belief. You only had to look at him to realise that this city and its citizens were completely alien to him. Faon and Sted had once had to concern themselves but…

There I go again, she told herself, allowing myself to be sucked back into the city's way of thinking: becoming obsessed with the trivial because that was all they had to concern themselves with. But wasn't that the point? Tenebrians had no say in their life because everything was done for them whereas Reznor had had nothing done for him and had had to decide his own life. He had survived whereas she knew that she wouldn't have known where to start. Now she had been given a chance to live the life she wanted: with Albie and others. For the first time in her life she felt alive…present. It felt good.

She snapped back to the image on the wall she had, out of habit, previously ignored. Reznor was quietly tapping the image's frame, deep in concentration. She knew what he was going to ask so she jumped in before he even reached there.

"Listen, I've no idea where anything in this block or any other block is because I never went anywhere else but school and the shopping /entertainment level floor: you just didn't go anywhere else. Perhaps we should see if any of the others have come up with any ideas." Reznor was pleased she had said that because he didn't want to admit to not having a clue how to get out. The world below may have been hard and dirty but there was beauty down below that all these gleaming glass towers and perfectly arranged squares couldn't match. All he could think of now was getting out of Tenebria: anywhere was better than all this false perfection.

"At least we know where to get transport even if we don't know how to get to it..." He added.

They were about to return to the school room, when two dusty troopers appeared, one with a limp, and these new arrivals certainly looked pleased to see them.

"Now, place the domitor down slowly this time and no funny business." ordered the trooper with the limp, training his domitor straight at Reznor.

Reznor realised that he was trapped. He froze and cursed himself for letting his guard down.

22

Albie was wishing he'd curbed his curiosity, he should have sat down in one of those floating chairs but instead he'd had to go exploring and look where it had got him. The red lights grew closer and Albie slowly lifted himself onto his feet.

"If those are eyes..." He mused "...that's one big fellow there..." He frantically searched for a way out but the only way out he could see was past the rapidly approaching eyes. The eyes grew closer and larger and under the glare of the lights above he could make out the shape of a man…except it was nearly twice the size of a man (well twice the size of a small man but that was still considerably bigger than him. The tapping noise came from a stick that it was using to nudge along a hard rubber ball. The stick had a flat blade at one end and a long metal handle. The creature's boots had four thrusters on their base: two rows of four on each shoe, and the 'man' was now gliding effortlessly towards him. Albie could see that 'the man' was made of metal and his arms and legs were wider than Albie's shoulders. He was about to cry for Ordenne but noticed the door to the school room had shut behind him, she'd probably be too busy saving their lives…the irony of the situation gave him a wry smile.

"What's the point of having a new identity if you are not alive to use it?" he mumbled but the moment he opened his mouth he wished he hadn't as the new arrival, who hadn't taken its 'eyes' off him suddenly boomed:

"Speak up …!" it called out. "Come for some exercise? Where's your kit? No anti-grav skates? You must be confident…" With that he drifted over to one of two long seated areas that Albie hadn't noticed built into the panelling with low boards in front of them. He, Albie had decided it was a 'he' judging by the arrogant swagger, reached over the board easily and produced a stick similar, but much smaller, to his own and a pair of boots. Had he called them skates? "You'll need these," advised the metallic voice that was somehow familiar, but Albie couldn't figure out from where. "You're a skinny little wretch but we'll soon work you into shape. No pain...no gain. I'll make you sweat!"

He had taken his eyes off Albie and was now gliding up and down in front of the opposite tunnel entrance. Albie saw an escape route and was about to make a dash for it when the panelled doors swung shut sealing the two of them in together. Albie cautiously walked over to the boots, picked them up and examined them.

"Put them on!" came the order, patient but expectant. Albie found they fitted over his ordinary shoes and that once they were on the skates adjusted to fit snugly. "Come on, let's sweat!"

Albie thought his nervous state was managing to make him sweat quite nicely as it was without any help but decided it would be wiser to do what he was told. The next problem was the getting up.

Gingerly easing himself onto his feet, he noticed a round dial with markings on each of his skates. Studying the figure gliding slightly above the cool floor he studied the dials once more. Bending over he turned one of the dials and his left feet rose from the cool floor, toppling him face-first onto the cool surface. Sitting down he turned the second dial and felt his right foot drift up, as the metal monster continued to glide back and forth with growing impatience. Leaning against the transparent panels he pushed himself onto both feet and was happy just to be upright.

The next stage was to attempt a step forward. As the figure in the background continued its skulking vigil, Albie watched how he moved his feet. Albie pushed one foot forward but as it slid forward the other foot seemed reluctant to follow and he crashed to the floor, ending up with his feet further apart than he imagined they could go. A stab of pain shot through his body: this was not going well.

Recovering a little he watched as the figure casually drifted a few centimetres off the ground: it certainly looked easy. Easing himself back onto his feet, Albie took a deep breath and tried to follow suit. To his surprise he too was gliding over the floor, this time angling the boots to use the thrusters to push against the ground. Too late he realised he had no idea how to stop and crashed into the transparent boards, collapsing into a bruised heap, oblivious to the taunts being aimed at him from the other end of the hall.

There wasn't any time to recover when a black spherical object smacked into the board above him. He instinctively pulled his head in then rolled over as another slammed into the panel to one side of him.

"I said I want to see some sweat…! Get up!" there was an edge to the voice now – he was at the end of his patience. Albie grabbed hold of the nearest panel and leaning on his stick he managed to pull himself up. He fought his feet as they tried to drift in different directions. Another ball flew at him and glanced off his hip. He gasped, turning to see his opponent picking out another ball from a bag on his back. This time he got the message and managed to make his way slowly towards the far net, he had no idea what he was going to do but decided it would be better to get as far as possible from this maniac. Another ball thumped into his shoulder but he only winced, preferring to concentrate on keeping moving.

"So, fancy yourself as a goalie, do you?" it snarled and bizarrely it was at this moment that Albie realised where he recognised the voice – it was the voice that he had heard when he had first learnt to talk: the same voice that he had mimicked as a child then forgotten until his refresher course. He hated that voice and now it was flinging objects at him for fun.

He was finding it easier to move in his boots and as he drifted down to the metal netting an idea came into his head. Another ball whizzed past him. In the background the jeering continued but it suddenly stopped when Albie turned around to face him. Albie simply stared at him, trying his best to not to look annoyed.

Another ball was unleashed from the giant's stick but this time Albie used his stick to deflect it aside, he repeated this a second and third times before he heard his opponent congratulating him…or was he goading him?

"Good block boy, but let's see how you deal with these…" Albie held his breath as another shot blurred straight at his head; up came his stick and the ball pinged away. The next shot rocketed into his chest and he was thrown back, his spine crashing into the box that the net hung down from.

"Didn't like that, did you?" sneered the shooter

but Albie said nothing; instead he pulled himself up to his full height, trying to look undaunted. This only spurred his opponent on. "See how you like these…" With that he emptied the remaining balls in his bag onto the floor and like a whirlwind fired ball after ball at Albie. By the time the bombardment was over Albie lay on the floor, blood dribbling from cuts to his head and body. His legs and arms ached and he just couldn't summon up the energy to get to his feet.

"Get up you, lazy worm…nobody lies down in my lesson!" He started speeding towards Albie, still pouring insults at him, telling Albie he wasn't sweating enough.

A need to survive took over and Albie pulled himself wearily to his feet, the giant was heading straight towards him. Albie skated himself, slowly building up his momentum, this seemed to please his opponent.

"So, you've got guts after all have you? I like a good fight." Albie had no intention of fighting and as they drew near each other, he threw himself full length to the side of the careering body. Metal body crunched into metal bar and as the chain netting rattled its disapproval Albie could see red eyes growing darker, angrier. Ignoring the pain from his many bruises and cuts he managed to drag himself to his feet.

Glancing at the balls lying randomly about the metal man's feet he realised what would happen next. Turning as quick as he could, he tried to get as much distance before the inevitable happened. Ball after ball screamed past him, even they seemed to be angry with him, he daren't turn around and just kept skating until he reached the far end. He hadn't noticed the balls had stopped but as he collapsed onto the floor once more he thought about Ordenne feverishly working on the computer: still blissfully unaware. How long could he keep this up? It was an effort to stay upright, never mind the psychopathic robot trying to pulverise him…oh, and there were the cuts and bruises as well!

His heart sank once more as the tap-tap-tapping resumed: this time it was the sound of stick on floor. He had to try something. He couldn't keep on avoiding it for much longer. Summoning his energies, he pulled out his faithful rope and tied it around the bar he had been leaning on. Skating slowly at first, he built up his speed and managed, miraculously, to stay on his feet whilst holding the other end in his hand. He was delighted when he made a move to swerve to his left, narrowly avoiding the stick aimed at his stomach. Albie then skated to the creature's opposite side before looping back around to its front, ensnaring it in his rope. With one last desperate tug he pulled it tight and the huge body tumbled to the ground, momentarily stunned.

Albie didn't have a clue what to do next but a shout from the seats above told him "…Back of the head!"

Without looking to see whose voice it was he raced over and could make out a panel in the flailing monster. Before it could swing a fist or stick at him he yanked it open and speared the tangle of wires inside with his stick. All its struggles ceased: arms and legs drained of life. Albie collapsed on top of it and panted – every part of his body throbbing with pain.

In his head he heard another type of throbbing, totally different – a beating sound…clapping…yes; that was it, clapping…someone, and it was only one person, was vigorously applauding him.

He raised his eyes slowly and although he was having difficulty focussing, the voice of Ordenne filled the hall, reverberating with its shrillness.

"That was brilliant – I've never seen anybody beat him like that…way to go! I wished I'd seen it all"

Albie couldn't believe she'd not helped him before now and as the transparent doors swung open once more his mind drifted away into a world where he wasn't battered, bruised, being shot at or hanging above a gaping chasm.

"How about you put that 'borrowed' weapon of yours down on the floor, just where we can see it? This time if there is any funny business from you, big man, it's your little friend who will be the one to suffer." warned the further – most of the two filthy troopers. Tissa shrunk back against the wall but that was as far as she got as she bumped into an armoured body that grabbed her and pushed her to the floor. Reznor knew he could take no chances and gingerly lay the domitor down. The moment he did so the corridor was filled with the sounds of radios. Orders and reports were exchanged with unseen commanders but they knew exactly who would get to hear about them.

Reznor was pushed forwards and a boot, dirtier

than normal, was placed firmly upon his head. He didn't give the slightest bit of resistance as he looked at Tissa's panic-stricken expression. Responsibility overwhelmed him, much the same way it had when he had discovered Faon and Sted, he knew she was looking at him, almost pleading him not to do anything silly: they'd been lucky once but now was the time for restraint. He found himself surrounded by more and more shiny and well-cared-for boots. Out of the corner of his eye he could see Tissa's temporary sigh of relief replaced by fear, her memories of factory-life still strong, if a little hazy.

The next moment he was being roughly lifted to his feet, a black gloved hand clasped tightly to each arm. Both arms were then wretched behind his back; resisting the urge to fight back he ignored the pain and focussed upon Tissa. Catching her attention, he winked and she responded with a put-on smile. Troopers swarmed in between them and soon all he could see was the back of her head. Tissa had six troopers circling around her and Reznor became desperate to keep her in sight, not knowing how she would cope if they were separated. She looked back at him, pleading for him to follow and he found wishing himself forward; he was beginning to panic: he was failing her.

She had trusted him to protect her.

Albie had trusted him.

How could he protect her if he wasn't with her?

His mind was filled with escape but he fought every instinct.

Just as Tissa's guard stepped out of sight he felt

his own group move: following. Relief swept over him. They headed back along the corridors, past angry onlookers who appeared to enjoy assuming the worst: some shouting "terrorists", others claiming they would have "murdered us as we slept". The troopers embellished everything warning them to stay away for their own good. There was none of the restrained and timid abuse from earlier on: Tissa's and Reznor's scruffy appearances undoubtedly didn't help but once the troopers had them under close control the two prisoners were fair game: the voyeurs appeared like a pack of animals sensing a fallen prey: easy pickings for those who wanted to vent any pent-up aggression. Volleys of abuse, food and drink rained down. Not one drop or piece of food hit any of their escort. Reznor couldn't see whether Tissa was coping with the abuse but he knew she'd be thinking about the unfairness of it all. It was a relief to leave the residents behind as they stepped through an anonymous door and into a cold, draughty shaft. Ladders with moving rungs rattled upwards and downwards in front of them before being swallowed by the dark. It was at this point that they were both released and Reznor could see Tissa was visibly shaken by the experience. All he could do was smile encouragingly; a line of troopers still forming a barrier between the pair. Two troopers stepped onto the rungs heading downwards, leaning back onto the rungs as they did so.

"You! Now!" Ordered another; pushing Tissa forward. Unsure, she shuffled forward so she was standing next to the ladder. Glancing back, she was given a further shove. Steeling herself she stepped onto a rung, instantly grabbing hold of another as she did so. She clung on as the floor disappeared beneath her. More troopers followed swiftly behind her, along with Reznor and his guards.

They emerged into a plain lobby with metal grilles on the floor, still surrounded by their guard. There was none of the colour or vibrancy of the front; this was most definitely the worker's entrance. If only they had been real workers, things would have been a whole lot better!

23

Somehow Faon and Sted found themselves back at the stairs that curled down to the front entrance of the block. Crouching at the top, hidden by the broad, ornate balustrade, they thought through the alternatives.

They knew the moment they wandered down the broad foyer stairs there would be a multitude of socialising residents messaging the troopers because their evening had been spoilt by *another* sight of someone who wasn't in the least bit pleasant to look at or fashionably dressed. What was the city coming to if you had to see these lower lifeforms?

The alien pair had thought their disguises as workers would serve them better than their escaped prison outfits. How wrong could they have been? They had been below ground so long they had forgotten that workers were never meant to be seen. Lights were fixed, appliances repaired but nobody ever saw anybody actually doing anything. There must have been another way for the repair teams to move around.

"Did you notice any ways into the building, other than the one we came through?" mused Faon as they both studied the revellers mingling freely below them. Sted shook his head and pulled his bottom lip over his top one just to add extra emphasis to his answer. Faon expected this answer and simply turned her head back to the crowd. The lights in the foyer had now been lowered so that the only illumination was provided by the coloured flashing lights that winked hypnotically to entice more clients to make use of the drinking points manned by patiently attentive and efficient robots. The humanoid-looking figures mirrored everything about the figures demanding their attention except for their metallic faces that shone in the flickering illuminations. The tables both inside and out were surrounded by groups of young adults coolly chatting nodding in time to both conversation and musical beats, preening themselves and their clothes whilst continuing to run the rule over each other: always on the lookout for someone interesting to talk to. Faon had decided that they could easily have made it back to the door they had originally come through but she wanted to check out a theory that was throwing itself around her mind.

"Can you hit that light with this driver?" she asked, pulling a metal tool out of her pocket and pointing it at a lamp positioned at the end of the banister below them. It was dimly glowing to indicate the start of the steps but could clearly be seen. Sted nodded, sizing up the driver in his hand, turning it over before gently throwing it up and catching it a few times. He took aim at his target. Faon held her breath: not wanting to admit to doubting her friend's ability. She clutched the metal bars of the banister before her as the bar flew through the air, striking its target dead centre. The sound of exploding glass was masked by the beats that bounced around them and as both bar and lamp fell, Faon pointed at it with great satisfaction. She indicated her own eyes and then the smashed object to tell Sted to keep his eyes on it.

Her own eyes were scanning the walls but every time she tried to focus coloured blotches swamped her: thanks to the lasers that were now projecting the names of drinks and snacks on every available space; safe in the knowledge it would increase their sales for the night. Blinking constantly, she just couldn't see past them and wished she could blow them away. Rubbing her eyes, she took one more look in some vain hope that she could spot anything but her eyes just wouldn't help her. Disheartened, she planted her chin onto the rail of the banister as she slowly closed her eyes. She drifted away: remembering. Her rescue from the cave, the factory and re-capture, Bara Abus and Albie, their escape from the underworld: the more she remembered the more her head began to swim as lack of rest began to catch up on her.

It was just then that she felt Sted nudging her. Pushing her memories aside she shook herself awake, following the finger pointed at the remains of the light he had vandalised. There at the foot of the banister, unnoticed by all the revellers, were two SPDRS, one sucking up all the glass shards with a pipe attached to its abdomen while the other appeared to be scanning the damaged object. A young couple drifted hand in hand to the foot of the stairs and as they did so the two metallic creatures scuttled into the plants at the side of the stairs and the pair drifted upwards, oblivious to everything but themselves.

With the couple out of sight, the repairs continued as did the spying mission. They watched expectantly as one creature scuttled back into the synthetic foliage and returned with a new plexi-glass piece that it carefully screwed into place. Sted carefully eased his way down the stairs, maintaining visual contact while Faon watched the workers from above, hoping to see where they went. To her delight she watched the pair scuttle back into the imitation plant-life but sighed as they disappeared from sight. Checking nobody was watching, she hurried down the stairs herself, using the banister to provide some cover. Pulling plastic leaves away from the spot she had last seen the metal insects she joined Sted. He was peering into a small flap in the wall, just big enough for a person to crawl through.

"Bingo" she whispered gleefully before grabbing hold of him. To his surprise, she kissed him firmly on his cheek. In the dark, Faon never noticed the smile that spread across his face. She pulled herself through the tight gap unaware of the way his eyes followed her as she disappeared.

The irony of the situation they found themselves in wasn't lost on Reznor: here they were in front of the back door they had been fruitlessly searching for but had as much chance of leaving by it as they did of being accepted by those revellers upstairs. Reznor could sense Tissa's fear even though they were still separated. She was just staring stoically at the ground. He began studying their surroundings, praying for a miracle, but kept glancing occasionally at her wishing she would return his glance.

It wasn't that they were being pushed around or treated roughly by the guards; rather the sinister threat of their weapons, armoured bodies and visor-covered eyes. They didn't know if they were watching or not but neither prisoners nor guards moved so the longer the apparent stand-off continued the greater the tension rose and the more Reznor worried about his young accomplice.

Above them, the constantly rattling rungs disappeared into the gloom. Reznor was starting to fidget, tapping his foot to imaginary beats and whistling silent tunes: surely, they couldn't hold them like this much longer. What were they waiting for? Were they waiting for the others? Had they been caught? Two overall-wearing shapes emerged clinging to the ladders, chatting as they descended. Their laughing voices filled the hushed lobby but once they caught sight of the silent group the arriving workers' amusement faded away to be replaced by a respectful silence.

They couldn't bring themselves to look at Tissa and Reznor and waited at the foot of the ladders for permission to continue. A trooper shouted across at them; making no secret of his disgust for them.

"Where are you going?" he demanded with a sneer. The lead worker lifted a SPDR he was cradling in his arms as an explanation but when the trooper refused to respond he knew he was going to have to reply. He hated talking to the troopers – they held his kind in such contempt that he knew every word he uttered would probably be ignored and a waste of his breath but it was the end of his shift and a bed was waiting for him: not as comfortable or bright as the ones up here but it was his home. He was lucky because it had a window in it and was away from the sewers. It would take him a while to get through the tunnels to the outer regions of the city where the worker classes were housed so he wanted to get going as soon as possible.

He sighed before explaining.

"Been repairing one of the stair safety lamps in the main entrance." The trooper nodded slightly. Pleased with this response the overall-clad worker continued: "Got to take this little feller to be emptied..." He looked to see if his story was getting any further reaction: it wasn't. He carried on regardless. "Strange one…just blew as if something had been thrown at it." At this the trooper stirred and suddenly looked interested.

"When was this?" he snapped. The man on the step was flattered that he should be asked two questions in one night and forgot about the difference in class.

"Just an hour ago: auto sensors detected it, all cleaned up in record time and nobody saw a thing."

"Go on, but stay away from these two or you'll be joining them." replied the trooper curtly and they hurried off, pleased to be away.

The instant the order had been given he forgot about the pair scurrying away: it was bad enough he had to be in here, having to smell them, let alone talking to them.

"Control, have we footage from the foyer cameras where the safety lamp blew?" There was a low hum followed by a crackle as the radio sprung into life.

"Confirm that, watching it now…nothing unusual…lamp replaced…SPDRS away…wait a minute…worker out of position…on the stair…sending through enlarged image now." Holding the communicator, he opened the front panel and studied a screen, his mouth curled into a sneer as he waited expectantly.

"Inform Lord Abus that we have two of the escapees and have a sighting of a third, could be worth sending SPDRS to investigate."

"Confirm. Lord Abus is on his way." Replied the voice and he clicked the panel shut.

Turning to Reznor and Tissa his sneer became a contemptuous smile. "There's someone who wants to have a word with you." Reznor steeled himself as Tissa's head remained glued to the grill at her feet but he could see her hands were clasping tightly together like a vice: she was still fighting.

Albie lay on the floor, his anti-grav skates had been taken off and it was a great relief to be able to walk again. Ordenne was putting repair-strips, taken from a medi-bag kept in the school room, on his various bumps and bruises. The sudden cooling and antiseptic effect of the strips brought tears to his eyes. The robot still lay a few metres away: the wires Albie removed still dangling out of his head.

"So, did you manage to kill us off?" he asked as she dabbed at a long cut on his leg with a cloth.

"Yep, we are all officially dead – escaped prisoners, shot in the attempt. Funny though, couldn't find any record of Reznor. He just doesn't exist but now he does – he's called Rioch, a vid – seller. I found your record too: there was only one Albie who disappeared when he was seven along with his mother."

He looked expectantly at her, waiting for any news she had uncovered. "Oh...it's good news: your mum is still active: that's their word for alive. She's in the older female camp… not the one I was in. It's the one where they put the mothers of older children." Albie smiled with relief and nodded his thanks but his eyes still wanted more and Ordenne's chirpiness disappeared. "Tissa's mother is there too – they're both at the recycling factory!"

She paused to let him take in the news and her voice dropped as she began to tell him the rest.

"Your dad is a strange one. It was impossible to find anything about him; other than he is highly sought-after. It didn't say anything else: I've no idea why. I'm sorry I can't find out more." he shrugged and she squeezed his shoulder slightly.

"I didn't even think he was still alive, but it would have been nice to know more. I know one person who'd be able to tell me more…there's something familiar about that tall one." With that, Albie seemed to get lost in his thoughts.

Ordenne quickly thought how she could lift him and tried to be enthusiastic, piping up to break the silence:

"I've got you a new identity. You aren't called Albie any more, you are now called Addus and you're still at school. The others proved no problem, cross referencing the factory with their names – that was a well-spent night in that hideaway of yours, listening to all your stories, just as well I'm a good listener. Hope they don't mind but I thought it would be quite useful to have the others as lowly workers, thought it might come in handy sometime; hope they aren't too mad at me: I gave them good clearance levels. It seemed like a good idea at the time. Despite the fact that there were nearly ten years between them, Ordenne was babbling excitedly like a schoolgirl about her electronic achievements. Looking at Albie nursing his wounds she stopped. "Anyway, how are you healing?"

"Painfully."

Albie turned his attention to the metal man that had tried to kill him.

"What is he?" Albie said, pointing at the robot. He pulled himself to his feet and started poking and prodding the creature.

"Oh, he's one of the robot educators. Someone must have left him switched on; they usually get switched on just before a lesson by the central computer. I once snuck in during a lunch-time and reprogrammed the maths educator to show us vid-coms instead of having a class. I was nearly expelled for that one." She laughed but Albie was only half listening.

"You mean you can reprogram these to do to them what it did to me?"

"Sure: no problem. There are more over the other side. We had a different one for every sport, equipped with the specialised gear for their sport: the gymnast was very nimble and doubled as our kick boxing educator, there was the athletics educator – boy, could he throw…" Albie was away, rooting through the far changing rooms and staff rooms and his eyes lit up as he took in the rows of silent robots.

"But I want them only to attack the troopers…" he added as she withdrew to the school room to find some tools. She left Albie mulling over her information.

"So, mum is still alive and there's one person who can tell me more…" His train of thought was interrupted by a loud horn that echoed around the room as if it was being relayed to every room in the block.

"Attention citizens!" The moment she heard the source of the voice, she ran back to the room Albie was in. There was no mistaking the cold, evil strains of Bara Abus. Albie's face twisted to one of complete hatred and stared at the speaker positioned innocuously in a corner. "There has been an intrusion into the block by six escaped terrorists. Two have been apprehended. It is only a matter of time before the others are caught but if you see any intruders it is your duty to report them or you will be punished. Both faces dropped, who? How? They both knew there was more to come. "This is a compulsory message from Lord Abus." the voice continued. They sat motionless in anticipation. They knew there was worse to come as the pause grew.

"This is Lord Abus with an announcement for the terrorist called 'Albie' remaining in the building," His voice snarled then paused "We have your young friend, such a shame she will have to be executed along with her companion: unless you are in the plaza at daybreak. If you appear with your other friends then their lives will be spared. I do dislike wasted lives." The horn rang once more and with that the voice was gone: his insincerity plainly evident. It was still dark outside, but the full moon and the lights from the buildings that towered above the plaza lit up like day. In a few short hours they'd either have to give themselves up or put into operation a rescue bid. Spurred on, they tirelessly set about the robots, fully aware that they couldn't stop the rising sun.

24

Stepping out of the maintenance duct they had crawled through, Faon and Sted's first reaction was amazement. Multiple ducts stretched in every direction: transparent tunnels disappearing once they were out of range of the pale orange glow of the lamp above their heads. Each duct was big enough for two people to fit comfortably through with two tracks of moving rungs to cling onto: one track moving upwards whilst the other headed downwards: like two moving ladders. The whirring of motors and rattling rungs could be heard from each duct above the thudding music from the passage they had just crawled through. Although Sted didn't seem bothered by them, Faon winced as the beats invaded the calm of this secret world. She was able to breathe a sigh of relief once she had pushed the door closed. In doing so the outside world disappeared behind them and they relaxed for the first time since arriving onto the surface: soothed by the gentle rumbling of the rollers pulling the moving ladders along. Sted felt compelled to move to the nearest one and absent-mindedly started stroking its outer casing like it was a soft carpet. He could now feel the vibrations as he studied it.

"This is amazing, we could probably get to any other part of this building if we wanted…there must be about ten ducts coming from this one spot."

"How do we know which one to take?" Faon shrugged. There were no signs to read, the only difference in them was their colour. They were all different shades of red: running from a deep red: almost maroon, to a light, almost pink red. Trying to see into the dark was pointless as each disappeared long before its end was in sight.

"Try pot luck? What do you reckon to these colourings: what do the different shades mean?" Faon mused as Sted took a step onto a medium shaded track, clinging onto a rung as he slowly rose then disappeared from sight.

"Sted: no! We've no way of telling…" Faon's words were lost as his feet finally vanished but she could just hear his voice telling her something about "nothing ventured" and decided to follow.

There were small dots of light every so often but not bright enough to see further than their hands. Even feet became swamped by the blackness, so there was no way Faon could see her partner ahead of her. All she could do was hold on and prepare her speech about why Sted should have consulted her before he leapt onto the first track. They could end up anywhere she kept telling herself. This was so unlike him: what had come over him, he was normally so safe and predictable. The more she thought about it, the more she realised that what scared her was not that he had acted so rashly but that he could make decisions without first thinking of her. Ever since they had first met he had only thought of her and looking after her – she didn't need his help anymore, she was more than capable of looking after herself: was he making a point? She felt strange thinking that they might not be so inseparable but at the same time excited that a new stage in their relationship might be starting; a stage in which they were equals and not one person reliant on the other.

Glancing ahead of her, Faon could make out a brighter and larger orange light growing larger by the second. Her arms were starting to tire and the thought had crossed her mind of how high up she was and how far it would be to fall if she let go: which she had decided was not such a good idea. She also wondered how far ahead of her Sted was. She didn't dare call out in case she attracted any unwelcome attention. By now she could make out that the glow ahead was some kind of room and also the end of the line. She was able to breathe a sigh of relief as she made out a dark figure rolling off the track before quickly composing itself. She'd recognise Sted's figure anywhere: there weren't many who were as skinny as he was, even inside the factory.

Her eyes drew level with the room and she suddenly realised she didn't know how to get off. Her hands would soon lose their handholds and then what would she do? Walk them forward along the floor? Attempt to roll forward into the room? Neither method would convince anybody that she was meant to be there. Her hands walked their way down from rung to rung until her body was virtually folded in half and her back was scraping along the back of the duct threatening to pull her back down. At the last minute she neatly performed a forward-roll-come-belly flop onto the floor.

It wasn't much of a floor: more a platform hanging in mid-air. It was one great metal grille and being able to look at what was directly below wasn't comforting in the slightest because there was nothing there. The only sound they could hear was the chattering tracks as they disappeared into the ducts that led away from the platform. Sted had assumed, since he couldn't see much of anything, that there were no doors or walls here and that the only way off the platform was through two metal ducts either side of him that led off on the same level and another opposite that led higher still with more rungs to hold onto. The ducts that led away on this level were walkways that one person could stand up in but Sted wanted to go higher. The pair stood silently, catching their breaths in the middle of the systems of tunnels that surrounded them.   It was Sted who finally interrupted the amazed silence.

"Sorry for charging off, just thought one of us needed to do something." The apology made Faon feel a lot happier and she found herself dismissing it with a shake of the head.

"No, we could have been down there all day if you hadn't. Where do you think we are?"

"I think we're nearly half way up the building, judging how long we've been going so I think we'll need to take one of these ducts."

"Why's that then?" she was really beginning to be amazed by the way he had become so resourceful and realised she liked sharing the decision-making, letting somebody else do some thinking.

"Did you not notice the photos on the wall?" he asked but Faon looked blankly at him, unable to think about anything else but her aching hands and the soothing noise of the moving tracks.

"They were all showed various camera views of the block. The same views in every corridor." He was very pleased with himself and carried on, ignoring the bemused look on Faon's face. "Look at these ducts – they go upwards." He pointed at the ducts ahead then after pausing to organise his thoughts. "On the sides are the walkway ducts for this floor level." His thoughts were tumbling out but lacked any sort of order so Faon still wasn't following. He resumed the explanation. "The screens on the walls showed what was outside the building as well as a view from the roof…. on the roof of each of the blocks are rows of Predavators: our way out!" With that he pointed at the pipe opposite inviting Faon to go first.

"Okay but I want you to think of a better way of getting off these things because I don't fancy rolling out of these ducts and off the platform. So, you better get those gears in your head moving!" With that she vanished up the duct opposite. Not wishing to be left behind, Sted quickly followed: a not totally unfamiliar position for him to be in.

The only thing that changed was their exit method. They arrived at another platform with ducts leading off in four directions, but this time they worked out that as the track approached the platform there was a handle on the right-hand side which you could grab onto before one could put step onto the platform relatively successfully as you rose.

There was still no-one about, but by then it was the middle of the night: the best time for them to move around. The familiar shades of red surrounded them but there was still nothing to suggest where to go. They hoped that they were approaching the top of the building but there was nothing to indicate how far they had come or needed to. So, they took a few moments to rest their hands and catch their breath; simply listening to the chuntering rhythms all about them as they sat on the platform.

Sted investigated the ducts opposite and was surprised to see a pair of boots, then a pair of legs appearing. He relaxed slightly when he saw that the legs wore workers' overalls but he still hissed at Faon to warn her. She sprang up but there was nowhere for them to stand to make it look as if they were doing anything but standing around doing nothing. A face soon appeared and it was joined by another body seconds later. Sted backed away to allow the new arrivals some space and also because he had no idea how the new arrivals were going to act. He didn't fancy the idea of being pushed or grabbed by anybody on a platform with no walls and plenty of space to fall through.

The two groups eyed each other, trying to read each other's minds at the same time. The others both carried backpacks and were eyeing the duct behind Faon as she and Sted moved instinctively out of their way.

"Caught you!" laughed the first arrivee as Faon

exchanged nervous glances with her partner. "What are you slackers supposed to be doing? Travelling light?"

"Errr…" they both wracked their brains for an explanation but it was Sted who came to their rescue.

"Just in the middle of a job: need to get a couple of broken SPDRS." He coolly replied and he was relieved to see smiles materialize.

"Yeah, isn't that the truth, they've got all these ways for us to get in and out without being seen but can they get the equipment for us? Fat chance!" The taller of the two sat down on the edge of the platform with legs dangling over the side. "Good job there aren't any cameras here: perks of the job! We've been up top, helping with the Predavators, it's no wonder everybody behaves themselves: there must be at least 15 Predavators on every block roof." Faon joined him on the edge of the platform, making a determined effort not to look down and keeping a close eye on the other worker to see he wasn't too close.

"That's our next job after that: some tricky circuit problems." She piped in; making a quick mental note of the duct the pair had emerged from.

"I'd watch what you do up there, security is tight. They say Lord Abus is in the block: couldn't make out much but something about escaped prisoners from one of the factories, very dangerous apparently. A bit of excitement, eh? Better them than us!"

Faon nodded and jumped as he slapped her on the back, her hands instinctively gripping onto the gaps in the platform grill. Her heart was pounding: not daring to move but wanting to scream at the thought of plummeting over the side. She managed a strangled smile and tried to remain calm as the pair headed for the duct to take them down.

"Well, that's us done, off for a well-earned rest, when I manage to get home. Good luck and I'd get those ships finished before his Lordship arrives." With that they both left to continue their journey down and Faon was able to relax and take a deep breathe. Sted simply whistled.

"Do you hear that: it's this way to the roof. Let's get going." Forgetting her early nervousness, she swung her legs back onto the platform before springing towards the duct. Sted was more cautious but his call of "What about the security?" fell on absent ears as Faon's boots rose out of sight.

25

Bara Abus appeared through the only lift doors that opened onto the back-entrance foyer, flanked by four troopers. His upright form dominated the cool light that emanated from the lift. He took a cursory glance around, reminding himself how disgusting this area and those that used it were. He focussed on the two pitiful individuals surrounded by his troopers. This was the most secure place to hold them after the earlier fiasco so it would have to do while he interrogated them. It wouldn't take too long judging by the sorry state of the female. Yes, he'd start with her: no point wasting any time with the male. He would enjoy breaking him later but time was of the essence. The big one, however…he looked familiar: but from where? Abus stared at Reznor's face. Even in the gloom he could make out a weather-beaten face scratched out by the winds that whipped around the underworld and scarred by the chemical spills that littered it. This one had never lived above ground, unlike the girl who had known little else. He didn't remember the young female from the factory: but why should he? But the male? Abus marched up to Reznor; troopers rapidly parting to escape his piercing half-robotic glower. Abus's gaze never wavered.

"Yes, I remember you but there's more to you than our last meeting isn't there?" With that he brought out his domitor above his head, still studying Reznor's blank expression, before bringing it across his head. There wasn't a flicker of emotion as he watched Reznor crumple to the floor. Reznor lay motionless, tensing every muscle so that Abus couldn't gain any satisfaction from seeing the big man squirm. This angered him more so he kicked Reznor in the chest who groaned and that brought a smile to Abus's face.

"I'll enjoy continuing our friendship later but for now I need you in one piece." Turning to Tissa, who was unable to raise her eyes, he enjoyed seeing her shake with fear. Abus studied her; soaking up her fear. Clicking two slender fingers he held his palm out and one of the troopers who had arrived with him in the lift strode forward before placing a dark, transparent object on it. It had an abdomen from which protruded six silver, segmented legs and two long antennae with suckers on the end. His cold gaze concentrated on the shuddering girl. Stepping forward, his long legs needing only one stride to reach her, he held his open hand next to Tissa's shoulder and the creature did the rest, scampering onto her then climbing nimbly up her hair and onto the top of her head. Its antennae felt their way to her forehead before clamping themselves onto it. She gasped then tried to pull it off her but both antennae were stuck firmly and its legs had twisted themselves around her unkempt hair. She began to scream as she pulled frantically at it with no success.

"Now, I'd like you to think about your friends. Who are they? Where did you meet them? And most importantly where are they now?" snarled Abus. She dropped to her knees: screaming in pain. Reznor made a move to help but a light blue bolt from the nearest trooper paralysed him.

Abus pulled out the communicator that had been slung on his belt. He studied the screen and smiled as he saw pictures emerging of her first meeting with Albie. "There's a good girl, just keep thinking about him and the others…"

The track drew closer to the brightest light the pair had seen in this labyrinth of ducts. Faon suddenly wished she hadn't been so rash in following Sted as her courage deserted her. Shielding her eyes from the white glare she could make out the shape of four troopers standing idly around the door that she assumed led to the hanger. Trying to act coolly she leaned forward as her hands came away from the rung. Counting down she waited until the last minute to step confidently onto the platform. A thrill swept through her body as she managed to avoid stumbling or falling over, it was an emotion that wasn't shared by the waiting troopers who watched with a complete indifference. Sted followed with a slight stumble then they stood side by side wondering whether to approach or not: feeling extremely vulnerable and awkward. It was too late to back away without raising intense suspicion but they had lost the nerve to bluff their way in. Sted started fidgeting, realising that Faon was still carrying a commandeered domitor. It was then that the standoff was broken.

"Well, come on…let's have your retina scan…move it!" growled the obviously most senior trooper. "It was bad enough being posted this side of the door, never mind having to breath in your smell and that of your friends."

Neither of them dared make the initial step to approach the trooper holding what looked like an oversized light pen. Faon could only think about how they could possibly get away from these four and the domitor she had attached to the back of her overalls belt looked to be the best bet. The chances of them both surviving a shootout with four troopers was remote, especially given the fact that two of the four troopers were tapping their domitors irately and looked seconds away from shooting anyway. She started edging back but was amazed to see Sted stepping confidently forward even though inside his stomach seemed to be churning louder than a Predavator's engines and he was sweating profusely. Luckily, he was able to control himself, avoiding the urge to break down, throw himself on the platform and beg for mercy.

The foot and domitor tapping stopped and he held his breath, praying that Faon was ready with her domitor. He readied himself, running through a plan to kick their legs away, grab a weapon and…his mind went blank. He suddenly thought the plan had no chance of success and he was going to die: at least it would be quick.

He blinked furiously as the pen was shone into his eye, much to the guard's further annoyance but the bored trooper persisted, desperate to get rid of the two weirdoes.   His partner looked casually at the screen on his communicator in complete contrast to Faon and Sted.

"Don't you people ever wash?" one of the troopers taunted. "No wonder you aren't allowed out when normal people are around." The others ignored these comments as if it was his usual sport to insult the lower classed workers.

Faon's finger was twitching on the activation button when the lead trooper muttered:

"Here we go…" Sted's fists were clenched tightly and he could feel the sweat running down his fingers he was going for the one who told him he smelt, first. "This one's cleared. Come on then…" Sted was too stunned to take a step forward; it had to be a trick. "Come on you, you're next." Still clutching her domitor she stepped calmly forward, her heart was racing as she stared into the light: Ordenne had done it. For a brief moment her heart missed a bit as the offhanded trooper told she was cleared and the door swung open and wind whipped around them. The air felt so fresh, even fresher than the stifling heat at ground level and blowing as if beckoning them out. She felt like closing her eyes and inhaling deeply until she was brought back to the present. "Go on then, get out. We're freezing…Do some work will you?"

"Take your festering bodies out of here…" another called. Giving the troopers a broad beam they both stepped through and as the door slammed they were alone in the night: their first sight of the night sky in over ten years. What's more, in front of them stood fifteen silent Predavators moonlight glinting on dark fuselages, with nothing behind them but open space and freedom…the most beautiful ideal either of them could imagine.

<u>26</u>

Reznor held onto the nodding Tissa. It was just over an hour since exhaustion had brought an end to the stream of tears that had followed her interrogation.

"Why did I tell him about Albie?" She had sobbed over and over, rocking with the pain that had overcome her. She had been unprepared for the mind probe, as Reznor kept on repeating it was no coincidence Abus had chosen her for the probe. It made no difference: she still felt as if she had betrayed the others. Their faces had appeared on the computer screen in Abus' hand and even though she had tried to fight the creature it was like having it rummaging inside her head. Once Abus was sure he had extracted all the information from her, the creature had detached itself, leaving her shaking on the floor, its smooth surface absorbing any warmth she had left. She had remained there shivering and ignored: her innermost thoughts had been ransacked. Abus' pitiless indifference made her feel helpless. Soon after Bara Abus had gone, Reznor had been allowed to comfort her. However, she couldn't be consoled.

He hadn't tried to talk, realising she was beyond it. All he could do was keep her warm: protect her from the shock. Reznor had knelt down next to her and she, in turn, had welcomed the support he had offered. Every sob she had made had ripped through him; fuelling his rage. Bara Abus would pay. If Reznor was to die he would make sure Abus joined him.

There they lay, surrounded by their silent, motionless guard, Tissa's head resting on Reznor's folded leg. In front of them, in spite of it being a shaded glass panel door, the entrance to the building told them how much longer they had before any probable elimination. The light grew until shadows appeared, gradually creeping further into the foyer: a bitter omen for their doom.

The troopers barely seemed to be breathing around them, the occasional crackle on their radios the only sign that they were there. Needless to say, they were oblivious to Tissa's tears. Reznor's mind turned to the others, Albie and Ordenne – How had they faired getting into the schoolroom? Had the others found some escape? His mind raced through the rescue possibilities, for all he knew they would be meeting them as fellow prisoners, if they weren't dead already. Despite the anger boiling within him, the feeling that their situation was hopeless grew and grew. Even if he managed to knock out a trooper and use his weapon there would still be many more troopers. Tissa's despair was evident but he was finding it increasingly harder to hide his. The sunrise had been and gone and they were still waiting to find out their fate. The lack of news on the others was unnerving him even more. Reznor was sure if they had been killed their bodies would have been paraded triumphantly in front of them so; no news was good news. Even in her sleep, Tissa let out the occasional sob, her body shaking from the shock of the mind probe. Not many young girls had been subjected to the probe and she hadn't actually revealed much; Albie was trying to get into the schoolroom – they would easily have worked that much out for themselves but she hadn't revealed why… and she didn't actually know where the others were.

Reznor found himself stroking Tissa's pony tailed hair: no longer the fashionable tower it had been before she had set out on this adventure. Even though it was pulled tightly and neatly together the tips were still rebelling, twisting defiantly, curling even. The dye that had coloured it had now grown half-out, giving her a two-tone effect: green and black. Her grimy complexion, despite being young, had been toughened by the month spent under the city and as Reznor studied her he realised that this girl had more fight in her than he had given her credit for. Whatever they were about to face, she'd find a way to cope, which would give him the chance to think of an escape route.

Without warning the exit door was thrown open and the troopers, whose motionless posture had been unnerving to say the least, sprang into life. They instantly closed ranks around their prisoners. Everything that had happened in that room faded as if part of an unreal dream and as Tissa was woken with a start neither of them had a real understanding of what was going to happen to them or what was out there. Tissa stood up first, straightened her back, before rising to her full height. She was still easily dwarfed by their escort, then she extended a hand to Reznor who was having difficulty getting his legs to respond: hours spent kneeling had cut off his circulation; making him stagger. Realising it had been taken as a sign of weakness on his part he took a moment to compose himself and, resisting the temptation to leap about until his blood returned to his legs and feet, lifted his hand towards Tissa. Helping him up she looked into his eyes and he could see the defiant girl had overcome the frightened one.

They both strode towards the light streaming through the doors, the rays forming a tunnel for them to walk towards while the morning chill greeted them, making them shiver as they shielded their eyes.

Between the buildings that rose around them, the sky was blue: a deep, warming blue that lifted them. The sun was just poking between the enormous buildings. How could anything bad happen to them under such a glorious sky? Tissa squeezed Reznor's hand to tell him she was alright and they marched towards the surprisingly empty square.

A loud siren began to fill the square, reverberating, growing in strength as it reverberated from one side of the square to another: announcing the arrival of the actors in that morning's show. It sent a shiver down both their spines as they marched out of the doors, hand in hand and defiant.

Emerging from the shadows, the chill air of the lobby vanished to be replaced by a muggy, dry heat. The tall, slender trees that lined the edges were perfectly still and they hardly felt a breath of air. In the centre of the plaza three steps lead up to a raised concrete dais but, apart from their guard, not a soul had dared venture outdoors. Instead, every window was open from the first floor upwards and curious faces leaned out as they ate breakfast bars or sipped their morning wake-up mixtures. Bleary – eyed revellers from the night before propped themselves against window frames: no more than casual observers.

Half-hearted jeers greeted the two terrorists as they were marched towards the centre of the square. The troopers on guard formed a ring around the bottom steps, nervously clutching the weapons they held across their chests: it wouldn't do to be too intimidating in front of this number of citizens. They had to be the good guys disposing of the evil terrorists. Once in place, the expectant buzz stopped as the plaza held its breath in anticipation...but of what?

It didn't take long for the crowd to get restless: this wasn't as entertaining as they'd expected...nobody was doing anything! Idle chatter began to fill the air. The main characters below them remained perfectly still. As if on cue, the strains of a Predavator could be heard and slowly a craft dropped down, landing in a corner of the square. It was the blackest ship and its perfectly polished hull suggested it belonged to one person: Lord Abus. The reverence returned once more and those who had been hanging or leaning casually out of their windows straightened up and slunk briefly back into their rooms. Nobody wanted to be noticed by Him.

The Predavator whipped up dust around them and their faces were blasted by the hot down draft from the engines, only the troopers took no notice; their visors allowing them continued vigilance.

Tissa's heart was racing and she clutched Reznor's hand tight, determined not to be separated from him. She felt stronger knowing that he was there and wondered whether this was what it was like to have a father that stayed with you and wasn't forced to stay anonymous. If she had been able to know her father, she hoped he could have been like Reznor. The crump of the Predavator landing announced Lord Abus' imminent arrival and she felt Reznor stiffen. She could see his eyes narrow and that he had defiantly straightened up to *his* full height – he wasn't going to let Abus see any weakness in him.

The landing ramp dropped, gradually revealing the dark interior. Gas jets filled the bottom of the ramp: pushed out from the pistons that had lowered the ramp. Tissa wondered whether it was for dramatic effect as she began to feel that their presence was designed only to entertain the masses in the blocks around them: a diversion to their pointless lives. Hovercams began circling them: they were live on TV.

Nobody emerged at first but as their eyes focused they could make out Lord Abus' form, flanked by two troopers. He held Reznor's gaze as he marched purposefully towards him, each determined not to break their stare: cold blankness met fiery hatred. Reznor stood defiantly, a stance that Tissa mirrored exactly as she held Reznor's hand even tighter.   Lord Abus rose effortlessly up the steps to square up to him. Standing a metre away from each other, the pair matched up about the same height but Reznor was definitely broader, a fact that changed the cold expression on Lord Abus and for a split second he mirrored the fire in his opposite number's eyes then the blank coldness returned.

Lord Abus let out a laugh like a cough as he remembered who had the upper hand. Reminding himself of his superior position made him feel better.

"Where are your precious friends?" he taunted, "So much for their loyalty…Friendship?" As he said this he studied Tissa who couldn't bring herself to return his gaze: the probe's sift through her mind had left her innermost thoughts and feelings exposed. Instead she focussed on a tree that was waving gently in the draught from the Predavator's engines that were still powering down. An industrial breeze rippled around the square that made their eyes smart. Lord Abus quickly picked up on this and this time his laugh was mocking. "Your boyfriend…is he coming? Shall we ask him, eh?" She stared at her feet nervously but felt Reznor's hand grip hers even tighter.

Disappointed with the reaction, Lord Abus turned his back on them, turning his attention to the crowds that had reappeared at the windows. His eyes skipped from face to face still cowering safely out of reach above him. He felt only contempt for those he was supposed to be protecting from these 'terrorists'. Activating a switch on his belt, Lord Abus' stern and joyless tones reverberated around the square: amplified through the stationary Predavator's speakers either side of the cockpit.

"Citizens, you see before you two of the terrorists who have only one intention: to destroy our beautiful and well-ordered community. They are jealous of the good life we have. This city that emerged from the chaos of war and disaster…and all they want to do is return us to those dark ages: thankfully long gone!" There was a murmur of agreement in the sombre crowd and half-hearted nodding of heads. In truth, it really was too early for most of them to be out of bed and they only wanted an end to the spectacle so they could escape any consequences for them. They also wanted to continue recovering from the previous night's excesses. Bara Abus would have expected nothing else: no-one dared challenge his will: they really were so easy to control. He turned his attention away from the crowd and decided it was time to address the missing Albie.

"Albie! Yes Albie…I am talking to you! Is there no honour amongst criminals? Not going to rescue your friends from their impending execution? Lost your guts?" His goading was met by silence, only the hushed muttering of the interested but frightened audience stunned by this free show reached his ears. All around them conversation revolved around whether there would be an execution, a rescue or worst of all: nothing eventful to talk about.

"Yes, Albie…want to know about your father? I knew him. You want to know about him, don't you? Show yourself and I'll end your search for information." A private buzz swept above the plaza followed by an outcry:

"Nobody knows their father!"

"It's forbidden"

"There's just no need for it…"

"What does he want to know that for? It's disgusting!"

"If I'd known my father I'd get him for my huge feet!"

"You cheeky…. What about *your* clumsiness?"

"Yeah, someone's *got* pay for *that* all right! Last night on the dance floor was too messy!"

The conversations raged, completely oblivious to the drama waiting to unfold below. As Reznor looked past Lord Abus' head he had to smile as he studied the screens flashing on the building walls, forming a ring around the square. Each of them blinked from a picture of a red drink to bright red words "Drink Doop, it'll kill you!" He started to smile at the irony of it all but then his smile grew further as just above one of the screens a hole had appeared, unnoticed in the uproar of arguments raging, and small pieces of masonry crumbled onto the plaza below. Lord Abus spun around and all eyes were focussed on the increasingly widening hole.

Taking this as his cue he leapt across Tissa, pulling her down, before catching a distracted trooper unawares. His kick knocked the guard off his feet and a swift punch released his weapon. As if she had been waiting for the right moment to strike, Tissa swept it up as Reznor, still stranded on the ground, was set upon by another trooper. He deflected this attack with two well – placed kicks to the midriff and the trooper flew over his head. They both made a break for the protection of one of the many trees about them.

As they did so a series of metallic creatures emerged from the hole to drop heavily but undamaged into the square. A stunned silence fell upon the scene. The robots stood motionless, towering over the smaller troopers. A nervous muttering drifted around the square. Their interest pricked, the crowds returned to their balconies to casually lean out and observe the action. It didn't take long for them to recognise the robots that had instructed them in their school days. The painful memories began to trickle back of tortuous

physical education lessons at the ends of these metal
beasts but seeing them from their vantage point, the
gathered adults could at last feel relaxed in their
presence.

Suddenly, they sprang into life.

The tallest, a skater, gracefully swung a stick in
an arc about it and in the process pole-axed a pair of
troopers unlucky enough to have been close to its
landing spot. Behind it, a smaller, human figure
dropped down before scrambling onto the robot's back
as they began to advance steadily.

It was some minutes before Lord Abus noticed
his prisoners' escape but by then his intended target
had most definitely changed. There, riding atop what
he assumed to be a teacher robot sat Albie. The robot
carried a metal stick that glinted in the sunlight,
dazzling Lord Abus but another flick of a switch on his
belt put an end to that particular problem. A visor
dropped over his eyes. He glowered at the pair who
had leapt from the first floor and were now skating
towards the dais. He had always hated the sports robots
and all the pointless games they had made him play.
Jogged by painful childhood memories, Bara Abus
focused his attention on the two great hatreds in his
life. The one he had come to hate the most was Albie
but he needed him alive so he watched the pair calmly
and waited.

As the tall robotic figure skated towards him,
Lord Abus remained still and patient, watching the
smiling figure on top shooting at his troopers. He
ignored his minions who had taken position around

him and were busy returning Reznor's fire on one side while trying to desperately topple the speeding figure. Maybe he should not have insisted the boy was simply incapacitated as he watched his guard struggling to bring the darting figures down.

He stood and glowered as Albie's head briefly popped up to take shots before hiding behind the silver structure he was riding. But then it was there: Albie was in his sights, Lord Abus felt the button beneath his finger; he couldn't miss, years of frustration against Albie that had unwittingly ruined his only friendship, he had only been doing his duty…fathers couldn't contact their children: it was the law…all that could end now with the end of that grinning fool. Although it pained him, he needed the boy.

Lord Abus's smile lasted a mere fraction of a second as a solid object slammed into his padded shoulder. Caught by surprise, he shot skywards, incinerating one of the screens that was still telling people to drink 'Doop'. Fizzing sparks shot in all directions sending residents scurrying from the vantage points for cover.

Lord Abus immediately took aim in the direction of the attack and was just able to throw himself down the steps as a metal ball flew over him before colliding with a trooper's arm. Positioned at the hole in the wall stood another metal figure that was hurling, with deadly accuracy a selection of sports equipment: long poles, balls, boots... Behind it a female dressed as a technician was hurrying about supplying it with anything she could pile in front of it as ammunition.

Now that the action had started there were more watching from the higher floors as the casual observers below withdrew slightly for their own safety. They watched amazed as more robots jumped from further holes in the windows and walls, there were kick boxers, wrestlers and martial arts instructors dropping down before charging the small cluster of troopers still huddled in the middle. All the while, Reznor and Tissa were adding to the confusion with an attack from the other side. Laser blasts whizzed backwards and forwards. Reznor and Tissa had to keep moving to new trees to protect themselves as the troopers found their positions.

Sheltering behind a new tree, an out of breath Reznor took a moment to check on his partner who was still getting the hang of using the weapon she had picked up.

"The buttons on the top – use the darkest one." He called in between the shots that fizzed by. A thumb's up sign told him she understood before shooting in the general direction of the attacking troopers.

Just as the attackers seemed to be gaining the upper hand, the corners of the plaza became flooded with more and more troopers who had been waiting nearby.

Albie had nearly reached Bara Abus but one look at the incoming troops told him what his priority was: his friends. Turning, the skating robot reached the centre of the plaza but at the last minute, before the steps, both skater and rider were sent stumbling.

Managing to launch itself onto the dais, dispersing troopers in the process, the skater came to a rest next to two delighted figures. Albie added to the mayhem with a few well-placed shots of his own before coming to rest in front of his two colleagues. The metal figure provided some extra cover as Albie grabbed hold of an overjoyed pair, pulling them onto its back once it had righted itself.

"Grab hold of the legs: use the rim of its shoes to stand on and hang on, we're going to Ordenne, we'll stand a better chance together with one front.

The three clung on as they zipped across the battlefield; stick swinging wildly and domitors blazing. They forced their way through the crowd, miraculously without serious injury, and with various metal bodies forming a barrier they took what cover they could in front of the building.

Despite their best efforts, the troopers kept coming and one by one the robots started to be overpowered. They realised they were losing the fight.

All around the square, smoke from burning trees hit by misplaced shots added to the dust from fallen masonry making it harder for Albie and the others to see. Their eyes were streaming. The troopers had worked out that the way to stop the robots was to aim for the joints of their arms and legs and there were now downed robots littering the square. In the background, the nervous but interested crowd was cheering them. Albie knew that however much he disliked them, the crowd's presence and the troopers' desire not to risk having any of their citizens injured or killed was preventing any aerial attack.

Ordenne began throwing any furniture she could get hold of onto the steps below and a makeshift stockade began to take shape. Both she and the hurling robot jumped down to join her friends behind the stockade. The robot had just used its last javelin so after climbing over the piles of plastic it began to take on the advancing troopers. Demonstrating great skill, it attracted admiring glances from the martial arts robots that were uprooting trees to act as weapons. But they knew it was not enough. Cowering behind their makeshift stockade of plastic furniture their only hope now was Faon and Sted but where they were, was anybody's guess and whether they could help was another matter.

27

Faon was finishing the checks to their chosen craft while Sted kept a close guard on the door they had earlier emerged from. A cooling breeze blew gently across his head. It seemed to call to him. A glow lit up the skyline behind him from the endless rows of identical buildings stretching towards the horizon.

"Do they end or is this all there is? Does Tenebria stretch across the whole planet?" Sted wondered, abandoning his watch to amble over to the side of the building. A featureless, smooth concrete wall circled his level: just high enough for him to lean his elbows comfortably on. Above him drops rhythmically dropped down from the hydroponic farm above. There he stood, dreaming of the city's end where concrete and metal didn't strangle everything…or so he hoped. Perhaps there was water that danced in the sunlight and that hadn't been constantly polluted or reprocessed or maybe there was land…with trees, not the organised and manicured rows below him but trees of all different shapes and sizes and other plants: wilderness, that he had once seen pictures of. Closing his eyes, he could see it all. There was a wooded hill that looked out onto strange creatures running free and wild amongst fields of long grasses. Lush mountains and valleys stretched out into the horizon wherever you looked. Paradise was pulled from his thoughts by a sharp jab in his back.

"Hey, what's the…" Caught in mid-sentence, his jaw refused to budge as he stared open-mouthed into the barrel of a trooper's domitor.

"You're not paid to admire the view!" snapped the trooper; the sun reflecting off his armour and momentarily blinding Sted.

"We'll have to teach you a lesson, won't we?" goaded another, swaggering towards them, his armour glowing red with the rising sun. Pulling Sted upright, he shook him before pushing him back towards the side of the building so his head was staring at the drop to the square. His feet began kicking while his hands vainly tried to pull himself back onto the roof but the trooper had tight hold of his back, pressing it down onto the wall. Sharp ripples of concrete dug into his chest. Sted started gasping: the breeze that had lulled him was now replaced by the stale heat from below that he struggled to catch hold of. His eyes blurred but he could just make out two familiar forms being led into the middle of the plaza – Reznor and Tissa – before everything became swallowed up into a mass of swirling colours. He fought the urge to give in, convinced that the only way out for him if he did was down.

Just as he felt he was giving up Faon's familiar voice came to his rescue.

"Do that and you'll never get that ship ready in time: he's the best computer engineer on the staff." He felt himself being lifted then dropped unceremoniously back onto the tarmacked ground. His eyes had cleared enough for him to make out his partner's silhouetted body, the red glow of the rising sun also radiating from her but with more power, warmth and beauty. A shadow fell over him as one of them stepped over him. Sted could see them standing, sizing up the lithe figure that had challenged them.

"Well, well, well…look who it isn't…Miss do-gooder herself. Thought you were sent to the camps for your meddling: trying to help people..." at that, Sted heard the trooper spit and felt something land centimetres from his nose, he shuddered.

"Got promoted, did you?" laughed the other trooper before turning his attention to the forlorn Sted. "See she's still helping the low-lifes." For good measure he stood on Sted's hand as he began to stand up. The trooper was about to twist his foot to increase the pain when a sudden blast struck his back shooting him to the foot of the wall. Sted saw his chance and leapt at the other. The frustration at having his blissful moment spoilt and his treatment at their hands, and feet, to give him added strength. He crashed the remaining trooper into the nearest Predavator, knocking him out cold.

Faon looked at him, impressed as she surveyed their handiwork.

"You do surprise me these days you know." She commended him, giving him a squeeze on his arm, as she walked casually over to pick up a discarded domitor. He was beginning to like this attention. He had to bring himself back to reality suddenly remembering what he had seen.

"It's Rez…they've got him…and Tissa. Come on, have a look." He blurted out before dragging her over to the wall. A giant shadow drifted down and past them as they hurried and for a moment they froze, not knowing whether to dive for cover or try to act normally. They drew closer to the edge and watched the darkest Predavator they had seen drop centimetres away from the wall towards their captured comrades.

Even after it had sunk from view they found themselves unwilling to move; convinced that any second it would rise before them and they would come face to face with Lord Abus. Tearing themselves away from the scene below they crept away from the edge of the building, not wishing to end up tripping over the side.

"I've disabled the automatic computer, I'll be able to fly it and you'll have to do everything else." She warned him. "Give me a few minutes to disable the other ships and we'll be there. Keep an eye on the square...and the door."

Sted watched her as she ran away before murmuring:

"You surprise me too: no doubt about that." Clutching the dropped domitor he peered over just as Lord Abus emerged from his ship.

Sted watched amazed as masonry rained upon the plaza and he felt like cheering when Albie emerged, mounted upon what looked like a huge metal man that bore down on Abus and his troopers. Albie was a whirlwind gliding everywhere; balanced effortlessly he was picking off troopers at will while his mount cut wide paths through the swarming troopers; seemingly immune to their blasts as they flew off its stick. Sted thought about taking a shot from his vantage spot but resisted the urge, not wanting to give away their position. He kept glancing at the door and the two fallen troopers, not wanting to be caught out by either but the door remained shut and the troopers were still: the battle below was pulling all available troopers towards it. Relieved, he turned his attention to the plaza and realised that above the sounds of the laser fire he could hear cheering. Across the higher levels of the block, well out of reach of the smoke, projectiles and gun fire, crowds were baying for blood.

Cheering as troopers were catapulted into trees or sent reeling by well-placed missiles from an unseen force; Sted had a strong feeling (or was it hope?) that Ordenne was behind this.

Although pleased to hear someone cheering for them, Sted still felt sickened by the noise of the crowd. That same crowd had, a few hours earlier, been repulsed by the sight of them but was now cheering the others on as if it was a gladiatorial contest for their entertainment. They ringed the square, coolly eating breakfast; steam rising from hot drinks and food bars in the early morning: the full strength of the sun still to be felt.

Cheering and laughing, they had made sure they were quite safe in the upper floors. Once the contest had grown in its ferocity and the smells of overworked lasers and smoke from burning trees had become unpleasant the crowd abandoned the lower levels. They were enjoying themselves but self-preservation was high on their list of priorities: they still feared the reaction of the troopers. They certainly wouldn't want to be caught up in any backlash and definitely didn't want to be seen to be involved in any way. Sted watched Bara Abus seemingly follow Albie but the luck was always with the youngster; trees, robots and flying troopers thwarting the older man's efforts but Sted could see this only infuriated him more.

The battle was taking a downward turn as Albie's army were being forced back by sheer weight of numbers and a good many of the robots had lost arms and legs enabling the troopers to overpower them, deactivating them with single well-placed shots. Troopers stood triumphantly on top of the fallen metal masses before using the extra height to get clearer shots.

Sted turned to let Faon know how the battle was changing but froze. There she stood: like a statue. Behind her, with his arm wrapped firmly around her throat, and blood trickling down his face stood the trooper Sted had knocked out: obviously he hadn't hit him hard enough. With domitor embedded into the side of her head, Sted could see beads of sweat covered her forehead as she fought to stay calm.

"That's right; if you don't want anything to happen to Do-gooder you'll do exactly what I say." He growled, blood from the gaping head wound dried but smeared across his face where he had initially wiped it. His body armour hung loose where Sted had grabbed him but he took no notice. His eyes burned with rage.

"Put the domitor down, you low-life scum…slowly. You're going to wish you hadn't crawled out of your hole." He nodded to the ground and slowly Sted did as he was ordered, keeping his hands in full view and his eyes fixed firmly on the domitor aimed at Faon.

"That's good, low-life, you do have some brains then. Not much; but then you do live in the dark, don't you? You two are coming with me." He nodded again, this time in the direction of another lift door that Sted hadn't noticed.

Sted walked cautiously backward, maintaining eye contact as their captor pushed Faon forward into a stumble.

"Keep your hands where I can see them: above your heads." The trooper followed them in the direction he'd indicated but his head had started bleeding again and he was becoming irritated by the blood trickling into his eye. He brushed it away but more seeped down. He was becoming more and more incensed that anybody had dared to do this to him.

Sted heard the click as he set his domitor to another setting and judging by the trooper's increasingly irate state he knew it wasn't set to stun. They had reached the lift doors when he stopped barely an arm's reach away.

"Move to the side," he ordered as he waved them away from the doors with the domitor in one hand, wiping streaming blood from his face with the other. "What are you looking at you scum? I should have let you drop…" His voice tailed away as he pointed his weapon at Sted.

Sted could see the blood flowing more freely. He was beginning to shake: his finger now hovered over the trigger button. Sted knew what he had to do. Steeling himself he sprang at him, his hands clutching at the weapon as he knocked the blood-stained trooper over. The moment he did so a single shot echoed round the rooftop.

He felt free.

He never felt the thud as both he and the trooper hit the concrete roof. The pain from the shot didn't register either. There was a floating sensation …into the breeze, the heat of the sun filled him. All his cares and discomfort had gone as he soared upwards: mind and body cleansed. Faon and the roof top fell away beneath him. He had so wanted to tell Faon how much he loved her but maybe she'd know that anyway.

Faon heard the crunch as the trooper hit the concrete then felt the dull thud as Sted's body jumped with the force of the blast before he too hit the ground. They both lay still. The wind whirled about her, and the warmth of the sun tried to fill her. She shivered and began to shake uncontrollably. She couldn't take a step. The sounds of the battle still raged far below, it might as well have been a different world for all she cared.

She forced herself to edge forward, slowly at first, but then found herself charging towards her friend but he just lay there. She wanted to cry out…scream, make any sound at all but her mouth failed her.

Kneeling down next to him she rolled him onto her knee. The trooper lay on the tarmac: the indignation still etched into his face. But Sted was smiling. In all their time together, in the bunker then with Reznor and Albie, she had never seen him so happy and at peace. Putting her cheek next to his, tears dripped onto him, wiping away the dirt and she rocked him, carefully wiping the dirt away until she could gaze at him: unsoiled. They were alone.

The battle sounds grew. She forced her mind back to the present. As gently as she could, she dragged Sted into the Predavator she had prepared, surprising herself at her sudden presence of mind and increased strength despite the tears that streamed down her filthy face. Laying his body across the seats in the hold she placed a blanket across him: she didn't know why but it just seemed the right thing to do. She prepared for take-off.

"I'm coming Reznor and we're going to your wilderness, Sted. Nobody better get in our way." She thought as she revved the engines up and armed the guns. "This is for you, Sted." Glancing at the closed door to the hold. She paused as the Predavator rose effortlessly. The bodies of the two troopers still lay where she had left them. She didn't care whether they were dead or not: revenge was the furthest thing from her mind. Escape was all she could think of so Sted's sacrifice wouldn't have been in vain.

The roof sunk from the screens and the rescue had begun.

28

Fighting side by side, Reznor and Albie had reached the same conclusion…their chances were bleak. Only a few robots remained and they were dropping quickly. The four humans were struggling to pick off the troopers that had made it through the barrier of robots, so effective just half an hour earlier. Now, there was no barrier any more.

The final robot dropped as its circuits were disconnected. It had served them well but without any legs or arms there was very little it could do beyond spitting sparks from its exposed wires. A familiar sound filled the air. The crowds above them had become extremely subdued. It had been a fun morning, a diversion for them to talk about that night, but that was all. After all it didn't do to cheer terrorists, did it? Audience support had gone for Albie's band now that they looked to be staring defeat in the face. They decided to callously change to the winning side and began cheering as the troopers took charge.

The troopers gathered in a semi-circle metres away from the impromptu barricade that Albie and co had been defending. Firing ceased and they withdrew as a Predavator dropped lower. The downdraft threw dust clouds into the sky. Lord Abus still stood in the middle of the plaza from where he had been directing the waves of attacks and now he was looking extremely smug and superior. It was time for his victory speech and his venom was directed at Albie, the whole plaza fell silent, reverently waiting in anticipation as the ripping sound of the Predavator grew. Albie stood tall as he emerged from behind the makeshift blockade.

"This time I have you just where I want you, caught like the rat you are," boomed the amplified voice of Lord Abus, "you have wriggled away twice but the next time we meet you will be in a prison cell awaiting execution. There are people who would like to meet you before you die…extremely slowly." Lord Abus glanced above him watching the Predavator, a quizzical look briefly drifting across his face but dismissed out of hand as his visor shrank out of view. His long red gash and robotic eye caused a stir above as he did so but it barely registered as the red light in his left eye burned into his enemy. "I never got to thank an old friend of mine for this…" the words "old friend" hung on his lips as he tapped his eye that shone through the dust and dirt; a red laser blazing straight into Albie's mind. "…So isn't it lucky I can thank his offspring instead!" His robotic eye was now pulsing in time to the throb of the Predavator that was now hovering just in front of the stockade.

This new addition was beginning to irritate Abus, Albie noticed. He had to admit it did seem strange that the ship should hover just above them for so long. But there it remained, ignoring the landing site that the waiting troopers had cleared for it to take the prisoners away. The troopers meanwhile had begun to get nervous at the lack of a landing and the even more irate mood of their leader. The crowd that had slunk into the buildings slowly re-emerged sensing that there was something not quite right and maybe there was to be a final twist to the morning's 'fun'. None of them dared speak but their silent vigil resumed.

Lord Abus was now swiftly tapping his leg with his domitor, wondering how much longer that fool of a pilot could be. He decided that he would see that he or she was dispatched immediately to the factories the instant they landed. Nobody kept him waiting like this! He studied the cockpit, his red eye trying to pierce the cockpit without success.

"Find out what that idiot is doing and get me

their serial number." He ordered, whacking the nearest trooper on his helmet. Just as a group began moving towards the craft, the bay door opened so that its tip was just touching the highest point of the plastic barricade and the approaching group stopped, unsure of what to make of it. Heads turned towards Lord Abus, who simply stared at them; annoyed that they had dared to stop carrying out his instructions. They immediately hurried towards Albie, who had been joined by an equally bemused but nevertheless defiant Reznor, Tissa and Ordenne.

Reznor stood defiant to the end: chest out with weapon resting casually upon his shoulder. Tissa on the other hand was crouching down, crouching down behind a heavy table, catching her breath while Ordenne, defiantly, stood legs astride two chairs holding a domitor across her waist in two hands. All four were staring uncertainly inside the Predavator.

Lord Abus was about to order their immediate capture when the ship's laser cannon devastated the approaching party. Reznor gleefully leapt into the ship the moment that happened, followed by the two girls. Albie joined in the fire-fight, dropping to his knees, picking off the trooper charging towards them. Reznor's hand reached down for him just as a sudden searing pain swept though as a hot blast of laser fire glanced across his thigh. He screamed angrily at the deep burn; inadvertently dropping his domitor. Powerless, Albie watched it disappear into the melee of plastic and metal. The next thing he knew he was struggling to stay upright as a gloved hand had grabbed hold of his ankle: the hand felt cold and inhuman. The mound he stood on began shifting and he fell flat on his back, the hard plastic of a chair's arm digging into the small of his back. A sudden downward jerk dug the chair arm even further into him. He was being dragged down and he was powerless to prevent it. Reznor's arm reached out lower but Albie continued to sink further away from him. As he sank he came face to face with the hand's owner: Abus, his red eye piercing and pulsing.

"You are going nowhere, boy," he hissed. The pain in his thigh suddenly disappeared and Albie felt a surge of power course through his leg. Still sliding down, Albie, the unkempt boy, kicked out at his elder: his boot landing squarely and powerfully upon Abus' chin.

His kick was filled with the rage that Albie felt, now the pain had virtually disappeared but he was able to channel it as if he had been made for this. However, the hand clung doggedly onto his leg. Behind Abus his troopers were streaming towards them and despite the constant fire from the Predavator they were steadily closing in on Albie. Abus' domitor swung down onto Albie's leg, retribution for the kick. Albie could see Abus seething. Another strike followed by another drag and Albie was at Abus' feet. Abus' knee was on his chest and his domitor was pressing into Albie's temple.

Try as he might, Albie couldn't get rid of the arrogant, gloating expression that looked down upon him. Abus' domitor was motionless; aimed directly at

Albie. Anger and hate seemed the only emotions he was capable of and he hated Albie...or did he? Albie somehow could sense there was a struggle in Abus' head. He needed Albie...but at the same time there was anger. But it wasn't anger at Albie...it was with his father. Abus was right, he had known his father...and his mother!

Albie had no idea how he knew these things, just that he could sense the feelings and emotions: the conflict taking place. Suddenly, his connection was broken.

A single shot rang out and Abus fell back, holding his gun hand, blood trickling through his fingers. Albie's chest was freed. The domitor that had been aimed at his head now lay next to him. Albie stared at this man who had been his father's friend. Why had Abus been so determined to kill him? Gone was Albie's hate; replaced by stunned amazement. Cannon shots rang out around them but Albie was miles away, his mind completely oblivious to the sound of approaching troopers' boots. He thought he heard Reznor's voice in the background but he couldn't take his eyes off the seething, spinning Abus sinking to the floor, another shot striking his shoulder; revealing not flesh and blood but open circuits and spitting wires. A pair of hands pulled Albie away from the battle and into the bay of the waiting Predavator.

Guns still blazing, the craft rose as the ramp closed; drowning out the cheering crowd above. The fickle crowd had once more rallied behind the little bunch. The blasts from below had little effect on the

Predavator as they disappeared into the sky.

Behind them was a scene of silent devastation. The crowds vanished the moment the Predavator passed their respective levels: once again fearing reprisals. Abus lay motionless surrounded by his minions; staring.

"Bring that craft down!" He ordered as he came to. Troopers rushed off in every direction, leaving him alone in the square: his useless shoulder sparking; arm hanging limp. The anger he felt overcame any pain.

"That boy and his friends will pay." He cursed as he pulled himself up. Taking a brief moment to smooth himself down with his one good arm, he limped for his craft: the final figure to leave the battleground.

It took a minute for their eyes to adjust to the dark of the cargo hold once the closing ramp had cut out their last view of the chaotic plaza and its surrounding blocks. There was a brief call of "Hang on!" before the Predavator lurched forward. It was only when they began strapping themselves into their seats that they noticed Sted's body peacefully strapped opposite. Reznor was first to the body. Slowly pulling back the simple blanket, he could only stare at Sted's familiar features: unable to take it in. He beat his fist against the fuselage then dropped onto his knees, stroking his dead companion and friend's face. He looked so peaceful that all Reznor could do was pull the blanket over his face.

"I'm sorry, man. I hope we can find what you

were looking for." He whispered, strapping Sted's body as best he could. Without thinking he casually punched Sted's shoulder as he had done so many times before and headed for the cockpit.

On the flight deck, Ordenne felt awkward. She hadn't really had time to get to know Sted or any of them really and felt like a visitor at a wake, feeling the sense of loss but not able to share it. Faon would need her help, she decided as she tried to busy herself. Sitting in the spare seat she pushed her feelings aside, concentrating instead on the computer before her. She relaxed as she put her mind into getting to grips with the ship's computer fire system.

Albie gazed at Sted's body. Shaking his head, he adopted a vacant look, unable to do anything more than stare at the far wall. Gradually that faded and he was able to manage the beginnings of a half-hearted smile as he looked at Tissa. She looked up and he realised how little he knew about her; despite having endured so much to save her.

"Thanks," was all she could say before resting her head on his shoulder and closing her eyes, as much to avoid looking at Sted's body as through sheer exhaustion. She had changed beyond belief in such a short space of time. Now she was in exactly the same boat as Albie, alone but with a mother out there: in one of the camps.

Albie stroked her head as it rocked on his shoulder with the motion of the Predavator. He tried to visualise the girl he had watched staggering about, smiling at all those 'beautiful people' in the city without reply. Maybe they had been destined to meet. Easing himself from under her sleeping head, he picked up a blanket folded in a nearby compartment then laid it over her.

Stepping into the cockpit, Reznor could see how easily Ordenne had settled into the role of computer operator. He held onto the back of Faon's seat as the Predavator sped across the city.

"It was quick," she said, "he saved my life…" She was going to say more but words failed her as she began to well up with tears. Keeping one hand on the joystick, she pulled her sleeve over her fingers before wiping two single tears away from her reddened eyes.

"He was a real hero." Reznor tried to comfort her but his words choked in his throat. Why did he have to die? After all he'd been through, why now? He had to ignore the questions that were fighting in his head to be answered; there would be plenty of time for that. "What can I do to help?" he asked as calmly as he could.

"There are two sets of laser cannons that can be mounted on the sides. Ordenne will open the hatches for you…it won't be too long before we have visitors."

Reznor returned to the hold where Tissa lay, now sprawled over two seats. Seeing her safe was now even more important than before, if he wanted a reason for Sted's sacrifice it was so that they could all have that new start that they had each dreamed of.

A panel either side of him slowly dropped open and the air stream from outside whipped at him.

"Come on Albie…things to do." His friend made

sure Tissa was secure then focussed his tired mind on Reznor as he showed him a control console next to the open panel. "I think this is how you do it…" He decided as he pressed a series of buttons that had Albie bewildered. To their delight a laser cannon swung from the outside of the fuselage where it had been embedded and Albie couldn't help but be impressed.

"Whoa…" was all he could manage as he studied a screen that sat in between two metre-long laser cannons.

"You just have to point it and the computer will try to do the rest…press these buttons to fire. If you get the hang of it and want to try it without the computer; flick this switch and you'll be on manual." Albie nodded and stroked the top of the computer: for some reason it all felt very familiar. Next, he grabbed hold of two padded handles with the fire buttons placed handily for his thumbs. He swung left and right, up and down, scanning every spot of the sky and was amazed at how responsive the cannons were. Reznor reached across and gently punched his shoulder in encouragement. He briefly stopped as he caught sight of Sted's form lying serenely, metres away.

"This is for you, man." he murmured as he readied his own cannons, mimicking Albie's sweeping motions with his own cannon and took a deep breath, "Let's pray it wasn't all in vain."

There had been no sign of any other craft coming out to intercept them as they sped away. In fact, Albie was beginning to feel a bit bored by the endless rows of identical blocks with identical squares, trees and flashing signs they skimmed across. Most had one or two Predavators sitting idle on their roofs but nobody was in sight: a bit of an anti – climax. He may as well be sitting having a rest with Tissa for all the action he was getting. Reznor tapped his shoulder as they stood back to back. As Albie turned around, he indicated a pair of headphones nestled below the panel so he put them on. He instantly heard Faon reeling out instructions.

"…coming towards us and there are lots of them so keep focussed, my guess is we are approaching the maintenance ring where the workers are housed. They'll be more likely to attack us away from the residential zone…not so many witnesses…and hey, they're only workers…" Suddenly Ordenne's voice jumped in:

"Gun positions approaching…multiple Predavators on their way…"

After passing the last residential blocks and the wall that separated them from the outer reaches of the city; it was as if the sun had been blotted out. Everywhere they looked dark dots were massed waiting for the order.

Albie and Reznor gripped their weapons tightly, not having the slightest inkling the fire storm they were flying into.

"Missiles!" cried Ordenne and suddenly the sky around them was filled with anti-aircraft fire that tossed them furiously from side to side. Albie felt the heat as black explosions ripped barely metres away and the hold was filled with the acrid stink of the exploding shells. On top of that it was impossible to hear the others through his headphones with the ear – splitting noise of the shields ripping themselves apart. A sudden lurch knocked him off his feet. He crashed onto the gantry as the little craft strained to dodge the missiles hurtling towards it.

"Albie!" Cried Reznor, mesmerised by something outside. Albie sprung back to his position as a missile zipped towards them. He fumbled for the triggers but his flustered fingers just couldn't find them. Before he knew what was happening they dropped like a stone and Reznor watched as the missile hurtled into the ground, destroying a run-down building…somebody's home. There was no time to dwell as they both had missiles bearing down on them. This time Albie had control and began firing at the incoming targets, quick as the missiles appeared he was equal to them and one by one he was able to destroy them: each explosion turning the temperature up a notch as smoke built up to distort their view. Their faces were now blackened and they had received numerous cuts from pieces of flying shrapnel but they were becoming quite adept at ducking after every explosion. The longer the bombardment continued the more in tune with each other they grew, ducking together to avoid being caught by the shrapnel flying from their respective targets. As suddenly as the attack had started, it stopped: leaving them with a myriad of scrapes and scratches but with their faculties intact. The fuselage hadn't been breached and despite the ferocity and sounds of the battle, Tissa slept on, head lolling about with every dip and soar.

29

The dilapidated buildings, the best the city could provide for their manual labourers, stopped abruptly as they headed towards the black shimmering horizon. A featureless wall charged into view at the edge of the expansive no-man's land that blurred below them, imposing metal gun towers were suspiciously silent: brooding.

Albie and Reznor took the opportunity for a quick rest. Their arms ached from pulling the hefty laser cannons from left to right and their thumbs were sore from near constant firing: the thought that that was just a taster wasn't comforting. Albie tried not to look at Sted's body and was thankful that it had been strapped before they had set off. He wasn't feeling confident about their chances of escape as he leaned on the barrel of his cannon. Surveying the dark masses ahead, he was so intent on the formations ahead that it was several seconds before the burning sensation from the hot barrel of the weapon registered. He leapt back, tripping over the metal grooves in the floor. He landed centimetres from the still unconscious Tissa: the only calm body in the eye of this storm. He had no way of knowing what she had been through the previous night but having Reznor with her he hoped would have been some comfort. Jumping off the grating he felt the engines slow and they were no longer moving forward but hovering.

The slowly rotating Predavator was hovering just out of range of the gun towers. Below them lay an expanse of rocks and discarded military equipment. Nature had filled the gaps with its hardiest plants – spikes and thorns adding to the obstacles for anybody who thought they could make a quick dash for the looming wall. Abandoning his gun, he followed Reznor into the cockpit where Faon and Ordenne were discussing the next move. Ordenne was studying a screen with a black dot in the centre and a thick ring around the outskirts. Seeing them arrive she filled them in:

"It's not good. In the centre is us…and this ring is them."

"How many of them are there…roughly?" Reznor asked, not really wanting to know the answer but hoping he might be pleasantly surprised: he wasn't. Ordenne was calm and matter fact as she announced the bad news:

"…about a thousand Predavators, maybe more. …No way of telling how many missile launchers on the ground or gun emplacements." Reznor pulled a calm studious face as if he were trying to think of a plan but all he could come up with was:

"We're dead, aren't we?"

Faon simply pushed her lips together and rolled her eyes.

"It's a bit tight, to say the least. There is no way back, there is a fleet of ships following us that was scrambled from each of the city blocks and the others have taken off from the bases along the wall," added Ordenne, still flicking through charts of the landscape ahead of her on her screen. She slid one after another onto and off the screen. As she grew more desperate she dismissed them quicker and quicker.

As they tried to figure out their next step, the fleet around them remained at a distance: studying the little craft as it spun slowly: waiting for it to make its move. "We aren't that far from the edge of the city…if we could get that far there may be a chance…" The looks around her weren't hopeful so she continued with her search of the maps. "There are pulse fences around the perimeter of the…" Albie gave her a blank look so she changed her tack, simplifying the explanation. "…electric fences circle the city and if anything tries to break out they will drag it down using a kind of tractor ray," More blank looks followed "…they'll make us crash." Albie smiled, pleased to have understood. However, the three faces looking at him soon wiped the smile away: heads were shaken before returning to the screen.

"Where does the power come from?" Albie butted in and they turned once more to consider him. First reaction was to ignore him but Faon backed him up:

"He's right…there must be a power plant somewhere, knock that out and we can get out…" she was about to continue when the screen with the respective positions showed a change as the band of Predavators behind them began to advance ominously.

Spinning the ship round to face the oncoming attackers there was no doubt in Faon's mind that to stand and fight was not an option, speed was their only chance. She didn't have an inkling of consulting the others before swinging into action.

"No time to explain…just trust me." Faon dropped back into her chair, swung her legs under the circuit panel and they sped towards the wall and its patiently waiting guns.

Albie and Reznor rapped knuckles while they headed for their respective guns. They knew that it was all or nothing but they were beginning to realise that if there was anybody who could fly them out of this: it was Faon.

The moment their speed picked up, the barrage from the wall ahead set the air about them on fire. Molten chunks and clouds of thick black ash battered the hull as they were tossed about by blast after blast. Reznor and Albie didn't dare approach the open windows as the hot debris flew into the hold. Albie glanced down at Tissa but incredibly she still slept. With no targets to fire at yet they remained behind the protection of the thick fuselage, safe for now.

That all changed when they were thrown to the floor by the biggest eruption so far. Albie was thrown headlong, his skull connecting with both the hull and the grating on the floor. He felt a sudden breeze he hadn't felt earlier and as he lifted his head he was confronted by a gaping hole in the bay door. It was large enough for him to see the massed Predavators closing in behind them following at a safe distance, the thought of being hit by their own guns holding them back. All of a sudden, his left hand felt unusually warm despite the through draft. They were rocked once more and glancing down at it he shouted to Reznor for help as something next to him was on fire. Ignoring the flying shrapnel, his friend pulled him away, trying to stamp out the cinders that had set Albie's sleeve alight.

"Put it out, put it out!" screamed Albie hysterically, any resemblance of cool disappearing in the seconds of panic.

"Just chill, man…I'm in control," Reznor reassured him as he smothered the last embers with a flameproof blanket. Albie was staring at Tissa whose blanket was the object on fire. Trying to mouth to Reznor, the shock prevented him getting a word out. The sleeping mass that was Tissa stirred slightly as the flames warmed her legs and she mumbled unintelligibly. She suddenly sat bolt upright, staring at the flames creeping closer, screaming as she struggled with the straps that held her to her seat. In her panic she tried kicking the blanket away but only succeeded in tangling herself further. In the nick of time Reznor sprayed the burning cover with a fire extinguisher he had pulled from the wall. As Reznor did that, Albie, still carrying the flameproof blanket and without a thought for himself, threw himself over Tissa smothering the flames in the process.

"Thanks," she said rubbing the bruised shins he had just given her "I really do appreciate it: honest."

Apart from the hole in the rear they had remained reasonably intact. Faon's flying had bettered the accuracy of the wall's gunners and now the closer they got to the looming wall, the fewer guns could bear down on them. Albie and Reznor resumed their vigils and Tissa joined Albie as they approached the wall.

"Hang on, here's the inner wall!" Ordenne cried out and all three braced themselves as they lurched upwards, eventually ending up as horizontal bodies pressed against the scorching metal hull. They hadn't banked on having to hold on quite so much as they gradually slipped towards the gaping hole.

"Quick fasten yourself in! Shouted Reznor as Tissa hung onto the seat she had just left with one hand while the other was being used as a mooring by Albie to stop himself plunging through the ripped fuselage. The temperature outside was now searing and despite the through-draft the air was becoming stiflingly hot and acrid. They could hear Ordenne's forward guns pounding away and could only guess at how many Predavators were closing in from above. The views from their lasers were even more obscured by pungent smoke and flames that made their eyes smart.

Managing to wedge their feet onto the grooves in the wall, Albie and Reznor resumed their gun positions. More and more Predavators appeared on either side of them, skimming the walls as they swarmed towards the lone craft. The ends of the cannons were starting to glow red from their near-constant use so Reznor unclipped himself before grabbing a fire extinguisher. With it hooked firmly under one arm he began crawling back towards them. The guns hissed as they were covered with the cooling foam.

A sudden explosion next to him rocked the Predavator. Reznor was sent flying towards the teeth of a newly-appeared, glowing hole. His hands flailed for a hand hold. Every time he managed to grab something his momentum pulled it away from its mooring. Finally, his battered fingers managed to cling on and this time his handhold didn't move. His fingers were wrenched as his body slammed into the hull but he clung on.

Unable to make it back to the safety of the seats or the weapons, he wedged himself between the hot wall and the floor. His body moulded to the ship's hull, every pull and strain contorted his body further as did every explosion and vibration. Panels of the hull rattled and moaned their dissatisfaction but the Predavator remained in one piece. He was now constantly jarring: stomach frequently lurching one way while the rest of him was thrown the other. Still he clung on until they reached the top of the wall. The sudden dip of the craft, as they plunged down the other side of the wall, sent him freefalling towards the cockpit door.

Luckily it remained tightly shut as he thudded into it. He was just about to wedge himself in again when they straightened out and he simply slid upside down onto the grilling before rolling unceremoniously over; finishing up at his gun position. Albie was already there.

"Stop rolling about and grab your gun; there's Predavators aplenty!" ignoring the pain from his flying lessons he straightened up to his full height. The temptation to toss his friend cheerfully out of the aperture was great; but he managed to overcome it. For a moment Albie thought he might actually do it when he lunged forward. Instead of grabbing him, Reznor took firm hold of the laser and began firing at the Predavator he had spotted closing in. Blue bolts zipped towards it and despite all he had been through, his accuracy was true. The Predavator was soon ablaze as it plummeted towards the ground. There was no time for him to stop as Predavators whizzed straight at them, bolts screaming past them. Albie, opposite, began firing as they swung past.

The sky grew dark once more as swarm after swarm of craft took it in turn to attack, sweeping across each other in well-calculated patterns so that not one ship crashed into any other despite their head-on charges. The luck they had had with the missile attack hadn't lasted and the hull was now riddled with holes. A fully awake Tissa ran from back to front, putting out any fires that started and every so often dowsing down the cannons as they threatened to overheat. Their faces were black and it was a fight to breathe but still the ship whizzed on.

Up in the cockpit Faon guided them across the armoured buildings in the military zone. Ordenne guided her towards the outer wall while blasting anything that headed towards them. Black smoke had started to seep under the door from the hold but they ignored it: the engines still worked and that was all that mattered.

Ahead of them rose the outer wall of the city, much larger and better armoured than the inner one. It slowly drew closer; the whole ship shaking: straining to escape. It was as determined as they were to stay together and escape. Despite the rattling hull and the now-frequently shorting circuits Faon's mind was focused upon reaching this final barrier. She pictured Sted's face and expression: willing her on. Her years in the factory, her emotions on taking charge of a Predavator once again and escaping from the mine: all leading to this. None of them had seen what was outside the electric beams that flashed from wall pylon to wall pylon but this is what she and Sted had dreamed about ever since they had met, hemmed in *that* cavern by *that* fateful rockslide. He was cheering for them, somewhere and she wasn't going to let him down. Returning back to the ongoing flight, the slow motion sped back to real time. Once more they were engulfed by a swarm of Predavators and streams of laser fire crisscrossing their craft.

Every so often they found themselves rewarded with a brief respite before the next attack gathered in front of the sun, almost blocking it out. Faon turned to Ordenne.

"Have you found the power plant yet?" demanded Faon; urging her partner to work faster. Ordenne simply shook her head so Faon returned her attention to staying in one piece. "We aren't going to last much longer up here, have to drop to ground level;

the buildings will give us some cover." With that, they banked, flying parallel with the immense, domineering wall. Suddenly, the damaged craft dropped and flew through a gap between two windowless factories that was just wide enough for them. The guns on the rooftops were only momentarily able to shoot before the Predavator dipped below the roofline. For the moment they were safe, trusting in both Faon's skill at the helm and Ordenne's navigation.

"Got it!" cried Ordenne pointing at the on-screen map. "I can guide you but it'll be tight…" She paused to take a breath then began her directions. "Sharp right here," she began as Faon responded immediately, putting every muscle into pulling the joystick back and to the right. The hull squealed as they banked right, scraping the underside on the corrugated metal factory wall. Sparks flew from the Predavator but still they carried on. Above them single Predavators swept down but the closeness of the neighbouring buildings prevented anything more than that. A smile spread across Faon's features while Ordenne could only sigh in relief, her face screwed up in concentration. Reznor appeared at the door but said nothing as Ordenne called out bearing after bearing and Faon responded with great skill and composure until at last they bore down upon the electric fence's powerplant.

"There's a lot of drag from the holes at the back, Rez. You'll need to plug as many of them as you can." Faon advised, surprising him that she knew he was there.

They emerged from the protection of the buildings and raced across another open wasteland of discarded debris and thorns. Swooping down behind and above them, Predavators launched missile after missile at the low-flying craft. The missiles slammed into the ruins of buildings around them, sending dirt and metal soaring. The air around the fleeing Predavator turned grey: the pursuing pack were somehow failing to destroy them. Reznor and Albie dodged the shards of metal and lumps of rock that poured through the openings. Faon's voice buzzed in their ears as they ducked their way back down the hold. Crouched on the floor they listened to her plan.

Once she had finished, they and Tissa set to work pulling the laser cannons back into the moorings before closing the panels they had been firing through. Once this had been done they were dismayed to find that they could still feel the wind whipping past them. It was only then that they realised the extent of the battering the Predavator had taken. The metal hull was littered with great gashes where laser blasts had burnt through. They could see the missiles still racing towards them and the blackened sky of Predavators waiting to pounce once more. All the time the air whipped at them: forcing them to cover their eyes from the steady stream of debris as they fought to fill the many rips in the hull.

"...Plug as many of the holes as you can with anything you can lay your hands on!" ordered Reznor as the ship continued to rock under the ongoing assault.

Anything that could be lifted was crammed into any holes that were found; spare clothing, strapping, medical supplies, tools: all became makeshift plugs. The flow of air through the hold dropped as more and more of the rips in the hull were blocked up.

Taking a brief pause for breath, they momentarily admired their handiwork and checked there wasn't anything else they could cram into the final gaping hole before turning to strap themselves in. They looked forlornly at the breach at the back. Through the gaping hole they watched their enemies swooping out of range to launch wave after wave of missiles, all the time waiting for the killer blow that would end their escape. Thankfully, Faon's flying kept them on target and in relatively one piece.

Three pairs of eyes scoured the hull for something to block the gap but they had used everything that could be removed, there just wasn't anything big enough. Suddenly Tissa, looking helplessly at the cockpit brought her eyes on a piece they had overlooked.

"The door, the door to the cockpit!" she squealed "It would just about cover it. Have we got any cutting…?" she hardly had a chance to finish her idea as she caught sight of Reznor, grinning manically behind a pair of dark goggles, staring at the already lit cutting torch in his hand. He expertly attacked the bolts holding the cockpit door and seemed to revel in the sparks that flew around him while the others tried to stay as far from both the manic cutter at one end and the gaping hole at the other. The ship continued to bounce as missiles erupted close by, each blast tipping Albie and Tissa closer towards either cutter or gaping hole. They both clung on to whatever strapping remained attached to the hull as they bounced from each other to the sharp edges littering the hull. Every exposed piece of skin was ripped with cuts as were the remains of their blood-stained clothing. Reznor ignored both this and the metal that dug into him as he wedged himself against the hull, concentrating all his efforts on cutting the bolts that held the cockpit door in place. Sweat poured down his face and into the goggles with the heat of the flame, stinging his eyes while making it harder to see what he was doing.

A missile erupted as it hit the scarred ground below the escaping Predavator, showering the craft with a shower of sparks. Barely noticing the bombardment on his back, Reznor carried on cutting. It was Albie who first noticed Reznor's shirt catch alight but Reznor still failed to notice, until Albie set about him, furiously beating the quickly spreading flames with Tissa's blanket.

Wiping his forehead with his spare hand, Reznor started to feel the heat of the cutter as the metal holding the door in place began to glow a molten red then blacken and crack. It felt like his whole body was on fire but he had to keep working: if he didn't have this door off then they would all be burnt to a crisp. Suddenly he felt something whip his back. This time he felt a scorching sensation and swinging round, through his sweaty goggles, could make out the shape of Albie shouting furiously at him. His back was ablaze. Dropping the blowtorch, he was immediately attacked by a pair of frantic friends who covered him from head to foot in foam. Grateful for its cooling effect, he quickly wiped as much of it off as he could and sat up.

The three sat panting amid the carnage. Another explosion shook them back to their task and despite now feeling the pain from his burns, Reznor sprang up, and set to the door once again. Once more, sparks were flying but this time nobody was alight.

Finally, with a triumphant yell he threw down the torch and ripped off his goggles as the metal door fell menacingly towards him. Albie flew across the compartment and with Reznor's help dragged the slab towards the hole at the back.

Surprising Albie and Reznor, Tissa then produced a welding torch and set about the door that her companions had placed over the opening. Flashes danced when flame met panel. With Albie and Reznor taking it in turns to hold it steady and stamp/beat it into the required shape, despite the buffeting from outside, the gap was eventually sealed.

Neither of the flight crew took any notice or even seemed aware that they were doorless.

"Hold on…" called Faon without a backward glance, "We're coming up to the power plant's…" One blast from Ordenne's front lasers instantly destroyed the perimeter fence.

"…okay, so that *was* the powerplant's perimeter fence."

Ahead of them loomed the dome-shaped powerplant, linked to enormous towers either side of it by a multitude of crackling blue electric rays that stretched away to both left and right: the city's final barrier to their freedom.

The glow of Tissa's welding job had barely had time to cool when there was a cry from Faon to brace themselves, followed by the sound of missiles speeding towards the defenceless powerplant.

The small Predavator banked sharply, skimming the surface of the city's electric wall making it spit and fizz as the craft fought to escape the wall's pull. Tissa felt her grip loosen and she was flung onto the door she had seconds earlier been welding. Her body shuddered with the pain of landing on her back but before Albie and Reznor had time to react, the craft swerved to avoid a deserted factory building and she was once more catapulted across the hold. Without thinking she covered her head, wincing as metal dug into her arms. The others picked her up, battered, scratched but alive.

Ordenne's shooting had destroyed the giant conductor from which all the power surged to the electric wall. Bolts of electricity from the powerplant were now arcing randomly skyward, angrily lashing out at anything it could: the pursuing fleet, their lonely Predavator… Predavators spun to escape the pulses so collisions and near collisions filling the blackened sky.

The pursuers gave up the chase and so the

lonely, battered craft looped around and sped once more across the bare ground towards the spitting powerplant, low enough to avoid being hit by any of the electric bolts. A further barrage of missiles streaked towards the main body of the powerplant: a large dome from which the conductor had stuck out. The little craft once more banked away but this time it carried on through the city's final defence: now deprived of power. The powerplant quickly disappeared beneath an angry red frothing fireball, erupting in every direction, destroying both factories and defences.

Obscured by the intense flames and smoke, a single Predavator hugged the surface of the wall before looping over it and dropping sharply mere centimetres from the edge of the city's foundations. It instantly disappeared, swamped in the darkness of the underworld.

The following day, a dark Predavator landed next to the burning remains of the power plant. Only the foundations remained after the inferno had burnt itself out. The fire had been seen from all over Tenebria and smoke had reached a hundred metres into the already blackened sky: blotting out the sun for kilometres. The official word was that terrorists had caused an explosion on the edges of the city and had perished as they tried to leave the city but rumours sprang up. Rumours were whispered of a battle that had raged in one of the residential squares, a battle that had left Lord Abus severely wounded. Other rumours had spread that two of the terrorists were little more than children and that they had embarrassed Lord Abus and the city's forces.

Bara Abus had heard all of these rumours and dealt swiftly with those who he had caught spreading them. The talk would soon die down but he knew that this band had not perished in the inferno. Not a trace had been found of the stolen Predavator or the terrorists; despite constant searches of the surrounding area.

He knew they'd be back. This time he'd be ready. He would search tirelessly for them. Destroy the others but the boy, Albie, had to be caught in one piece and alive. His domitor tapped slowly against his leg as he scanned the scorched earth about him, the twisted black shapes and the burnt stubs of bushes that had spread the fire to part of the military zone. Kicking at the ashes that covered the bare ground, he bent down to touch them. Wincing, he tried to move the new hand he had been given: it would be a long time before his bone adjusted to the metal grafted on to it. His new shoulder didn't work that well either, he'd already sent the surgeons to the factories but that hadn't helped the pain, only added to the anger and frustration boiling inside him.

Blowing the ashes off his gloved hand, he watched as the wind picked it up, carrying it into the sky, lifting it over the tangled steel and concrete remains of the wall and out to the clear blue waters of the sea. Disgust filled his face as he looked through the gap in the wall at the crawling waves. He shivered uncomfortably in the breeze before returning to his craft: he hated being this close to nature.

Only Reznor had seen such trees and plants: towering above them, their leaves making a natural canopy above their heads. Every imaginable colour glistened in the early morning sunlight and dampness covered the ground: Reznor had called it dew. Unseen creatures called out to each other all round them and the air was fresh, whipping through the trees. Whispers in the trees calmed the small group below with their soothing soundtrack. This was Sted's paradise!

Either side of them mountains rose into the clouds, covered with a carpet of green and grey that rose up the mountains before giving way, at their tips, to the cleanest, whitest white they could have imagined. Reznor had called this a valley and it was along this valley they had flown in their scorched and battered Predavator.

They had flown over the power plant before the worst of the explosion but had still been momentarily engulfed. It had been to their advantage as they emerged out of the city unseen, able to drop into the city's underworld and skirt its monstrous metal rim, only re-emerging into daylight when they had escaped all pursuit. Reznor and Faon alone had ever seen what lay immediately beyond the city limits but only Reznor had ever seen the wilderness. It was he who had guided them across the bluest water that had positively shone with the sunlight that beat down upon their stuttering craft. The land that stretched before them was the dream that had kept them going and now it was there: a land devoid of metal and fumes where man had not dared journey: away from the constricting safety of the city. The sea had given way to huge banks of rock and they had finally felt at ease: protected by the steep slopes that led down to the valley. Creatures ran freely below them as the craft limped on; as frightened of the new arrivals as the arrivees were of this unfamiliar land.

Choosing an open space, next to the largest trees they had ever encountered, they had landed.

Emerging from one of the side holes in the Predavator they realised how lucky they had been. The hull was completely black and covered in the splices of shrapnel that had ripped through the fuselage. Faon patted it in thanks as she left, quickly pulling her hand away as her hand smarted from the heat of the metal.

"Will you ever take off again?" she had mused.

One by one, they emerged into an unfamiliar sky. Gone was the brilliant blueness of Tenebria but in its place a soft white blanket rippled and rolled over their heads. Glimpses of a more natural blue sky peeped occasionally through in-between the fluffy cover.

Breathing deeply, they tasted nature in all its glory: a kaleidoscope of smells and sensations. Faon sank to the floor and began crying: it was as beautiful as Sted had promised.

"You were right...yes you were. It is amazing

and I finally feel alive! I wish you could be here with us now." Looking back into the gloom of the hull, she could just make out Sted's body, virtually untouched after their ordeal.

Reznor, emerging from behind her, wrapped his arm around her shoulder. She turned to look at him then rested her head on his shoulder. Tissa and Albie wandered slowly around the tall grasses. They were in complete shock. They could never have dreamed this place up in their wildest dreams. Its seemingly endless grass plains faded into the horizon whereupon the mountains rose up. They kept glancing back at each other to check it was all real but couldn't manage a word. Finally, they returned to the Predavator where Faon and Reznor were studying the damage suffered during their miraculous escape.

Carrying Sted's wrapped body on their shoulders they made for a clump of trees on a mound in the middle of the plain: the two girls at the front with Albie and Reznor at the back and Ordenne bringing up the rear. As Reznor would later tell Albie; he had arrived at their cave a boy but had acted like a man ever since and so it was that they walked solemnly: the softness of the ground a welcome feeling. Laying his body under the shade of the largest tree they set to work, digging. It seemed appropriate to place Sted into the land that he had dreamt so much about but as the body was lowered into the ground it also felt completely alien to them.

Faon looked at her friend and she knew she would remember his smile until the day it was her turn to join him.

"Under these trees is just where he would have liked to have ended up" she told them. "lying in this...grass." she paused and glanced quickly at Reznor who smiled and nodded in agreement "listening to this..." once again she paused to take in the leaves rustling, the unseen animals chattering in the trees above and in the valley about. She took a deep breath, inhaling and began to cry. Reznor put an arm around her, remembering their state of health at the first meeting and Faon tucked her head into his chest. "Thanks to you, Sted, we are all able to live at last...we owe you everything...I love you; a real hero." Tears overcame her and she couldn't stop sobbing. Tissa and Ordenne dropped some flowers onto his body then left the others at the graveside and sat at the edge of the copse feeling thankful that they had made it.

"We must help the others in the factory, we owe them that much," said Ordenne after a few minutes silence. Tissa nodded. She had no idea what they could do but knew their guilt at reaching paradise would grow.

"We will, we will," nodded Tissa "this is just the start, I can feel it. Albie and I have unfinished business..." looking across at Reznor and Faon still clutching each other. "I have a feeling that they have as well."

Albie had now joined them and was leaning

against the tree that shaded them. Glancing up, Ordenne smiled at Tissa before getting up to wander into the valley. Tissa smiled back but looking up at Albie she felt her cheeks redden slightly and she had to turn away: her feelings towards him were changing.

"We'll find them; you know…your mum… and mine. This is all my fault, if I hadn't…" Albie began but Tissa stood up and put a finger to his lips, shaking her head.

"Today is the first day of our new lives and we owe it to Sted to make the most of this chance. No regrets. What has been, has been. No regrets for the things we can't change."

He looked at her and nodded but noticed a look in her eyes, a look he didn't recognise but it made him feel special. He hugged her briefly and sighed, watching Ordenne as she strolled across the grass.

"It'll all be worth it - you'll see." He concluded.

<u>Epilogue</u>

A loan figure in an ancient peaked cap watched the battered craft land. He saw the figures emerge from its shell but remained hidden. He was good at that. He had seen these craft before: visiting the valley-dwellers and they usually meant trouble but this one was different. He swung the rounded bat in his hand gently though the grasses around him. They bowed but swung back into place again. He looked for more craft but there were none: that was very unusual.

Turning his cap round so the peak was facing the back, the hulking figure climbed down from the rock he usually sat upon. It offered the best view of the plains and the best protection amongst its folds and outcrops. He'd wait until night and then investigate further. They'd never know he was there. For now, he'd report their presence: *he*'d know about them already but it was not worth keeping them to himself. That would never do!

Albie Volume II: The Progeny League

<u>1</u>

He realised the weapon was pointing straight at the girl. She was dressed in ill-fitting mechanic's overalls but her face wasn't that of a worker's: it was proud and defiant. Seeing her held in the trooper's grip, weapon embedded in her head, he was rooted to the spot. Chill winds tugged at him. The city shimmered below them. Behind them stood rows of Predavators. Something was said, he had no idea what, but his only thought was to save that girl. He would do anything for her. He put down the weapon he held in his own hand and the trooper relaxed slightly. The girl was pushed over to him but the domitor remained trained on them both. Blood trickled from the trooper's wound, just above his eye. Brushing it away, the black figure appeared to sway then stagger as the blood poured even faster into his eye and his mouth. He spat the blood out. The weapon in the trooper's hand shook and he heard the click as it was set to kill.

Steeling himself, he leapt, knowing that he had to save this girl: he had no idea who she was but he knew he loved her and she had to live.

"No!" he screamed, gripping his chest as if it had been ripped open. The chill wind wrapped itself around him, tugging at him then there was the warmth of another body close to him, holding him, rocking him…he felt loved. Finally, an intense relief spread through him. The pain in his chest vanished as quickly as it had begun: he was free. He was rising higher, away from the scene but he could smell engine fuel…it was so strong.

His hands feverishly scrambled to find a wound but there was none. The blue sky had faded away, broken rafters and cracked walls returning. Only the wind remained, tugging at feet that stuck out of the thin blanket barely covering him. Realising he was lying on his own dirty mattress in his own room he mopped his soaked brow with his blanket. Xean sat up and studied his world. The dirty overalls he had forgotten to remove clung to him like a second skin. As usual, he had collapsed into bed after his previous shift and fallen straight to sleep. Pulling his greasy hair back into its tight pony tail, he tried to smooth himself down: make himself more presentable. He could freshen up at work, after all they regularly had running water there: luxury!

His was the Tenebria that didn't exist. The squalor of the crumbling four walls Xean called his own was just an official secret. It wouldn't do to bother the city's well-groomed citizens with minor details about slums, boarded windows and poverty. After all, his kind were only manual workers so were lucky to even be above ground: privileged to serve in their gleaming city. Xean still felt grateful, although he sometimes wished the wind didn't find it quite so easy to rip through his room.

With his boots in his hand he pushed past the piece of wood leaning over his doorframe: a make-shift door. He winced as it fell back into place, catching his bare foot.

"Too slow," he thought as he stepped into the hallway and positioned the wood back over the opening to his room. He always remembered how lucky he had been to have that piece of wood; his brother had found it for him in resyc just before he had disappeared. Xean tried not to think about him but it was hard. They'd worked so hard to keep their relationship a secret: how had the troopers found out? What was so wrong with having a family? His brother had always been the more intelligent one, that's why he'd been allowed to live in the city. Xean was simply glad they had found him a job working on the Predavators: he was good with his hands and for a while at least he had been able to see his brother regularly.

A series of coughs from one of the many rooms on his floor brought him back to reality. Clinging to a swaying metal hand rail he guided himself past the holes in the wooden stairs; keeping alert to any fresh obstacles. An occasional blast of air through a gap in the wall diverted his senses away from the stench of a rotten building.

Not a soul stirred as he reached the foot of the stairs. The others in his block worked on various clean up brigades: only coming to life once the 'beautiful people' had finished their night time merriment and were recuperating in their plush apartments. Stepping off the rotten timbers and onto the cracked concrete walkway separating his building from its neighbours, he pulled his boots on. It didn't do to wake the neighbours with his clomping feet. He checked the road in both directions.   Just something he tended to do, he didn't know why. After all he had nothing to hide. He realised his brother had been on his mind a lot recently: something wasn't right, he could feel it. Shaking his head, he stumbled off in the direction of the inner city with his mind filled with that dream he had been having on and off for the last four months now.

He didn't live far from the wall that separated him from the elite. He could see the glow of the screens that constantly decorated the enormous blocks on the other side of the wall. Each illuminated the city with the same images. Ahead of him stood the eight-metre-high wall dividing the haves and the never-hads and never-dreamed-they-could-have. Its smooth concrete sides gave way to an array of metal spikes jutting out of a rounded summit: aimed at deterring any ideas his kind might have of sneaking in uninvited. Two guardian robots hovered in front of a pair of black studded gates. Even though he had made this journey hundreds of times it never ceased to amaze him how they came to life the moment he reached that spot.

A screen and a keyboard emerged from inside one of the metal bodies. After that the creatures remained immobile. Xean barely glanced at the screen before reaching out to scan his pass. He hesitated, studying both robots as his pass loitered above the screen. Tensing himself, he drew in a deep breath and closed his eyes as if he was praying. The moment his pass touched the screen, Xean's body jerked as he was engulfed by a jet of transparent gas from the guardian's partner. The next instant he was being doused from the other side, still unable to control his body's reaction as he emerged from the sterilising cloud that had engulfed him. One day, he told himself, he'd get his own back: blasted machines. One day he might not flinch. It would be a start, he told himself. The iron doors swung open ahead of him.

Still wiping his smarting eyes, he realised what another glorious day it was going to be on this side of the wall, weather control made sure of that. A good way to keep the people happy. Stepping onto a transparent walkway, he looked down upon the communal exercise parks, dropping away below him, which ringed the residential zone of the city.

Immaculate grass lawns and trees were crisscrossed by a maze of circular paths. He'd never been allowed to watch anyone using them but he often dreamt about what it would be like to relax under the shade of the trees or play games on the manicured lawns. Leaning against the handrail, he could picture the open spaces filled with couples holding hands and chatting as they walked or sat.

Returning to the present day, the people disappeared and the empty grounds were restored. Xean studied the shadow of the walkway that stretched across the grass and noticed the shape of a figure speeding along it behind him. The shadow wasn't walking but gliding; propelling itself towards him.

Turning sharply, he shook his head: the walkway was empty. Glancing down, the shadow had gone too. That was not normal, he told himself. He carried on, this time taking the occasional glance below. Xean was sure of it now: there *was* someone, or something, following him. One of the guardians? He had made this journey across the city's transparent walkways for the last ten years and never seen a soul: just him and the ad screens. The messages had stayed more or less the same in that time: buy this, drink that; use one of these to be a hit with the ladies. Only the names had changed: victims of ever-changing fashions.

However, every time he turned around, a figure would merge with the long shadows. Was it a trick of the light? A guardian wouldn't bother hiding, would it? The screens taunted him; teasing his barely-awake eyes in the way they usually did this early in the morning. The longer it went on, though, the more anxious he became. Walking quicker, he strained to hear the sound of steps behind him but there was none: just a faint whooshing sound. Spinning, he stumbled against the walkway's edge, his fingers tightly gripping the cold metal rail. His head began to spin: he stood half way between two enormous tower blocks. Five hundred metres below, he could see the trees in the empty plaza swaying calmly in the morning breeze: he did not like heights. Every window was blackened and would stay that way for another two hours, when everybody was expected to wake up. For once he wished there was someone there. Someone he could call to for help: but there wasn't. Gripping hold of the hand rail, he steadied himself and tried to focus on the images of a big-muscled man spraying himself with a black and gold bottle. The words on the screen blurred and he felt his knees buckle.

"Get a grip" he told himself "Remember: you've done nothing wrong... that they know about. We've made sure of it." Inwardly he raced through the possibilities. Surely, they weren't on to him. If they had wanted to take him: why bother trailing him like this? Couldn't they have easily taken him from his apartment? Were they hoping he'd lead them to the others? He wiped his forehead with an oily rag hanging out of his back pocket, completely unaware of the black smear that it left.

"Remember to breathe slowly...in...out...in...out..." He managed to focus on the screens once more, forcing himself to breathe steadily. Stealing another glance along the walkway, he was sure he could make out a shadow underneath him, just behind one of the bridge's immense supports. As he strained to focus, his head began to swim and he began to lose his balance. The tower blocks around him appeared to swirl and he staggered back from the edge. The figure immediately moved and he could see it was a slim figure, almost flying towards him.

Xean forced himself to stumble on and as he did so he could clearly make out the whooshing sound as the figure sped after him. Ahead of him, at the end of the walkway, loomed his workstation. The sight of the large plain pillars either side of the enormous double doors meant he was almost safe, if he could only reach them. By concentrating on his goal, he was able to run but his pursuer was gaining on him.

Any second now, he thought, the doors will open automatically. He would be able to smell the engine oil and spent Predavator fuel in the workshops where he had toiled for most of his life. But the doors never opened. Instead he felt someone grab him round the waist and momentum carried plummeting over the side.

To be continued in….

Albie Volume II:
The Progeny League

Printed in Poland
by Amazon Fulfillment
Poland Sp. z o.o., Wrocław